"With witty writing, sharp characterizations and a killer premise, *The Anomaly* is escapist fun perfectly tuned to our age of conspiracy theories and alternative facts."

—Thomas Mullen, author of *Darktown*

"Brilliant. Thrilling, tense, dark, funny. Michael Crichton meets Indiana Jones."

—C. J. Tudor, author of *The Chalk Man*

"'Michael Crichton meets Stephen King' is what was promised—and boy, does it deliver."

—Simon Lelic, author of *A Thousand Cuts* and *The New Neighbors*

"An exciting, intriguing, and often distinctly frightening story."

—Nudge Books

"If you like your sci-fi intertwined with a bit of horror and a bit of knowledge, you will definitely love this. (Did I just describe *The Da Vinci Code*?)"

—Booker Than You

"Rutger writes with such vivacious energy—blurring the line between historical fact and fiction so deftly...Rest assured, you'll struggle to find a more thrilling page-turner this year."

—Alternative Magazine Online

THE
POSSESSION

ALSO BY MICHAEL RUTGER

The Anomaly

THE
POSSESSION

A NOVEL

MICHAEL RUTGER

GRAND CENTRAL
PUBLISHING

New York Boston

Grand Central Publishing
Hachette Book Group
1290 Avenue of the Americas, New York, NY 10104
grandcentralpublishing.com
twitter.com/grandcentralpub

Originally published in hardcover, paperback, and ebook by Grand Central Publishing in July 2019
First Mass Market Edition: February 2020

Grand Central Publishing is a division of Hachette Book Group, Inc. The Grand Central Publishing name and logo is a trademark of Hachette Book Group, Inc.

The publisher is not responsible for websites (or their content) that are not owned by the publisher.

The Hachette Speakers Bureau provides a wide range of authors for speaking events. To find out more, go to www.hachettespeakersbureau.com or call (866) 376-6591.

LCCN: 2019941727

ISBNs: 978-1-5387-6188-5 (mass market), 978-1-5387-6189-2 (ebook)

Printed in the United States of America

OPM

10 9 8 7 6 5 4 3 2 1

This is for the Essex Witches:
Tes and Eleanor, Matthew,
& Bex and Kurt and Pip.

The unseen exists and has properties.

—Richard Ford, *Lay of the Land*

FROM THE FILES OF NOLAN MOORE:

SAN FRANCISCO CHRONICLE—AUGUST 14, 1904

PROLOGUE

She walked along the side of the road, and she walked fast.

Her legs were stiff, her arms crossed tight. Her head hurt. Badly. As if a metal band was clamped around her temples. Tightening. Her cheeks were stinging. Her neck felt naked and hurt around the back like a burn. Her best sneakers and her new jeans were getting soaked from the wet grass, and the gray-black mass of sky said there was more coming. Let it.

Everybody she saw was ugly. She had never felt more alone in her life.

And none of this was her fault.

She kept stomping homeward but after a while started to slow down, feet turning heavy and miserable. Her head ached worse than ever and her cheeks were wet now, too. And none of this was fair. She'd been so happy. She'd climbed such a big wall and all she wanted to do was share the view on the other side—not discover that somebody else thought they already owned it, that it wasn't hers.

Her vision was blurred with angry tears, but she'd walked this way so many times she could have done it with eyes closed. She didn't even notice the man sitting on the bench until she was level with him.

"Hey," he said.

Old guy. Gaunt face, black hair, bags under his eyes. She knew who he was immediately. Had seen him a hundred times. He'd been in their house, stood by the fireplace talking with her dad, drinking one of his beers. He'd always been in the background of her life like a dusty piece of someone else's furniture, but she didn't want to talk to him now. Him or anybody else.

She kept going.

"You okay?" he asked. He stood, started walking with her. Not right beside. But at the same speed.

"I'm fine," she said, keeping her head down, wiping the back of her hand across her eyes. It was probably too late, but she didn't want him to see she'd been crying. She was fourteen. That's not a child anymore, whatever dumbass old people might think. Parents and teachers, everyone— but friends most of all. All they ever want to do is keep you small. They're scared of who you're becoming.

Of what you know. Of who you *are*.

"That's good," the man said. "Just being neighborly. That's all. I wouldn't want your dad to think I'd seen you out here, upset, and not checked if you're okay."

"I am totally okay, thank you."

"Is it a boy thing?"

She stopped walking, stared at him, hands on hips. "Uh, that would be none of your business."

He stopped too, looked apologetic. "Sorry. You're grown now. I get that. You got your own world. And I don't mean to intrude."

"So don't."

"But it's cold. It's going to rain. Probably before you

get home. I'm just saying why don't I get you there. You look like you're having a bad day, is all."

"I don't need help."

"I know. Look, fine, I'll leave you to it. But I'll tell you one thing before I go, and you should believe me. Okay?"

"What is it?"

"Tomorrow's another day. And there's always a chance it'll be a good one."

She opened her mouth to retort, but closed it, suddenly feeling very tired. And dumb and guilty and small. She wanted to be at home, and warm, and dry. To start working out how she was going to fix this. Make it so she could start feeling happy again.

"Where's your car?"

She knew as soon as he made the first turn that something was wrong. This wasn't the way home.

"I've changed my mind," she said. "I want to walk."

He didn't look at her but she saw him smile, and she knew she'd made a mistake and it was too late to do anything about it. That it would always be too late.

She was his now.

PART ONE

We take the measure of being; indeed, it is so much that in and out—strongpoint—is always uncertain... more overthinking.

—Robert Lowell, "Eye and Tooth"

PART ONE

We take our measure of being from what surrounds us; and what surrounds us is always, to some extent, of our own making.

—Robert Pogue Harrison, *The Dominion of the Dead*

CHAPTER

1

You have reached your destination.

Kristy pulled gratefully to the curb and peered out the window. "Thank God for that."

She was alone and so said it quietly. The vehicle made no response. Kristy hadn't bonded with it yet—a loaner while hers was in the shop—not least because it adamantly refused to deal with her iPhone. On the eight-hour drive north the built-in navigation system had twice tried to lead her off the freeway, then retreated into panicked rerouting, before abruptly changing its mind and pretending the whole incident never happened. The car smelled pleasant and yet odd, as if doused with a scent designed to be an averaging out of the entire world's conception of "fresh," rather than pleasant to any single person or culture in particular. It was like being trapped in an elderly person's guest bathroom. Having the windows open above forty miles an hour caused an unbearably percussive *whap-whap-whap* sound. There was a blind spot on the left that hid overtaking cars in a way that seemed specifically designed to cause accidents.

It was a dumb car. Right now it seemed confident of one thing, however.

Destination: 243 Shasta Avenue, Birchlake, CA

It struck her how often we refer to machines not merely for information but also reassurance, as we once would have with a parent, and put a pin in the observation for a short think-piece at some point, or maybe never.

She got out of the car, wincing. It was dark and cold outside her cocoon. Both sides of the street were lined with buildings, few above a single story high, most fronted with wood and all weathered in old small-town style. Trees dotted along the sidewalks, leaves thinned into late-fall mode. A dim streetlight on the corner revealed a small but aspiringly upmarket grocery store. Beyond that, another couple blocks, a liquor store, then town kind of ran out.

Closing the car door sounded loud.

Birchlake looked pretty much as she'd expected. Thick forest on one side, river on the other, with further forest beyond. The narrow highway entered over a bridge at the southern end of town, passing an old motel and gas station. At the other end the road followed the river further into the mountains. The kind of place you'd blow straight through on a road trip without noticing, unless you were desperate for coffee, a sandwich, or the restroom.

243 Shasta Avenue was dark.

One of the handful of two-story buildings, the street-level space had fairly recently been an antique or bric-a-brac store, now shuttered. Originally the building looked like it had been a general store. The business next door was a hipster-style coffee shop, complete with intricately hand-chalked price boards and ironic hashtags, closed for the night. Convenient for the morning, though.

Kristy walked up to 243, stretching her arms and back. Three-quarters of the building's wide frontage was taken up by display windows flanking an old glass door, all of which had been whitewashed into opaqueness from the inside. On the right was a featureless wooden door with a large deadbolt. 243a. It looked secure but hardly welcoming. All reassuringly recognizable from the Airbnb listing, though a good deal less enticing at nine thirty on a dark, chilly night, a long way from home.

She pulled up the confirmation email on her phone, already wishing she'd booked into the B&B at the north end of town instead.

Pick up key from Stone Mountain Tap—ask for Val.

Kristy turned and scanned the other side of the street.

The Tap looked like it had been a bar for a long time and knew its business and had few regrets. There was a dedicated drinking area on the left, stools along a counter, and a long and low-ceilinged restaurant section on the right, with heavy chairs and tables, booths along the side, and maybe twenty people spread among the seating. The floor was battered wood, the walls randomly dotted with tarnished mirrors and neon beer signs and murky retro advertisements in frames. The lights were low. The music was not. Right now it was Joni Mitchell—who always sounded to Kristy like a cat trying to communicate that it was dying, and sad about it. Shelves behind the bar held bottles of every hard liquor known to mankind. There were a dozen beers on tap, too, half from the local microbrew and called things like pInePA and Cold River. It was the kind of place her ex-husband would like, Kristy knew.

There's a rare, fine line between anodyne and sketchy, he would have said. *And this is it.*

A lean woman in her early fifties stood behind the bar. Cropped gray hair, nose stud, wearing a T-shirt that revealed tan, muscular arms dotted with Celtic-style tattoos. She had the loose, easy stance of someone who'd done years of non-dilettante yoga, and gave Kristy an appraising look as she approached.

"Are you Val?" Kristy asked. "I'm looking for—"

"Dangit," the woman said. "Thought my luck was in." She glanced at a scrap of paper thumb-tacked to the bar behind her. "I am indeed Val. Kristy?"

"That's me."

"Okay, so. Normally I'd let you in and give you the tour, but the Crown Prince of Uselessness didn't show up tonight, and so I'm holding the fort by myself. I imagine it'll be self-explanatory. You look like a grown-up."

"I wouldn't go that far."

The woman took a while fishing a key out of her jeans. In the meantime Kristy cast a glance around to see if anybody was eating, and whether it looked edible. Nobody was. A tall, gaunt man in his sixties sat on a stool at the end of the counter. There was no glass in front of him.

He turned to look at her. Cloudy gray eyes, bags that spoke of a liver past its best, unnaturally dark hair scraped back from a high forehead. He looked so much like the kind of guy you always see in small-town bars that for a moment it almost felt as if she knew him from somewhere. Kristy realized she wasn't in the mood for a solo meal even if it was an option.

"So what brings you to B-lake?" Val asked, as she finally produced a key. Kristy could imagine her asking the same question, in the same knowing way, of every stranger who walked in the bar.

"Just exploring."

"Ha. Hope you brought something to read, because exploring will use up all of ten minutes. If you take your time. And to answer your next question, the kitchen closes at eight thirty on weeknights out of season. Sorry. The food's not bad, though, for future reference."

"Good to know," Kristy said, as she took the key.

"All part of the service. And don't lose that, cos I can't find the spare."

The door to 243a opened onto a narrow stairwell. Kristy found the light switch and carried her bag upstairs.

The apartment looked exactly how it had online, which shouldn't have been a surprise, but they didn't always. A five-second tour confirmed it had a small kitchenette and a desk and a door to the bedroom/bathroom—which had looked nice on the website and was an area on which Kristy wouldn't compromise. The furniture was old, but both it and the rug and pictures had been selected well enough to pitch the place convincingly toward shabby chic, rather than merely shabby. A bay window. Good enough.

She dropped her bag and went back down to the street. A woman was pulling in the sidewalk sign outside the grocery at the corner, but thankfully it hadn't closed yet. Organic vegetables. Local honey. An excessively wide selection of artisanal vinegars. The problem with seeing a lot of places is they all start to seem the same, especially the ones that are trying to be different. Kristy gathered up milk, snacks, a pre-made sandwich from the cooler. It featured an unnecessary amount of alfalfa sprouts, but she believed she'd be able to struggle through. A middle-aged woman with thick glasses took Kristy's money and gave her a bag without recourse to speech.

By the time Kristy stepped back out onto the street it had started to drizzle. The road was deserted, or so she thought at first. Then she saw a figure on the other side. Tall, thin. Hands hanging down by his sides.

He was lit, then unlit, by the flashing sign of the Stone Mountain Tap, and it took Kristy a moment to realize that he'd started crossing toward her.

He stopped a few feet short of the curb. His head still had to tilt to look down at her. Kristy was barely 5′4″ and slim of build. Which was why, in situations like this, she always spoke first. "Can I help you?"

The man said nothing.

"You were in the bar, right?" She phrased it as a question only because most humans are straightforward animals and a trick that simple usually got them to respond more quickly.

Not this guy. He sniffed, wetly, looked away down the street. Remained silent. Kristy was not afraid. There was a dozen feet between them and her reactions were fast. She'd worn her running shoes for the drive. It seemed unlikely this man ran at least a 5K every day of the year, as Kristy did, or that he'd be able to do it anywhere near as fast. She was watchful nonetheless. You just never know, and there was something about this man that she didn't like.

"You're here about her," he said. His voice was quiet, unthreatening.

"Who?"

"The missing girl."

"Like you probably overheard me say: I'm just exploring."

"People sometimes disappear for a reason."

"What kind of reason?"

"You'd be better off leaving in the morning, exploring some other town. But I don't suppose you'll listen."

The man turned away, and started to walk back across

the street. Stopped after a couple of paces, half-turned back. He paused a moment, lips pursed, looking at her.

"What?" she said.

"Sometimes it's better if they stay gone."

When he got to the other side, he turned left and disappeared around the corner.

CHAPTER

2

I t's still early," Molly said.

"It's really not."

She checked her watch. I'd done the same thing, less than a minute before. And a few minutes before that. "It's not eight yet. Your slot's until half past."

"Tell me, Moll. Have you observed the ebb and flow during the last hour, and been able to come to any conclusions regarding changes in the population density of customers in this retail establishment over time?"

"It's . . . less busy than it was?"

"There are exactly three people here, not including the comatose clerk at the register or the one hiding in the cooking section." I turned in his direction. *"I know you're there,"* I said, loudly.

Molly swatted me. "Shh, Nolan."

"Two customers wandered past without glancing at my book. The third picked up a copy and had a long, hard look, before putting it back as though worried about contagion. He's currently browsing the photography section, presumably in quest of artsy pictures of naked ladies. If I get any more bored I'm going to go give him the good news about the invention of the internet."

Molly made a face. "I'm sorry," she said.

"I hate to embarrass you, that's all," I said. "I know you pulled a favor to even get me in here."

Posters on the walls showed that Bookshop Santa Cruz's events generally featured literary A-listers, best-selling genre scribes, or winsome-looking people who'd written one achingly awesome short story and won a shit-ton of awards for it. I am none of those things. Normally their events involved an audience and a Q&A and wine. I'd been given a table behind the local history section from seven until eight-thirty, which on a drizzly Wednesday evening in late October is the bookstore equivalent of exile to a labor camp in Siberia.

Molly grew up in Santa Cruz and knew somebody in the store. Perhaps anticipating that my event might not lead to a long line of excited customers snaking away down the street, she'd volunteered to come along for the ride on the pretext of hooking up with some old friends.

"I'm not in the least embarrassed," she said. "People are stupid. Come on, nuts to this. Let's go get a drink."

"Now you're talking."

"Wait though. Didn't she buy a copy earlier?"

A young woman had come back in the store from the street, and was headed our way. "*The* copy, yes."

I smiled when she got to us, reaching for my pen. "Decided you'd like it signed after all?"

"Well no, actually," the girl said, looking awkward. "It was for my boyfriend. He's really into unsolved mysteries and stuff? But I just gave it to him and he said he only likes to read things by actual experts, sorry."

She held the book out to me diffidently.

"You'd like a refund?"

"If that's okay."

"And he sent *you* back to do this?" Molly asked.

The girl shrugged.

"You'll have to take it to the register and deal with them," Molly said. "Oh, and FYI? Your boyfriend's a dick."

The girl backed warily away.

Molly helped me put the books back in the box and then in my car, after which we went and got pretty drunk.

Or I did, anyway.

Molly had a single beer and then went for a late dinner with her friends. I kept meaning to leave the bar and kept failing to follow through. I remembered after a while that I'd got drunk in the same establishment, years ago, when passing through town after visiting my parents up in Berkeley. The bar hadn't changed much. Neither, it appeared, have I.

Eventually I managed to go, and eleven o'clock found me on a lounger by the tiny swimming pool of my motel, smoking in front of the no-smoking sign and drinking from a large bottle of local beer that I seemed to have purchased along the way. The drizzle had stopped but it was pretty cold. The motel was called the Bayview, despite not having one and in reality being situated a brisk five-minute walk from the ocean.

I was sufficiently inebriated by that point to find this glumly metaphoric for something or other.

Hi. My name's Nolan Moore. You may have heard of me from...

Who am I kidding. Of course you haven't. Unless you ran across me in my previous life as a journeyman screenwriter in LA, my sole claim to fame is being the host of a very slightly popular YouTube show called *The*

Anomaly Files, which investigates unsolved mysteries. The problem being that though it briefly looked like we were going to move up to cable, it fell apart for extremely complicated reasons that I won't get into right now, and so we're back on YouTube.

The problem with *that* is people who're interested in the subjects we cover don't *go* to YouTube, because it's the province of youngsters who want to watch other young people jabbering on about their inconsequential days. I'm aware that makes me sound old. I don't care. My point is most people go to the site to see their pre-existing worldview reflected safely back, not to have their eyes opened to new things, or be shown what's going on in the shadows.

And this, as my producer/director/friend Ken has pointed out, more than once, is why our business model sucks.

In an attempt to generate PR for the show (and to bump my income to the level where I could continue to pay for the apartment in Santa Monica that had been home since I separated from my wife) I'd written up some of our previous shows. These had just come out in a large-format book from a real publisher, and that's what I'd been trying to sell tonight. The net result—after the reversal with the girl with the shitty boyfriend—had been zero (0) sales.

There were a dispiriting amount of zeros in the book's sales ranking on Amazon, too. I honestly hadn't realized there were that many books in the world. It seemed altogether possible that books that didn't even *exist* had sold more copies than mine. After spending a few confused minutes trying to figure out whether asking the publisher to withdraw the book from sale might push me higher up the bestseller list, I realized I'd drunk more than enough and should call it a night, especially if I was hoping to drive Molly and me the six-plus hours back to LA tomorrow.

I dislodged my phone from my jeans pocket during the process of standing, but managed to catch it before it crashed to the floor, somehow also avoiding flipping it into the pool. Buoyed by this evidence that I was in fact totally at the top of my game, I noticed I'd missed a call.

It was from Kristy. My ex-wife. Or, as it hadn't quite got to that point (and we'd recently been cautiously experimenting with walking back from the split) the woman from whom I was presently separated.

Our current policy of playing it cool meant neither of us expected the other to leap straight onto calling back. We'd had a few good evenings together in the last couple months, including one when we'd added each other back to the Find Your Friends app, as a cocktail-fueled declaration of...I don't know. Openness to a future. Or something. The fact that I'd not felt drawn to use the information, however, nor entitled to, showed there was still distance to cross.

It was late. I could have left it until I got back to Los Angeles. But I didn't. Despite the hour, and having been no stranger to alcohol, I went up to my room, made some very bad coffee, and called Kristy back.

Mistake.

CHAPTER
3

I wasn't worried about waking her. Kristy switched to no-ring mode when she was done with the day. Not worried, either, that the delay in her picking up (necessarily) meant she was electing not to take my call. Kristy makes a point of leaving her phone on the other side of the room, usually somewhere precarious, to show how non-addicted she is. I've pointed out this shows she's thinking too much about her phone, but my wisdom fell upon unresponsive ears, as it so often does.

I waited patiently, picturing how she would lever herself up out of her chair and pad quietly across whatever space she was in, tucking her hair behind her ear in readiness. It's weird how someone not-answering their phone can remind you how much you know about them.

"Hey," she said, eventually.

"New phone, who dis?"

"Nolan, that doesn't work. You called me."

"I know. That's why it's funny."

"Pretty experimental use of the word *funny*, but let's move on. How did the book signing go?"

"Really badly."

"I did warn you it might."

"I know. But I wasn't sure whether that was genuine concern or merely you being mean to me for sport."

"Bit of both, if I'm honest. Well, that's disappointing."

"I'll survive. So, what?"

"Huh?"

"Before I called you, you called me, remember? Where are you anyway?"

"Town called Birchlake. Forty miles from Shasta."

"Okay. Why?"

She didn't answer, and in that pause I heard an echo of previous pauses. Most of them good—the everyday beats of silence in a relationship that's past (or before) the "somebody has to be talking or it's not working" phase. Others not so good, like the hesitation of a person choosing whether to tell the truth, and if not, which untruth—something that would be consistent with previous untruths. You never understand those pauses for what they are at the time. Only in retrospect. And once you've learned that bad things live in the gaps, and the world may not be as it seems, it can make you paranoid.

"Ten days ago a girl called Alaina Hixon disappeared," Kristy said, and I realized all she'd been doing was marshaling information. "Fourteen. From Birchlake."

"Name rings a bell," I said. "The town, not the girl." And it did, now I'd heard it a second time.

"Can't imagine why. It's Nowheresville. Alaina lived a mile up the road. She and a couple of girlfriends went walking in the woods after school. It started getting dark and one of them turned to Alaina to suggest they head home. She wasn't there. They called out and looked for her, but got freaked and bailed."

"Nice."

"They didn't know what else to do, Nolan. And they

went straight home and got their dad to call the police, so...The county sheriff and his guys were there fast. Then the Feds, and dogs. Nothing after five days of ground search. Nothing since. Nothing on social media. No contact with family or friends. Just plain gone."

"I'm surprised I didn't hear about it."

"Bad timing. The day before she disappeared was that Walmart shooting in Chico. 'Only' four died, but—"

"There was that huge manhunt, right. That I do remember."

"Exactly. Very bright and shiny. Took twenty-four hours until they pinned the guy down and blew his head off, then there were days of media analysis and hand-wringing after. Alaina missed her spot in the news cycle. She fell between the cracks."

I tried to imagine what it must be like to have your child disappear like that, and realized it was nowhere I wanted to go inside my head. "Don't they say that..."

"The first day is critical, yes. If a child turns up deceased, in three-quarters of cases death occurred within three hours. Movies are all about hidden cabins and the drawn-out playtimes of evil geniuses. In reality it's a panicky act committed by someone who's broken and vile, and it happens fast. But we shouldn't leap to that anyway. About eight hundred thousand people are reported missing every year."

"Seriously?"

"But eighty-five percent are under the age of eighteen, and the vast majority resolve quickly. People operate on a hair-trigger, understandably. Most of the time the kid's just late, or at a friend's, or goofing off. They come home, everybody shouts at each other, then someone calls for pizza and it's have-you-done-your-homework."

"What about the rest?"

"Family cases are often custody-based and more likely to involve children under six. The probability of harm increases markedly from family to acquaintance to stranger, of course, but in the end only one in ten thousand missing children are not eventually found alive."

"Dying is not the only deeply shitty thing that can happen to missing kids."

"Of course. And those dangers are higher with acquaintance or stranger abductions, which *also* become more likely if the missing child is female. Like Alaina."

"But why are you on this? It's terrible, of course. But you're not a detective."

"I was researching a piece on cyberbullying."

"Hasn't that been done?"

"Yes, it's been 'done,' Nolan. But, bizarrely, that didn't make the problem instantly disappear. And it's not only kids. Students do it to teachers, too—setting up sites to hassle them. It happens even more *outside* the school system. You don't want to see my mentions on Twitter any time I write something a teeny bit critical of the patriarchy, or suggest not having so many assault rifles in circulation might be a cool experiment."

"Well, you know my theory about that."

"Remind me."

"People are assholes," I said. I'd gotten to the end of the pot of coffee and couldn't decide whether it would be a good idea to make another, especially as the first seemed to have stirred ominous harbingers of tomorrow's hangover.

Instead I left the room and lit a cigarette on the walkway, looking over the wet parking lot. A homeless guy lurched along the road outside, shouting vaguely at someone who wasn't there. "So—is this girl's disappearance related to cyberbullying?"

"It wasn't," Kristy said. "Though I called the sheriff yesterday morning and suggested he look into it. Because, check this out."

My phone pinged. She'd texted me a picture. A pretty young girl. Pale skin. Long dark hair. Black jeans, black hoodie. She was standing in front of birch trees, with thicker forest behind. "That's her?"

"Yes," Kristy said. "Keep looking."

The image she'd sent was a screen grab, much taller than it was wide. I scrolled past the image. It'd been posted by "htilil♥2005" and had received precisely one like. I did the math and worked out that 2005 would have been Alaina Hixon's birth year. "What's with the white space underneath?"

"Somebody, or more likely two people, have posted comments. That's what those random sets of letters on the left side signify. But the comments are blank."

"That's a little strange. Unless it's just some pointless thing the young folks are doing this month."

"Not that I'm aware. On her other account there are normal comments. I've traced those posters back to kids at her school. But these? No idea. And keep scrolling."

The blank lines of empty post went on for a couple of inches of screen space. I was finding it hard to see this as cyberbullying worth the name (or Kristy's time), and was about to say so, when the comments changed. One of the same random-character accounts had posted a single word.

Witch

"Huh," I said. I kept scrolling. Something—the cold and dark, or a more atavistic response—was making the hairs on the back of my neck stir.

Witch

Witch

Witch

Witch

And then, at the bottom of the image, a final comment.

Time to join your mother.

"Okay, sure, that's a little weird," I said. "Any idea what the mother thing signifies?"

"Alaina Hixon's mother was in a car accident eighteen months ago. She's dead."

"Oh," I said. "Yeah. You should look into that."

Half an hour later I was at the tiny desk in my room. In the meantime I'd made and drunk more coffee and also—with the aid of the vast collection of notes I have stored on my phone—recalled in which context I'd previously encountered the general environs of Birchlake. I'd also had time to think about Kristy, and to wonder what she was really doing up there in the mountains, and why.

I checked my watch. Quarter to one. Late. But you never know. I dialed a different number. It rang for quite a while. I was about to bail when it finally picked up.

"What," Ken's voice said, "the *fuck* do you want?"

Ken is a late-fifty-something pug of an ex-Londoner, and at times somewhat brisk in his social interactions.

"Are you awake?"

"Well I am *now*, you twat."

"Good," I said. "I think I've found our next show."

CHAPTER

4

After the call with Nolan, Kristy spent ten minutes tending her digital garden. There wasn't much to do. She scheduled a couple of tweets promoting upcoming pieces and dealt with her mentions. And that was that. The outside world had been dealt with, leaving only the inner one.

She wasn't even sure why she'd called Nolan. Reassurance, probably. Grounding. But she still wasn't sure it'd been worth coming all the way here.

Or if it had been a good idea.

She should go to bed. She didn't feel like it. It was very late, though. One last cup of tea. Then bed.

She put the kettle on the stove and a bag of chamomile tea in one of six identical mugs. There were six sets of silverware, six plates, and six bowls. None were chipped. All were perfect, patina-less, as if freshly minted. The distorted reflection of her face in the kettle showed Kristy's own patina was coming along fine. Only those few lines around the eyes, as yet, and that one outlying gray hair. But age happens. Thirty-five is not the first draft of being a human. There are editorial marks in your margins.

She turned off all the lights except for the lamp and sat in the chair by the window, cradling the hot cup in her hands, slowing her breathing, trying to feel her way toward sleepy, watching nothing much happening in the street.

From up here she could see along it in both directions. An evening of drizzle had slicked the sidewalk into black, shiny pools, reflecting the streetlights. She considered taking an artsy picture of the scene for her loyal 120K Instagram followers. She'd left her phone right on the other side of the room, though. And she'd surely paid sufficient homage to the gods of social media for one night.

She yawned, at last believing that sleep had become a feasible endeavor.

There was a very loud crashing sound.

She froze. First out of shock—the noise was sudden, and extremely loud, seeming to come from somewhere very nearby—and then with confusion.

She'd been close to the window. Yet she hadn't seen anybody walking the sidewalk toward the building.

She only realized this after she'd turned toward the door to the apartment. She did this even though she knew that wasn't where the sound had come from. That's what you do. You check the perimeter. Hers was fine, but her heart was beating hard.

She pressed her face up against the window. Looked up the street, then down. Five, maybe ten seconds had passed since the noise. Nobody could have made it to either corner in that time. She wasn't even sure that's where the noise had come from—it had seemed to judder up straight through the core of the building, almost to start *inside* her—but it was the only explanation that made sense.

Which meant they were still down there. And that

the most likely explanation for the noise was someone hammering on the front door.

So, now what? Call the cops?

Not for someone banging on a door. Nobody's coming out for that unless it's a *very* quiet night, and if they do, they're going to make you feel small about it. And—if you're a woman—they'll take the time to patronize the living crap out of you, too.

Kristy waited, braced to hear the noise again. If you bang on a door and nobody answers, you bang again, right?

Individual seconds passed, one by one, then thirty seconds in a block. Then a minute. And another.

If you bang on a door *that hard* in anger, it's unlikely you're in a patient enough mood to wait two minutes for a response. So it was only somebody walking home. Fresh from an argument with their spouse, or randomly furious with the universe in general. *Bang-bang* on a door: that's showed everyone. Then stand there, fists hurting, head bowed, realize you're being lame, and lurch home.

Kristy let these rational, comforting explanations stroll around her brain, feeling her heart rate tending back toward normal. It didn't get down all the way, though— and her hands were still gripping the back of the chair.

Still no sign of movement on the street. Must be over five minutes now. She could open the window and look, sure. Hard to imagine what would be gained by this apart from the opportunity to ask them to go away—which would just confirm to them that somebody was inside. Not so smart.

And then her calm, measured thoughts skidded to a halt.

What if they were inside the building?

*   *   *

She stood in front of the door to the apartment, holding her breath, eyes closed, mouth half open. Doing everything she could to make her hearing as acute as possible. No sound from the other side.

Because there's nobody there.

There was no way they could have gotten in. Of course. But was she going to feel comfortable getting into bed until she was sure?

She slowly and silently opened the door. The stairwell was empty. The street door at the bottom was still closed. She padded down. Hesitated behind the door, then unbolted and quickly pulled it wide. Stepped out.

Just a cold, dark street in the mountains, late at night.

She went back in and relocked the door, feeling very silly, then went back up into the apartment, relocking that door, too. The annoying thing was she'd been ready for sleep, and now she was going to have to reboot the entire frickin' process. She headed to the stove to put the kettle on.

But stopped halfway. Her phone was in the middle of the floor.

She glanced up at the counter near the stove. She was prone, she knew—and had been hassled senseless about it by Nolan—to leaving her phone a little close to the edge of things. Tables. Nightstands. Counters, like this one.

In the year in which she'd lived alone, however, without someone to mansplain phone care to her, she'd made an effort to curb the habit. She was *sure* the phone had been six inches from the edge. Couldn't picture it—and knew how misleading that kind of mental image could be anyway, how easy it is to make yourself believe you saw something you never saw—but confident nonetheless.

And even if it *had* been there, hanging off, gravity

works straight down, right? It would have taken something to cause it to fall. The thud when whoever banged on the door downstairs? Maybe. Except the phone hadn't been lying on the floor when she crossed the room to the door.

She picked it up. The front was shattered, glass twisted with lines that looked like branches against sky.

The screen was cloudy gray.

CHAPTER
5

Alright then," Ken said, as he steered my car one-handed out of San Jose airport, his other meaty paw clutching a quadruple espresso in a tiny paper cup. "You have against my better judgment lured me up to Northern California, fetid lair of pot-drenched hippies and start-up wankers hell-bent on game-changing and disrupting things that were perfectly fine as they are. To be honest, I was drunk when we spoke last night and had no memory of booking the plane tickets until I saw the email when I woke up."

"You didn't," Molly said patiently, from the back. "You phoned me and told me to do it. At one thirty in the morning. I also booked a motel."

"Oh," Ken said, as he aimed the car firmly across several lanes of traffic toward the exit for 680, the freeway that would take us north of the Bay Area. Though we were in my car, when you're with Ken, he drives. Twenty-five years of directing commercials and low-budget horror movies has brought him to the point where he doesn't suffer fools gladly. Or anybody. Especially me. I've given up trying to argue the point and simply handed over the keys as he and Pierre came out of the airport. "Good. I'm sure you did a much better job. My point is, Nolan, compelling though your argument must have been, I'm hazy on the fine detail."

"We spoke for half an hour, Ken."

He thought for a moment, shook his head. "Nope. 'Come to San Jose,' you said. That's all I've got."

"I wouldn't mind hearing," Pierre said. Our cameraman was in back with Molly, an unusually small bag of equipment—he hadn't been able to bring his usual ludicrous amount of gear on the hop from Los Angeles—stowed in the trunk. He looked a little more annoyingly handsome and tan than when I'd seen him a few weeks before. "All Ken would say is 'It's some stupid idea that Nolan talked me into.'"

"Nice. Well, I apologize to Molly," I said, "who heard some of this over breakfast. But to teach you to pay attention, Ken—here's the soup-to-nuts."

Everybody's heard of the Nazca Lines, in Peru. If you haven't, look them up. I'll wait. Okay, you know what? Just listen. The Nazca Lines are hundreds of extremely straight lines of scraped earth—embellished with vast parallelograms and narrow triangles longer than a skyscraper is tall, along with massive animal and plant geoglyphs of eerie sophistication. Believed to have been created between 500 BC and AD 500, the lines are assigned to the usual alleged yesteryear obsessions of celestial observation or "ceremonial walkways," though neither makes much sense. Erich von Däniken and allied ancient astronaut nuts went all in on the idea that they were interstellar landing strips, but it's hard to imagine why you'd require so many, that are so long, and repeatedly and chaotically cross, or why you'd need vast, stylized pictures of spiders and monkeys and hummingbirds for this purpose (unless they were the logos of alien cruise ship companies).

Much less famous are the Sajama Lines in Bolivia, again formed by scraping away rocks to reveal lighter undersoil and stretching for up to twenty kilometers across arid and unforgiving landscape. There are none of the cool geoglyphs found at Nazca, but they spread over twenty-two thousand square kilometers, making them fifteen times the size. There are further examples that are barely known beyond academics in the relevant countries—like the Big Circles, twelve massive rings of low stone walls in the Jordanian desert, ranging from seven hundred to fifteen hundred feet in diameter. Nobody knows who made them, or why.

The area around the nearby Azraq Oasis has hundreds of more complex circular structures dated to around two thousand years ago. Still in Jordan, there's a ninety-three-mile-long wall called Khatt Shebib, which stretches across a random stretch of desert. It is not (and has never been) high enough to form a barrier against anything. At times two walls run in parallel, pointlessly. Over in Kazakhstan, meanwhile, there's a collection of two hundred mounds, ramparts, and shapes—including a vast square with a diagonal cross, and a three-legged swastika—known as the Steppe Geoglyphs, some of which are believed to be eight thousand years old.

And so on and on. There are famous examples in Europe, too—like the stone lines at Carnac in France. More are being discovered every year, now that people have access to Google Maps. But this kind of thing is only found in other, dusty and ancient countries, right? The weird foreign ones?

Wrong.

*   *   *

There are lines in the United States, too. I'm not talking about odd collections of megalith-type structures such as Mystery Hill in New Hampshire, or Gungywamp in Connecticut—or even the stone chambers in New England that conventional archeology airily dismisses as "root cellars."

Stranger, to me, are the stone walls.

There's no question that the scattered communities of sixteenth and seventeenth century New England would have needed to organize their environment, and likely spent some time piling up rocks for that purpose. A significant number of stone walls may be merely that. But in 1872 the US Department of Agriculture estimated there were 240,000 miles of walls in New England. Yes, all those zeros are correct. And still better than my Amazon sales ranking. A further report in 1939 nudged it up to 259,000 and still didn't factor in several areas that have especially large numbers of walls: modern researchers put the figure closer to 500,000.

That'd get you to the moon and back.

That's *a lot of walls*.

Let's put this in the context of the times, too— the period when (according to the few archeologists who've considered the phenomenon for five seconds) early settlers allegedly erected these features. In the highlands of Massachusetts there's a town called Hawley, for example. It was settled in 1770 and has never been large: its population in 1790 was 539, it peaked at 1,089 in 1820, and then it slipped back to 600 by 1879. These were farmers living in a harsh, rugged landscape—chopping wood, growing food, performing all the disappointingly tiring tasks required to hack out an existence in the New World.

Yet this small community apparently also had the time to build over *a thousand miles* of stone walls.

Their walls share odd characteristics with others across New England, lines that could circumnavigate the Earth twenty times. Let's run with the idea they're to keep wanderlusting sheep or errant chickens in check. In which case, why are some twelve feet high? And yet others built so low that they wouldn't form a barrier to a determined toddler? Why do some veer all over the place, in jagged or curling or looping lines? Why do so many start and stop suddenly and without apparent reason, failing to form a useful boundary? Why do others go through swamps, or up cliffs, or over mountains that were never farmed, sometimes scaling slopes that are hard to navigate without going down on hands and knees?

Dunno, right? So let's just ignore them.

That happens a lot. In the *New York Times* of December 18, 2002, you'll find a piece about a group of scientists diligently mapping the bottom of the Hudson River with sonar. They found evidence for several hundred of the ships recorded to have sunk there over the previous four centuries, which is doubtless fascinating if you have a thing for old boats, which personally I don't. There's a wealth of chatty information about the wrecks and items that divers had found—including leather, clothes, and food (blueberries, and a potato) that'd been held together by the mud for a couple hundred years.

But then, in the middle of the piece is an odd little paragraph. In throwaway style it's revealed that the survey also found "submerged walls more than 900 feet long, that scientists say are clearly of human construction," adding that the last time the water levels were low enough for building on dry land was...*three thousand years ago*.

Then they go back to drooling over the wreckage of Revolutionary-era ships, and the wall's never brought up again. If you don't believe me, look it up—though you'll have to head straight to the *NYT* piece because it's not mentioned anywhere else that I can find, and it's my job to look for this stuff.

Doesn't that seem *weird* to you? Half a mile of stone wall, built three thousand years ago, cited in the *New York Times* as discovered and mapped by real, named scientists—and yet everybody's "Huh, whatever"?

As *The Anomaly Files* has pointed out on many occasions, there's an awful lot of "Huh, whatever" in American archeology—especially when it comes to the country's prehistory. Which is curious.

Almost as if there are secrets we're not being told.

CHAPTER

6

By the time I'd laid this out Ken had gotten us around San Francisco and was heading up a smaller highway into the mountains of the real Northern California. Pierre had fallen asleep, which I was struggling not to take personally, as he'd been the one to ask the question I was diligently answering. To be honest, while he's a great cameraman and a relentlessly good-natured human being, laser-like smarts is not what we pay Pierre to provide.

Molly, as assistant producer, seemed to be paying attention—doubtless alert for things she might have to budget for or source or shout down the phone at somebody about. Ken was evidently listening, too, when not snarling at other road users or suggesting unrealistic sexual maneuvers they could perform upon farm animals, inanimate objects, or themselves.

"Alright, fine," he said. "Thank you for the only slightly boring travelogue. But we're not going to Nazca, or France, or even New England, on our budget. So presumably you're saying there are lines up here, too."

"I am," I said. "Not only that, but they're one of the most little-known mysteries in the entire country."

*   *   *

If people have heard of them at all, it'll be the Berkeley Walls—which run in sporadic sections up in the hills on the east side of the San Francisco Bay. But these are only a fraction of the lines in Northern California: there are far larger clusters around Shasta, the Sutter Buttes near Sonoma, and other sites. In total there are over eight hundred miles—and those are just the ones that have been located and mapped. Obviously a much smaller number than on the East Coast, but they share the characteristics of odd variations in height, failure to enclose, and a tendency to run through or over things like lakes and mountainsides.

Not only that, but California has been home to European settlers for a far shorter period. You can't shrug the structures off to crack teams of unusually wall-obsessed farmers in the 1600s, because there weren't any.

"That should make them easier to explain, though, right?" Molly said.

"You'd think," I said. "But no."

The area's original inhabitants, the Ohlone, were a sparse population of nomadic hunter-gatherers completely unknown to throw up stone walls for which they had zero need. It's alleged that Russian traders and even Basque shepherds wandered the territory in the distant past, but with scant evidence. Others have claimed the walls were erected under the auspices of the Spanish mission set up in San Jose in 1797, using conscripted Indian labor. This explanation fails for me on the grounds that (a) the Franciscans kept meticulous records of the many and various ways in which they oppressed and brutalized the region's inhabitants, and yet there is no mention of this bizarre undertaking, and (b) some sections of wall are over two hundred miles from the San Jose mission: the same distance we were driving. That's a longish schlep in a modern SUV—a wholly incredible distance to flog embittered Native Americans with no history of stonemasonry.

Slightly less fanciful—and the closest thing to an agreed on or sensible explanation, though again, nobody seems to be paying much attention—is the idea they were built more recently by farmers harnessing cheap labor available in the form of abundant Chinese laborers at loose ends after the gold rush. But I don't buy this either. A 1904 article by a Dr. John Fryer, professor of Oriental languages at UC Berkeley (and another on August 14 of the same year, published in the *San Francisco Chronicle* and written by Harold French) make it clear that the walls had already been regarded as a mysterious phenomenon for some time, likely decades. French's article, which points out that the walls serve no discernible "modern" purpose, is titled "Who Built the Pre-historic Walls Topping Berkeley Hills?" He says they'd been a source of mystery to the original prospectors in the region.

That they were there *before* the gold rush, in other words.

But put that aside, because I haven't been able to track down corroborating accounts. Consider instead that the gold rush ended around 1855, just fifty years before these pieces were published in reputable newspapers. There's no question that shorter periods of time were sufficient for history and purpose to be forgotten back then, but *really*? If the walls had been the product of locals taking advantage of Chinese labor, some of those farmers—or at very least, their children, or neighbors—would have still been alive. This wasn't Jebediah Farmerdude hiring a couple of guys to throw up a pen for his couple dozen sheep. This was building enough wall *to stretch from San Jose to Seattle*.

And nobody remembered this happening?

Nobody at all?

And none of which comes close to tackling the bigger question of their failure as boundaries. Yes, some of the stone has been repurposed over the years, but it's a trivial archeological undertaking to tell where that's occurred.

So why are some walls—like those around Modoc and parts of Shasta—formed of dotted lines? And what's the deal with the ones that go up sheer hillsides, twenty miles from where anybody's ever farmed?

Then there's this.

Around the time Fryer and French were penning their curiosity pieces, the walls also allegedly attracted the attention of Sister Mary Paula von Tessen of the Dominican Order at Mission San Jose. She studied them for twenty-five years, reportedly producing a number of maps and drawings. And yet when Dr. Robert Fisher—who'd been personal physician to the order for decades before starting to take his own interest in the walls—asked to see the late Sister Mary's notes, then (if you'll pardon the pun) the mission firmly stonewalled him.

The order's archives still hold her writings on religious subjects. But the product of a quarter century's obsession with the walls has completely disappeared.

"Okay," Ken said. By now we were within forty miles of Birchlake, steadily ascending into the mountains and forests. It was getting dark and the wipers were on against a persistent light rain. "So there's a bunch of walls. And in typical Nolan fashion, you've provided a bunch of non-explanations—things that you say that they are *not*. So what *are* they?"

"No idea."

"Mate—unless you can say those two words *really* fucking slowly, it's not going to fill an hour-long show."

"What do the walls look like?" This was from Pierre, now awake once more.

"Well, stone walls, I'm assuming."

Ken turned his head ominously. "You haven't seen them?"

"Not these exact ones."

"Have you seen *any* of them?"

"Sure. The ones outside Berkeley. Once."

"Are those . . . not very good walls?"

"They're fine."

Ken was still staring at me. "Then why the *hell* aren't we doing this back down there, near one of California's highest concentrations of excellent restaurants, past which I drove over an hour ago? Why are we instead going all the way up to this Birchlake shithole?"

"These are . . . better walls," I said, holding on to my seat as the car started to veer into the other lane. "Ken— eyes on the road, maybe?"

He gave me one more deeply suspicious glare, but then turned his attention back to the dark highway.

CHAPTER
7

Getting a new phone had required Kristy driving thirty miles to the Chico Mall. She walked down the central concourse without looking in any of the stores. She didn't like malls. Everything about them, from the drearily predictable array of potential possessions, to sparsely occupied food courts dotted with people whose shape suggested they shouldn't be eating fast food at eleven a.m., made her feel lonely and sad. And snide, and body-shaming, and elitist. A bad combination.

The guy in the Verizon store confirmed what Kristy already knew from fiddling with the phone. It was bricked. "And you dropped it, you say?"

"Well, it slipped out of my hand. As I was getting it out of my purse."

The guy frowned at the device. He had sandy hair and glasses and appeared determined to get to the bottom of the problem. Kristy didn't care about the bottom line, only the executive summary: she needed a phone that worked.

"Weird thing," he mused. "It doesn't look like an impact shatter. See the initial break? It's way up on top, near the edge—where the case protects it best. You'd've been super-unlucky for it to land on something at that exact spot." He turned it over in his hands. "It looks more like it cracked from an energy surge or something."

"Maybe," Kristy improvised. "It did feel warm when I got it out of my bag."

The guy was nodding now, as if sensing a mystery that would raise him above men and women of similar occupation, perhaps into the exalted echelon of Awesome Phone Dudes that are celebrated in legend and song, and on Reddit. "Never heard of that happening on this model before, though. It would probably be a good idea to—"

"It's an enigma," Kristy agreed cheerfully, to divert him from whatever horrifically protracted process he was about to suggest. "I should set my ex-husband on the case."

The guy looked up at her over his glasses, as though sensing the threat of a rival. "Is he a tech?"

"No. He hosts a YouTube show called *The Anomaly Files*."

"I've seen that. It's...well, it's kinda, not very..."

"I know. Look—so what happens next?"

He started to explain that he could maybe get her a replacement sent in a couple days. Kristy in turn explained that wouldn't work for her, and directed him to look at her account, where she knew that—courtesy of previous encounters with customer service—there was a note saying something along the lines of "Give this woman whatever she wants, right away, seriously: pissing her off is shit you don't need."

She walked out of the mall with a brand new phone fifteen minutes later.

*   *   *

On her way out of Chico she stopped at the sheriff's department. The sheriff was grateful for her previous tip concerning Alaina's second Instagram account, but other than confirming that his men were keeping a close watch for any sign of the girl, seemed disinclined to discuss the matter further.

She grabbed an early lunch in the Stone Mountain Tap back in Birchlake, working through a plate of surprisingly good nachos and waiting for her replacement phone to download all her crap back down out of the cloud. No sign of the old guy who'd spoken to her the night before. No sign of Val, either. Two guys were holding down the bar, one middle-aged and bald, the other a very good-looking dude in his twenties that Kristy immediately guessed might be the missing bartender from the previous night.

She heard him referred to as Kurt. The number of reminders required to get Kristy's check, however, suggested Val's nickname summed him up better.

After that she walked to a park on a bluff above the river. The sky was clear and blue, and she was glad to have her coat. Glad, too, for the coffee she'd bought from the place by her apartment. The roast was green and sour, an affectation she found annoying, but it was hot.

Apart from a scattering of benches the park held a faded-looking play structure in primary colors and a short, low section of old-looking stone wall of no evident purpose. A rusted chain fence on the bluff spoiled the view down to the rocky river. A sign at the gate indicated that it was dedicated to someone in particular, a woman who had doubtless achieved notable civic things in days of yore. It felt like the space had been somebody's brainchild a decade or two ago and the subject of many hard-fought town meetings, but had received little or no attention since.

Kristy saw two MISSING posters, both already weather-worn. The photo of Alaina Hixon made her look as if she couldn't possibly ever go missing.

After a while she saw a harried-looking figure striding down the path, so she got out her notebook and pen, and laid her phone next to them on the picnic table.

"I'm not sure what I can tell you," Principal Broecker said, taking a hurried slurp from a small thermos. His coffee smelled better than hers. "And I've only got twenty minutes. Sorry I'm late. Hi, by the way. Call me Dan."

He thrust a beefy hand across the table, and Kristy shook it. She suspected Broecker was one of those men who would always be running late, though not for want of trying. Forty-something, a little burly, a little hectic, shaggy dark hair and a beard. New-looking jeans, shirt in an ill-advised shade of mustard, a tweedy jacket that wanted nothing to do with either of the other garments. Either he dressed in the dark or was canny enough to give his students (and staff) an easy target for covert derision.

"Don't worry," she said. "I'm on vacation."

"Huh," he said, looking at her shrewdly, and she knew he'd seen right through that. "Well, so, what would you like to know?" He shivered. "It's chilly."

"Why didn't you want to do this at the school?"

"You know what they're like," he said. "Or maybe you don't. Schools are a little universe to themselves, and as such very alert to any disturbance in the force. It's taken this long to get back to where it feels anything like stable.

If I'm seen talking to an unknown person on campus—
or anywhere, because I'm Principal Broecker wherever I
go—the bush telegraph would start jangling. And look,
issues of privacy and confidentiality apply, as I'm sure
you understand."

"Of course."

"Good. Then fire away."

"What was your impression of Alaina?"

The principal exhaled. "It's a small school. A hundred
and fifty students, from here in town and houses further
up in the mountains. I have a name for every face."

"But you're busy."

"I am busy," he said, not defensively. "And apart from a
class I teach on early US history—which I know for a fact
is universally regarded as the most tedious elective available—I'm an administrator. I don't have the day-to-day
contact. Some pop out, naturally. The kids who're more
often sent to my office—one of whom is, disappointingly, my own son. The academically exceptional. On the
opposite extreme, I try to keep an eye on the children who
disappear, and Alaina definitely isn't one of those."

"Excuse me?"

"Sorry—terrible choice of words. Look, do you mind
if I have a cigarette? I allow myself one during working
hours. I can go stand over there, if you prefer."

Kristy smiled. "Doesn't bother me."

He pulled out a battered pack, lit up, and quickly
looked more relaxed. "Thank you. Obviously I didn't
mean 'disappeared' in that way. I meant..."

"The ones nobody notices."

"*Exactly.* The kids who don't excel but aren't tanking.
Who don't speak up in class but aren't self-evidently ex-
periencing issues. Who are neither popular, nor loners."

"And Alaina wasn't that kind of kid?"

He shook his head. "Grades in the upper middle of the pack. Plenty of character. Perfectly noticeable. She was taking my class and actually appeared to enjoy it, which is very unusual. Enough friends—she and the Hardaker twins seemed very close. I've discussed her a great deal with the staff in the last ten days, but none seem to have much more than that, even Gina."

"Who is..."

"In eighth grade each student has an advisor who's charged with keeping an overview of their progress. In Alaina's case, it's Gina."

"Can I talk to her?"

"I'm not sure why you'd need to. What with you being on vacation." He smiled briefly, and knocked out the end of his cigarette on the side of the bench. After confirming that the fallen embers were extinguished, he neatly folded the butt and stowed it back in the pack, each motion a fussy little secret. "Anything else?"

"Did she ever say anything about being bullied?"

"What?"

Kristy took out her phone and unlocked it. The picture was ready on screen. The principal stared at it. "Have you told the police about this?"

"I called them yesterday morning."

"Uh-huh. That explains why the sheriff came to see me in the afternoon. I told him what I'd told him before. That we'd never seen anything of that sort. In the school. Ever. So how come they didn't find this?"

"That's not her main Instagram account. I spent a few hours tracing back from her regular one. Seeing who'd commented. Where else they'd commented. If the commenters seemed to have secondary accounts—which kids do, to slip around prying parental eyes. Eventually I found this."

"What'd the police say?"

"That they'd look into it. I stopped by earlier. They say it's a dead end, and probably doesn't mean anything."

"Well," Broecker said. He was still frowning at the picture. "I guess there's not actually much *there*."

"Nope."

"And the last line could just be a mean joke."

"It could."

"Any idea who the commenters are?"

"No. For all I know they could be sock puppets owned by Alaina herself, to make her look more popular, or play out a role. It's unlikely the site would give me any information, and I haven't asked because I don't want to trigger them into taking the accounts down. It doesn't look like the police have, either. I got the sense they weren't taking me very seriously."

"I'm not sure they've ever taken Alaina's disappearance as seriously as they should, to be honest."

"What do you mean?"

He shook his head. "That's not fair. They had a lot on their hands with the mess in Chico. I'm sure they're doing everything they can." The principal put Kristy's phone back on the table. "But, so, what's your interest? And drop the 'on vacation' malarkey. I googled you. You're quite well-known online. Good, too—that piece on permafrost was very sharp. Are you intending to write something about Alaina's disappearance?"

"No. Or at least, not yet. She happened to pop up on a search when I was looking for something else."

"Los Angeles is a long way from here."

"I was bored."

"You must have been," Broecker said. "Look. I can see why you'd find that image intriguing, but I don't think it proves anything. Certainly not a culture of bullying."

"I didn't say anything about a—"

"No," he said, politely but firmly. "You didn't. But other people will. There are no 'isolated incidents' when it comes to bullying. It's always a 'culture.' A disaster for a school. It's appalling that Alaina has gone missing, and I'll do everything in my power to help anybody trying to find her. But right now it seems to me there's no additional story worth telling the rest of the world. Let me know if that changes."

He stood. "And one more thing. You asked what kind of girl Alaina *was*. So far as we know, she still *is*, yes?"

Kristy watched him stride away back up the path, a man on his way to be slightly late for the next thing, feeling as if she'd narrowly avoided being given a detention.

CHAPTER
8

Afterward Kristy walked along the forest-lined road into the mountains. About half a mile along was a cleared space in the forest on the right. A large, wooden two-story building stood there, a partially overgrown parking area behind, a creek running down to the river along one side. It had once been a restaurant and/or bar. Possibly somewhere to stay, too— there were tattered curtains hanging in the three pairs of windows on the upper floor. A sign indicated it had been called Olsen's. It looked like it had been out of business for years, but had long ago been a place you could reliably find a good time—to a possibly disreputable degree.

Kristy walked around it, including the back. At one end was a river rock chimney. The remnants of a 1940s sign on one gable said FOOD, and a matching one on the next said COCKTAILS. All the windows and doors had been covered from the inside with wooden boards.

She left and walked farther along the two-lane highway. It took her ten minutes to find the narrow road she was looking for, snaking off into the woods.

Fifty yards up it was a driveway with a weathered mailbox, HIXON written on the side with Sharpie.

The drive had been blocked by three rusted oil drums.

Back in the trees she could see one corner of an old, two-story wooden house. It hadn't been repainted in many years. A deceased pick-up truck lurked in the bushes, on flats.

It was very quiet in the trees. Also cold. A bank of low cloud promised more rain. With the positioning of the drums as a barrier, Kristy knew this was not the time to call unannounced on the family of a missing teenage girl.

She walked back to town. On the way an idea occurred to her. She got out her phone to do some quick research.

Twenty minutes later she walked up to a house a couple of blocks off Birchlake's main street. Broecker had mentioned a first name. The school's website provided a surname, along with a picture of a pleasant-looking brunette in her mid-thirties, smiling in that blandly reassuring way teachers do. Finding an address for the only Gina Wright in the county had been the work of moments on a website Kristy subscribed to.

The woman who opened the door was instantly recognizable from the school website. The resemblance was eerily exact, in fact, as though the teacher had just come from having the picture taken. A brighter smile, though that faded quickly, to be replaced with uncertainty.

"I wondered if I might ask a couple questions?"

"About what?"

"Alaina Hixon."

The teacher looked apologetic. "It's heartbreaking. But I honestly think I've told everything I know."

"It'll only take a moment."

The inside of Gina's house was tidy—the portion Kristy saw, anyhow. The hall showed no signs of kid

detritus or dust. The living room was tastefully deco-
rated, a large 1930s-style radio on the mantel the only
discordant note. The cushions on the couch were plump
and perfect and precisely equidistant. Kristy sat. Gina
remained standing.

"Just three things," Kristy said. "Two of which you'll
already have covered. But I wanted to get my own
impression."

"Of what?"

"Alaina at school."

"High middle of the pack. Better in humanities than
math/science. Not backward in self-advocating. At all."

"What about her home life?"

"So far as I know everything's hunky-dory, given the
circumstances. I've met her dad at school events, and he
seems nice enough. Though stretched a little thin. You
know what happened to her mom?"

"Died a year and a half ago. Car accident."

"Right. The rumor was alcohol was involved, and
I certainly saw Jenny in the Tap from time to time.
Alaina's dad has been by himself since. I think recently
maybe there's been a little friction. But she's a teenager, so..."

"What about Alaina's friends?"

"She hung out with Maddy and Nadja mainly. A
couple others. She was never alone in the yard. Seemed
to stay clear of the clique stuff, too."

"And you never saw evidence of bullying?"

"Are you kidding? Any hint of that in the school and it
would be a *huge* great deal with Dan. The principal. And
honestly, I'd be surprised. It's a small school and a small
town, and everybody keeps an eye out for everybody else.
Too much so, if anything. Why do you ask?"

"Nothing else springs to mind, anything different about her before she disappeared?"

"Only what I already told the investigators."

"Do you mind repeating it, in your own words?"

"The last few weeks, she'd been...I don't know. Distant. I spoke to a couple of the other teachers about it, but nobody else seemed to have noticed anything. I guess maybe I was more sensitive to it, because we'd always got on well before. But, like I said, she's a teenager. They can be weird. It doesn't always mean anything."

Kristy left the woman with her card. As she walked away, two things seemed clear. Kristy had interviewed enough people to have a sense when they were concealing guilt. She hadn't gotten that vibe, though she had gotten the sense *something* was up with her. Odd for Gina not to ask to see ID, for example.

As she turned into the side street that would take her to Shasta Avenue and her apartment, Kristy noticed somebody she recognized in the distance. He was approaching at a steady rate, as if he had somewhere to go. Kurt, aka the Crown Prince of Uselessness. He winked at her in passing.

Kristy ran out of steam when she got back to the main street. Being here was dumb, and not helping anyone. Least of all herself. But then what? It was far too late to start the drive back to LA. She was stuck here another night.

As she passed the Stone Mountain Tap she saw someone wave at her. Val, bussing a table in the window. She went inside. The place was empty in the dead zone between late lunchers and early drinkers.

"How's the exploring going?"

"I'm done," Kristy said.

"I warned you that nobody comes here for the excitement. You're booked three more days, though, right?"

"I'll let you know when I leave."

"Sounds good. Not gonna refund you, though."

Kristy smiled. "Fair enough. By the way. There was a strange noise last night."

Val glanced up from lining the table's ketchup and hot sauces in a neat row. "Noise?"

"Late. It might have been someone hammering on the front door." Kristy had thought about it a lot since, however, and realized her first impression felt correct. "But sounded more like it had been an impact on the interior wall. Underneath."

"Huh," Val said. She moved on to the next table, sweeping the cloth slowly and methodically over its surface.

"No way anybody could have gotten in there?"

"Nope," Val said. "It's locked up, front and back. I'm using it as storage. Bunch of furniture and old junk I need to figure out whether I can use for another reno, or should just take to the dump."

"Well, you might want to check if something fell over. It was kind of loud."

"I'll do that," Val said.

Kristy went back out onto the street and walked toward the apartment. As she unlocked the door, she glanced along the street.

Val was still standing in the window of the Tap. It looked like she was watching her.

CHAPTER
9

The motel was an L shape on the edge of town opposite a two-pump gas station. Ken parked at random in the middle of the lot—he has a tendency to own a space—and we three guys stretched and looked around as Molly headed over to check us in. The parking lot featured a number of cracks through which tufts of grass grew, dropping away at the end to the cold river twenty feet below. There were no other cars. The motel was beat up and very brown and backed up against a forest that looked like it went on basically forever. The rusting coke machine had an OUT OF ORDER sign that might as well have been written in cuneiform.

As Molly came back out of the office and returned to us, Ken shook his head. "I did my best," he said. "I know you had such dreams. Such hopes for life. I'm sorry it turned out this way."

Molly frowned. "Who are you talking to?"

"My younger self."

"Ha ha. The only other option was a snooty B&B where you and Nolan would have had to share a bed. And pay four hundred dollars a night for the privilege."

"I'd rather sleep standing up in this parking lot."

"Co-sign," I said.

*   *   *

It took two minutes to throw our bags into the rooms, five to walk to the center of "town" and find an establishment called the Stone Mountain Tap, and not much longer to get ourselves settled at the table in the window.

I decided immediately that it was a good bar, despite the excessively self-confident young guy who declared himself our server for the night. He confided to us that his name was Kurt. I've never been sure why I'm supposed to care about that information, as it's impossible to use without sounding either overly familiar or as if you're trying to start a fight, which I seldom am. Once Ken had communicated to Kurt that what he required of a waitperson was not personality but speed, we spent a drink laying out a plan of attack for the next day.

Ken had a map purchased from the gas station—which turned out to be under the purview of the same taciturn oldster who ran the motel. In the database on my phone I had rough diagrams of the positioning of (possibly) anomalous walls in the area, along with links to Google Maps overlays that would enable us to be more accurate when on the ground. The overlays had been compiled by amateur online enthusiasts, who claimed to have located only about thirty percent of the local walls, but it was a start.

We agreed that a couple of small clusters fifteen miles up the road would be a good place to try, and I left Ken and Molly discussing whether we could be bothered to get permission from the landowners (or just hop over the fence and hope for the best) and went outside for a cigarette. A woman with short gray hair behind the bar winked at me, presumably spotting a fellow social pariah.

It was, disappointingly, drizzling again, in that annoying spitty way that's almost rain. The weather in California is famously good, but when it decides to be wet—especially in the north—it can take a while for it to get the impulse out of its system. It was chilly, too.

I wandered along the street, wondering what it would be like to live in a place like Birchlake. Not exciting, but okay, probably. Small grocery store on the corner. Nice-looking coffee shop. But next to it something that had once been a large general store, windows now white-washed—never a good look in the middle of a main street. There was a faint glow from a window on the upper floor. Somebody's apartment, presumably. The rest of the street was dark apart from a liquor store up the end, with a guy standing weaving outside, steadfastly ignoring the NO LOITERING signs. As I passed he suddenly raised his head and shouted into thin air, then took a hurried step backward, as if someone or something had come right back at him—something bigger and scarier than he'd been banking on.

When I was most of the way back to the bar I noticed something out of the corner of my eye, and looked back at the upper window of the former general store.

A moment later I saw the shadow again, farther back into the room. Probably the inhabitant wondering why some guy was standing looking up at *them*. I waved to indicate that I was harmless (because I basically am) and walked on, meanwhile starting the phone call I knew I had to make.

"New phone, who dis?" Kristy said, when she picked up.

"Oh, so it's funny when *you* do it?"

"No," she said. "This actually is a new phone. The old one blew up."

"Seriously?"

"Something like that. So—to what do I owe the pleasure? Speaking to each other two days straight. People will talk."

"Let them," I declared, crossing the main street toward the bar. "Just wondered if you'd made any progress on the missing girl thing."

"None whatsoever," she said. "In fact I'm bailing tomorrow. I am bored and crave civilization."

"Oh."

"What? You sound weird."

"Well, I may have done something ill-advised."

"Plotting to overthrow the government again? We've talked about that. You'd be a dreadful dictator."

"No," I said. "Not that."

There was a pause. "Oh, for God's sake, Nolan."

I was now outside the Stone Mountain Tap. Confused, I looked up... and saw Kristy was sitting inside, at a booth in the back. She was staring at me, and looked exasperated.

At the table just the other side of the window I saw Ken look at me, frown, half-stand to peer in the direction in which I was obviously staring, and then turn back.

He looked pretty exasperated with me, too.

It's a good thing that I am fundamentally very lovable.

A couple hours later Kristy and I left the bar. The others had departed for the motel a little while before.

Ken and Kristy have met before and so merely exchanged "Nolan is an asshole" eye rolls when she joined our table. It was a first for Molly and Pierre (*The Anomaly Files* started after Kristy and I split up) but both have decent interpersonal skills and said hi and shuffled their chairs around to make room, managing to avoid asking, "Okay, we get that you guys used to be married or something, but WTF is she doing here now?"

I explained to Kristy about the rock walls in the area. She acknowledged that was our kind of thing. And so then we all basically ate and drank and hung out.

As I walked her along the street afterward, however, she stopped and turned to me. "Seriously, though."

"What?"

"Why are you really here?"

"Last night," I said. "You sounded…quiet. I wasn't far. I have been known to cheer people up."

"I recall such a thing, and that's sweet of you. I'm leaving tomorrow, though. I'm already packed."

"You said. We'll still go look at the walls. I should have warned you. I just hoped it'd be a nice surprise."

She smiled. "It is. And I'm booked here another few nights, so what the hey. Maybe I'll try one more poke around tomorrow, then come and get drunk with you guys."

"Sounds like a plan." I noticed she was wearing a necklace I hadn't seen before. A thin, plain chain, with a small silver cross on it. "Is that new?"

"No. Old." She saw I was still looking at it. "What?"

"Not the kind of thing you normally wear, that's all."

"I've had it since I was a teenager."

"Always useful to have something to hold up in the face of vampires. Because you just never know. So. How far is it to where you're staying?"

"We're already here. Airbnb. That's me." She nodded toward the old department store. "I'd invite you up for coffee, except I'm not going to."

"Good. Saves me coming up with a polite way to

decline. But wait." I walked back a couple of paces, looking at the window on the upper story. "You're staying up there?"

"Yes."

"And there's just the one apartment?"

"A spacious getaway of approximately four hundred fifty square feet, if I recall the listing accurately. Why?"

I hesitated, not knowing whether I should say, but figuring I had to. "Right before I called you earlier. I may be wrong, but I thought I saw somebody up there."

"In the apartment?"

"A shadow. As if someone was back in the room, blocking a dim light. And you were in the bar at that point, as I discovered moments later. So it couldn't have been you."

"Huh."

She opened a locked door, and I led the way up the side stairs. There was nobody in the apartment, and no sign that anybody had been there.

"Sorry," I said. "Hope I haven't freaked you out. Just my imagination, I guess."

I walked into the lot of the motel to find Ken, hands in pockets, looking into the dark of the forest. He held out one fist with two meaty fingers extended. I put a cigarette between them, and one between my own lips, and lit both.

We stood in silence for a few minutes before Ken asked the question. "So what's the deal, monkey-boy?"

"Honestly, partly that I think there could be a show for us in these walls."

"But also?"

"A teenage girl disappeared ten days ago. Kristy came

up here to look into it. She says it's related to something she's writing on cyberbullying."

"But you're not sure that's why she came, and so you thought why not be in the area, too. Partly because, despite what everybody says, you're a half-decent bloke. Also you're hoping it might make her take the idea of getting back together more seriously. Especially if you get her drunk."

"Sometimes I wonder why I bother saying things out loud to you."

"Me too." He winked. "Maybe you should stop."

CHAPTER
10

We drove out of town at the crack of ten o'clock the next morning. Normally Ken has a tendency to insist we get started stupidly early, a legacy of his days directing movies but also related to a policy of getting the day's work done as early as possible, so he can go to the bar. I'd slept badly and was already standing on the walkway at seven when he emerged from his room looking like a disheveled owl. We watched the rain for a while, then he muttered "Bollocks to that" and went back in his room.

It was still raining when we eventually got on the road, though less heavily. Cloud cover remained dark and low, however, and with the forests looming on all sides, the drive along the main street felt like going through a tunnel. I glanced up toward Kristy's apartment as we passed but couldn't tell if she was there. We'd agreed I'd give her a call late afternoon. After the main drag petered out there were a couple more blocks of houses, a school, then forest. We followed the highway along the river for a few miles before Molly directed Ken off a side road.

This forged higher still, at times through trees, at others with flat misty meadows either side, and would doubtless have been attractive if it hadn't still been raining. It was due to stop within the hour, but the weather station providing that information was fifty miles away so we weren't taking that as a guarantee. Ken's confidence in the project was declining steadily, and he'd already begun asking me about backup mysterious phenomena in the region. There weren't any. It was the walls or nothing.

"Okay," Molly said, eventually. "Well, we're here."

"Here" presented as a stretch on the left that was bereft of trees. A low wooden fence divided it from the road. Other than that—and shrouded in mist—it looked pretty much exactly like everything else we'd seen.

Ken pulled into the first available spot by the side of the road. "Go check," he said, to me.

"Check what?"

"The wall."

"I say again, check what?"

"That it's actually here."

"It's *not* here. This is the nearest we can get to it. Or to them. There's more than one. But now we have to hike."

"It's pissing down."

"It's barely a heavy drizzle."

Ken turned in his seat. "Nolan, I'm from England. Just as the Eskimos or Inuit or whoever the fuck are said to have a hundred words for snow, we Brits are perfectly capable of describing rain. Some days we do little else. Regardless of how you'd rank the current conditions on the Nolan Moore Scale of Shit Weather, I'm not getting out of this car unless you're sure there's something worth pointing a camera at."

"I'll come," Pierre said. "We'll want some start-of-the-expedition footage."

"And it'll need sound," Molly said. "So I'll come, too."

"Thank you both," I said. "I'd just like to say it's a pleasure dealing with true professionals."

"Likewise." Molly grabbed her backpack and the boom mic. "Shame to muddle on without the decisive and visionary eye of the show's director, though."

"I know," I said, sadly. "But it is what it is."

"And what it is, is *bollocks*," Ken muttered, wearily undoing his seatbelt. "God I hate Californians."

"Hey," Molly and Pierre said, in unison.

"Not you two," he said. "Just him."

We walked together back to the middle of the wooden fence, and peered into the gloom.

"All this mist will look pretty cool," Pierre said. "If we actually find…"

"Look, *there are walls*," I said. "For fuck's sake. And we will find them. Have I let you down before?"

All three looked at me. "Well, yeah," I admitted. "Okay. But for now, dare to believe."

"We'll need some of the introductory crap you said in the car yesterday," Ken said. "But let's tape a heavily condensed and less boring version later, when and if the weather gets better. For now say something short, then let's go look for these things. Oh—and coat off, Nolan."

"Seriously?"

"The weather's 'fine.' You assured me earlier."

I took off my coat, revealing the billowy off-white shirt that Ken insists I wear on camera, partly for continuity but mainly so he can make fun of it.

I handed him the coat. He put it on. "Ooh, toasty."

I stood by the fence and Pierre raised his camera. He winced, but nobody asked if he was okay. We all knew he'd injured his shoulder on our last expedition, deep in the Grand Canyon, and that we all preferred to leave the events there in the back of our minds. Molly stood to the side and lifted the boom mic. Ken pointed at me, and Pierre nodded.

"So here we are," I said, trying to look relaxed and committed and not at all freezing. "And if this isn't technically the middle of nowhere, it's certainly the back of beyond. We're in the Sierra Nevada mountains, and the last place that looked like a real town was Birchlake, which is"—I raised my hand and pointed—"thirty minutes back that way. That doesn't mean this area's always been remote, however. Humans introduce paths into the world. Sometimes in response to environmental features, like bridges across rivers or tracks along ridges. Others merely to join settlement A to settlement B. If those places stop being a big deal, or fade entirely, the paths can vanish, too. Our lives and landscapes are written by time, whose invisible hand in shaping our world is only evident in retrospect."

I saw Ken was frowning at me as though I'd started speaking Japanese, and decided to cut to the chase.

"Nonetheless, this area has never been anywhere in particular. And that's why what we're about to show you…is rather mysterious. Follow me."

"Cut," Ken said. "It'll do. Just one tiny note for the next section, though, Nolan."

"What's that?"

"Be better."

I got my coat back and clambered over the fence. The others followed. Funny thing about climbing a fence. Doesn't matter how unimportant the structure is, how close to collapse, or if you're miles from anywhere, going from one side of a fence to the other always feels like a trespass, which I guess it sometimes is—but also as though you've traveled farther than the tiny distance involved. You were over there, and then you're here. You are somewhere different now.

I considered saying something along these lines in the next to-camera chunk, but found it all too easy to imagine the irritably puzzled way in which Ken would stare at me.

Molly got centered on her GPS unit, and we set off into the mist.

CHAPTER
11

California is celebrated for beaches and surfing in the south. In the north are the epic redwoods—and in old growth areas these ancient and astonishing trees may have trunks wider than a car and growth rings laid down before the birth of Christ. It's home to majestic mountains, too, as at Yosemite, and alpine water spots like Lake Tahoe, where—especially if on a terrace getting into your second cocktail—the beauty is arranged with such eerie perfection as to suggest you are not in a natural environment but instead spending your designated annual vacation in the carefully designed recreation sector of a vast starship, bound for the far side of the galaxy.

It's a big state, though. There are other parts. The endless extent of the Central Valley, with nothing to see for hour after hour except more of the same, and where in summer it's so arid and hot that your only desire is to not be there anymore. There's the California desert. And then there's...

"This is the most boring bit of California I've ever seen," Ken said, after fifteen minutes.

"Seriously?" Pierre said, who'd been filming for much of the time—clips of me striding manfully up and down minor hills and gullies, along with atmospheric shots of mist curling into the trees. "I think it's great."

"It's not ugly," Ken admitted, gesturing vaguely. "There are trees doing that whole tree thing. Tons of the bastards. And there's shrubs, or whatever they are. Bushes, whatever. I don't care. And craggy rocks, and mountainy bits. But a little of all that goes a long way, and there's a bugger of a lot of it. Are we there yet, is what I'm saying."

"Should be soon," Molly said. "About a couple hundred yards, around the crag over there. I think."

We kept trudging onward. The drizzle had stopped, or at least become so fine that it was like walking through cold, wet air. The meadow eventually narrowed, trees pressing in on the left, a bare, rocky prominence on the right. I was beginning to worry the GPS overlays we were relying upon were either inaccurate or simply made up, when we turned a corner.

"And there it is," Molly said, quietly.

"Fuck's sake," Ken said. "You have got to be joking."

I'll admit that at first glance it wasn't impressive. In all honesty, it didn't become much more impressive after you'd spent ten minutes looking at it from all angles.

Walking around the rock face had revealed a further extent of meadow. If you were to imagine a green/gray/beige blanket thrown over an unmade bed, with hills and depressions caused by hidden pillows underneath, that's what the terrain looked like—assuming you'd also surrounded the bed with ranks of cold, silent pine trees, built to scale. Okay, forget the bed thing. It was a dumb comparison.

But there, in the middle, was a wall. About forty feet long, less than three feet high, and basically straight.

As we got closer, further detail became evident. It had been constructed by piling gray, lichen-covered rocks on top of one another, some large, others small, the latter used to plug gaps between the former. It was consistently about a foot thick along its length. The end closest to us was vertical: the other ran out over the course of a couple of yards, gradually getting lower, before stopping.

Without needing to be instructed by Ken, Pierre and Molly followed me as I walked around the wall. I'd love to be able to say more about it than what I've already said, but there isn't much to add. At the far end there was evidence the wall had originally extended further: scattered rocks in an approximate line, a couple of small pits in the ground where it seemed like large stones from a lower layer had once been bedded. The other end looked like it had always been designed to simply stop as it did.

Aware that Ken was standing out of shot, waiting in a silent way that was nonetheless very loud, I stopped wandering around the wall and turned to camera. When Pierre looked locked and the light went on, I started to talk.

"We purposefully brought you first to an unremarkable portion of wall," I lied, "to give you a sense of what they're like in isolation. You'll note that no magical level of technology is involved. Let's dismiss that idea right away. You see this kind of dry-stone wall all over the world. Rocks piled on top of other rocks. Some of the people who've tried to explain away the New England walls have claimed they are literally that: farmers dealing with a phenomenon called frost heave, where stones are raised to the surface by successive cycles of frost and thaw. The idea being that farmers dealt with their fields getting rockier by picking up the rocks and throwing them in a pile. But I don't buy that."

I squatted down. Pierre smoothly mirrored my movement. His knees didn't make cracking sounds, unlike mine.

"Because, look," I said, running my hand over the wall. "This isn't haphazard. Bigger rocks form the bulk of the structure, but smaller stones have been used to ensure a fairly uniform surface. You don't bother to do that if you're throwing rocks out of the way. This is a wall, and designed as such."

I straightened and pointed over the wall at the nearest portion of forest. "Over there is the basis of another attempted explanation. The walls of New England are rarely mentioned until the late eighteenth or early nineteenth centuries. Some have speculated that excessive forestation in the early years made frost heave more and more of an issue, and that they simply ran out of wood to build enclosures. So they killed two birds with one stone...and built them out of rock."

I turned toward Pierre and used a below-frame hand signal to indicate I wanted to switch to a walk-to-you. He dutifully started backing away, as I ambled toward him.

"We can't wholly dismiss that idea. It's possible some of the walls came about that way, and for those reasons. But then let me ask you this."

I stopped at the end that had a neat, vertical upright. "As you can see, the wall stops here. Back at the other end, there's evidence it continued for some distance. Somebody, at some time, removed some rocks, perhaps to build something else. But not here. Almost as if there was supposed to be a gate. But there's no evidence that a further stretch of wall ever started after a gap. This wall simply stops. Why?"

I went around the end and started back in the other direction. "And if you look back along its stretch, you'll see the top is exactly the same weathered gray color, and covered in lichen to the same extent, as the sides. It's not proof, but it suggests the wall was never any higher than this. So what on earth is the point of it? To mark off one person's land from another's? Possibly, but look around— does that seem likely, in this mountain pasture, miles from anywhere? Every time you think you've answered something about these walls, it raises another question."

I stopped walking and looked straight to camera. "Questions that *The Anomaly Files* is going to try to answer."

"Cut," Ken said. "Nolan—can I have a word?"

We walked together toward the trees, leaving the others to go on ahead toward where there was supposed to be a small cluster of further walls.

"What's up?"

"How," he said. "That's what's up. Or that's my point, anyway. *How.*"

"How what?"

"How the hell *are* you going to answer these questions? You've admitted, often enough that it's becoming tedious, that nobody knows who built the walls, or why, or when."

"That's why it's a mystery, dude."

"I know. And mysteries are our business, for better or worse. But we're not here to just say, 'Weird, huh?' Nobody's going to watch an hour of that. I signed on for this wall idea because it's less dangerous than the last thing we did, and it's cheap. But cheap is no good if all we get is you peering at orderly piles of rock and shrugging. And don't trot out your line about it not being important to find, only that we continue to seek. Finding is television. Seeking is just you twatting about in a wet field."

"I know," I said. "Look. Half a mile from there there's a couple of longer sections. Maybe we'll find something to work with. If not, then you're right. We might just have to bail on this idea and it be one of those things you give me endless grief about forever."

We rejoined the others and trekked farther into the wilderness. The walls weren't where the overlays said they would be—my confidence in the maps was waning steadily—but only another quarter mile further. There were three. One much like the wall we'd already seen, albeit only two feet high, though easily a hundred feet long, adrift in the middle of open space. Both ends were straight, as though leaving space for a gate or door, without evidence of a continuation.

The second wall was much shorter, only about twenty feet, but higher—about four feet. It went up a steep stretch of hill, close by some trees but running diagonally away from them in a way that was hard to fathom. It curved.

The third wall was close to it, and the same height, and again curved, but in the opposite direction. They would have looked like a pair of brackets from above, where one had slipped lower than the other. Taken both in isolation and together, the walls made no sense. It was weird they were there. But that was about all that could be said.

So I said it, to camera—finishing about two seconds before it suddenly started raining, hard.

We ran together into the trees and took what shelter we could until it slackened, passing around a flask of coffee that Molly had thought to bring along, because she is awesome and basically should be president.

Then we trudged back to the car.

CHAPTER
12

At around the time Nolan's crew was filming the first wall, Kristy was walking to the Hixon house for a second time.

She'd spent a couple hours exploring Birchlake—at first during her run, during which she circumnavigated it twice; then on foot, grid-walking the eight blocks of main drag along with side streets that were clean and well maintained and held a few decent Victorian houses and a small Safeway and a boarded-up Masonic hall. The local history museum was cozy and dull, apart from a room about the main street in previous eras, with photos of the old stores that had once lined it. Evidently the Tap had previously been called the Stumptown Saloon. The art gallery provided further evidence for Kristy's theory that proximity to natural beauty is inversely proportional to the quality of the art it inspires.

Wikipedia had meanwhile informed her the town was first mentioned in the early 1800s as a spot used as an occasional camp by passing trappers—the location previously having been known to local tribes for a thousand years (*citation needed*). The logging industry brought permanent settlement, then a further brief boom through being on a route to Gold Country, though it never incorporated. Gradual decline into the twentieth century, but currently holding steady.

On the way to the Hixons', before turning up the twisting side road that would take her to their drive, she took another look at the building on the side of the highway. Her time on the web had also turned up the information that Olsen's Tavern had been built to take advantage of the logging boom in the early 1900s, on the previous site of a small old house. It had been extended over the years, but the original stone fireplace was preserved. It had a checkered history—the place to have the kinds of fun that best took place discreetly outside town, and often closed for long stretches after infractions of legal or moral kinds—before closing for good in the late 1990s.

There was a story there, of a quiet sort: the settler family who'd built the original house by a mountain track along the river (why here, rather than in town?), the change to tavern (by the same family?). Some attempt to scratch out an existence after a previous occupation had dried up, or a brave leap into the unknown? Expansion. Rowdy, intermittent popularity. Eventual closure. Abandonment.

Not Kristy's kind of thing, though, and only interesting if read near where it happened, so you could feel how the human and geographical stories intermingled. The style of ill-punctuated memoir you'd find self-published in a local bookstore, if places had local bookstores anymore. Birchlake didn't. It would have no resonance elsewhere and so would join the growing number of stories that had nowhere to be told. What some pop star ate for breakfast gets a billion likes on Instagram. Several generations of some non-famous family's life? No market for it. Nobody cares.

Kristy shook her head, surprised at her mood, and

turned away from the dead building. It wasn't her job to stand in mourning for it. Screw that building.

She considered bailing back to Birchlake. She could have a bath or read or write and basically stay out of this dismal weather until Nolan called to say they were ready for dinner and drinks.

But no. Without trying to talk to Alaina Hixon's father she had nothing, not even enough to write an open-ended thinkpiece. And something she believed she'd taught Nolan was that you stick with a story until there's undeniable evidence that you're wasting your time.

She walked up the road.

She'd tried calling ahead, without success. A message had not been returned. The three oil drums were still in position near the top of the drive. After checking nobody was watching, Kristy opened the mailbox. It was empty. This increased the likelihood someone was in residence, but it was impossible to know by how much. A neighbor could be taking in the mail. Kristy wouldn't blame Alaina's father for not being able to bear sitting here while the probability that his daughter was dead slowly ticked up from 90 percent to 99.9.

She walked past the drums and up the drive. It was covered in wet leaves and banked hard to the right. On the left, that old truck, once green, now faded, rusted wheels without tires, up on cinder blocks. It was quiet. The sky felt low and heavy.

After another thirty feet the drive curved back left again, passing an old and overgrown set of yard furniture. A tire hanging from the branch of a tree on old, gray rope. The house had once been painted a cheerful yellow, now turning curdled cream and gray. A few boards had slipped.

A sudden crashing sound on the right.

Kristy jumped, and for a moment thought it had been made by a figure, coming rapidly toward her—but it was only a misleading shadow between two trees, set in motion by the real cause of the sound. A doe and two younger deer emerged chaotically from the undergrowth.

All turned their heads, blinking, assessing her, before walking stiff-legged in the other direction.

"They're allowed here," said a voice. "You're not."

A man was on the porch. Early forties, short hair and stubble, both starting to gray. He was sitting on a low, battered armchair, largely obscured behind the rail.

She stopped a couple yards from the steps. "My name's Kristy Reardon. I tried calling," Kristy said.

"What do you want?"

"I'm a journalist."

Many people wouldn't have led with this information, but Kristy had found that being upfront was the best policy. Bryan Hixon didn't seem to have a response to the information. There was an overflowing ashtray on the table next to the ratty couch, and a glass half full of something that could have been iced tea, but probably wasn't. The man's eyes were bleary, rims pink from lack of sleep. In other circumstances he would have been handsome, with an evenness of features reflected in the pictures Kristy had seen of Alaina.

"Can I come up?" she asked.

"No."

"Can I ask a couple questions from here?"

"Is it going to help find my daughter?"

"I'm a writer. Not a detective."

"Seems to me journalists aren't good for much except stirring trouble and blowing their own horn."

"It's a point of view. I don't necessarily disagree."

"Where were you when Alaina disappeared? Chasing that psycho down in Chico? Going for the money shot?"

"I'm not from here. I live in LA."

"So why are you on my property now?"

"Can you think of any person who might have wanted to harm your daughter? And were you aware of any unusual interactions in the days before she disappeared? Things out of the ordinary? Things that might cause her to behave distantly toward people? A teacher, for example?"

"No, and no. So I guess we're done." He picked up his glass. He'd already dismissed her.

"I guess," Kristy said. "One other thing, though. I've been in town a couple days. The night I got here, a man came up to me in the street. An older guy. Late sixties. Tall, thin. Black hair. Ring any bells?"

"Nope."

"He told me some people disappear for a reason," Kristy persisted. "He implied I'd be better off leaving this be. Any idea why he might do that?"

"None at all," Hixon said. He raised the glass to his lips and slowly drained it. Then set it back on the side table and crossed his hands in his lap, still without looking at her. "I'd like you to leave now."

"Final question. What's my name?"

"You told me but I wasn't listening."

"It's Kristy Reardon. I've run out of cards but I'm easy to find online. I hope you find your daughter."

"She's gone." His voice was flat.

"I truly hope not. But if so, all the more reason to hope you find her."

"You don't get it," he said. "Even if she comes back, she'll never be the same."

Kristy stared at him. She tried to work out how to respond to the idea that, should Alaina get away from the person or people who'd abducted her and come home, she'd be beyond repair, damaged goods, not his daughter anymore.

"You don't mean that."

"Go," he said. "And don't come back."

CHAPTER

13

It was a soaked and bedraggled little gang of searchers after truth that returned to our motel. The plan was to get dry and thaw out before reconvening to check Pierre's footage, then find somewhere for me to tape an outro. Preferably under cover, as the cloud was heavy and the rain didn't look like it was going to let up any time soon.

I ran a deep bath and lay in it, drinking coffee in the dim light while I waited for the tips of my fingers to return to their normal hue. The expedition felt done. Though the question of why the walls existed remained intellectually interesting—maybe, to a few people, or possibly only me—it was not visually arresting. One wall looks a lot like another, and as Ken kept pointing out, it wasn't like I had an explanation ready to roll.

Some stories are short stories. This one was barely a haiku. We'd spent money on a couple of airfares, two nights in a motel, day rates for Pierre and Molly, miscellaneous expenses (beer). We had stuff in the can from previous abortive ideas and could throw this into a bucket show of Things That Are Mildly Intriguing. It wasn't the end of the world, and frankly I wouldn't be unhappy to leave.

I was allowing myself to doze off in the warmth of the water, believing there was no harm in catching up on last night's patchy sleep, when the two dim bulbs either side of the mirror flickered. I ignored them. A minute or two later there was a strange and quite loud cracking noise from the main room. I ignored that, too.

But then I heard the sound of dripping.

I clambered out of the bath, wrapped a towel around myself, and padded out into the main room, shivering as I left the coziness of the bathroom. At first I couldn't work out what had happened, and I was on the verge of heading back to the warmth when I saw that the glass pot on the coffee machine was lying in pieces around the hot plate.

The coffee previously inside was pooling over the desk and dripping in large quantities off the edge onto the floor—directly into the bag that held my laptop.

I hurried back into the bathroom to grab another towel.

"One of those science things, I assume."

"I hate science," Ken said. "It's full of annoying shit like that. I was in a hotel room in Liverpool once that was freezing. Took a shower. When I came out, the warm air from the bathroom was hitting the cold front in the bedroom and it was literally raining in my hotel room."

Ken had determined that the motel rooms were "too cheesy, even by our standards" to tape my remaining sections, without coming in so tight as to seem like we were on the run from the police. We'd spent a few minutes trying to find somewhere photogenic around the motel exterior—achieving nothing but being stared at with suspicion by the gray-haired guy lurking behind the desk in the office—and so were now intrepidly heading into the woods behind.

The forest was pretty thick, and after about a hundred yards the ranks of tall pines reduced the rain falling onto us to a negligible level. The floor was uneven, large boulders here and there, and it was gloomy and misty but still light enough to shoot if we got onto it quickly.

Ken looked at me. "Sure," I said. "And then, I guess?"

"Yeah. Sorry, mate."

He called Molly, telling her to bring Pierre and his gear. While we waited we wandered around the wood.

"Tell me to fuck off if you want," Ken said, after a while. "But I've got to ask."

"Soon after Kristy and I got together," I said, "she got overinvested in a missing person case down in LA. I mean, obsessed. Talking to friends of the family. Hassling the cops. Going *way* overboard for what was supposed to be a simple 'the dangers to our kids' piece for a free paper. So eventually I convinced her to back out. She's steered clear of that kind of story since then, at least while we were together."

"Yet now, here she is."

"Hence me jumping on the walls as an expedition. But she texted me earlier: she talked to the missing girl's father. Got nowhere, so she's leaving tomorrow, too."

"Job done then, mate."

"I guess. Sorry there's no show in it."

"Does leave us in kind of a hole. On the other hand nobody's tried to kill us this time round, so I'm prepared to call it a win overall. Aha—here we go."

I turned to see Molly and Pierre coming toward us. "What do you think?"

Pierre made a seesaw motion with his hand. "It'll do,"

he said. "Let me have a scout around, though. See if there's something better nearby. Like a glade."

"A glade?"

"Yeah. Or a glen."

"Just get on with it," Ken said. "I am very ready for an adult beverage."

Pierre strode off into the gloom. I started putting together a form of words that would summarize the walls, a capper piece to consign them to the world of Things We May Never Understand.

Meanwhile Ken was frowning at Molly. "You all right, love?"

"Of course. Why?"

"Dunno. You just look a bit something-or-other."

"I'm cold," she said. "Previously I was wet. Then I was dry, and warm. Now I'm getting cold and wet again. This is a retrograde step, and it saddens me."

"This won't take long," I said. "Then the burgers and beer are on me."

"Hey, guys." This was Pierre, shouting from some distance away. "You might want to come see this."

He'd gotten a couple hundred yards deeper into the forest, and it was clear what he was talking about before we'd got halfway to him. "Nolan," Ken said. "You are a moron."

Pierre was standing by a wall.

It was four feet high along its length, made of rock—much like the ones we'd seen earlier, except taller, and made of smaller stones, giving it a more finished quality. It was thirty yards long, though longer in extent, because rather than being straight, it undulated like a snake.

There was no sign there had ever been a continuation. It was just a wavy wall, standing by itself, in a forest. I spent a few minutes walking around, looking for signs of further construction, but couldn't see any.

"So," Ken said, when I rejoined the group. "Just to be clear, we spent half the fucking day traipsing about in the rain looking for walls miles away, when there was in fact one *right behind our motel*. And dare I say it, though I'm using the word loosely, a more interesting wall, at that."

"Not my fault," I said.

"Looking forward to hearing why. You're the twat with the map."

"And as I explained, nobody's made an exhaustive catalog. A few segments were recorded on the ground years and years ago, but the majority were plotted using Google Maps—often by people who've never even been to California. And look up."

The three of them dutifully tilted back their heads. Old pines towered above, tiny scraps of dark gray sky beyond. "What?" Ken said.

Pierre got it. "Online maps of wilderness use satellite imagery. In forests, they can't see the ground. So nobody spotted this wall, or put it on a map."

"Which means they could be all over the place," Molly said. "All around town. And nobody knows about them."

"The locals probably do," I said. "But they've always been here. Nobody knows why, or cares."

"Well, on that, to be absolutely honest..." Ken said.

"I hear you," I said. "Okay, time to wrap. Props to Pierre for finding the perfect backdrop."

Pierre gave Ken a light to hold. I positioned myself at one end of the wandering wall, and when he nodded, started walking and talking toward him as Ken and Molly tracked alongside.

"People always want to talk about the big mysteries," I

said. "Are the pyramids spaceships (no) or ancient power plants (also no)? Have we been visited by aliens? Maybe, but that guy in the Safeway lot who says he's been abducted is still crazy. What happens to us when we die? Dig up a grave, there's your answer. Actually don't, because it'd be illegal and weird. But the fact is that the existence of heaven or hell is not something we're ever going to know." I stopped for a moment. "Or be able to evaluate on a YouTube show with a very limited budget."

I started walking again. "But that's where the smaller, lesser-known mysteries are important. They evoke aspects of everyday human experience that are curious, or wonderful. They shed light on the real forces in our lives. Time *does* exist, regardless of what hip physicists and stoned people might claim. It's how pyramids get built, and how they fall apart. It's how people fall in love, how broken hearts heal and how things get forgotten and lost—much like the original purpose of these walls. A gulf of time is like looking at something through the wrong end of a telescope, making everything strange, as the black and white photography of yesteryear makes it easy to believe that people back then dressed and dreamed in grayscale. That they were different from us.

"But they weren't. The past is *not* a foreign country. The past is close by, always. You simply have to be prepared to find the invisible path to get there—and it's often the smaller mysteries that show the way. Thanks for taking another walk into the weird with *The Anomaly Files*."

I stopped talking. Ken nodded.

"Not too shabby," he said. "And now, I could not help but overhear, the drinks are on you."

*   *   *

We set off back the way we'd come, walking in silence, spread out among the trees. It was getting dark, and mist was thickening between the trunks. Pierre was soon lagging behind as he grabbed a few last artsy shots. I didn't have the heart to tell him that if this expedition got thrown into a bucket show, there wouldn't be space.

"Who's that?" he said.

In the distance, half shrouded in mist and shadows, someone was heading purposefully further into the trees. A fit-looking woman with short gray hair. She had a bag over her shoulder. From the way she was moving, it wasn't light.

Molly peered. "Doesn't she work in the bar?"

"Yes," I said. "What the heck's she doing out here?"

"She could ask the same," Ken said. "And I wouldn't have a good answer. She's probably looking for mushrooms or communing with tree spirits or some other hippie bollocks."

"What have you got against hippies?"

"We really don't have time for that, Moll."

The woman looked up and saw us. She raised her hand in a semi-wave designed to acknowledge our presence while making it clear that she had no desire to interact.

I waved back, and we carried on toward the motel.

CHAPTER

14

Birchlake on a Friday night was a little more like an actual place, as though there were a bunch of extra people kept in storage somewhere and only allowed out to play one night a week. Most of them seemed to have headed straight for the Stone Mountain Tap, but luckily Kristy got there early.

She'd staked out a big table on the opposite side of the room from the bar. I pointed out what a tactical error this had been, but by then the place was too busy to move. Luckily the smarmy young bartender remembered Ken and checked in on our table frequently, initially at least.

Ken, Molly, and I spent a while trying to thrash out an idea for a next show. Most of the options on our list would require a full week to shoot, and though I'd been sanguine about money while relaxing in the bath, the truth was the pot was nearly empty. "So we stay local," I said.

"We've done most of the obvious ones in LA," Ken said. "And non-obvious ones. And no, we're not doing the Subterranean City of Lizard People. Partly because it's obviously a load of cock, and because if it's not, you're not getting me in a cave again any day soon. Or ever."

"Not leaping at the idea myself," I admitted.

Kristy meanwhile sat at the other end of the table,

people watching. Though I'd been firmly instructed not to describe the event in its entirety, she knew the bones of what had happened in the Grand Canyon. Certainly enough to chip in with something like "And I wouldn't let you!" and I found myself vaguely irritated that she did not. Which was dumb, I knew—but the end of an expedition, especially a failure, can leave you tired and grumpy.

"My round," Molly said.

I stood to help—we hadn't seen the Kurt guy in a while—glancing at Ken. He looked surprised too. Molly is generally the last person to force the pace of drinking.

He raised one eyebrow a quarter inch, and I nodded.

For a few minutes I focused on getting Molly into position at the bar. When we'd ordered, Molly turned to me. "Who's driving tomorrow?"

"Ken."

"Seriously?"

"Hangovers only make him stronger."

"But we're definitely leaving."

"I think we're done here."

"Good."

"You're not feeling it for Birchlake, I can tell. Any particular reason?"

She hesitated, and in that moment I saw something over her shoulder, a glimpse across the crowded room to the window onto the dark and rainy street. The glass was fogged with condensation, but I saw something dark moving slowly across the view. Then it was gone.

"Your coffee machine," she said. "What exactly happened?"

"I don't know. I came out of the bathroom and the pot was in three pieces on the desk. Leaking everywhere."

"And your room door was shut."

"Well, obviously. And I always make sure it's firmly locked when I'm getting naked. There was this one time at a hotel in...never mind. Why?"

"So what made the pot break?"

"Glass on a hot plate. Cold air. The former causes the inside of the glass to expand. The latter makes the outside contract. Enough differential between the two, and—"

"Girls understand science too, Nolan. And it happened to me once when I was a kid, with my dad's treasured whiskey tumbler. I washed it under boiling water, trying to be helpful, and it shattered. I thought being heavy would protect it. But he explained it takes thick glass to cause the effect. His glass had just had a bunch of ice in it. Bing. Cheap, thin glass is fine unless there's an extreme temperature difference. Was it *that* cold in your room?"

I shrugged, knowing I wasn't capable of doing the math and also that the fate of my coffee pot wasn't the issue here—hoping she'd get to saying whatever was on her mind. But then our drinks started arriving, and so we got to picking them up and carrying them to the others.

Ken raised his eyebrow again when we got back. I shook my head and sat next to Kristy. "The hell's happened to that waiter?" I asked, for want of anything else to say.

She was looking thoughtful. "Table behind you," she said, quietly. "But be subtle about it."

I inclined my head. The table behind us held a couple in their thirties. A thickset, affable-looking guy attacking a large plate of food, chatting as he did so: looked like it was an infodump on his day, or possibly entire week, or year. The woman was listening with a rather fixed smile, a large glass of wine in her hand.

"Huh?" I said.

"I'm developing a theory. Tell you later."

"Does that mean I might be getting an invitation?"

She shook her head. "I want to be on the road early. Speaking of which, I need to talk to Val."

"Who?"

"The bar woman. It's her Airbnb I'm staying in."

"Okay. Well, maybe now's a good time."

She looked at me. "Everything okay?"

"Sure," I muttered. "I'm going for a cigarette."

Ken followed me out. We walked up the street and smoked in silence for a while, watching mist curling along the street.

"The womenfolk are in odd moods tonight," Ken said.

"You can say that again."

"You didn't ask Molly what's up?"

"I did. But she started obsessing about my coffee pot. I'll try again, though I should try to figure out what the deal with Kristy is first."

"I'll confess that the atmosphere between you two is not making me want to shout 'Get a room.'"

"And I have no idea what's up with that. Since you engineered us re-meeting, we've hung out a dozen times. Plus regular texts, emails, some long calls. I honestly thought we were getting somewhere."

"Having an audience doesn't help."

"Maybe. I guess it's probably . . . what?"

Ken was looking over my shoulder. "Hell's that?"

At first I couldn't see anything except a cold, wet street. Streetlights weakly illuminated patches, but by eighty yards into the mist it was nearly impenetrable.

Within that was a dark shape. "I have no . . ."

The shape resolved into a person. Some unconscious

part of my brain got this several seconds before my mind and had my feet in motion down the street toward it.

At first the figure didn't seem to register my approach. Then he or she started wandering off to the side as if to elude me. I changed angle to cut them off, and they started back the way they'd come.

"Nolan," Ken said. "Fuck are you doing?"

I could see now that it was a woman with long wet hair, wearing a long coat. I pointed Ken to head to the left, cutting her off. She started turning slowly on the spot, as if trying to see a way out between us.

"What the hell's up with her?"

"Must be drugs," I said. There are a lot of meth labs hidden in the California mountains. I grabbed her shoulders, gently, not wanting to scare her, trying to hold her still. Her hair was soaked and clinging to her face.

But finally I got a glimpse. "Holy crap. Go get Kristy."

"Why?"

"Just do it, Ken. Be fast."

He hurried up the street back toward the bar.

The woman suddenly wrenched her torso from side to side, nearly slipping out of my grasp. I knew I wouldn't be able to hold her securely from where I was, and so slipped behind her instead, clamping my arms around her stomach and chest.

The door to the bar slammed open and Kristy came running. Ken followed, but Kristy runs fast. She slowed as she got closer, mouth dropping open.

"Is it?" I said.

Kristy crossed the final yards, hands held out in a reassuring way. "It's okay," Kristy said. "It's okay."

She reached up and moved the hair from the side of the woman's face, though by now I suspected it wasn't a woman. I could tell by Kristy's reaction that I was right.

It was a girl. *"Alaina?"* Kristy said.

Behind Kristy, Ken stood looking confused, one hand out to the side to keep Molly and Pierre back. Pierre came forward anyway, taking off his jacket.

I let go of the girl, hung the jacket over her shoulders and moved around so I could finally see her face.

"It's her," I said.

The girl's eyes swiveled to look at me. Her face was pale, tinged almost blue. "I don't remember you."

"You don't know me. But you know who *you* are, right?"

"I'm Alaina."

Kristy was grinning. "That's right," she said. "You're Alaina Hixon. Where...where have you *been*?"

"In the woods. All by myself."

"Well, you're home now. And you're okay."

"I'm not okay."

"You are," Kristy said. "Whoever took you, whatever happened...it's not your fault. *None* of this is your fault. There will be people you can talk to, who'll help you understand that. It's going to be fine. You're okay."

"I'm not okay," the girl said. "I'm different now."

Kristy looked wary. "What do you mean?"

An expression spread across the girl's face. Slowly, and lopsidedly, as if she was having to remember how it went. It took me a moment to realize it was a smile.

"I died," Alaina said. "But now I'm back."

PART TWO

Sickness begins here. I am a dartboard for witches.

—Sylvia Plath

CHAPTER
15

Alaina started to wander away from us, as though she'd lost all interest and remembered she had to be somewhere else. Her movements were faltering, however, and by the fourth step she was staggering. Pierre moved fast and caught her.

"Hey," she said, voice slurred. "You're cute."

"She's really cold," Pierre said, struggling to keep her upright.

"Bring her to my car," Kristy said. She started across the street. I followed. "Are you taking her home?"

"No, ER. She's sick, Nolan." She pulled out her phone. "I'll text you her address. Can you call her dad? Explain what's happened. I'll take Alaina to the nearest hospital."

"Which is where?"

"Probably Chico. I'll let you know."

"What about the police?"

"Also Chico. I'll call them from the hospital."

"You don't thin—"

"*No*, Nolan, I don't. Who knows how long it would take them to get here on a Friday night."

Meanwhile Pierre and Ken had half-carried the girl to Kristy's rental and were sliding her into the back seat. "I'll ride along," Molly said, running around the other side. "Find out where the hospital is while you drive."

And that was the end of the discussion. Two minutes later Kristy's car was speeding away down the street. "She does *take charge*, doesn't she," Ken said.

"What's that expression about pots, kettles, and blackness?"

"No idea. It sounds stupid. But for once in your life you were right. We should be staying here with that girl and waiting for the sheriff to arrive."

"She'll be closer to the cops at the hospital."

A woman was standing nearby, anxiously waiting to talk to us. "Was that her? Was that *Alaina*?"

It was the woman Kristy pointed out to me in the bar earlier, the one tolerating a talkative husband. "Yes."

She stared at me, blinking. "You're *sure*?"

"Well, yeah."

"Oh, thank God." She ran back toward the bar, already on the phone. I got out my own and called the number on the contact info Kristy had texted me, reflecting that it's seldom you get to give a stranger such good news.

There was no answer. I tried again. Still nothing. Looked at Ken. "So now what?"

"Call the police," Ken said.

"Ken—"

"Seriously, Nolan. We call the cops and go back in the bar, where you have a sizable tab that needs paying, and there is more vodka that needs drinking. Kristy has made this her business, and good for her. But it's not ours."

I knew he was right. But also that Kristy had tasked me with informing Alaina's father, and she'd likely trust me to accomplish this, and so wouldn't do it herself. "Ken,

I'm not going to sit and drink while some father doesn't know that his daughter has reappeared."

"Nolan..."

"He's right, Ken," Pierre said. "That's not okay."

I started walking quickly back toward the motel. After a moment, Ken swore, and they followed.

All I knew was the Hixons lived up a road off the highway a mile out of town. The address Kristy had given me wasn't much help in the dark but after a few minutes I spotted something I recalled her mentioning—three oil drums blocking a drive. Ken parked, and I tried calling Hixon's number again. Still no response.

"I'm just going to put this out there," Pierre said, as we stood looking past the drums. It was very quiet and extremely dark. "Isn't it weird, if your kid's missing, to not pick up the phone if it rings in the night?"

"That would certainly be my take," Ken said.

"I don't know," I said. "I suspect in the first days you'll have your phone glued to your hand. But by now? You'll have gotten past expecting good news and are so exhausted that you turn off the ringer in hope of a few hours' sleep."

"Could be," Pierre said, dubiously. "It's only nine thirty, though."

"So hopefully he's still awake."

I held my phone up. Light from the screen showed glints of leaves, gnarled tree trunks, a drive that curved to the right. You know how woods feel at night, even near dwellings, and these were no exception. I remembered the last time I'd used my phone like this, however—trapped deep in a cavern in the Grand Canyon—and knew there was nothing to be scared of. At least, nothing in that league.

We followed the drive around a stand of trees, past a rusting old truck. After a further thirty yards it widened into an open spot in front of a house that loomed as a darker shape in the darkness. No lights were on. The house looked dead, like it had been left alone there a hundred years ago, as if it lived by itself in the woods.

I went to the bottom of the steps leading up to a porch. Turned off my phone in case this made it easier to see a glow within any of the windows. There wasn't one.

A sudden snapping sound. We turned to look. Couldn't see anything. A moment later it came again. "Hell is that?"

"Do they have bears here?" Ken said, his voice low.

"I don't think so," Pierre whispered.

"Actually, maybe," I said.

"Fuck's sake. Grizzlies?"

"No. There's only black bears in California now."

"And how dangerous are black bears?"

"I've never looked into it. But I'd suggest we err on the side of caution."

"Which involves what?"

"Staying still, and being very quiet. Unless it attacks, in which case we stay still but be very loud. I think."

"Oh, I'll be loud," Ken muttered. "They'll be able to hear me shouting 'I hate you Nolan' in *Canada*."

A moment later I heard the cracking noise again. I thought it was farther away, though in the woods in the dark it was hard to be confident. And when it came to bears, I wanted to be confident before choosing my next move.

"Go up on the porch," Ken suggested. "It might be less likely to attack up there."

"Okay."

I put my foot on the lowest stair. It creaked, loudly. It seemed certain the others would, too, so I went up the rest in one big step. Ken and Pierre followed quickly.

We stood together on the porch looking out into the murky darkness. After a full minute with no further cracking sounds, I lifted my phone and triggered the screen again, reasoning light might scare any animal away. A broken tricycle lay on its side in the bushes.

Then something came running straight past the house.

All three of us yelped like girls. I'm not being sexist—I mean the pitch was *much* higher than I would have believed any of us capable of. Especially Ken. Whatever it was, it moved fast. There was a rush of air, the sound of leaves shoved aside as it exited the clearing. Then it was gone.

"What the hell *was* that?" Pierre whispered.

"Coyote?"

"It was a *lot* bigger than a coyote."

"Fuck this," Ken said. "Anybody in that house *has* to be awake by now. Just knock on the bloody door, Nolan."

The top half of the door was constructed of smeared glass panes, one of them cracked. I put my head up close. No sound from inside. I knocked.

We waited a minute, then I knocked again, harder. No movement inside. No sound from upstairs. "Okay," Ken said. "Nobody's home. We're done."

On impulse, I put my hand on the doorknob and turned it. It wasn't locked. The door opened silently.

"Uh, Nolan," Pierre said. "You shouldn't—"

"I know." I pulled it shut again. "But isn't that a little weird?"

"This is the arse-end of nowhere," Ken said. "They

cleave to the old ways. Which probably includes keeping a loaded shotgun by the bed. Seriously, I'm done, Nolan."

I took a step back, wondering whether to try one more time. But it seemed either the house was empty or the occupant didn't want to talk to strangers in the night. Ken was right about guns, too. The parts of California that don't live on avocado toast and soy lattes have plenty of weapons at their disposal. "Okay, yes—let's bail."

"Nolan," Pierre said. "Check this out."

He was standing near an armchair a few yards along the porch. A similarly distressed side table was alongside. An ashtray overflowing with butts. A coffee mug.

"What?"

He indicated for me to come closer, and pointed. I leaned over, saw the mug was half full. Put the back of my fingers against the side. It was warm. Not was-hot-once, but still hot enough to drink.

"We should leave," I said.

When we got back to the car we stopped.

"So what do you—" Pierre said.

"No idea," I said. "But we're going with Plan Ken now. We came, we tried, we failed. The cops can let Alaina's dad know she's back."

"Nolan," Ken said. His voice sounded odd.

"What?"

He nodded toward the car. In the moisture on the windshield, someone had scrawled two words.

GO NOW

CHAPTER
16

At midnight the three of us were sitting in chairs on the walkway outside my room when a car pulled into the lot.

Ken dropped his cigarette to the ground. "You going to mention the message on the windshield?"

Kristy parked near the office and got out. I've known Kristy long enough to be able to tell merely from the way she opens a car door that she's good and pissed.

"Not right away," I said.

Kristy came storming over, Molly following more slowly. I caught Moll's eye and could see her stuck between trying to nonverbally communicate to me, as she normally might, then realizing this was my ex-wife, and so it might not be appropriate. Her face settled into an expressionless halfway house.

I stood. "Is Alaina okay?"

"I have no idea," Kristy said, tersely. "Molly called the cops while we were on the way. They got to the hospital ten minutes after us. At which point it was immediately 'Great, girls, thanks so much, run along now.'"

"Well, I guess you're not a relative," I said.

"I *know* that, Nolan. But I *am* the person who delivered a missing teenage girl to them."

"Did they manage to contact the father?" I'd texted Kristy to let her know we'd failed. I'd left it at that, without further detail about our trip to the Hixon house.

"Not by the time we left, I don't think. But they weren't sharing their every move. They took a statement and then did everything but shove us out the door."

"Getting their ducks in a row," Ken said.

Kristy turned bad-temperedly to him. *"What?"*

"Girl goes missing. Twelve days later, she returns. On foot. Which suggests she's been in the area the whole time."

"In which case," I added, "people may be drawn to ask how the hell the cops didn't find her *before*. Did they not look in the right places? Didn't they ask the right people the right questions? Did they *screw up*? Is this the kind of thing the newspaper or CNN or everyone on Twitter should hear about? Can we get #TheCopsFuckedUpAgain to trend?"

"The police will want to get a picture of their liability," Ken said, "before Alaina starts telling her story to anybody. Especially if they're not family."

"And most of all if they're an actual investigative journalist," I concluded. "Don't you think?"

Kristy visibly calmed. "One of the annoying things about you two is your occasional tendency to make sense."

"Infuriating, isn't it," Ken said. "It's our secret weapon."

"Did the doctors say what they thought could be wrong with her," Pierre asked, "before you had to go?"

"No," Molly said. "The ER nurse said she'd never seen anything like it."

"Alaina even told the doctor he was wasting his time," Kristy said. "On account of the fact she was deceased. She was quite calm and reasonable about it."

"I did find a couple of possible explanations on the web when we got back," I said. "Cotard's delusion is one. A rare condition where people think they're dead. Sometimes even that their internal organs are putrefied, or missing."

Kristy didn't say anything. "Well," Molly said, into the silence. "That does seem kinda right. What causes it?"

"Could be a particularly nihilistic form of depression. The French physician it's named after characterized it as *'la délire des négations,'*—a psychosis of personal negation. A couple of the better-known cases seem to be related to head trauma, though, so lesions of the parietal lobe might be implicated."

"Alaina had no sign of head injury," Kristy said. "And nobody has mentioned her being depressed."

"Good. And basically nobody knows for sure. It's not a recent fad, either, like identifying as being dead. Cotard's case was in 1880, but the first known description is from 1788. Chances are it happened before, too."

"It's not Cotard's," Kristy said.

"Well, option two is confabulation. Basically a memory error when someone's trying to paper over the gaps of something they can't process or can't remember. Something won't fit, so they create a fake memory that feels absolutely real."

"It's not that, either."

"I see. And you're sure of this because...?"

"Being with her in the car, and in the hospital, before they made us leave. It's not a delusion."

"Uh, yes it is. She's not dead. Ergo, it's a delusion."

"No, it's a *diversion*," Kristy said. "I don't think she really believes she's dead. Or that she *was* dead."

"So... why's she saying it?"

"To cover up for someone."

"That doesn't make a lot of sense, Kris. And who? Didn't she specifically say she'd been out there alone?"

"Yes," Molly said. "I asked her again in the car, and she said the same thing."

"Exactly," Kristy said. "Which *is my point*. Why would a girl disappear in the forest? How would she stay hidden from search parties? Why would she remain out there *for twelve days*? Someone drugged her, and she's confused, blanked the experience—or is trying to bury it in real time. She's trying to avoid facing what was done to her, or she's covering for someone. And I want to know who that is."

Once again I was aware of Molly looking meaningfully at me. "Well, I guess it'll come out in the next few days," I offered, as blandly as possible. "When the—"

"Oh, it'll be sooner than that," Kristy said, with a fierce smile. "I'm going back tomorrow morning."

"Is that wise? Aren't you done here? You came looking for someone and now she's back. End of story? Happy ending?"

Kristy glared at me and walked away to her car.

CHAPTER
17

Fifteen minutes later I was standing outside the building that held Kristy's Airbnb. My phone was in my hand. It'd gone to voicemail four times already. In contrast to when I'd called from Santa Cruz, I was confident she was ignoring me in the hope I'd go away. That wasn't going to happen.

"What?" she said, when she eventually picked up.

"We need to talk."

"I'm tired, Nolan. And you've had some drinks."

"So have you."

"Not as much. I never do."

I considered reminding her this was a discussion we'd had more than once in the bad days. That dismissing anything someone might say on the grounds they've had a few beers was a dubiously *ad hominem* way of making the other party's opinions inadmissible, even if they might be right. I did not make the observation. It never worked then and it seemed unlikely it would now.

"Are you still there?"

"Yeah," I said. "And I'm going to keep being here, and simply call you back if you end the call."

"So I'll turn off my phone."

"For God's sake, Kristy—why are you being like this?"

"Why are *you*?"

"Because *I'm worried about you*."

I hadn't known I was going to say it until the words were out of my mouth. When they were, I knew it was true.

The line went dead.

I stood there wondering whether it was worth calling back—or if it would only make things worse.

I didn't wonder for long. My dad has never tried to pass on many life lessons: his theory is you have to make the mistakes yourself to understand what count as mistakes, and how they happen. He told me always to choose the beef option on long-haul flights. He told me that you haven't finished cooking until the kitchen's cleaner than when you started. But the main thing he's adamant about is that you never, ever go to bed on bad terms. You travel far while you sleep, he says, and when you come back the world may have changed. Differences have time to solidify. So always get to the other side of them before you say goodnight.

Just as I pressed Redial, the door in front of me opened. Kristy looked very tired and her cheeks were wet.

I took a step toward her but her eyes said that wasn't what she wanted. "Kris," I said, instead. "Alaina's *back*. It's all good. So what's going on?"

"I told you once about a friend I had at school," she said. "Helen."

"Right. Her family moved away when you were fourteen."

"Yes, I did tell you that."

"But?"

"I lied."

*   *   *

I made chamomile tea—I'm not a fan, but Kristy will not suffer instant coffee to be in a house and so there wasn't any choice. She sat in the chair by the window meanwhile, staring down at the wet street.

I gave a cup to her and sat with mine on the sofa. And waited. Sometimes it's worth nudging people. Sometimes it's not. Kristy is not nudgeable. I'd learned that.

"You remember what it was like," she said, eventually. "Though I think maybe it's different for boys."

"What is?"

"Boys...I don't know. They grow up in parallel, it seems to me. Even if it's a super-close friend. They play and talk and hang out a lot. And I'm not saying that isn't just as meaningful, or rich. But I get the sense boys stay separate. They walk side by side. Whereas girls, at that age...they blend."

"In what way?"

"A girl and her best friend will create a world, with them as the only inhabitants. When they're little, it'll be a fantasy realm. When they start to grow up it's an ante-chamber to the Big Wide World, somewhere they can experiment with grown-up feelings. A private universe, a safe space, though it can get intense in there, and if it goes bad, it's *bloody*. It's risky letting someone hold your soul when you're not even sure what shape it has yet. I don't think boys do that. Until they fall in love."

"Perhaps," I said. I wasn't sure she was right. Boys forge intense bonds, too, and create worlds of their own. You could argue that high school shootings conducted in pairs were terrible proof of this, or, more positively, the world's most successful rock bands. But I understood her point and wasn't going to get in her way.

"So," she said. "Helen Fincher. Her family lived a half

mile away. We met in first grade. Hit it off. And after that…Didn't agree on everything, were different in a lot of ways, but that was okay. Better. Even the fact that we didn't live next door worked. As we got older it gave us a first step to a shared independence. Our families were friends by then, and when one afternoon when I was eight I announced I was going to Helen's, my parents looked at each other and said, sure, be back for dinner. I walked over, by myself, feeling *amazingly* grown up. And after that, Helen's dad used to say, we became the Quantum Kids, the Kristy and Helen Show. The grown-ups never knew where we'd be at any given time, but they could be sure it'd be in one house or the other. We wound up eating with the other's family at least once a week. If the other kid happened to be there at mealtime, our moms would set another place without thinking about it.

"By then the families were going on vacation together, too. A week a year, a couple long weekends. Every Memorial and Labor Day my dad and Helen's dad would be affably bickering in one of the yards about how to grill ribeye, getting slowly wasted on Coors. And with Helen and me, it was the whole nine yards. Talking into the small hours. Lying on our backs looking at the stars. If you'd put it all in one of the scripts you used to write, the producer would have said, 'Okay, Nolan, we get it—they're BFFs. This is too on-the-nose, tone it down, sheesh.' Even now, twenty years later, I find it impossible to recall my childhood without a visceral sense of Helen standing beside me, a presence at my shoulder."

She stopped. Gathered herself smaller into her chair. "Well…I suspect you know where this is going."

"Tell me."

"It was the October of eighth grade. One Saturday

Helen and I went to the mall. We did it every week-end. You talk about ritual walkways? We had one, to the Garden Mall, even when it rained. We plotted about outfits to buy when we had more money. We had burgers. We hung out. We were about to leave when I remembered my dad's birthday, and for once, instead of letting my mom handle it, I had an idea of my own. I'd noticed he seemed to get into this one song whenever it came on the radio. The Fugees. That cover they did of 'Killing Me Softly with His Song.' Remember? Totally not his kind of thing, which is why I'd noticed. I went into the Sam Goody. Helen waited on a bench outside. I found the CD. I stood in line, paid. The whole thing took less than five minutes. When I came out, Helen wasn't there."

"Jesus," I said. "What happened?"

"I waited. Then I looked for her. But you know what it's like in those places—if you go searching for some-one there's a high chance that you're going to miss them because they're on the move, too. And of course in those days kids didn't have cell phones—so you can't call or text or Snapchat saying 'WTF are you?' I gave it fifteen minutes, then I ran home. My dad drove me straight back and we looked and looked together and then we talked to mall security and they called the cops. It was on the local news every day for weeks. But they never found her."

"Shit, Kristy," I said. "Why didn't you *tell* me?"

"I try not to think about it. It was the end. Of everything up until then. Of that life. The end of having a best friend. I don't think I ever had one again. Until you, I guess. The end of the families, too. At first everybody was supporting each other, but after a while... I was *there*, you know?"

"But it wasn't your fault," I said. "They must have understood that."

"Intellectually. But how would *you* feel? Don't you think some part of you would resent the child who *didn't* disappear? Even if you never said it out loud?"

"I don't know," I said. "I hope not."

"Everything died. Stopped dead. And then gradually it started up again. As it does. Helen's family moved to another town. That part was true. She didn't go with them, that's all. She got stuck. Like a lot of things. When my dad died, I found the CD I'd bought that day buried deep in a drawer in his study. It was still shrink-wrapped." She drank the last of her tea. "And that's why I didn't tell you, and why I don't ever think about it anymore."

"Except you're here now. In Birchlake."

She smiled briefly. "Yeah."

"And it didn't go that way this time. Alaina's back. She's okay. She's alive."

"And I'm happy for her, and her dad, and for her friends. *So* happy. But think about it, Nolan. If she'd just got lost, she'd have made her way back out of the woods long ago. Or the cops would have found her. That didn't happen, which means somebody *took her*. Somebody tried to steal a girl out of her own life. That is not okay. That *cannot stand*." She looked at me, eyes bright. "You understand that, don't you?"

"Get some sleep," I said. "It's late. What are the names of the girls who were with Alaina when she disappeared?"

"Madeline and Nadja Hardaker. Why?"

"You're going to the hospital tomorrow morning. I get it. Not even going to try to stop you. But if Alaina doesn't want to talk, then you need to back off—and we need to go home to LA. Right?"

"Of course," she said, not very convincingly.

I sighed, and kissed her on the top of the head. "At least try not to get arrested, okay?"

When I got back to the motel the lights were off in Ken's and Pierre's rooms. I was surprised to see Molly still up, sitting on a chair on the walkway outside her room.

"Kristy okay?"

"She's fine," I said. "Were you trying to signal something earlier?"

"Only that she, well."

"It's okay. You can tell me."

"She was *really* going off at the hospital, that's all. I mean, notably so. Angry, tearful...really big."

"We just talked about it," I said. "It's bad backstory, that's all. She'll be right as rain tomorrow."

"Good. And we're still leaving bright and early?"

I hesitated. "Probably."

She nodded, looking glum.

"You okay, Moll?"

"Fine," she said, with a smile that wasn't a smile. Then she said goodnight and went into her room.

I heard her lock the door, then check it.

Twice.

CHAPTER
18

W hen I went to knock on Ken's door in the morning I found a Post-it note saying he'd gone to hunt down breakfast. I'm no Sherlock Holmes, but I know Ken is both a creature of habit and economical with effort, and so I surmised that—like a wily old predator in the veldt—he would likely have returned to the last place he successfully ate.

I walked to the main street, and when it became clear the Stone Mountain Tap was very not-open-yet, I turned on the spot and spotted the coffee shop on the opposite side of the street. It was open.

Ken was inside, lurking in a corner, a pot of coffee and an untouched croissant in front of him.

"Are you on a diet?"

"This place claimed to do breakfast. They lied," he added, loudly. The young hipster behind the counter ignored him. "As any fool knows, breakfast has at least one dead thing in it. This has no dead things and is therefore not breakfast. But they don't have anything else. Fuckers."

I sat opposite. "So," I said.

"I hear you. In your position, I'd do the same. Do you know what it's about yet?"

I gave him a summary of what Kristy had told me the night before. He breathed out heavily. "So she's going to do what she's going to do."

"Already on it," I said. "Her rental isn't out there. She'll be at the hospital right now, taking names and kicking ass."

"And because you laughably feel you might be able to offer emotional support, you want to stick around."

"Did you get return flights?"

"Yes, Nolan. I didn't fancy walking back to LA."

"Nuts. I was going to suggest you took my car. Though I guess you could leave it at the airport in San Jose, and I could get Kristy to drop me off there."

"Yes. Or, here's the thing," Ken said. He took a mouthful of croissant, and grimaced. "Why do they even make these things? Pierre and I have seats for tomorrow afternoon. Molly's more than scary enough to get the flight moved up a day and put herself on the plane, too, but I did some deep thinking in the small hours."

"That sounds ominous."

"These stone walls of yours, though not the most interesting thing I've ever seen, aren't wholly without intrigue. Yesterday we even discovered one in the woods behind the motel. There may be more. The fact they're closer to town could mean they're just eldritch pig pens or whatever, but checking them out might bulk up this thing to a show after all. Which would be good. Because we have spent money on it."

"I know. And if I didn't know you, I'd think that was the actual reason you were thinking of staying."

Ken winked approvingly. "Nobody says you're stupid, Nolan. Okay, of course they do, but you're right on this occasion. Point one—what do you think would be the very least effective way of getting me to leave a place?"

"Suggesting you should go. Like someone did via a message on the windshield last night."

"So there's that. Who did it? Why? Also, we're flailing for mysteries we can afford to investigate. And let's also face this—*The Anomaly Files* is struggling to maintain a financially viable audience. Or an audience of any kind. So why not hedge our bets and double up?"

"Meaning?"

"We look for more walls. But there's a real-life mystery here, too. Okay, it's not a pyramid or lost gold mine or aliens or whatever. But a girl went missing. She is now back. This is an *actual* mystery, and one with a happy ending. People might want to watch a show about that. And we're here, complete with a crew and an experienced and attractive journalist."

"You're not talking about me, are you."

"Do you think Kristy would be up for it?"

"I don't know. This is personal for her."

"All the more likely to be worth watching."

"We can ask. Molly's not going to like it, though. She really seems like she wants to go."

"I'll talk to her. How about you?"

"My ego is robust enough to cope with having a guest presenter on the show."

"Even when she turns out to be much better at it than you are?"

"Remind me why I spend time with you?"

"No idea, mate. I keep trying to give you the slip. I'm one step away from buying a disguise."

I thought about it, but not for long. "Let's do it. It's a break from our usual schtick, but maybe that's not a bad thing. And I've even got an idea of where to start. The girls who were with Alaina when she disappeared."

Ken shook his head. "They'll have told the police everything they know."

"I'm sure. But law enforcement are maybe not the only people who wanted their ducks in a row. Think about it. You're fourteen. Your friend vanishes. You freak out, run home. The cops ask you what happened. What do you tell them?"

"What happened."

"Right. But in the context of a crisis in which you feel horrifically guilty for being okay. Kristy's friend disappeared when Kristy went into a store. She said something like 'It couldn't have taken five minutes.'"

"So?"

"Nobody goes into a record store in a busy mall on the weekend, finds the thing in the racks, heads to the register, stands in line and pays, in five minutes. It's going to take ten, at least. Five extra minutes isn't much, but how long does it take to get hit by a car? A single second. These girls say they searched for twenty minutes. It could be they only looked for ten—but it *felt* longer because you're in the woods and freaked out."

Ken looked thoughtful. "I see what you're saying."

"Nobody's lying. But you underestimate how long it took for someone to vanish, overestimate how long you searched. Because you unconsciously want it to be known that you did the right thing, that the horror show isn't your fault. But now? Alaina's back. It's different."

Ken nodded. "The pressure's off. And so if somebody asks the same questions they might get a more accurate timescale."

"That's my thinking."

"For you, it's not bad thinking. Alright, I'm game. You going to tell Kristy before we try to talk to the girls?"

"I was considering making it a nice surprise."

"You live dangerously, Nolan. I admire that. Can I have all your stuff after she kills you?"

"It's a very bad idea," Molly said.

"Oh," I said. "Why?"

"Seriously? I have no idea how old you are, Ken, but the days of you being carded in bars are long gone. Probably back when shoulder pads were a thing. And Nolan, with respect, nobody's going to mistake you for a teenager, either."

"Ageist, dude."

"No," she said. "Not my point. You're both fine examples of...well, you're both men, anyway. And *that's my point*. The two of you cannot go try to talk to two young teens by yourselves. Not looking like...that. I'd call the police myself, and I *know* you."

"You have a point," Ken said. "Of course. Which is why you're coming with us."

"I don't *want* to," she said. "If I had a car of my own, I'd be long gone. I don't want to be here anymore."

"Ken," I said. "Let's multitask. We're not going to stick a camera in these girls' faces right away. So why doesn't Pierre stay here, scout out the woods, get a sense of what else is there to be found. That way we can come back later and launch into it with a head start."

"Nice," Ken said. "I'll go tell him."

He strode off toward Pierre's room looking for all the world as if it had been his idea. When he was out of earshot I turned to Molly. "Moll. Just tell me what's up, okay?"

"You're going to say I'm just being silly."

"I really won't."

"Okay. Well—"

"You're just being silly."

"You're a funny guy, Nolan—but shut up. Yesterday after we got back to the motel, we went to our rooms. I took a shower. I was frozen. When I finally got out, the bathroom was full of steam. I wrapped the towel around myself and used a washcloth to clear a spot in the mirror. And…"

She stopped talking.

"And what?"

"There was somebody in the shower."

"What?"

"I jumped and turned around. The shower was empty. I looked behind the curtain. Nobody. But I know what I saw in the mirror. Somebody was standing there behind me."

"The bathroom lights are very dim," I said, carefully.

"I know, Nolan. But that wasn't it. It wasn't a shadow, either. There was *someone in my shower*."

"Okay," I said. Simply telling her she was wrong wasn't going to work. I needed a more roundabout approach. "What did he look like? I assume it was a he?"

"I don't know for sure," she said. "The head was tilted forward, dripping. I couldn't see a face. I turned in half a second. Gone. But… it felt like a him."

It felt a little as though she was being evasive on that point, but I didn't push her. "So what did you do?"

"Checked behind the curtain again. Looked back in the mirror. Nothing. So I opened the door to the main room. Poked my head out. It was empty. And really, *really* cold. I double-checked—the door to the outside was locked."

"Huh," I said.

"Do you believe me?"

"I believe that you think you—"

"Oh, get lost, Nolan. And tell me. What really happened with your coffee pot?"

"Christ, that again?"

"What I mean is—*why did it happen*? It wasn't science. And it must have happened about the same time that I saw what I saw in my shower."

I spread my hands, hoping to suggest an openness to the world and its odd quirks, with a hint that she should do the same. Molly's face said it wasn't working. Even a little bit.

Thankfully Ken and Pierre were on their way toward us now. "Look, Moll," I said, quietly. We can talk about—"

"I saw what I saw, Nolan."

CHAPTER
19

When Kristy parked in the lot a news truck was already in position, though it seemed they were packing up. The first people she encountered inside the hospital were two policemen on their way out: the sheriff from Chico and a sleepy-eyed deputy she'd encountered with him last night.

"Good morning, Officer Tindall."

Kristy saw Tindall registering the fact she'd remembered his name while he couldn't pretend he was in the same position. Kristy had talked to enough cops over the years to know the ones who were on the take or racist were a minority outnumbered by men and women who turned up day after day and night after night to do a difficult job for which they received little thanks. She wasn't looking for a fight. Just respect. "Kristy," she said. "Reardon."

"Right. So, you're back."

"Sharp. Didn't realize you were a detective. I'd've been less snappy with you last night."

The sheriff smiled. "Touché. Obviously you're back, Ms. Reardon. And look, I get that we probably seemed officious, maybe even rude. We're grateful you got Alaina here so fast. We just needed to make sure everything was done right."

Ducks in a row, Kristy thought. "And was it?"

"Seems so," the sheriff said, missing the hidden question. "She's in good shape, according to the doctor."

"Physically."

"What do you mean?"

"Well, she did keep saying she'd died."

Officer Tindall laughed. "Right, yeah. She dropped that soon after you left. She was joking."

"Strange joke. I see local news are on the case."

"Of course," the sheriff said. "But Alaina doesn't want to talk to them. They were getting pushy, but when her dad arrived they got the message. He believes they didn't do enough when Alaina went missing. He made that real clear. He feels the same about us, and made that equally plain."

"And did you?"

The sheriff looked at her. "Excuse me?"

"A girl in the woods by town. For twelve days. It's unfortunate she wasn't found. Maybe even surprising."

"When you get back to LA," the sheriff said, "spend a while with a map of this county. Birchlake backs onto hundreds of square miles of mountain forest. Some parts very steep. I can understand why Bryan Hixon got frustrated. But we looked. Hard. The Feds looked. People from town looked. As I explained yesterday."

"Is Alaina's dad still here with her?"

"Yes. But they won't be for much longer."

"She's being released *already*?"

"No reason not to. They gave her an exhaustive physical and ran bloodwork and monitored her through the night. She's in good shape. She's a very lucky girl."

"But where's she been?"

"In the woods."

"Who with?"

Officer Tindall hesitated. "Well, nobody."

"For twelve days? Evading police and civilian searches? And without losing a ton of weight? Twelve *days*?"

"That's what she says," the sheriff said. "And we've got no reason to think otherwise."

Kristy was struggling to keep her voice level. "You know it can't be true."

"We talked to her. Child services talked to her. The doctors examined her, along with a psychiatrist. No signs of physical or sexual abuse. No evidence of restraint. She says she was alone. She said it multiple times."

"So...was she *hiding*? If so, why? From who?"

"No, she was *lost*. Once you get away from town, those woods are thick. A dozen experienced hikers a year wind up lost. Alaina had no map or experience."

"But she *lives* around there."

"You can drown in six inches of water and you can get lost a mile from home. She got messed up in the dark and turned around and got more lost. Woke in the morning and set off in the wrong direction and made it worse. But now she's back. And she's okay. This is what they call a happy ending, Ms. Reardon. Most people seem glad about that, not determined to go to the dark side."

"I'm not most people."

"I can tell."

"And you, as a police officer—you've no interest in making sure you know what happened?"

"Our job is to investigate crimes," the sheriff said. "That requires a crime, with a victim. Alaina Hixon says there wasn't one, and she isn't one. So we're done."

"Even though she could be *lying*, which means there's someone out there who might do this again, to some *other* girl? A girl who might not be so lucky? Who might *not* come back? Ever?"

"The Feds will interview Alaina this afternoon," he said. "They'll ask her the same questions and let me know if anything warrants further investigation."

"Great. I assume you have no objection to me trying to talk to Alaina before she leaves?"

"Nope," he said. "But judging by how she and her dad dealt with the other newshounds, I'd say it's a longshot."

"My grandmother told me you should ask for what you want," Kristy said. "And if they tell you no, always ask again a second time. To check they're sure."

"I can believe that," the sheriff said, with a touch of weariness. "And I'll also bet a lot of folks have come to wish your grandma had kept that wisdom to herself."

Kristy asked at the nurses' station on the second floor if it was okay to visit with Alaina. A nurse went to check. To Kristy's surprise she came right back and said yes.

The room was small but private. Alaina was perched on the edge of the bed, dressed in clean jeans and a gray hoodie. She turned when she heard Kristy enter. "Hey," she said.

The touch of frostnip she'd had the night before had gone, and her cheeks looked flushed from the warmth of the room. Kristy was glad to see her looking well, though it made it even harder to believe her account of what happened.

"I thought your dad was here."

"He's gone to bring the car around. The police said they'd go keep the news people busy for a few minutes."

"You're slipping out the back? Cool. I've always wanted to do that."

"My dad says journalists don't give up easy," Alaina said, with the trace of a smile. "I guess he's right."

"Guilty as charged." Kristy sat on the end of the bed. "So how come you let me say hi?"

"You brought me in last night. That was nice of you."

"Anybody would have. I'm glad you're back."

The girl's eyes were pale and blue. "I can see that."

"And you're feeling okay?"

"Fine. Why?"

"You were saying some strange things."

"Like what?"

"You told us you died. Seemed pretty insistent. But the cops said you stopped saying it."

"Well, yeah. People were being weird about it."

"Well, it's kind of a weird thing to say, right?"

The girl shrugged. "I guess." She was looking down at her hands as if unsure about them in some way.

"You okay?"

"I'm fine," Alaina said. "Just, when I leave here, it's all going to start. No going back."

"What's going to start?"

The girl shook her head, then seemed to get distracted by something in the corner of the room. Kristy glanced in that direction, but there was nothing there to see.

"I know what you mean, I think," she said, to prompt her. "A lot of people are going to want to see you, talk to you. Your friends especially. They're going to be so happy you're back, Alaina. Just take it slow. Don't try to do it all at once."

Something in Alaina's expression said Kristy had missed the point by a mile. "You should go now," she said.

Her tone was friendly, but firm. Kristy was about to ask why when the door opened and Bryan Hixon came in.

"Let's get out of here, baby," he said, before spotting Kristy and stopping. "Oh."

Kristy stood. "It's okay, I'm leaving."

He came and stood in front of her, however. "Thank you," he said. He still looked exhausted, but his eyes were clear. "For bringing Alaina here last night. I owe you."

"Glad to do it."

"I'm taking her home now, though," he said, maintaining eye contact. "She needs rest. To get back to normal life. Without being bothered. By anyone."

Hixon's tone was a lot like his daughter's. As if, perhaps, she'd heard it from him many times.

Kristy glanced at Alaina, but the girl was looking back into the corner of the room, moving her head from side to side, as if watching a fly.

"Goodbye," Hixon said.

By the time Kristy left the hospital the cops and the news truck had gone. The lot was almost empty, as if being sick was unpopular on Saturdays. The sky was dark and low.

She got in her car. Breathed out. That was, she guessed, that. If everybody was going to be dumb about it, there wasn't a lot she could do. The only hope was that when the Feds debriefed Alaina they were less incurious. But they, too, would be ready to move on, disinclined to push hard on a case that seemed to have solved itself.

Let it go.

She sat staring out across the asphalt until she realized the trees dotted around it were blurring. Wiped her cheeks. Wished she had a coffee. Started the engine. As she steered toward the exit she noticed a car parked away from all the others, in the far corner of the lot, under a tree.

A figure she recognized stood at the front, leaning back on the hood, smoking.

She drove away.

CHAPTER
20

The Hardaker residence was a few blocks from the school—a well-maintained Victorian, originally the lair of someone who'd most likely paid other people to cut down trees rather than doing it himself. We'd made contact with the girls pretty easily. Molly had the idea of reaching out on social media and established that both had Instagram accounts in variants of their given names (maddyhard and naddyhard). Evidently they had notifications turned on, too, as Madeline came straight back, saying they'd be happy to meet. Mindful of Molly's qualms, Ken suggested doing so at their own house, with at least one parent's permission and presence. There was a longer delay in response to this, but eventually a message pinged back saying that was fine though the opportunity was time limited.

The door was opened by a brisk, fit-looking guy who was, disconcertingly, exactly the same height as me. In every other regard Greg Hardaker was clearly the upgrade: clear of eye, smooth of skin, obviously prone to forms of exercise that went beyond my semi-regular half-assed runs.

"My wife's at Safeway," he said. "And I have to be gone myself in half an hour, so..."

"That's all we need. And thank you."

I introduced the team and we followed him into the house. It was soon evident that, whatever this guy did, he also earned a lot more than me. Actual art on the walls, Restoration Hardware furniture, a side room filled with more high-end computers than it seemed reasonable for one person to need. "Alaina's really okay?"

"Far as we know," I said. "Kristy—she's our presenter—is at the hospital now. How did you hear Alaina was back?"

"A couple we know were in the Stone Mountain Tap last night," he said. "One's a teacher at the school. Gina. She called us right away. Which was thoughtful. The girls...well, you can imagine how they've been feeling. And it's been worse the last couple of days, for some reason."

"Maybe it was starting to sink in," I said. "It must have been tough. For all of you."

"You can say that again." He paused, in front of a door at the end of the hallway. "Where's she been? Alaina?"

"That's not clear yet."

He nodded. "Okay. Look, I've agreed to you talking to my daughters because, well, basically because they really want to, and on the rare occasions when they're on the same page they're frankly unstoppable. Also because...I think it'd be good for them to tell their side."

"Their side?" Ken asked.

"Alaina disappeared. They didn't," I said. "People can be judgmental. As if it must somehow be the fault of the people left behind."

"Exactly," Hardaker said. *"Exactly."* I got the sense my remark had been enough to allay any lingering doubts. "How come you don't have a camera, by the way?"

"This is just a recce," Ken said. "When we do the thing properly we'll need lights, release forms, the whole she-bang. And it won't be on spec, on a Saturday morning."

"Ah, okay. But look, I don't want them hearing anything that's going to upset them. Anything bad. About where Alaina's been, or what might have happened to her. Okay?"

"Don't worry," Molly said. "Far as we know, it's all good."

A few minutes later Ken and I were sitting on a couch in a large, pleasant room. They'd expanded the windows on the back, so the wall was almost entirely glass. Beyond lay a tidy yard, a fence with a gate in it, forest beyond. The fence was high and solid. The gate was basically a door.

Madeline and Nadja Hardaker sat together on the opposite couch. Despite the similarity of their Insta handles, it was clear that being the non-identical kind of twins was not sufficient: they'd leaned hard into every turn where further distinction could be made—clothing, hairstyle, and attitude.

Madeline's hair was in a tight ponytail. She was wearing jeans and a black T-shirt with the letters WTF on it, upside down. "When can we see her?"

"We don't know," I said.

Nadja's hair was long, unconfined, and she was wearing an actual dress. "Is she okay?"

"She was taken straight to the hospital, and the police were there soon after."

Nadja was well aware this wasn't an answer to her question. "But did she *seem* okay?"

"She was cold," I said. "She was a little intense. Other than that, I'd say she seemed fine."

"Alaina's *always* intense," Madeline said. "So. Do we get paid for doing this?"

"No," Ken said.

"These are just a few initial questions," I said. "I know your dad doesn't have much time. And we've read the reports. I want to clarify a couple things. Then hopefully we'll be back later with our cameraman. At which point, sure"—I glanced meaningfully at Ken—"there may be expenses. For which you'd be reimbursed."

"Oh, okay. So what do you want to know?"

"You must have heard all this a hundred times," Molly said to Greg. "I'd love to see the garden."

"Uh, sure," he said, glancing at his watch. "You girls going to be okay?"

They gave him identical eyerolls.

"So," I said, once Molly and their father had left the room. "We're going to need to dramatize a couple parts of the story, for the show, so I need to make sure I've got a clear picture of what happened."

The girls nodded in unison.

"So could you describe that? Exactly where you went?"

"We left school," Madeline said. "Dropped our bags on the porch here. Then walked down the street."

"The main street?"

She looked at me as though I was being obtuse. "Well, obviously."

"To where?"

Eyebrows raised now. "The...motel?"

I sensed I was missing something. "Why?"

Madeline turned the irony levels up to stun. "Because...that's where we went into the woods?"

Her sister was frowning. "If you've read the reports, how come you didn't know that?"

"They weren't explicit about the exact location," Ken said. I have no idea if this was true. "Which is why we're glad to be talking to you, love. Exactly the kind of detail we need. Why'd you go into the woods down there?" He nodded out the window. "Why not behind your house, for example."

"They're boring," Madeline said, glancing out at the fence. Molly and Greg were ambling close to it. "I mean, okay, it's all the same forest, but we know that part way too well. And it gets steep so you can't really go anywhere."

"They're the little woods," Nadja added. "We wanted to go into the big woods. Well, Alaina did. She'd been all about the forest for weeks beforehand."

"Any idea why?"

Maddy shook her head. "History," Nadja said, however. "Principal Dan's class? He went on and on about the forests, religion and stuff."

"Sounds interesting."

"It's more boring than you can possibly imagine."

Maddy sniggered. "Dan's a dork."

"Okay," I said. "So, the three of you walked through town. Did you stop anywhere?"

"No."

"See anybody you knew?"

Madeline had now decided my IQ must be in single figures. "Seriously? This place isn't exactly Chico."

I managed not to smile. "Indeed. Or San Francisco, or New York. Okay, so it's a small town and you're bound to see people you know. Do you remember anybody in particular?"

Nadja shrugged. "Just randos."

"We saw that dyke who works in the Tap," her sister said.

"Val, right. We did. Though she's not a dyke. You're not allowed to call someone a dyke unless you are one."

"Whatever," Madeline said. "She does it with women, either way."

"You don't know that," Nadja said. She looked at me. "Val's only been in town a couple years, keeps to herself, and has scandalously short hair. That has led some of the more parochial residents to leap to conclusions."

"Plus, she's an actual lesbian," Maddy said.

"Great," I said. "So you got down to the motel. And went into the woods behind there. What time? I know you'll have been through this before, but I want to be precise."

"School finishes at three," Madeline said. "We hung around, then walked . . . we thought around three thirty?"

"Wait," Nadja said. "I texted mom." She pulled out her phone and started flicking through it. "Keep talking, I'll find it. It's a way back."

"Can you describe what happened? What you did while you were in the woods?"

Maddy shrugged. "Just chatting. Goofing around, taking pictures for Insta. Wait." She bent over her own phone.

"Three twenty-six," Nadja said, holding hers up. "I texted mom at 3:26, saying we'd be back for dinner. I was in the motel parking lot when I did it."

Maddy held her phone up, too—displaying a selfie of the three girls, grinning, on the edge of the same lot. "Taken at 3:28," she said.

"Mind if I take a copy?"

She shrugged, and I took a picture of her screen. "Did you post anything once you were in there? I'm asking because it might help nail the later timings."

"No. Data signal sucks bad enough in town—it's dead in the woods. We checked out the walls, stuff like that."

"The walls?"

"Yeah, the stone walls. You must know about those."

"Of course," I said. "We saw one yesterday. Kind of wavy."

"Right! That's where we were. There, and then we went deeper. There's more in there."

"So then what?"

"We'd been like, maybe forty minutes," Madeline said. "Alaina had wandered off to take pictures. But it was getting cold and we were kind of over it. So we went to where we thought she'd be, but she wasn't there."

"How long had it been since you saw her? I know you'll have answered that question before."

"About ten minutes."

"Or maybe fifteen," Nadja said. The girls looked at each other, and Madeline nodded. "Could be, probably. It might even have been twenty."

Ten was the figure they'd given before. So here was an extra window. "And then what?"

"We called. And looked around. And kept calling."

"I know it's hard to be sure," I said, "but for how long, approximately?"

"Half an hour," Nadja said. "We called, we looked. We waited. We called and looked some more."

"And then?"

"Thirty minutes is a long time," Madeline said, sounding defensive. "If you're waiting for someone to come back."

"Hell yes," Ken said. "I wouldn't have stuck it that long."

"Even if it was me?" I asked.

"Especially not," he said. "Five minutes, max."

The girls laughed. Ken's better at this stuff than me. "Well, okay, it was probably closer to twenty," Madeline said. "But still long, and she just, you know, *wasn't there*. And it was getting dark and starting to rain, and we couldn't *find her* so..."

"We freaked out," Nadja said. Her voice was flat, and I guessed that if someone had asked these questions of Kristy twenty years ago, following days of people carefully not mentioning she was still here when her friend Helen was not, it would have sounded about the same way. "And we ran home and told Dad and he called the cops."

"Speaking of Dad," Ken said. He nodded toward the window. Molly and Hardaker were heading toward the back door. "Looks like we're out of time."

Everybody stood. "So when are you going to do the real video?" Madeline asked. "Because I am going to need new jeans for that."

"Very soon," I said. "We'll be in touch."

I shook her hand, and turned to do the same with her sister as Madeline and Ken left the room. Nadja was looking out of the window, however, toward the fence. She frowned.

"Thank you," I said.

She turned to me, looking confused, but then smiled brightly and shook my hand.

We walked together back toward the main street.

"Good work, Molly," Ken said. "That was smooth."

"Did it help?"

"Maybe," I said. We'd talked on the way to the interview about her trying to get the girls' father out of the room, in the hope they might be more relaxed—and leave space for them to diverge from previous accounts. "The gap was a little longer, the search a little shorter."

"But that's basically what you suspected anyway."

"Yeah."

"So did you actually learn anything?"

"Maybe."

"Okay, what?" Molly said, irritably. "There's something you two aren't saying. Spill it."

"They're lying," Ken said.

"About what?"

"We don't know yet," I said.

CHAPTER
21

At around the time Ken and Nolan were talking to the Hardaker girls, Pierre was thinking he probably had enough film now and might as well go back. Before leaving the motel he'd reviewed what had been shot the day before, transferring the footage to his laptop. First, the material from the mountains in the morning. It was good and moody, and some of the stuff of the mist curling into the trees was genuinely pretty great.

Then the to-camera section they'd done in the woods behind the motel: a little dark, but he'd worked with Nolan long enough to understand he was unlikely to respond positively to being asked for a redo unless absolutely necessary, and also to know the presenter's first take was generally the best take. He made a note to check with Ken whether he thought they could grade it into acceptability, and backed it all up to one of the stack of portable hard drives he'd brought from LA. Reassured that he now had two copies, he erased the files from the camera's drive.

Then he went into the woods to see what he could see.

He found the wavy wall where they'd done the outro, and he shot further clips of it from a variety of angles and distances as a safety measure: worst case, they could use these as intercuts under Nolan's audio from the kinda dark sections. This wouldn't have occurred to Pierre a year ago. It occurred to Ken as naturally as breathing, however, and picking up that kind of trick made working on *The Anomaly Files* worthwhile, despite barely being paid industry standard rates. And being shot in the shoulder on the last expedition.

When he'd got everything they could possibly need, he lowered the camera and looked around. He wasn't entirely sure what he was supposed to be doing. Yesterday, it'd seemed like they were bailing. Ken hadn't explained if that had changed. He just said, see if there are more walls out there.

So Pierre walked further into the woods.

The terrain soon started to get steeper and more rugged, but for a while there was nothing to see except a lot more trees. His dad would know what they were called. Pierre's childhood hikes had featured a constant stream of background facts, the comforting hubbub of parental observation. Some kids would have absorbed a portion of it. Pierre had not. He'd trusted his father to hold that information, with the result that he had taken none of it into himself.

He was okay with that. He was about pictures, not words. It didn't matter what the trees looming over him were called, nor the various types of damp moss that covered most of the ground and occasional fallen trunks. It mattered how they looked. What you see is the mind's best attempt at making a picture out of the information it has. Nolan had said something like that once. Sometimes knowing too much prevented you from being able to *see* it properly.

He walked another twenty minutes. Nolan had said the local area had been extensively logged a hundred years or so back, but you wouldn't know it in here. Maybe this was an old growth section that avoided being felled. The trunks were thick and straight, a mix—though Pierre didn't know, and wouldn't have cared—of Douglas fir and sugar pines. Clumps of redwoods, too, though not the giant kind: they needed the fog found along the coast. That he *did* know.

It was easy to find a path and enough light filtered down from above that it didn't feel too gloomy. It was quiet, though. Very quiet. Pierre didn't think this was just because his father wasn't alongside, saying stuff. It was all just...very still. Suddenly he stopped walking.

"Whoa," he said, quietly.

The wall closest to him was low, barely two feet high and mainly obscured behind the fallen trunk of a once-massive tree—which is how he hadn't spotted it earlier. There was a bunch of rocks just in front.

He switched on the camera and got a few shots, taking a moment to log the GPS coordinates. The upright part of the wall was about six feet long. It could have been as much as ten before the other rocks fell down.

As he went back to walking, more slowly now, he came around the side of a thick knot of trees.

He stopped again. "You're going to want to—" he said, half-turning, before remembering he was alone. Which was weird. He always handed this kind of thing up the ladder.

This second wall was much higher. Had to be close to four feet. Over a foot thick. And long, too—stretching seventy or eighty feet away into the woods, ignoring marked changes in terrain. Straight to start, then curving back hard on itself. From above it'd look like a fish-hook, but—Pierre established by looking up—you were never going to see it from above. And so it wasn't going to be on Google Maps. Unless some of the locals knew about it, this was new. Nolan would like that. A lot.

Pierre walked along the inside of the curve. He noted—and filmed—the fact that at the end, the part where the pointy bit would have been on a real fish-hook, it seemed again like stones had been dislodged. Then he went around and started filming the other side, though he stopped walking, and lowered the camera, when he saw there was *another* wall beyond.

About two feet high again, but long, and this time completely straight—heading off into the trees like a single, wide train track, straight across a gulley, running straight into kind of a cliff. It had to be a hundred and fifty feet long. It looked bizarre.

He took some more footage, but only a few quick shots. Nolan and Ken were going to want to see. So far as Pierre had been able to tell, all Nolan had to say about these walls is nobody knew what the heck they were. It didn't seem likely that what he'd found changed that, but if your point is that something's mysterious, then the more mysterious you can show it looking, the better, right?

And these were mysterious, there was no doubt. Even to Pierre, whose tendency to reach for the unknown was less acute than most. Partly it was the fact they made zero sense either individually or together, and certainly not out in the woods like this. Also, they just seemed weird.

The walls they'd filmed yesterday had seemed odd, sure. But there was something different about these.

*   *   *

He checked his watch and was surprised to see he'd been out in the woods for well over an hour. Closer to two, in fact. He'd found enough. Time to go.

He realized the light might not be as good when they came back, however, and decided to lay down a final piece of footage as a master shot they could cut against: taken standing on the spot and slowly turned in a circle, to show how the walls stood in relation to one another.

He found the position where a panning shot would be least obscured by trees. As he found it, a bird floated hectically down from above and started arcing gracefully between the trees. Pierre quickly raised the camera, knowing this would kick the shot up straight to A+. He locked on the bird as it entered frame. Panned steadily across with it, ignoring its fluttering side diversions, tracing the overall arc of passage. Turning smoothly at the waist, legs balanced—

He stopped, suddenly.

The bird wasn't in shot anymore.

He turned back, trying to find where he'd lost track of it. Presumably it'd flipped upward, higher into the trees. But there was no sign, up or down or on either side.

Had it gone deeper into the woods? He held position, ready to restart filming. The bird didn't come back.

Pierre lowered the camera, disappointed. That would have been awesome. Plus now he was going to have to do the whole thing again, without the bird.

"I'm lost," said a voice.

*   *   *

Pierre turned.

There was no one there. Nothing except trees and that higher wall, thirty feet from where he was standing. Dust, spinning languidly in shafts of light.

The voice had sounded as though it was only a few feet behind. Perhaps closer. It was hard to believe somebody could have got out of sight in the time it'd taken him to turn around. No, it was impossible.

So it hadn't happened. Pierre decided that he hadn't heard anything after all—at least, not outside his own head. That happens, sometimes. An unbidden thought bubbles up from deep inside, unexpectedly. So unexpectedly that its articulation may sound as though it was said out loud.

Why "I'm lost," though? He wasn't lost.

And why would his inner voice sound like a little girl?

He decided that he didn't need the panoramic shot right now after all. It'd actually be a lot better if Nolan himself was in the space when it was taken. It kind of summed up the whole walls thing, and the presenter would provide a sense of scale, too.

Yes. Good idea.

Pierre started back the way he'd come. As he got closer to the higher wall, however, he heard the voice again.

"Help me," it said.

Definitely a little girl. Pierre quickly covered the last of the distance to the wall. If some kid was out here by herself, hell yes he was going to help.

But when he looked around the end of the wall, there was no one in sight.

Then he heard another voice. Not loud. "I don't trust her," it said. An older voice this time, female.

"She promised," another replied. A man. "She made a

deal. The stones are down. And some of us are already abroad."

These voices seemed to be coming from the *other* side of the wall. Pierre felt relieved. Obviously there was a family out here with him. He figured he ought to at least say hello, to avoid startling *them* as he passed by.

He walked back to the end and poked his head around. "Hey," he said. He was looking down into the curved area, toward the fish hook part.

There was nobody there.

He could hear something else now, though. Not voices. Music. It was very faint, as if coming from the other end of a long corridor. There was a slight echo on it, too. Pierre cocked his head. What *was* that song? He couldn't quite recall.

"You found me," the little girl said.

She sounded much closer. Right behind him.

She tapped him lightly on the back. "Now I'm yours."

A sensation rolled down Pierre's spine as though someone was tracing it with a fingernail, then seemed to sink into him. For a moment it was like that awkward, leaden feeling you get if you strain your back and it refers round into your stomach muscles. A kind of bloated anxiety.

Then it was gone.

He turned. Nobody there.

No little girl. Nobody at all.

Pierre decided firmly that he didn't need to talk to these people after all.

He walked quickly away, back through the trees toward the motel, as a soft, cold rain started to fall.

CHAPTER
22

Kristy took a roundabout route back to Birchlake, driving empty roads that wound apparently aimlessly through miles of forest, and—when presented with a choice—selecting routes to make the journey even longer, hoping that a period in movement might help her reset. It rained for a while, stopped, then started again. Eventually she came upon a barely there town, realized she was hungry, pulled over in front of a diner. She ate a sandwich slowly, staring out the window across the highway into the trees. Got out her phone. Scant data signal. She used the website she'd previously employed to find Gina Wright's address to locate another.

But then put the phone down.

She knew from both writing and life that nothing ends and nothing begins. Everything is structured and textured by what's come before—and will pass on a diluted version of this foreshadowing, along with its own flavor, to everything after. What your grandfather or great-grandmother did and experienced will influence your choices far more than you'll ever know or could bear to believe. A trick Kristy had learned long ago, when she finished a piece, was to go back and cut the entire first paragraph. It might need tweaking afterward, but generally you found little of substance had been lost and the result felt more direct. Less mediated. More like life.

The length of our stories is arbitrary. You choose where they begin and when they have ended. Alaina's story was done, on any rational level. All Kristy had to do was accept this and be grateful, and get back to her own life.

So that's what she was going to do.

The phone buzzed. A notification popped up to say Nolan had emailed her. She flicked up the screen, assuming that it would be an invitation to join them in the Stone Mountain Tap and contain enough autocorrect errors to suggest they'd already been there a while.

Instead Nolan explained he and the team were considering changing the focus of their show from the walls to Alaina's story. He wondered how she'd feel about presenting it.

No, she emailed back. *It's done. Leave it.*

But by the time she got back in the car, she knew his email had arrived at exactly the wrong time.

It was midafternoon by the time she got back to Birchlake. She drove to the address she'd tracked down and parked outside. Walked up a short path and knocked on the door. It was answered by a woman in middle age, whose hands were covered in flour.

"Hi," Kristy said. "Sorry to disturb you. I wondered if I could have a word with your husband?"

"Well, that'd be up to him," the woman said, cheerfully. "He's with his lover."

"Oh," Kristy said.

The woman laughed. Down the corridor behind her, a

boy in his mid-teens was at the kitchen table, apparently doing homework. He smirked at his mother's remark.

"I'm kidding," the woman said. "Well, maybe not. He's at the school. There are principals who manage to keep it to a weekday affair, I've heard. Dan's not one of them. What did you want to talk to him about?"

"Alaina Hixon. You know she's been found?"

"Thank God."

Her son looked up. "Maddy's going to be on YouTube about it," he said. "Maybe even TV."

Mrs. Broecker frowned at him. "Says who?"

"Some people interviewed her and Naddy this morning," he said. "They have a show about mysteries and stuff."

Oh for God's sake, Kristy thought. "Exciting. Okay, well, I guess I'll go to the school."

"Are you with the TV people?"

"No," Kristy said. "And tell your friend not to get her hopes up."

Before the principal's wife closed the door, she gave Kristy a look. "If you see Dan, do me a favor."

"What's that?"

"Tell him I'm cooking something he likes, and he should come home."

A single car sat in the school lot, a tired-looking Subaru. Kristy parked next to it and walked to the main door. It was unlocked.

"Hello?"

The lobby was lit only by light coming through the glass wall and door to the yard beyond. It felt the way the kitchen does when you can't sleep and come down in the middle of the night. Artificial light was coming from the open door of an office at the end of the corridor.

Principal Broecker was behind his desk there, surrounded by papers and peering at his computer screen.

"Hey."

He jumped, looking caught out. "Christ."

"Sorry. I called out earlier. You look absorbed."

Broecker pushed his hand through his hair. "I never seem to get the time for this stuff during the week."

"You can't do it at home?"

"Too many distractions."

Real life, you mean, Kristy thought, but knew that she was no one to talk. "Great news about Alaina."

"Oh, God, isn't it? Part of why I'm here. Everything's been so out of kilter that I'd got behind. There's a fundraiser for... well, you don't need to know about that, but the point is life can get back to normal. I suppose this means your 'vacation' is over?"

Kristy smiled. "Yes. But my mind doesn't stop working on the weekend, either. Wanted to check something."

"Sure."

"What's the story with Alaina's mother?"

"Not a happy one," Broecker said, sitting back behind his desk. "She was out driving, late. And drunk. Jenny— Jenny Hixon, that is—was one of the people who'd been most welcoming to our family, too. I have to admit we maybe didn't do enough to try to keep the connection going. I'm not sure why. She drove off the road a few miles from here. The car plummeted into the river. She died instantly. Extremely sad."

"There was never any question that there was anything suspicious about it?"

"Not at all. At least, not in the sense of third parties, which

I assume is what you're getting at. The local grapevine suggested she'd been depressed for some time. Personally I never saw any sign of it, but I guess often you don't."

"And since then it's just Alaina and her dad?"

"Far as I know. Why?"

"I went to their house a couple days ago. And encountered him again this morning. He seemed a little... controlling."

Broecker's eyes were wandering back toward his computer, and he still hadn't offered Kristy a seat. "He's sole-parenting a teenage girl. And he's just got her back, after thinking he'd lost her forever. He's bound to be a little possessive for a while, don't you think? If that happened to my son, I'd be locking him in his bedroom until he's thirty."

They said goodbye, and he wished her a safe journey home. But at the door, Kristy turned back.

"Did you manage to speak to her?"

The principal was halfway through moving a sheaf of papers and didn't look up. "Speak? To whom?"

"I was at the hospital in Chico this morning."

Broecker didn't say anything, but his hands stopped moving. "As I left," Kristy continued, "I passed a Subaru. Same color as the one in the lot. There was a guy by it, smoking. Head down and turned away, as if he wanted to make sure he wasn't seen. Pretty sure I know who it was, though."

The principal finally looked up.

They sat on opposite sides of one of the picnic tables in the schoolyard, sheltered by a tree.

The principal pulled his cigarettes from his jacket. "It'll be two, today."

"You didn't drive thirty miles for a covert smoke," Kristy said. "So?"

"It's inconceivable I might simply have gone to check on a student who'd been missing? To see how she was?"

"No. Though I would have thought it could have waited until Monday, and you're considerate to have given the family space unless there was compelling reason to talk to her."

Broecker smoked in silence for a moment.

"Was it what I showed you on her Instagram account?"

He grunted. "You are sharp."

"I had a conversation with someone a couple days ago. They suggested bullying is a big deal for you. And not just because how it might reflect on a school."

"Who was this person?"

Kristy didn't answer. "Protect your sources," he said, with a wry smile. "I get it. But I have moments of acuity, too. I'm quite capable of working it out for myself."

Kristy saw in his face that he already had. "I hope you won't make it a problem for her."

"No. And Gina's right. I was a narrow-shouldered and unbecoming child, remarkably untalented at sports. So I spent a certain amount of time being shoved around. It happens. I survived. More relevant is what happened to my sister, Melissa. She's three years older and three times as smart, and I looked up to her enormously. I still do. In high school she went to a party one night—secretly, against our parents' wishes. She was sexually assaulted. She couldn't tell our parents, or thought she couldn't. I didn't know how to help her. Didn't think I could. I thought that was the grown-ups' job. That was bad enough."

He knocked off the end of his cigarette. Ground the ash

to invisibility with his shoe. "Ten years later she applied for a prestigious, career-defining job. When she arrived for the interview, one of the men in the room was the boy who'd assaulted her. She didn't get the position. And she couldn't explain *that* to our parents, either. I remember sitting there while my mother, trying to be kind, gently suggested to Melissa that she should set her sights a little lower."

"Christ," Kristy said.

"This, or something like it, happens all the time. Not necessarily assault. Being sidelined, spoken over, interrupted, overruled. *Bullied*, effectively. But I'm sure you don't need me to mansplain mansplaining to you."

"I do not," Kristy said. "But how does this relate to..."

"My history class. It's outside the core curriculum and purely for students who might find it interesting. A cultural overview of early American settlement. One topic tends to be quite popular. Alaina in particular appeared taken with it."

"And what's that?"

"Witchcraft."

"Huh."

"Specifically I deal with how accusations of witchcraft have been used as an instrument of social control. Of gender control, especially—a way of dealing with uppity women. Of disempowering. Conversely, it's certainly true that taking on that mantle, claiming witch-like abilities, was for some women a means of *asserting* control, of coming into their powers. And sometimes that happened when girls were arriving into early womanhood. Girls of precisely Alaina's age."

"And when you saw the picture on Instagram, and the comments, you were worried she might have taken your elective to heart. And run with it."

"Exactly. And as a result come into contact with people online who do not have a teenage girl's interests in mind. There are strange people out there. Strange, bad people, invisible to the rest of us, lying in wait."

"Yes, there are."

"And so that's why I went. It was dumb, and I didn't get to see Alaina anyway. But after two days of feeling guilty and worried, I had to try. There's something not right about her disappearance. Over and above the obvious."

"*Thank* you," Kristy said. "I, too, have been saying this, to universal disregard."

"From whom?"

"The cops. Alaina's father. My ex-husband."

The principal stood. "The world is full of secrets. The question is whether it's a good idea to know them. Sometimes doors are better left closed. For the individual, for everybody concerned."

"I'm not good at that."

"I could tell that the first time I met you. And it's just as well there are people like you—though of course you take responsibility for whatever you release. I'm sure you recall the story of Pandora's box. It does not end well. Are we done?"

"Yes. Except your wife said you should come home for dinner. She said it's something you like."

"I like everything she cooks," he said. "Maybe one day she'll realize that."

"Perhaps she'll realize sooner if you're home more."

He smiled.

CHAPTER

23

Well, it had to be her dad, right?"

"Can't imagine who else," I said. "Could have been kids, I guess. But Hixon seems most likely."

Ken and I were in the parking lot of the abandoned tavern outside Birchlake. We were talking about the message that had been drawn on the windshield of the car the previous night. "Question is, what was it supposed to mean?"

"Interpreting it didn't stretch me, Nolan."

"But why?"

"Let's ask him."

"Let's not," I said. We'd come to see if we could talk to Alaina. Kristy had texted a few hours before, to say her father was bringing her home from the hospital. She hadn't yet responded to an email I'd sent later on, raising the idea of switching the show's focus, but the whole idea was moot if Alaina or her father were against it. Molly had declined to come along. Which was fine—we didn't need her for this—but she was nonetheless dragging her feet in a way I'd never seen before. "At least, until we get a sense of how the land lies."

The oil drums were still in place—or had been placed

back in position after Alaina and her father returned to the house. "Still not exactly putting out the welcome mat," I said.

"Unless she'll talk to us, there's no show. Better to know where we stand before we bother putting anybody on tape."

We walked through the gaps and along the drive. Followed the curve around a trio of redwoods, past the old truck, and a sagging bench, half overgrown with poison oak. In daylight—albeit a gray, weak, late-afternoon kind—it looked far more prosaic, the kind of unmaintained frontage you find with most houses in small mountain towns off the beaten track. A very ordinary nowhere-in-particular. Should have felt that way, too. But it didn't, and when I turned to Ken, his face was looking pinched.

"Is it just because we got spooked here last night?"

"Dunno, mate," he said. "But let's get this done. And then—"

He stopped, frowning into the trees. At first all I could see was a thicket of undergrowth, tangled around a stand of small trees, oaks or something. Then I saw it. The undergrowth was about three feet high, made up of plants that I mainly didn't have names for. It was pretty thick, which is why you didn't notice at first that it had achieved its height by growing over something.

At the left end, in between the distinctively lobed leaves of poison oak burnished with fall color, was the jagged corner of a chunk of rock. Once you'd spotted it, the others became more obvious. It was a stone wall.

"That one of yours?" Ken asked.

I went closer. It was distantly possible it had been part of some structure related to the house, an outdoor firepit, long-ago grill, product of many weekends of some dad's diligent labor. But the stones and manner of construction were the same as the walls we'd seen in the woods behind the motel. "I think it must be."

"They do get around, don't they."

The wall was about five feet long, curved as though it had once been part of a larger arc that would have taken it across the driveway.

We looked up at the sound of banging.

We stopped ten feet short of the house. A middle-aged guy was nailing a plank of wood over the top section of the front door. It was the third piece he'd placed, and his goal seemed to be to cover the entire upper section.

When he noticed us, he stopped—still holding the wood in position. "The hell are you?"

"The guys who found me last night," a girl said.

Alaina stood up from where she'd been sitting in the ratty armchair. Her arms were tightly folded. She kept them that way. "Two of them, anyway."

The man gave the lower nail one more whack, put the hammer down. Wiped his hands on his jeans and came down the steps. "Bryan Hixon," he said, as he shook my hand, and then Ken's. "I need to thank you guys. Sincerely, thank you."

"We didn't do much," I said. "Went out for a smoke, and there she was."

"Where's the other guy?" Alaina asked.

"Filming," I said.

"Shame. I'd like to see him again."

"We came out here last night," Ken told her father. "To let you know Alaina was back."

"Huh," Hixon said. "That was you? I was asleep in

back. Heard something. Assumed it was coyotes. Tried to go back to sleep. Then half an hour later I got a call from the cops saying somebody found my girl."

"The yelping was us," I said. "Something ran past the front of the house."

"Coyotes," he said again.

"I guess," I said. "Though it seemed big. And fast."

Ken nodded up at the house. "Why are you boarding up your front door?"

"Because he's a dumb-ass," his daughter said.

Hixon smiled tightly. "Alaina, go inside."

She didn't move. He turned his head. She stared him down, and in that moment I saw something I recognized from my own childhood. The moment when a long-held power balance shifts, when a kid gets old enough to question whether they actually have to do what a parent tells them, and lets that doubt be known. Puts it right there on the table, where it can't be ignored. I imagine it's a strange and perhaps even disturbing moment for a parent, a cold wind blowing across everything that's come before. Because yes, this is the harbinger of the adult who may one day be looking after *you*, but wrapped in the disguise of someone who's still a child: poised on the boundary between one world and another.

But then Alaina yanked open the front door, went indoors, and slammed it behind. The plank Hixon had been working on fell off with a clatter. There was a moment of silence.

"A few of the panes were broken," Hixon said, calmly. "Probably a couple more are now, too. I should get to finishing the job. It's going to rain again."

"We'll get out of your way," I said. "But we came to ask something. I'm Nolan—and that's Ken. We have a

TV show. Well, YouTube. It's called *The Anomaly Files*. It's about unsolved mysteries. It seemed to us that—"

"No," Hixon said. "First up, there's no mystery. Second, if there was, it's been solved. Alaina's home."

Ken is not someone who backs down easily. "Which is great, mate. But where's she been?"

"In the woods. She's back. End of story."

I could see the sitting room through the window. Mottled walls. An old-looking couch. Some pictures in narrow wood frames, including what looked like an old engraving of a woman. Alaina was in the middle of the room, apparently on the phone, but staring at me.

I tried a smile. There was no indication that she saw.

"You'll want to get back to town," Hixon said, as he walked back up the steps. "Like I said, it's going to rain tonight. Tomorrow too. Hard."

"Well, if there was a moment of that which wasn't weird," Ken said, as we walked away down the road, "then I missed it."

"I know, right? What was up with the door thing? I went right up to it last night. Sure, there was a crack. In *one* of the panes. So why not just cover that one?"

"He's not stopping there," Ken said. "Didn't you notice? There was a pile of planks over near that shitty armchair. Cut to length to cover the window."

"What's he going to do—board up the entire house? Why?"

"You got me, mate. And didn't things seem a little tense for a father and daughter who've been reunited?"

"And another thing. If what he said about last night was true, it wasn't him who put the message on our window."

"I know. Hang on—I'm buzzing." He pulled his phone out. "Moll," he said. "We're heading back. How about—"

He stopped talking abruptly. Listened.

"Stay there," he said. "We're coming."

CHAPTER
24

Gina Wright was in her kitchen, looking out the window. After seven years, the view of their yard was like that old wedding photo on a shelf. A rectangle of grass, flower beds with straggling roses, wooden fence on three sides. A tree, around the base of which—the summer they bought the house, in a fit of new-home enthusiasm— Derek constructed a rustic wooden semicircular seat copied from something he'd seen in a magazine. The idea was it would be somewhere for them to spend cocktail hour, but it fell down the first time they tried. He rebuilt it with a lot more nails, and from time to time it still functioned as a place to perch, though she'd always felt precarious on it. As Derek got slowly heavier he stopped using it altogether, though neither of them mentioned that. He worked later now, too, and so these days Gina conducted weekday cocktail hour by herself, standing here in the kitchen with her glass, or a second, or often third, looking back out onto the yard but only really seeing the fence.

Today was Saturday, though, and Derek wasn't at work. He was watching television. Something on PBS— a documentary about the history of American retail, by the sound of it. Who would watch a show like that? Who would even make it?

She checked the time. A little after six. Putting the meal together would take five minutes, tops, from leftovers and what had come home in a box from the Tap last night.

So really, she had no reason to be in here. She could go sit on the sofa. It wasn't like it was some boring sportsball. Derek was a smart guy, perennially fascinated by the world, eager to learn, eager to share. He wasn't the problem here. Gina wasn't sure what the problem even was.

Well hell, yes, she knew.

She'd allowed herself to get drawn into a situation, step by careless step. It didn't matter how you tried to dress it up, it was wrong. It was so easy, though. All it took was a quick and apparently loving text to check how Derek's day was going—his reply to which would confirm he was beavering away at work and would be for a while.

But that, as she well knew, only made it worse—the fact that it wouldn't even occur to the affable, perfectly nice guy watching TV in the living room to question what his wife got up to during occasional afternoons.

So there was that. Normally she managed to compartmentalize it, however, and yet now she felt unsettled. Maybe it was the fact Alaina was back. While she'd been missing, the town felt on crisis alert. Even after the initial shock of her disappearance had started to fade (which was terrible, but the human mind accommodates quickly in order to stay sane) there'd been an alertness. As if everyone was unconsciously waiting for bad news to finally fall.

But the hammer blow hadn't come. Alaina was back. Unharmed. And life could go on as before. Perhaps *that* was what felt strange. Life wasn't strange anymore and yet continued to *feel* strange, and that was somehow worse.

Gina shook her head irritably, helped herself to another glass of wine. Decided to take the bottle and see if Derek wanted more. Like a loving wife should.

As she left the kitchen she heard a line from the narration of the show Derek was watching—

"…became an integral part of the social scene of many young teenagers, a forum in which they could both participate in an increasingly consumerist society, and engage in socializing rituals in a relatively safe environment."

—and hesitated. It did sound *unusually* dull. But that could be entertaining, maybe? If they made fun of it together? Even though Gina felt she learned enough about the rituals of young teenagers during the average working week.

She was still deciding, adrift in the hallway, when Derek turned his head toward the door. "You okay, honey?"

"Yes, why?"

He smiled. "Nothing. Just heard you coming. And yes, I *would* like a splash more Merlot."

She went in, committing herself to the space, and leaned over the back of the sofa to refill his glass. The narrator droned on, the screen showing slow panning shots of the interior of airports. "Oh. I thought this was about malls or something."

"Nope. The evolution of airport architecture."

"Wow. Is it as boring as it sounds?"

"It's *stunningly* dull," he said. "It's so bad that it's got me in its tractor beam and I can't seem to turn it off."

Gina smiled, wondering why she didn't want to sit

next to him. Why the prospect filled her with a faint but very real feeling of repulsion. Even dread.

"Come," he said, patting his hand on the sofa. "I'll put the food together in a while. It's Saturday. You worked hard all week. Relax."

The fact that he'd say that, and sincerely mean it, when he worked much longer and harder hours, made Gina want to punch him. Or herself.

Thankfully at that moment her phone pinged from the counter in the kitchen. "I'll just see who that is."

She hurried back into the kitchen, anticipating another in the daylong string of texts and Facebook messages from people celebrating Alaina's return. She could take her time answering, then lay out the food. Derek would likely fall asleep on the couch after dinner. Another day would pass.

The notification was from Instagram, however. Someone had liked one of her pictures. She barely ever posted. Couldn't remember the last time, in fact. Some people evidently worked on a slow news cycle. She clicked on the notification out of curiosity. The app loaded, then flipped straight to the picture that somebody had liked.

Gina nearly dropped the phone.

It was a photograph of the front of their house. Taken late afternoon, judging by the light. Judging also by the fact that the picture showed the front door being opened, by Gina, to let in a figure that was unquestionably male and equally unquestionably not Derek.

"Fuck fuck *fuck*."

Gina looked to see who'd liked the picture. Only one person. A collection of letters she didn't recognize. She noted that the picture had gone up ten minutes before.

"You say something?" Derek's voice startled her so much that she almost dropped the phone again.

"Stubbed my toe."

"Klutz. A cute klutz, though."

"That's me! I'll be through in a second!"

She hurriedly deleted the photograph. She recognized the previous picture—a photo of the MISSING poster for Alaina, ten days previously: they'd all done it in the period immediately after she disappeared, posting on all the social media they could, in case it helped.

Gina hurried to the sink, convinced she was going to throw up. Stood bent over until the feeling passed, settling instead into a deep, grinding feeling in her guts.

She grabbed a glass from the drainboard and drank a lot of water, thinking hard. There were two things she needed to do right away. She used the phone to go to her Instagram account and change her password.

Then she went to the bathroom, locked the door, and used a little-known messaging app to send an urgent DM.

CHAPTER
25

Molly was in the middle of the motel lot. Two cars were parked there. One was mine. The other was Kristy's rental.

"Kristy's here?"

"No," Molly said. "That's what's weird. Well, one thing."

Ken and I had walked back to town as fast as we could. All he'd said was Moll sounded "freaked out."

"Is this to do with what you thought you saw in your shower yesterday?" I'd told Ken about this on the way.

"No," she said. "And *I saw it.*"

"Moll, love," Ken said. "Just tell us what's up."

"When I got back I thought I'd find Pierre. Hang with him. But he wasn't around, and it started drizzling, so I wound up in my room. And basically I fell asleep. I guess."

"You guess?"

She hesitated. "I was sitting on the bed with my laptop, leaning back against the headboard. Doing the accounts for this trip. Then it was half an hour later. So, I fell asleep. And I woke feeling cold. And I was sitting there on the bed, looking across the room, and it all seemed very...red. The murky red bedspread. That crappy faux-wood paneling. The red-brown carpet. I didn't like it. You know? It's all just all *very dark* and very *red*. I *hate* it."

I glanced at Ken, expecting to see him looking bemused. In fact, it seemed like he knew what Molly meant.

"So I thought I'd try Pierre again," she said. "I came out, saw Kristy's car. I thought that might mean *you* were here, Nolan, so I tried your room first because it's closer. No response. Or from Ken's. So I went back to Plan A and knocked on Pierre's. *Still* not there. This time, I really banged on it. He's *not there*, Nolan."

"Okay, Moll," I said. I was finding it hard to understand why this was such a big deal. "So he's not there. They've probably gone to get something to eat."

"Or drink," Ken said, pointedly. "Did you try phoning?"

"Of *course*," she said. "Three times. No answer."

I took out my phone. There was an email notification on the screen. "Ah, here we go. Incoming from Kristy. This'll…Oh. It's from a couple hours ago."

"And you've only just noticed?"

"It literally just came in," I said, as I loaded up the email. "Probably sent it from somewhere with crappy signal, and it got held up. Oh. She's…okay, well, she's very much *not* on board for doing a show about Alaina."

"Good," Molly said.

"The idea's dead in the water anyway," Ken told her. "Her dad told us to bugger off, and without her it'd be like doing a show about the pyramids without showing any pyramids. Which I admit would not be beneath us. Stop dicking around and call Kristy, Nolan. Find out if Pierre's with her."

It rang for a while, and then her voicemail message cut in. I tried again. Same result.

Molly frowned at me. "She's not answering either?"

I checked out Kristy's car, establishing it had been locked, and peering in through the windows. The interior looked like a vehicle piloted by Kristy always did. A high-tech water bottle in the cupholder, but otherwise as though it had recently rolled off the production line and then been cleaned again, to be sure. Ken and Molly came to join me.

We stood in silence for a moment, then all turned together to look at the forest.

"I don't see it," I said, a couple of minutes later. We were a few yards into the trees now. It was dark and quiet. "Kristy has zero interest in these woods."

"She might now, though," Ken said. "Alaina spent all that time somewhere."

"But she emailed a couple hours ago, saying the story's over, and to leave it. Her exact words."

"You heard her last night. If Pierre found something that made it look like maybe she was right, and Alaina *wasn't* wandering around in here by herself, then Kristy might decide it's back on again."

"But Pierre wasn't here when I got back," Molly said.

"So he comes out of the trees as she's parking. Tells her what he's found. Kristy's on it like a pack of rats. Back into the woods they go."

I remembered another option. Feeling a little sheepish, I fired up the Find Your Friends app. The others watched the screen with me as it said LOCATING, and the wait symbol whirled slowly around. And then stopped. "Location not available."

"Hate to point this out, Nolan, but you're separated. Have been for a while. It's not out of the question that she might have de-friended you on that."

"She did," I said. "I did too. Of course. But we put each other back a few weeks ago."

"Sweet. In which case, that's pretty much proof they're in the woods, mate. Those girls earlier said the data signal's fucked in there. With no data, her phone can't update the server with its position. Thus, location not found."

He was right. But I still took a couple of steps deeper into the woods and called out Kristy's name. Loud.

Molly and Ken both jumped. "Christ, Nolan."

"Shh."

We listened. Nobody called back.

We could have taken our pick of the seating in the Tap's restaurant. There was only one person behind the bar—the young guy from the previous nights—and he didn't have his work cut out for him. It was early, sure, but it still seemed kind of empty for a Saturday night. A few couples, widely spread out, not talking much.

We bought drinks and sat in a booth. "Not exactly a carnival atmosphere," Ken said.

"It's cold and dark and wet outside," Molly said.

"All the more reason to go *indoors* and drink and raise merry hell. And also—last night a missing child came home. You'd think that might lift the spirits, wouldn't you?"

As I watched, the young bar dude behind the bar got his phone out, looked at something, thrust it back in his pocket. He didn't look happy. Nobody did.

"Where the *heck* have you been?"

I turned to see Molly was talking to Pierre, who'd just come in. "The motel," he said.

"You just got back?"

Pierre looked confused. "No. I've been there for, like, an hour." He checked his watch. "Two, in fact. Fell asleep sitting in the chair. Just woke up. Wondered where everybody was, then I remembered what Ken and Nolan are like and realized there was only one possible answer."

"But I banged on your door," Molly insisted. "*Hard*. How can you not have heard? Or when I called you?"

"Must have been a deep sleep, I guess," Pierre said. He seemed pretty vague. "I didn't get much last night. My room was really cold."

"Have you seen Kristy?" I asked. "Or know where she is?"

"Nope," he said. "Why? Should I?"

"She's not answering her phone either."

"No clue, I'm afraid. Who wants a drink?"

I went up to the bar with him, and asked the bar dude if he'd seen someone answering Kristy's description.

"I know who you mean," he said. "But no. Not today."

"Kind of quiet here tonight, isn't it?"

"This whole town is a morgue," he said, his mind on something else.

I went outside for a cigarette. Mist was coming in from the woods, curling down the street. It was near dark and drizzling and the street was deserted. Small, old towns in the mountains can sometimes seem like sets, especially at night. This did more than most tonight.

I tried Kristy again. Had another look at the Find Your Friends app, with the same result. There's something unsettling about technology when it fails. It feels like a promise reneged. You trust the device to put you in contact with somebody, or the one in your car to tell you where to go, as you might once have trusted the gods to bring rain, or your priest to keep the community safe from harm. Then one day, for no obvious reason, they fail you.

I crossed the street. Even the little grocery market on the corner was closed. Why, early on a Saturday evening? People need organic tofu on the weekend, too. I went over and peered through the window. Nothing to see. Dark shelves.

As I backed from it, I noticed something I hadn't seen before. A ghost sign, on the high portion of the wall, the remnants of a previous name, now faded almost to invisibility. VANESKI GROCERIES.

I headed along the street to the building that held Kristy's apartment. Pressed the buzzer, heard it ring upstairs. Listened for the sound of the upper door to the stairway being opened. Nothing. I decided to try her one last time and then (really) call it done, but saw I still had the previous app up on screen, so jabbed my thumb irritably on the Update button for Find Your Friends instead. The whirly thing plodded dutifully around for a while, as it had every time before, electronic shorthand for "the magic isn't working."

But then it stopped, and a tiny icon of Kristy's face appeared bang in the middle of the screen. I was sufficiently surprised that it took me a few seconds to work out what it meant. Not only that it'd found her, but also where.

Right where I was standing—which meant she had to be inside the building after all.

I walked backward, looking up at the window on the first floor. No sign of light, still. I called out, feeling dumb. Certainly loud enough to be heard from within the apartment.

No sign. I tried phoning, but it wasn't answered and I didn't hear the sound of ringing from above. I was heading back toward the door to bang on it again when I saw something.

The wide street windows of the former general store had been thoroughly whitewashed. During the day it was impossible to see through. But now...for a moment it had seemed like there was a light inside. Not all over, as if a bulb had been switched on—but a small patch.

Maybe like the screen of a phone?

I went up close, shielding my eyes with my hands to cut out ambient light in the street. At first all I could see was variegated dark gray, the uneven strokes of a heavy coverage of whitewash on the inside of the glass.

But then I saw it again. A glow, moving. Deep back in the room.

I rapped on the window with my knuckle. "Kristy?"

The light stopped. It dimmed, too—not as if a flashlight had been turned off, but as though it had been slowly turned down to nothing.

I realized there was a padlock on the door. Which meant, of course, nobody could have come in this way. Feeling stupid, I glanced across at the heavier door giving access to the side stairs up to Kristy's apartment. The deadbolt was in place. She wasn't upstairs.

So it must be her inside the building. And she must have gotten in some other way.

I walked up to the corner and down the next street. An alleyway ran behind the buildings. Grimy dumpsters, a mistreated office chair, bad smells. I walked past the back of the grocery, two other buildings, the coffee shop— and got to the rear of the building holding Kristy's apartment.

There had been two windows here—small, utilitarian.

Boarded over long ago. A door between them, not boarded but reinforced. More recently, by the look of it: the wood was weathered but not as gray. Just a regular lock.

I knocked. No response. I grabbed the handle and gave it an exploratory tug. The latch didn't seem like it would stand up to concerted effort. Though of course I wasn't going to break in.

I heard footsteps and turned to see Ken sauntering along the alley toward me. "Fuck are you up to, Nolan?"

"Kristy's in there."

"Doing what?"

"No idea. She's not responding to calls or knocks."

"Well maybe that's because she's somewhere she's not supposed to be."

"So then what's she doing in there?"

"I asked *you* that." He went up to the door and listened. "I can't hear anything. What makes you think she's inside?"

"I saw a light. Through the glass in the front."

"To be honest, mate, I only came looking for you to ponce a cigarette. It's cold and drizzling, so if you're intending to lay in wait, you'll be doing it on your own."

"Wait for who?" asked a voice.

Ken and I jumped out of our skins.

CHAPTER
26

Kristy was standing behind us.

"Do *not* ninja up on people like that," Ken said. "Fuck's sake. My heart feels like it's being punched by a little bastard rabbit with metal paws."

"Where have you been?" I asked.

Kristy indicated how she was dressed. Ponytail. Air-Pods. Head-to-toe Athleta. Running shoes, hence having been able to arrive behind us silently. "Guess, Nolan."

"Chess club."

"Ha ha."

"So why's your car at the motel?"

"I came to see if you guys were back. You weren't. I went for a walk while I waited, realized I should catch up on the run I missed this morning. So I changed and went for it, figured I'd go back for the car later. What's the big deal?"

"Nothing," I said.

"I got back, saw Ken sneaking around the corner and wondered what the hell he was up to. What *are* you doing?"

"Looking for you. I tried calling. Knocked on your door. Then . . . tried the Find Your Friends thing."

"I'd forgotten we did that."

"Well, we did. And it said you were here."

"Well, I wasn't," she said. "But my phone is. It's on the table upstairs."

"The idea that you and your phone might be in different locations is an explanation I hadn't thought of."

"Still doesn't explain why you're creeping around."

"Nolan thought he saw somebody inside," Ken said. "And because of the phone thing, he assumed it must be you."

"What would I be doing in there?"

"We've all asked that question now," I said, irritably, feeling dumb and embarrassed, "and it turns out there's no answer, because you weren't."

"It's hard to be sure," Ken said, "but I think this might be the most boring conversation I've ever been part of. I'm unsubscribing. How about we head back to the bar, and—"

There was a loud crash from inside the building.

We stared at the door. It sounded like something very heavy had toppled—or been knocked over—in there.

"That happened before," Kristy said, quietly. "The night before you got to Birchlake."

"And?"

"Val said she stored stuff in here. She rents the whole building, I think. We should go tell her."

"She's not in the Tap," I said. "Or, she wasn't five minutes ago."

"In which case, that must be her inside," Kristy said, "and she could be hurt."

"So call the cops," Ken said.

Kristy pushed past us and grabbed the door handle. She gave it a tug. Looked at me.

"Fuck me," Ken said. "Am I the only person here who understands what the police are for?"

"Do it," Kristy told me.

I hesitated, but only for a moment. Whatever fell over in there had been very big, and landed hard. Kristy has a willingness to get up in the world's face that I don't share—I tend to let the world come and find me, and prefer it to make an appointment—but if someone was lying underneath a big heavy thing we couldn't just call 911 and hope they got here within the hour.

I braced my foot against the wall and took the handle with both hands. Yanked against it, hard. Then again.

On the third attempt the jamb splintered and the door opened, so fast it was almost as if something flew out.

Beyond lay a corridor, almost pitch dark. The far end glowed faintly—streetlights dimly visible through the whitewashing on the main street windows.

"Superb," Ken said. "So not only have we schlepped all the way to the arse-end of California and not got a show out of it, we're now merrily breaking and entering. Can we set fire to a church later? I've always wanted to."

"You're only pissed because it wasn't your idea."

"Yeah, I know. Let's have a look then." He took a step into the corridor. "Hello?"

No response. He glanced back at me with an expression that I assumed must be concern. I hadn't seen his face do anything like that before.

"Come *on*," Kristy said, impatiently, shoving past both of us and into the building.

"Careful," I said, as Ken and I followed. "You don't know what state the boards are in."

I got out my phone. Its light showed twenty feet of corridor with grimy walls. A doorway on the left. I poked my head in and saw an old desk, a couple of wooden chairs, a pile of old paperbacks. A bent spatula on the floor.

A further door on the right revealed another room of the same size. Nothing in it except for an old-looking safe in the corner, most likely from the store's original incarnation. Curling sheets of paper were thumb-tacked to one wall: staff rosters from its last inhabitants; a poster for a local fair in 1992; a sign telling people not to steal food from the fridge, specifically singling out a re-peat offender called Nick "Thiefboy" Golson. The more personal something left behind, the more it looks like it's from ten thousand years ago.

We walked to the end of the corridor and Kristy and I raised our phones to illuminate the space beyond.

Nobody said anything for a moment.

The room was forty feet wide, and maybe the same deep. A wooden counter ran along the right side, shelves behind. Both looked, like the safe in back, like they had been there a hundred years. The left side of the room was likewise lined with shelves. Some had things on them. It was hard to tell what they were at first, and our attention was taken by what was in the remaining space.

The floor area was empty, apart from a stone wall.

I stepped carefully into the room, directing the phone light more directly on it. The wall was about twelve feet long, maybe three feet high either end, with a pronounced dip in the middle. It looked like a work in progress. It had a pronounced curve. "Is that another one of yours?" Ken asked.

"Certainly looks that way."

"Why is it . . . inside a building?"

"I have no idea."

"Look here," Kristy said. She'd gone past the wall to the counter, shining her light at the contents of the shelves on the other side. Rocks. Some by themselves, others in collections of two or three. I went to where she stood, noticing that—hidden behind the wall—a few sheets of legal-size paper lay on the floor. I walked around the end of the counter to look at the shelves.

Each of the rocks had a scrap of paper wedged under-neath. A short set of numbers had been written on each. A scan along two of the shelves suggested the notes were all in the same handwriting. "The hell," Ken asked, "is this all about?"

I returned to the wall in the middle of the room. Squat-ted down to look at the sheets of paper. Sketches, more than one per page, most scribbled out. Crescents, wavy lines. A skewed rectangle. A lot of the crossings-out were jagged and hard, as if made in anger or frustration.

I stood back up. "We should go."

Back outside in the alley, I examined the damage to the door frame. The splintering around the lock was minor. You'd have to come up close to see it had been broken.

"So I guess we now owe somebody a couple hundred bucks," I said. "To get that fixed."

"I'm happy to have the conversation with Val," Kristy said. "We were doing the right thing. We thought she was hurt in there." She hesitated. "Though in fact..."

"*Nobody* was in there," Ken said.

"Which...is weird."

"Nolan's a muppet. He thought he saw someone, or a light, but there was always a chance he could have got it wrong or be on drugs. That's not the point."

Kristy frowned. "Then what? The rocks, or that wall?"

"Well yeah, partly. But something else. Did you see anything that looked like it had just fallen over?"

"No."

"So what made the noise we heard?"

We checked Kristy's apartment. No sign anything had fallen in there, either. Kristy headed for her phone, leaving me and Ken to double-check around the apartment.

"Expecting something?"

"No," she said. "Just checking it's working."

She said she'd shower and then join us in the Tap, and give the Val woman a call in the meantime.

As Ken and I smoked our way across the road to the bar, he turned to me. "We all heard that noise."

"I know. One of the buildings either side?"

"No way, mate. And what's the deal with the rocks?"

"I don't know," I said. "But remember yesterday, when we were walking back from filming the capper?"

"You're right. We saw her. Out there. Near the walls."

"Carrying a heavy-looking bag."

"But why would anybody steal stones from the walls?" He saw that I'd stopped in the middle of the street. "What?"

"Look," I said, turning to indicate in both directions.

He saw what I saw. Nobody. Empty sidewalks. No lights apart from in the Tap and the liquor store down the street. Nobody was loitering outside it tonight.

He shrugged. "The weather's crappy, like Moll said."

"But it's seven thirty in the evening, Ken. Saturday night."

"Christ—Nolan."

I thought he was just getting impatient with me pointing out what he'd already pointed out, but then he started running toward the Tap—and for him, running fast.

CHAPTER
27

As she approached the Hixon house Val felt her phone vibrate. The screen showed a number with a 310 area code. Los Angeles. Had to be Kristy Reardon, probably confirming she was leaving in the morning. Good. Calling back could wait. She set off up the drive.

The oil drums that had been in place since Alaina disappeared had been moved, and as she rounded the last bend to the house, Val could see why.

She slowed. Stayed back in the dark.

A car was parked in the space in front of the property. Not Hixon's truck, which sat beyond. Val recognized the vehicle. The owner was standing with Hixon on the porch, in the sallow glow of the bulb above the front door.

Val walked up the remaining driveway, staying as far to the side as she could get without having to push through undergrowth. She stopped when she couldn't progress further without risk of being seen.

Close enough. She could see through the only window on the side of the house that hadn't been boarded over. The job was half done, as though Hixon had been disturbed. The two men on the porch were speaking quietly, but she heard enough of the tone and cadence to know the conversation was stilted, men who weren't actual friends, Hixon waiting the interruption out so he could get on with the task he'd set himself. The four windows on the front of the house—two on each floor—had already been covered.

Val acknowledged the thinking behind this, and the effort, but knew it was a waste of time. There's no point building a wall when what you're afraid of is already inside.

The uncovered lower half of the side window revealed the living room. Old wallpaper, equally old pictures on the wall. Val recognized the woman in the engraving in the lower middle, and understood the family resemblance between her and the photo of a woman further along the wall, and also to the young girl she could see through the window.

Alaina Hixon stood in the middle of the room, head bowed. A girl of the same age stood on either side, watching her carefully. Madeline and Nadja Hardaker. Madeline glanced to the side, as though nervous. With the front windows covered, the three girls couldn't be seen by their fathers on the porch. But that might change if one of the men decided the reunion had gone on long enough and came to say so.

Val didn't think that was the only reason Maddy was nervous, however. Nadja also had the look of someone who was realizing that they were in danger of getting way out of their depth.

Alaina meanwhile had moved her hands so they were palms together, pointing downward. She raised them, still joined, until they were in front of her chest. She slowly rotated her hands about the wrist so the palms were facing front, and then—looking as if she was executing a tai chi move—straightened both arms to the side, until they were both straight, palms out.

Maddy and Nadja both diffidently took a step forward, until their chests touched Alaina's palms. The three held this position for a moment, and then Alaina raised her head, turning it to the right, and suddenly spat a ball of red phlegm straight into Nadja's face.

The girl blinked, but didn't move.

Alaina turned her head to the left and did the same to Madeline. Then faced front, eyes still closed, and stuck her tongue out, downwards, as far as she could.

Even from where she stood, Val could see that the girl had bitten it, and it was bleeding freely. A large drop of blood slid off the end and dropped to the floor.

Val felt her heart sink and her stomach turn. Pure theater. Who knows where from. Some dumb movie. But doing the wrong thing by mistake didn't stop it being wrong. Spilt blood always counts.

A gust of wind writhed through the bushes, curling round their bases, gathering force, then shooting up into the branches of the trees.

The two men on the porch noticed. "Storm's on the way," Bryan Hixon said.

Hardaker nodded, and called out for his daughters.

Val glanced back at the window. The three girls were standing with their faces crushed up close together, arms around each other's shoulders, hands held in tight fists.

Hardaker lost patience, and went into the house—leaving Hixon outside.

The wind started to swirl through the undergrowth again, this time slower, more insidious. It felt less like a product of the environment and more like something trying to push past. It swirled in a vortex around Val, thick as water, buffeting her so hard that she had to step rapidly to the side to stop herself from falling over.

Then it shot up into the trees again, dislodging an explosion of leaves that fell brown and golden around her.

Then suddenly someone was gripping her shoulder, and Bryan Hixon's face was right up in hers. Angry, but not only that. Afraid, too. "Get off my property," he said, in a low, hard voice. "And stay away from my daughter."

"Mr. Hixon, you don't understand."

"I understand everything I need to. I've been down this fucking road before. She doesn't need your help. She needs to be *left the fuck alone*."

"You're going to need *help*," Val said. "She's going to make mistakes. She has already. Can't you *feel* it? Let's *talk. Before it's too late*."

"We don't need anybody." He shoved her, hard. "Go."

Val hurried away down the drive before Hardaker and his daughters could come out of the house and see her.

CHAPTER
28

I arrived in the bar a few steps behind Ken, to see Molly right up in Pierre's face.

"Where have you *been*?" she said, when she saw us.

The few other people present were studiously ignoring the situation—apart from the young guy behind the bar, who was watching it very carefully.

"What the hell's happening?"

"God knows," she said. "I went to the restroom and when I got back he's going off at the guy behind the bar."

This was the most un-Pierre thing I'd ever heard of. "Pierre—what's going on?"

"I don't know," he said. "I was sitting there. Molly went to the bathroom. And I . . . I dunno. That guy, he just."

He glanced at the bartender. Kurt or whatever his name was.

"He just what?"

"Nothing." Pierre was staring down at the floor. He looked about twelve years old. "He didn't do anything."

"Okay then," Ken said. "Seems like there was a thing, but it's not a thing anymore, right?"

"Right." Pierre glanced at the bartender again. "Sorry."

The guy shrugged. "No biggie, dude. I should probably ask you to leave, though. Right?"

Pierre nodded, accepting this was reasonable. "Why don't we head back," Molly told him. "I'm tired anyway."

I walked them outside. "Seriously, Pierre," I said. "Are you okay?"

"I'm fine," he said—and he did look more himself. "I honestly have no clue what just happened. The guy really...I don't know. He's a bad person."

"Because...?"

Pierre smiled sheepishly. "Or maybe he's not. Shit, I don't know, Nolan. I felt angry at him suddenly. Sorry. Everything seems different, that's all."

"What do you mean? Different how?"

"Let's just go," Molly said to him, with the gentle, everything's-okay tone only women can muster convincingly. "Early night. So we can leave bright and early, right, Nolan?"

She looked me in the eye. "Sure," I said.

I watched them walk away down the street into the mist, or fog—I've never been sure of the difference. It was getting thicker, either way. I've known Pierre for two years. In that time, apart from being unnecessarily handsome and annoyingly personable, he hasn't caused me a moment's grief. I found it hard to understand why that might be happening now.

He's also extremely transparent, and so I was pretty sure he didn't know either.

Just before I went back into the bar, my phone rang.

"I see you," Kristy said.

I turned, saw her in the window of her apartment, a shadow against a dim glow. The edges of the window looked blurred. She waved, a small movement. I waved back.

"No response from Val," she said. "I left a message. I

don't expect anybody's going to happen by and decide to try the back door to the building tonight."

"Well, apart from us. So, are you coming down?" I knew what her answer was going to be.

"I don't think so," she said. "I've had a shower, I'm warm and dry, and I'm not sure I need another night in that bar. Every day here is beginning to feel like the same day. How about breakfast? In the coffee shop? Eight thirty?"

"Sounds good. And you're fixing to be on the road soon after?"

"That's my..."

I thought for a moment that the line must have dropped out, but realized I could hear her breathing. "You okay?"

"Yes," she said. "Just, be cautious with that guy."

"What guy?"

"I talked with him the first night I was here. He came up to me in the street. Said some odd stuff."

"Kristy—what guy?"

"For God's sake, Nolan—the one on the corner. Tall, older guy. Standing looking at you."

I turned toward the grocery store. Nobody there. Back the other way, toward the liquor store on the next block.

"Kristy, there's nobody out here except me."

"Nolan, he's *thirty feet* away. Opposite the grocery."

I turned. Even walked a few yards in that direction. The street was empty. "You're looking out from a lit room onto a dark and misty street, Kris. The light's playing tricks."

She was silent for a moment. "Oh. Okay."

"Do you want me to come up?"

"No. I'm fine. See you in the morning."

I didn't argue the point. I'd had enough of people being strange at me for one night. I went back in the bar.

CHAPTER
29

When I woke it was cold. Really cold. For a moment this caused a disconnect in my brain, taking me back to the last time I'd woken freezing—at the bottom of the Grand Canyon, in the dead of night on a small beach by the side of the Colorado River, scrunched up in a sleeping bag. Only when I realized I was swaddled instead in sheets that smelled faintly of bleach did I lock back to where I was. My motel room.

I didn't open my eyes because I find it harder to get back to sleep afterward. I could tell, in that way you can tell, it wasn't anywhere near time to get up. That it was still the middle of the night. I curled up tightly, trying to maximize my body's warmth, hoping to drift back.

It was working, too—until I heard the sound.

I ignored it. I've stayed in a lot of motels and hotels. Each has its distinctive chamber orchestra of unexpected noises. The whir and clunk of the elevator down the hall. The rustle of another guest careening along the corridor, listening to the television too loud in hopes of making their room seem less empty, or telling a child to get back to their own bed and go to sleep, for the love of God. My condo in Santa Monica has a string section of its own—people arguing as they walk along the beach, a sudden spasm of music from a boom box strapped to a homeless person's bike, distant sirens. Evidence of things unseen, each clear enough to picture them in your mind's eye.

If you try to ignore them they'll get on your nerves. So instead I listen, accepting them as part of the soundscape, and find it helps me back to sleep, a lullaby from the universe.

The sound of rain on the window. I was lying on my right side, so that was in front, six feet away. A sudden gust of wind, moving branches around the back of the motel, aspiring toward a howl but falling short, dropping into a slowly fading moan—taking me with it, I hoped, back to sleep.

Except…

There was that sound again.

Or still. I realized it hadn't ever gone away, only slipped briefly below the threshold of audibility, submerged beneath the steady patter of rain. Then I realized that it was music. A heavy beat, though tinny. A high melody, wistful. I knew it. But couldn't remember what it was.

As I listened, I realized it was repeating itself. Like a ringtone. I finally opened my eyes and propped myself on one elbow. I already knew there were problems with the idea, but I flapped out my hand onto the nightstand for my phone.

It wasn't there. Now that I had both ears off the pillow it was easier to lock on a direction and confirm what I'd already suspected. The music was coming from a source inside my room. And it still sounded like a ringtone.

The problem was that it wasn't *my* ringtone. I've had

the theme from *Halloween* as my call alert ever since phones became sufficiently advanced for you to have a say in the matter. I started by laboriously keying in the tones (it's amazing what you'll do when you're supposed to be writing the fifth draft of a bad script) and graduated via midi files to eventually using a sampled chunk of the real soundtrack.

That was the first problem. The second is that I always, *always*, have my phone on silent overnight.

And the third was, where the heck was my phone?

My eyes were accommodating to the darkness but there wasn't much to go on. A red LED on the coffee machine. The rectangle of the big window at the front of the room, only slightly lighter than the wall around it. I turned my head, trying to refine the direction of the sound. I always put my phone on the nightstand. I snatch a couple of pages of a book before sleep, and I do that on my device. I also use it as an alarm, checking it's set before turning out the light.

Still befuddled from sleep, I couldn't recall doing either, though that could also be because Ken and I had stayed in the Tap a good deal longer than was wise, before eventually lurching back to the motel.

When...yes, I read. I remembered it now. And I also set an alarm for eight a.m. While lying in bed. So where the heck was my phone?

I leaned forward querulously and peered over the edge of the nightstand. No sign of it on the floor.

I got out of bed, shivering. As soon as my feet landed on the carpet the music stopped—to be replaced with a muffled vibrating sound. I spotted a faint light on the floor, over by the end of the window by the door.

My phone, facedown on the carpet. Now doing what it

was supposed to—lighting up its screen, and vibrating—rather than playing a ringtone out loud.

But... on the floor. Over there.

Ten feet from where I now remembered placing it on the nightstand, before I went to sleep.

The screen confirmed I had incoming, from Ken. It also said the time was 1:44 a.m. I pressed the screen to accept the call.

"Nolan?" Ken's voice was low, scarcely above a whisper. "Is that you?"

"Well, yeah," I said. "This is my phone. Are you okay?"

"I'm in my room."

"Okay. But... why are you calling?"

"I need you to come in here."

"In your room?"

"Yes, where else, you twat?"

"I don't know. This is a weird conversation, Ken. It's nearly two in the morning."

"I know what fucking time it is," he hissed. "Seriously, Nolan. Just get in here."

"Why?"

"There's someone in my closet."

CHAPTER
30

I pulled on clothes and left the room. It was raining steadily, but the walkway was mainly protected by the overhang, and outside actually felt warmer than it had in my room.

I padded along to Ken's, tried the handle. The door was locked. A moment later the handle turned, however—and the door was drawn open a little.

I pushed it further. The room was dark. Ken was immediately inside, close up to the window, in PJs and disheveled hair mode. He had a finger to his lips.

I closed the door silently behind me. Did a "WTF?" mime.

Ken pointed at the closet. Like the one in my room, it was on the far side of the bed, forming the wall that demarked the bathroom from the rest of the space. Two sliding doors, both closed.

We stood in silence for thirty seconds. Nothing happened. My heart was beating pretty hard.

I looked at Ken. He was very still, very there, fully focused on the closet.

There was a quiet knocking sound.

Two knocks, like a knuckle rapped against wood. Not fast, about a second apart, and not hard. But yes, a knocking. Coming from inside the closet.

Ken looked at me—and pointed to his ear as a question. I nodded. I'd heard it too.

And I didn't need to ask why he hadn't gone over by himself to see what was causing it. No matter how much of a hard-ass you are, if there's someone in your closet in the dead of night, you want numbers on your side.

After about twenty seconds there was another double-knock. Same timing, but a little louder. As before, it seemed to be coming from the left side of the closet.

Ken indicated for us to approach the bed. He climbed onto it, carefully, so as to not cause creaks from the mattress or frame. I went around the end until I was in position between the end of the bed and the closet.

Another pair of knocks—this time faster.

Ken lowered himself onto the far edge of the bed and got his feet planted firmly on the floor. He reached across his body with his right hand, toward the handle on the left-hand side door. Got it in position, held it there.

Looked at me. I nodded. He threw the door aside.

It slid fast, crashing into the other end of the closet and revealing a space that held a few coat hangers, one with a pair of pants on it, a pair of Ken's shoes, and a tatty ironing board leaning against the back.

Nothing else.

I held up my hand, and slid the door back again, more slowly. Then indicated I was going to open the other half. Ken nodded. And I did it.

But there was nothing in there apart from Ken's overnight bag. Finally, I drew the two doors more slowly toward the middle, so the opposite sides were half open.

There was nobody there.

We looked silently into the space together. "No," Ken said quietly. "That is not okay."

"A coat hanger?" I suggested. "Swinging against the door?"

Ken gave it a try. The closet was too deep for a coat hanger in motion—even if you could come up with a rational reason for it to move—to swing against either the door or the back of the closet. "You heard it," he said. "And how many horror movies have I made?"

"Too many."

"Oi. But, yes. And back in the days when you didn't do it all in VFX but had to make things actually happen. And as the director of zombie cult favorites such as *The Undying Dead* and *They Eat Your Face III*, I'll tell you: if you want it to sound like someone's knocking on a door, you can piss about all you like but you'll wind up holding a microphone next to someone banging real knuckles on real wood."

"But there was no one in there."

"I know. And *that's* what I do not like."

"How long was it going on?"

"Dunno," he said. "About ten minutes. Must have woken me up. *Knock-knock.* I got out of bed. *Knock-knock.* Considered checking it out, but then thought—fuck that. Get Nolan in here. You can use him as a human shield."

He winked, and then we were both laughing. Quietly, and a little shaky, but it felt good all the same. When we stopped, we realized that we could hear a noise.

Knocking. But not the same this time. Three quiet sounds: *rap-rap-rap*.

Coming from the door to the room.

We very quietly and carefully crossed the space. This time it was me who reached for the handle. Ken looked around, grabbed the coffee pot from his machine, came and stood to the side of the door. Nodded.

I grabbed the handle and yanked it open.

Scaring the crap out of Molly, standing outside.

"So *now* do you believe me?"

"About what?" Ken said. I'd explained why I was there. Molly in turn had told us she'd been woken by the sound of closet doors slamming above her head—and, knowing it was Ken's room, come up to check what the hell was going on.

"I told you," I said. "Molly thinks she saw something in her shower."

"And what exactly was it?"

"A figure," Molly said. "Standing in the tub. I saw it in the mirror. But when I turned...it had gone."

"Nolan—what the fuck is going on here?"

"I don't know," I said. "And that's not all. When you called me...my phone was being weird."

"Weird how?"

"Playing the wrong ringtone. With the sound on."

"Not sure that's the strangest thing I've ever heard."

"It was on the floor, half the room away from where I left it before I went to sleep."

"Oh."

"And when I got out of bed it stopped playing the song, and went back to vibrating."

"Yeah, alright," Ken said. "You can be in the weird-events gang. But I'm going to repeat the same question."

"And I continue to not know the answer. It could still be science."

"*How?*" Molly said.

"Ken's closet backs onto his bathroom. There will be pipes in those walls. Old pipes. The temperature drops, they make a noise."

"Maybe," Ken said. "But do you think we should check whether someone else has had something weird happen?"

"Who?"

"Who's not here?"

We went downstairs and to the end of the walkway. Ken knocked on Pierre's door. Waited a while, then did it again.

"So I guess he's asleep," I said.

Molly moved up close to the window, however, shielding her eyes. "There's a light on in there."

Ken did the same. "Dim, though."

"It's from the bathroom," Molly said. "Why would he leave the bathroom light on?"

"Maybe he just does."

"He's not a child, Nolan. I doubt he needs a night-light."

"You'd be surprised," I said, thinking of Kristy, who used to prefer leaving a low light in the hallway outside our bedroom. She gradually got out of the habit while we were together. I had no idea what she did now, which felt weird.

"Fuck's sake," Ken said. "If we wake him up, so be it."

He rapped a lot louder on the door. Molly put her ear close to the window and listened. Shook her head. I was getting very cold and a little wet and increasingly keen for us to not be doing this. "One of you phone him."

"Where are you going?"

"Around the back."

I walked around the end of the building, taking a squall of bitey rain in the face in the process. I was aware this would look odd to anybody watching, but so far as I could tell we were the only people staying in the motel.

I went up to the narrow window, stood on my toes, and got my face up close. The dim light was enough to show something in the main area. The chair that, in my room, was pushed as far under the desk as possible, to save space.

Pierre's was lying on its back on the floor.

When I got back around the front Ken was knocking on the door again, this time with his fist.

"He's not answering his phone," Molly said.

"I think it'd be good to check he's okay," I said.

"How, mate? I'm not breaking down another door tonight."

"I'll go ask the manager or owner or whatever he is."

"He's not going to be happy about it."

I walked to the office, Molly following. "You think something's really wrong, don't you?"

"I don't know." I told her what I'd seen through the rear window. "Doesn't prove anything. He could have knocked it over and not bothered to put it back."

"No," Molly said. "I've seen how Pierre works a motel room. He keeps them shipshape. This is a guy who has been known to find someone to come back to them with him, as you know, and ladies do not wish to find dirty socks everywhere and the TV tuned to the porn channel."

"Right, but bear in mind he tried to start a fight tonight with a bartender, which is a long way from his standard MO, too."

The office was dark but had a sign with a number to call after hours. It turned out to connect to the apartment in back of the office—as we could tell from hearing the ring. After a while, a guy answered it. He wasn't delighted at being woken after two in the morning, but I laid it on pretty thick about being worried about a friend.

Five minutes later he emerged into the office wearing a bathrobe that looked even older than he did. I let Molly take point in the conversation, as she's a lot better at that kind of thing. By which I mean talking to people.

He came outside with us and along to Pierre's room. He knocked. No response. So he unlocked and opened it.

"Hello?"

He stuck his head in, and stayed that way for a moment. Then he pushed the door wide before setting off back along the walkway toward his office.

"I hope you boys brought your checkbook," he said.

For a while none of us said anything. Then Ken picked up the chair, and slid it into position under the desk. To be honest, that only made the rest of it look worse.

"Jesus," Molly said, eventually.

All the lamps were broken. The bed had been turned on its side and leaned against the closet. In the process, both of the latter's doors had gotten cracked.

The armchair was upside down, one leg detached. The clock radio from the nightstand was a pile of wreckage in the corner. The motel notepad had been pulled apart, pages shredded, strewn all over the room like confetti.

I went to the bathroom. One of the lights was broken. The other shed a weak glow upon a floor that was an inch deep in water, overflowing from the bath. I turned off the tap. When I got back Ken and Molly were each holding one of the scraps of paper from the floor. I picked up one too.

Ken's had a series of wavy lines drawn on it. Molly's was much larger, nearly a whole sheet. Someone, presumably

Pierre, had etched a design onto it. It had been gone over many times, at first calmly, and then with increased ferocity. Impossible to tell what it was supposed to be.

"Okay," Ken said. "We need to find Pierre, and we need to find him fast."

At that moment the phone in the room rang, scaring the crap out of us. Then I realized the phone in my pocket was vibrating, too. Molly cocked her head, and stepped over to the door, and then backed out into the parking lot.

"Ken," she said.

We followed. From the lot you could hear that all of the phones in the motel were ringing. They rang five times, and then stopped.

It was quiet for a moment. And then there was a sound, like thunder. It rolled toward us out of the woods, and slowly faded. Leaving a very loud silence.

CHAPTER
31

I t was not only the phones in the motel that rang. Most people in town slept through the event, but some did not.

One of those who heard was Gina Wright.

She'd already been awake. Lying, as always, on the right-hand side of their bed, listening to the gently snoring hump on the left side. The snoring wasn't loud; she was used to it, and it wasn't what had kept her staring up at the ceiling—nor what had her gazing unseeingly at the television after dinner, though Derek had been dozing on the couch and yes, gently snoring during that, too.

When they'd come upstairs she'd slept for an hour, but then: bang, wide awake. She'd had this a few times over the last three months. Nights where she woke and thought, *Oh God, what am I doing?* Because it wasn't like she didn't love Derek. And she knew what she was doing was dumb and wrong, and while affairs can have one of several outcomes, few of them are good, and pretty much *none* of them are good when you've wound up having sex with someone purely on the grounds it might be fun—rather than any sense that it was a connection worth burning your life to the ground over. The OGWAID sessions lasted half an hour or so, after which she would eventually drift off. Now it felt like she might never sleep again.

So she heard her phone ring downstairs.

She left it charging in the kitchen each night, as her nightstand held a cute 1930s-style alarm clock Derek found for her a long time ago. It didn't go with the rest of the décor in the room, but whatever. She'd said once she liked that kind of thing. He'd remembered. That's the problem with attentive partners. You say something, they listen, and you find yourself receiving ceramic squirrels or amusing golf memorabilia every birthday for the rest of your life. They love you for who you are and encourage you to stay that way, tending that wall around you, even after you've come to suspect that you may have been someone else all along.

Normally she'd figure the ringing was a wrong number and let it play out. Not tonight. The sound made her heart beat like a jackhammer. She slid out of bed and padded quickly down the stairs, but the phone had stopped by the time she got to it.

There was a notification on screen but it didn't relate to the call. Two people had liked her Instagram post.

"No," she whispered. "No, no no."

A new post, from an hour ago. When she'd been asleep. The same picture as before. She deleted it.

Then realized that wasn't enough and deleted the app from her phone, too. Then realized *that* didn't go far enough either—whoever was posting wasn't doing it from *her* phone, were they? All Gina had achieved through deleting the app was preventing herself from knowing if it happened again.

She went to the kitchen table, opened her laptop, and prepared to delete her whole account, knowing she'd be losing pictures going back five or six years, some of which she loved, many of which she'd struggle to find backups for. She hesitated, but only for a moment. Pressed the button, pressed again for *Yes, I'm sure*.

She got herself calm—or fairly so—and went back upstairs. Slipped back into bed. Derek remained oblivious to the seismic dangers unfolding, to the tectonic plates of utter catastrophe shifting beneath where he slept.

Because there was Facebook, too, she realized.

Now she'd cut off the Instagram route, what was to say whoever was doing this wouldn't switch tracks? She'd only had thirty followers on Instagram, a couple friends (she was trying to avoid remembering which exact ones, because then she'd have to confront the idea that some might have seen the picture), but mainly strangers who liked artsy pictures.

Facebook was different. Family. Old friends. Former colleagues. A whole network, including a couple of people who were supportive when she felt low. Still only three hundred people, but this wasn't a numbers game.

This was *her entire life*.

She'd have to do it, though—if there was the slightest hint the attack could switch to there: though she knew well enough that all it might do is shift things into an even more serious arena. If they couldn't harass her online, what's to say they wouldn't break it out into the real world?

She had to find out who it was.

Not Kurt. He was in the damned photo. Of course he could have got a buddy to take it, but why would he? And his response to her panicked DM earlier—he'd managed a single word, "fuck"—didn't read that way. She'd responded by telling him to be calm, she'd fix it. Somehow. His response to *that* had been "ok cool." Ironically, it had taken the clear and present danger of their relationship becoming known to show Gina what a pointless little prick he was.

Not the type to blackmail, though. She was sure of that. So, who?

A thought dropped into her mind then as if it had dripped through the roof and fallen straight through her forehead.

She closed her eyes. Visualized the picture she'd now stared at twice before deleting, twice. Saw it in her mind as clearly as she could. Focused in on the glimpse of upper body, in the doorway. She'd been wearing her teal shirt. The one thing she'd been able to find recently that she thought didn't make her look overweight.

Thursday, then? Yes. Definitely Thursday. The most recent time she'd seen Kurt. The memory connected with a feeling of jitteriness. More so than usual when he came around, because while she trusted him to be discreet, you just never knew—as the existence of the photo proved. Gina had been *extra*-jittery that day because, barely five minutes before, she'd let someone out of her house.

That woman. She was with…actually, had she even said? No—and Gina had been too flustered (she'd hidden it, she believed, but yeah—she'd definitely been flustered) to check. The woman had asked questions about Alaina. Then gone—just in time. But…perhaps *also* in time to see Kurt wandering up the road toward Gina's house.

Maybe she'd happened to glance back, saw Kurt slowing pace as he approached. And *maybe* the kind of woman who'd come in someone's house without saying who she was—taking advantage of a woman whose thoughts were elsewhere—could also be the person to pull out a phone, snap a picture.

Gina lay thinking about this. Thinking also about the fact that the woman had previously talked to the principal. Gina knew Dan would not only have remembered her name, but made a note, filed it.

Call Dan. First thing tomorrow. Establish who the woman is. From there it wouldn't be hard to find out where she was staying in town. Gina could pay her a visit. And let her know that if she was behind the pictures, she was making a mistake.

Then she remembered. The woman *left a business card*.

Gina didn't have to go through Dan. Where had she put it? She closed her eyes, trying to remember. It didn't take long.

She'd put it on the mantel, because she'd been standing right next to it. Hadn't thought about it since. Derek wouldn't have moved it. She didn't have to go down and check now, tempted though she was.

Gina eventually fell asleep comforted by thoughts of what she'd do to the woman—Christine? Something like that—if it was her posting the pictures. Images that were violent and bloody. Thoughts, Gina should have realized, that were nothing like anything she'd ever had before.

Thoughts that might not even be hers.

The rings were also heard by Greg Hardaker, up late in his home office, tweaking a pitch deck to present in San Jose on Monday, last step toward Series B funding. He knew the deck was fine already, but he'd found shifting the words around—even if they ultimately wound up in the same place they'd started—helped free the ideas, releasing them from a rigid verbal format, keeping him loose when he was in the room.

He was almost done when he heard the phone in the

living room. *Ding-ding, ding-ding.* It pretty much never rang. The whole family had cell phones, naturally. The house only had a landline at all because accepting one chipped five percent off the cost of the telecom package. Had to be one of those infuriating automated calls, screwing up the time zone.

The ringing stopped, but he walked in there anyway, thinking he'd leave the handset off the hook in case the spambot dialed again and kept dialing. The phone was on the sideboard right inside the door. He was on the way back out before noticing someone standing in the room.

He jumped, but managed to keep most of the movement inside. A slender figure over by the window. Wearing pajamas. Arms down by her sides.

"Nadja?"

She didn't say anything. He walked over. "What are you doing down here?"

She remained silent, looking out into the garden. "Phone wake you?" Greg knew that didn't make sense. She must already have been here when it rang. It was a question to ask in the hope of provoking a response.

It worked. She looked at him, frowning. "What phone?"

"The phone. In here. It rang, like, a minute ago."

"I didn't hear."

"You didn't... Naddy, what's up?"

She turned her head back toward the window. "Look."

Hardaker looked into the garden. Didn't get what she meant at first, then realized. "The door in the fence."

"I woke up. Heard a sound. A banging. Outside. I went to my window. Couldn't see anything. But then it happened again. I came down. And when I got here, the door was open."

"Huh," Greg said. "Okay. Stay here."

He went into the kitchen. His coat wasn't hanging by the back door, which was annoying. Come to think, he hadn't seen it for a few days. Whatever.

He stepped out into the yard. It was cold. Raining. Windy. He flicked the switch for the garden lights. They didn't do much but were enough to show there was nobody in the yard. Which was the main deal, after all.

But still, the door in the fence.

Bracing himself against the wet, he strode across the lawn. The back fence was seven feet high and sturdy, made of reinforced redwood. He knew because he'd had it built when they moved into the house, by Bryan Hixon. Before that the yard had been open to the forest beyond. Fine for the backwoods crowd. That wasn't going to play for Greg, a former city dweller. Good fences, good neighbors, all that. He glanced back toward the house and saw Nadja had been joined by Madeline, also in PJs.

He waved, smiled—both looked so grown-up these days, so much like young women, and sounded and acted that way, too, it was hard to remember they were still kids inside—and went to the door in the fence.

It was halfway open. There was a bolt, though from time to time it remained unbolted when somebody forgot. The latch was pretty deep and there was no handle on the other side. Presumably whoever last closed it failed to make sure the metal arm was safely in place. The wind could have been enough to blow it open. Also enough, most likely, to blow a branch against the other side of the fence and make a knocking sound. Everything tidily explained. That was Greg's job.

He stepped through the gap to find the most likely branch and snap it off. No obvious culprit. Whatever. It was cold and wet and he wanted to be done with this.

He turned back, fully outside the property for a moment, the other side of the fence. In the woods. Through the open door he could see the back of the house. And the window. And the three figures standing in a line.

He froze.

Then there were only two. His daughters. The figure in between had gone. It hadn't been his wife, he knew that. Taller. Thin. Something told him it had been male.

He moved his head to the side. The side of the bookcase in the back of the room moved into line of sight. That's what it had been. That's all.

He shut the gate. Made sure the latch was down. By the time he turned back the window was empty. They'd gone upstairs, back to bed. It was time Greg did the same. Though he thought he might have a bourbon first.

As he stood sipping it, looking out at the fence in the dark, he remembered something. When the phone line had been installed, Maddy had spent a while fiddling with the handset. She'd changed the ringtone. It didn't go *ding-ding*.

That was the phone in their previous house.

Kurt heard his own rings as he packed his bags in his tiny room above the Tap. He waited them out, phone in hand. He knew it wouldn't be her because she was in his contacts as G. No idea who else might be calling this late, because the phone wasn't saying "contact unknown." It said NO NUMBER. He wasn't sure what that even meant. Nor why it wasn't vibrating at the same time, as it normally did.

Whatever. It stopped after five. He put his phone on the bag he'd already packed. Been a while since he visited mom up in Portland. She'd be psyched if he stopped by for a few days. Which would give whatever situation might be brewing with the teacher woman time to play out. If it went nuclear he'd simply head somewhere else. Getting bar jobs isn't hard, and nobody needs that level of shit over a random MILF.

He looked out of the window. It was still raining, but not super-hard. Maybe now was as good a time to leave as any.

Ryder, the principal's son, also heard the rings. He was up late on his laptop, half-listening to a *Tomb Raider* walkthrough while using Photoshop to patiently recreate a sweatshirt design for a band Maddy Hardaker liked. She wanted the shirt, but the official merch was hella expensive. He hoped maybe a knock-off version might do instead.

The laptop binged to tell him a call was incoming, relaying the information from his phone. It binged four more times, then stopped. No notification came up on the screen, which was weird.

He dismissed the event and bent once more over his work, soothed by the comforting sound of someone explaining in detail where to find all the munitions packs in level 5.

And there were others. But most people slept.

The only phone in Birchlake that did not ring was Kristy's.

CHAPTER
32

In the end, Ken and I gave up. We walked the main street and did a quick but thorough grid search of the others, walking one road apart in hope of halving the chance of missing him. Went up as far as the abandoned bar close to the Hixon house, getting wetter and wetter. Came back, skirting the edge of town, sticking close to the river. By the time we were on the main street again, walking past the Tap, I'd lost all feeling in my fingers and we were both soaked through.

"This isn't working," Ken said. "We're chasing a moving target."

"We can't just leave him out here."

"I know, mate. But if he's not answering his phone, what makes you think he'll talk to us in person?"

"We don't know he's got his phone with him."

"We couldn't find it in his room. And I told Moll to keep looking. If she'd found it, she would have called. What?"

I was looking in through the windows of the bar. It was empty and dark. "Thought I saw something."

Ken came and stood with me. "Like, a person?"

"Dunno." Chairs. Tables. Lamps, none of them lit. We'd spent enough time in this bar that it should look welcoming even under these conditions. It didn't. Everything about it seemed unfamiliar. "Doesn't it look different to you?"

"Well it's shut, mate. And dark."

"More than that. Like you wouldn't want to go in."

Ken didn't say yes, but he didn't disagree, either— and when Ken thinks you're talking crap he's happy to let you know. "I don't like this town in general, to be honest."

"Me neither. But that's weird, isn't it? I mean, look at it. Okay, not right now, because it's raining and cold and the middle of the night. But apart from that, Birchlake is a three-dimensional postcard."

Ken turned from the window, huddling into his coat, and looked down the street. I persisted. "And the first night we arrived. It felt fine then, didn't it? Okay, it was the start of an expedition, which is always mildly exciting—"

"Speak for yourself, mate."

"But now..."

Of course everywhere seems different in the dark, as if whatever contract exists between being and place during the day is suspended. But this felt like more than that. I wasn't sure I even recognized it. The old, faint VANESKI GROCERIES sign on the side of the store. The line of tiles across the top of the coffee shop, each with the letters J&K. The buildings seemed not just arbitrary but insubstantial, as if we perceived them only because we expected to.

I said something along those lines. Once again, Ken didn't tell me I was being dumb.

There was a soft *whomp*ing sound. We turned and saw an owl flying down the street. I'm pretty sure it was an owl, anyway—though it was very black and very large. It flew past, and away into the darkness.

"Let's get back to the motel," Ken said.

Molly was still in Pierre's room. Thankfully she'd made coffee. My head felt vague and scratchy, and it was probably the last thing I needed, but that wasn't going to stop me.

She could tell that we didn't have any news, and she didn't ask. Instead she led us over to the desk, now covered in the scraps of paper that had previously been strewn all over the room. "Check this out."

She indicated a line of six pages placed together along the bottom row. Each had at least two, and up to five, drawings. They were hard to describe. Strong, confident shapes more like writing than pictures, albeit writing of a very stylized kind, curved letterforms flowing into each other—like tattoo designs. Some suggested symmetry while actually differing markedly between sides, as if there was a willful attempt to pull the mind first in one direction, and then another—to suggest order, then undermine it.

Two of the designs looked familiar—including a simpler sign of two Vs laid over one another. Others were presumably variations of the same kind of thing.

Ken looked at me. "Hell *are* those, Nolan?"

"Sigils and other apotropaic marks." I took a photo of the sheets and then swept them onto the floor.

"What do they mean?"

"Some are supposed to represent spells. Others are designed to protect, or curse. A few relate specifically to demonology."

"Really? The design looks kind of modern. Or at least, not ancient."

"The popular framework of witchcraft *is* relatively modern. Everybody thinks that whole Cotton Mather and Witchfinder General vibe of peasants brandishing Bibles and burning torches was the way it was, back to the dawn of time. In fact, the church was slow on the case. For a long time the official line was not only was it wrong to punish alleged witches, it was heresy to believe in them in the first place."

"Seriously?"

"*Secular* punishment of witches took place in the Middle Ages, and the church would sporadically get involved, but persecution was discouraged, and doctrinal thought leaders, including Pope Gregory VII, came flat out and said to leave them alone."

Molly frowned. "The church was *okay* with witches?"

"No," I said. "More like they had themselves in a tricky ontological bind. Think of the Christian church as a metaphysical start-up, disrupting the way in which people experienced the divine."

"Do I have to?" Ken said. "Only, doing that would make me feel like a complete twat."

I ignored him. "Up until that point, most cultures celebrated a pantheon of gods, with legions of minor demons and spirits on the side. Polytheism was the norm, with specialized local deities looking after distinct areas of human existence and experience. Judaism started the trimming process, partly because the Jews kept getting kicked around the Middle East and needed a nonlocalized god they could take with them. Eventually, forking off a new beta version of that faith developed by a bearded troublemaker of whom you may have heard, Christianity got the blessing of the venture capitalists of the Roman Empire and said, 'Hey, everybody, game-changer—

there's definitely only one God. Okay, he had a son who was a big deal, and also there's this nebulous Holy Spirit thing, but bottom line is we're shipping Monotheism 2.0. Worship him, and him alone.' The problem being that under this model Christianity *couldn't* take a hard line on witches, because that would admit there were other spirits sneaking around the place: hence the church announcing it was heresy to even *believe* in witchcraft. After a thousand or so years, though, people were still doing it, which bugged them. Added to which, as a circle-the-wagons tactic when Christianity started to fragment into factions, by the Middle Ages the idea of Satan as the ultimate adversary was gaining traction. Up until medieval times the devil wasn't actually a big deal in mainstream Christian theology—but when your grip on power is slipping, you need a common enemy."

"The script is only as good as your villain."

"Exactly. And this focus on Satan also *finally* gave them a doctrinally consistent rationale for attacking witches. Witchcraft was deftly repositioned as evidence of *Satanic* influence, and—bang, case closed. The big fifteenth century manual on witchcraft, *Malleus Maleficarum*, says right on the title page: 'Not to believe in witchcraft is the greatest of heresies.' A total reversal, and so now it's okay to throw women in lakes tied to chairs or set fire to them."

"So why did the witchcraft thing go so luridly nuts here in America, when there was none of that backstory?"

"This country was shaped by the fact that we've always been prepared to believe any old shit, the weirder the better. It was founded by Puritans, a group who operated on a loose trigger when it came to the idea of possession and evil spirits. Also bear in mind that these were small, isolated communities, and they weren't having a great time. The winters were much colder than they'd been used to back in England. It wasn't easy to grow food. There were periodic epidemics, and once in a while the local tribes—often with good reason—would stop by and kick the crap out of them. This was a hard, dangerous life, and suffering people reach for scapegoats and desperate solutions. Other factors. A distrust of any woman living alone, or women who were sexually proactive—especially a servant who might cause trouble by revealing that some of the fine, upstanding husbands in the village had up-stood inappropriately. More prosaic reasons, too. Poverty and greed. If a couple was childless and the man died, his house and possessions went to his wife. But if the wife should happen to meet with an unfortunate accident—like, say, drowning in a lake after being tied to a chair—then his goods went to the community instead."

Molly looked personally affronted. *"Seriously?"*

I shrugged. "It's a theory. I don't know a lot about witches. Never looked into them much."

"Why?"

"Because it's all bullshit."

I went outside. It had, miraculously, stopped raining, though the lack of stars suggested there was plenty more on the way. As I wandered across the lot I checked my watch. Four a.m. Not a good time, ever. Even in the dim and distant days when I'd have been up at that time because I was having fun, it'd be the point where you'd wonder whether you'd actually had enough fun now and should go to bed.

At the far side of the lot the asphalt stopped in a ragged line. Beyond was a couple yards of grass, then a bluff that dropped down a rocky incline to the frigid river ten feet below. The water was moving fast. It's a sound I love. Back in the days when we'd muse about such things, Kristy and I agreed that when we got old and gray we wanted a cabin in the mountains, with a creek. I'd build a deck (using skills I would presumably have acquired in the meantime) and we'd sit on Adirondack chairs and sip local beers and listen to the water and think serene thoughts. The smell of fresh bread was somehow mixed in with the idea, Kristy having presumably gone to baking school while I was learning carpentry.

This water didn't sound that way. It was loud, but there was a sibilant note, like whispering. Running water often sounds like it's a short sample, running on repeat. This didn't. It sounded like it kept saying different things.

I squatted down, head cocked, trying to work out what was strange about the sound. As I did so I glimpsed something in the water. Dark shapes. Like fish.

Though they couldn't be. They were too large. And when I tried to focus on one, it dispersed. The longer I stared into the water, the louder the sound of it seemed to get.

I heard someone coming across the lot and got out my cigarettes, assuming that would be why Ken had come out.

It wasn't him, however. Molly stood next to me. "Where did Pierre get those symbols from?"

"A book, I guess."

"Have you ever seen him read? And why'd you mess up the sheets of paper I'd carefully put together? Why sweep the symbols or sigils or whatever onto the floor?"

It was a question I'd asked myself. The gesture had not

been planned. My hand seemed to reach out and do it of its own accord. "I'm tired. I'm worried about Pierre."

"I know you are. But I don't think that's why."

"Oh?"

"You're a sensitive man. You know stuff. You feel stuff, too. Maybe things that other people don't feel."

"I don't really believe in that kind of thing, Molly."

"Belief is a funny thing, though. I used to get in these huge discussions about God with my grandmother. She was in the local church, forever trying to get me to come along even during the phase when I was too cool for *school*, never mind the freakin' Lutherans. I eventually snapped and said, 'Look, I don't *believe* in God," in that way teenagers do. As if they've proved something. And she smiled and said, 'That doesn't matter, Molly. What matters is he believes in *you*.'"

"I've heard that neat little metaphysical maneuver before," I said. "It's annoying."

Molly nodded, looking down into the river. "Irritated the heck out of me. But what if she was right? How about climate change? A ton of people don't believe in that. It's still happening. God might be the same."

She looked at me. "And if it's that way with God, it might work the same with the other side."

CHAPTER
33

An hour before this, Pierre had been standing in the shadows on the next street back from the main street, listening to the wind moving through the trees on the mountains all around, and the steady patter of rain. Mist was curling around the bottom of the buildings, but Pierre avoided looking into it for long.

The back door to the Stone Mountain Tap opened. Kurt came out carrying a couple of bags. He set them down, locked the door, bent to leave the key under the mat. The sound of each of these events was very clear. Pierre waited until he set off along the road, hunched against the rain, and followed as Kurt hurried to a car parked halfway to the next corner.

Kurt had thrown the bags in the back and was reaching for the front door when he realized someone was watching him. "Hey," he said, nervously. His first thought was that it was the husband and the night was about to go badly south. Then he realized the silhouette wasn't chunky enough. "Who's that?"

The figure stepped forward. It was the guy who'd hassled him in the bar earlier. Jeez, but this town was getting small all of a sudden. It really was time to leave. "Oh."

"You should go," Pierre said.

"Exactly what I *am* doing, dude," Kurt said, opening the driver's door, trying to act nonchalant, in case the guy was going to make any sudden moves. "Look, I still don't get what your problem is, but bottom line is I'm out of here, literally right now, so can we leave it at that? You win. I'm gone."

Pierre saw someone was standing the other side of the car, almost completely in shadow, very close to the wall, almost as if he was part of it. A man. Tall, thin. Old.

"You could hurt him," he said. The man's voice was calm, friendly. "Nobody would know. They're all asleep. You're invisible. You could do it and walk away."

Pierre shook his head. "I don't want to."

"It's what *she* would want, though. You could punish him. You *should*."

"She doesn't want me to."

"Sometimes girls don't know what they want. Sometimes men have to show them. It's always been like that."

"I'm not doing it."

Kurt meanwhile was staring at Pierre, confused. "Who...who are you talking to?"

"Him." Pierre gestured toward the old man, but he wasn't there anymore. Just stains on a wet wall.

"O-kay."

"Just go," Pierre said. "Go now and go fast, or I'll do what he told me."

Kurt hurriedly got into his car and drove away.

Pierre stood for a time, head bent. He could feel rain trickling down off his hair and onto his neck. See the circles as it fell into puddles in the broken surface of the backstreet. There was oil in these puddles, too, and when the raindrops fell it caused swirls in the iridescence, shapes that almost seemed to mean something. Symbols.

Then suddenly he started walking.

He didn't decide to walk. It just started happening, and the movements of his limbs felt jerky. When he got to the main street he paused. There was something in the mist on the opposite corner. It wasn't the first time he'd seen something like it. There'd been one in the motel parking lot when he left his room. It went around the corner, like a shadow, exploring. It was slow and slick, like the movements Pierre could feel in the back of his own skull. He knew there was nothing actually moving there, in his head, but that was the closest he could get to describing the feeling.

He looked up the street. Still and dead. It struck him that there should be a fountain up at the crossroads. People could sit around it while they waited. Then he realized that would make no sense, as it'd block the traffic.

He was about to cross the road when he heard voices. He shrank back into the shadows. A moment later two people came down the street.

A man—lean, a little above average height. Another who was shorter, rounder, older. It took Pierre a moment to realize it was Nolan and Ken. It seemed like they were looking for someone.

Ken said something. Nolan replied.

Hearing their voices made them seem far more real, and Pierre almost called out. They were his friends. Okay, bosses, but friends, too. People he knew. Who he liked. Who liked him. Probably. Whatever that meant.

They looked far away, though. And he didn't know whether he could trust them now. Them, or anyone.

Ever since he'd woken up in his room that afternoon, everything was the same but everything was different and wrong.

He stayed where he was and waited as they walked down the street and disappeared into the mist, until it was hard to be sure they'd ever been there at all.

Half an hour later he was in the woods near the walls. It was dark, but that didn't seem to matter. Closing his eyes didn't make a difference. He could walk through the trees safely, without banging into anything. He opened his eyes to check. It all looked the same. Closed them. No difference.

Walking with your eyes closed feels weird, though, so he kept them open as he tramped the last hundred yards through soaking undergrowth to the walls. In most cases it hadn't been easy to work out which the drawings referred to—one fairly straight or kinda curvy line looks much like any other—but the fish hook shape had been pretty clear.

He walked to a point in the middle of the long arm of it. Braced one hand against the wall, and shoved at the top of it with the other.

Some rocks fell off, tumbling down the other side.

He kept at it for a while. Then he went to the next wall and did the same. Looking over it from there at the first, he could tell he'd done enough. Rough though these structures had been, they'd had shape, integrity. They had been what they were supposed to be. You don't have to completely destroy something to stop it being what it previously was—and sometimes, like a mangled relationship, living in the compromised remains of something good can be far more harmful, more the opposite of what was there before, than wiping it off the face of the earth.

Like erasing the words "Do Not" from a sign on the highway warning "Do Not Pass." The remains are more dangerous than no sign at all.

CHAPTER
34

I spent a while thinking after we'd gone back to our rooms. I used the motel's flaky Wi-Fi to look a few things up. Then did some more thinking, sitting in the chair, wrapped in the cover from the bed against the pervasive cold. Finally I checked something on my phone, after which I did not sleep. Eventually at seven I texted Kristy, asked if she was okay with having an earlier breakfast. She sounded surprised—I am not celebrated for early rising—but said sure, half an hour.

Ken was standing in the lot when I left my room. He didn't look like he'd slept much either. The sky was low and dark. "What's up with him?"

He was talking about the motel owner, who was putting a battered overnight bag in the back of his car. He saw us watching and walked over. "Find your guy?"

"Not yet."

"I'm visiting with my sister for a couple days. Out of town. You're leaving today, right?"

"Assuming we can round up our friend."

"Leave your keys in the box. And a damages check for five hundred bucks."

"Okay," Ken said. "But what happens if the place catches fire while you're away?"

He was joking. The guy didn't smile. "It burns down."

As he drove past us, he stopped, wound the window down. "I've lived here my whole life," he said. "Third generation Birchlake. My uncle used to tell me stories. If I were you, I'd bail on your pal and get on the road early."

He drove away, leaving Ken and me staring after him.

I arrived at the coffee shop first, so I snagged the table in the corner and ordered. The drinks arrived as Kristy came in. I could tell immediately that someone or something had lit a fire under her and decided to let that unfold first.

"What's up?"

"Not sure," she said, putting her phone on the table. "But I just got a message from Gina Wright."

"Who is..."

"Teacher at Alaina's school. Says she's got something to tell me."

"On a Sunday morning? What kind of thing?"

"Didn't say—wants to do it in person."

"Kristy—Pierre's disappeared."

"What? Disappeared how?"

"Last night he got into some kind of altercation with the bartender. Molly walked him back to the motel. Then in the middle of the night we went to his room. He wasn't there. His room's a mess. A strange mess. You didn't hear from him? He didn't call?"

She shook her head. "I went to bed right after you and I talked. Slept. No missed calls, no messages. And, Pierre doesn't have my number. Seriously, he got in a fight? I mean, I barely know the guy, but he doesn't seem the type."

"He's not. Nor the kind to trash his room and cover a ton of paper with weird symbols."

"What kind of symbols?"

"Symbols that got me thinking. Have you still got that picture you sent me a couple of days ago? I deleted it."

"What picture?"

"The one that brought you up here."

Kristy scrolled through her photo app. "This?"

The photo from Instagram. "First I want to show you another." I found it on my own phone and slid the device across the table so she could look.

"What's this?"

"A photo I took yesterday, of another photo. The actual picture was taken by Madeline Hardaker at 3:18 p.m. on the day Alaina disappeared. Just before they went into the woods. Tell me if anything strikes you about it."

Kristy bent down over the screen. "Not really. A selfie of three teenagers. What am I looking for?"

"I don't want to lead you," I said. "I didn't get it when I first saw the picture. Then a couple of hours ago I was looking for the other one, saw this, and I got it."

Kristy sipped her coffee, frowning down at the screen. "Give me a clue, Nolan."

"Go back two nights. The night Alaina returned. Visualize it. Ken comes into the bar, tells you to come outside. You ask him why, probably."

"I did."

"And then?"

"He said, 'Nolan told me to get you out here.'"

"So you went. And what did you see?"

"The street. It was dark, foggy. You, about fifty yards away. With…"

"Don't backfill. See it as you saw it, in real time. You saw me there with somebody. So what did you do?"

"I came over to you."

"Just me?"

"No. You were with Al—"

"Seriously, Kris," I said. "Do it properly. You didn't know it was her immediately. So close your eyes and tell me exactly what you saw when you got to me."

"Nolan, you're being annoying."

"Do it. Please."

"Christ's sake. You were holding a woman, stopping her from getting away. Long dark coat. Long hair. She was struggling. Then she raised her head, and I saw who it was. Okay? Am I allowed to say it was Alaina *now*?"

I sat back, not sure whether I'd done a good thing or not. "Go back through what you just said. What you saw. Then look at the picture again."

She blinked, once, as she scrolled back through her recollection. Then looked down at my phone. Away, then back again. Then her mouth dropped slowly open.

"Got it?"

"Shit, Nolan. Why didn't you just say?"

"I wanted to be sure I wasn't misremembering."

"In the picture she's wearing a hoodie."

"Right. So if she was alone in the woods all that time, where did the coat come from?"

Outside it seemed to be getting darker. More rain coming. I hoped that, wherever Pierre was, it was under cover. He'd been gone for hours, and I was now genuinely worried. Ken had come most of the way to the coffee shop with me and was currently walking the streets, looking for him. Molly was back at the motel on a mission to ping

Pierre's phone at five-minute intervals and be there if he came back.

"That picture wasn't taken at the school? She couldn't have changed before she left?"

"No," I said. "Snapped moments before they went into the woods. Look—in the background you can even see the corner of the motel. Either she wasn't out in the woods the whole time, or she at least saw someone who gave her the coat. So why deny it?"

"Shit, Nolan. Text me that picture. This is *fantastic*. I take back everything I've ever said about you."

"Really?"

"Okay, not all of it. What was the other thing?"

"It's not such a headline. I'm not sure it means anything. But that Insta name Alaina has—htilil♥2005."

"What about it?"

"It stuck in my head. I remembered it a couple hours ago, wrote it down. Played with the letters a little. It took me two seconds. It's a simple reverse. Lilith. Ring bells?"

"Remind me."

"A figure in Jewish mythology. The name of Adam's undermentioned first wife—who Adam complained was a little too self-actualized, so God fired her, kicked her out into the wilderness, and cooked up the more pliable Eve instead. These days Lilith is usually positioned as a kind of demon or else claimed to be a mythical proto-feminist figure. But she's also a central icon in certain strains of witchcraft."

"Are you saying Alaina's a witch?"

"No, but she might *believe* in witchcraft. Might even think a witch was something you could *become*." I could tell from Kristy's face that she was joining up dots. "What?"

"The elective the principal teaches. He *covers* witch-craft. And, because he's a thoughtful guy, handles it from a politically correct perspective."

"Okay, so maybe there's a story there," I said. "If you want it. Though personally I'd just leave town. Which is what we're going to do as soon as we've found Pierre."

"The hell with that. I'm going to find out where Alaina got that coat."

"I really wouldn't go down that road."

"Why?"

"What got me thinking about witchcraft was the fact that—before he went wherever he's gone—Pierre covered a ton of paper with symbols of witchcraft and demon-ology, about which I'm prepared to bet Pierre knows nothing."

A woman was standing on the other side of the glass, out on the street, looking straight at Kristy.

"Oh—that's Gina. Order me another coffee."

"Kris—I'm not hanging around. I'm going to help Ken find Pierre and then we're out of here."

"Seriously, this will take two minutes."

She was gone. I irritably waved at the waitress, pointed at Kristy's cup. Then I phoned Ken. "Any sign?"

"No," he said. "Molly's got nothing either."

"I just realized something. We assumed Pierre did those drawings. He may not have."

"Huh. That's true."

"In which case . . ."

"If someone else did, Pierre might have an idea of who it was and be out looking for them. Here's a thought. That pretty boy in the bar last night."

"Why would he do something like that?"

"No idea, mate. But Pierre obviously had a problem with him, so maybe we should check in with the guy in case."

"Good idea. Where are you right...Christ!"

"What?"

I ran out onto the street, nearly flattening the waitress on the way.

What I'd seen through the window was Kristy being shaken by the shoulders. Hard. By the time I got out there they'd separated—Kristy on the back foot. The other woman looked furious—and ready to get straight back into the fight.

"Hell's going on?"

"She attacked me," Kristy said, bewildered.

The woman lunged forward again. I stepped in the way and took a fist to the side of the neck for my trouble. It hurt. "Look," I said. "Gina, right? Hell is your problem?"

"I will *take you out*," the woman snarled at Kristy. I held a hand to keep Kristy back. I could see her initial shock turning to anger and didn't want it to escalate. I've seen Kristy angry. You do not want to be in its path.

Meanwhile Gina shoved at me, trying to get past. Over her shoulder I saw Ken turning onto the main street. He started running in our direction. Then I became aware of another woman, walking fast toward us across the road. Val, the woman from the Tap. She got to us just as Ken did.

"Jesus," she said. "I heard about your pal getting in Kurt's face last night. What is it with you people?"

"Nothing to do with me," I said. "It's...actually I have no idea what's going on. I'm just getting in the way."

"That *bitch*," Gina shouted. It was right in my ear, and very loud. "Is trying to *fuck me up*."

"I have *no clue* what you're talking about," Kristy said.

Val turned to the other woman, who I now realized was the one I'd seen listening to her husband in the Tap a couple nights before. "Gina. It's a nice, quiet Sunday morning. Trying to beat up on another woman in the street is not a great look. For anybody. *Definitely* not you."

Something of this got through to Gina. She exhaled. Took a step back. "She hacked my account."

"*What?*" Kristy said. "What are you even *talking* about?"

"What account?" Val said.

"Someone took a picture three days ago, and..." Gina stopped, abruptly, as if finally realizing how the situation looked—and that whatever was exercising her wasn't something to shout about in front of onlookers. The customers and staff in the coffee shop were watching through the window as though they'd come across a new and extraordinary cable channel. We were strangers. The people inside weren't. Birchlake is a small town. They must know who she was.

Gina regrouped. Dropped her voice to half the volume. "She put up a picture on my Instagram account."

"When was this?"

"Yesterday afternoon, late. I took it down. She put it up again in the middle of the night."

Kristy had her hands on hips. "Gina. I don't know what made you think it was me, but it wasn't."

"You *must* have."

"Nope."

"Then..." Gina was staring at Kristy now, confused. You can tell when someone's lying to your face, especially when they're mad. You've got to be a sociopath not to betray a falsehood with a vagueness in the eyes. There was none of that in Kristy. She was telling the truth.

Gina put her face in her hands. "God, I'm so sorry."

"It's fine," Kristy said. "Clearly you're upset. Do you want to talk about it? You said you had..."

"No," Gina said. "I've got to go home."

She walked quickly away.

"Well that was weird," Val said.

"No kidding." Kristy was watching Gina go. I knew the look on her face. It meant she was trying to put things together in her head, with something just out of mental reach.

"Okay, well, bye," Val said. "I'm glad at least to see your boy has his shit back together."

"You've seen Pierre? Where?"

"When I was walking here. He walked by. Pretty fast. I said good morning. Didn't look like he was listening."

"When?" I asked. "And which way was he going?"

"Twenty minutes. He was headed into the woods. Why?"

CHAPTER
35

Molly got to the coffee shop quickly, and the four of us hurried up the street to the side road that held the bed and breakfast. A large, immaculately maintained Victorian.

"I bet *their* water pipes don't rattle," Ken said.

"What's it going to *take*?" Molly asked.

"A lot, love. I know how easy it is to spook people."

"You reminded me of that in the night," I said. "But you said it led you to believe that the noise you heard *wasn't* anything except what it sounded like. Somebody *knocking*."

"It was dark," Ken said. "You think differently. Sometimes, bollocks may be spoken. Even by me."

I knew he was right—that the absence of light changes the world in ways that feel bigger than simply not being able to see things. We all know this. Try walking around your house in the wee hours, with the lights off, even if you've lived there ten years. Something has changed, and that makes the whole place feel completely different. "You do," I agreed. "But the question is *why*. And—"

"Don't start, Nolan. Let's round up Pierre and get on the road, and you can bore the crap out of me with this when we're on the way down to San Jose."

"What are you all talking about?" Kristy said. There were only a few houses left to go. After that the road dead-ended at a low metal gate, with forest beyond.

Ken and I hesitated. Molly did not. "Ken heard knocking inside his closet in the night. Nolan's coffee pot exploded for no reason—about the same time that I saw…someone in my shower. Who can't have been there. Apparently this is all 'science.'"

Kristy slowed. "What?" I asked.

"It's probably nothing," she said. "But the second night I was in Birchlake, something happened with my phone."

"I know," I said. "You got a replacement."

"I didn't say why. I heard a banging sound from the store below the apartment, like I told you. I went down to check if it was someone hammering on the street door. When I got back upstairs my phone was in the middle of the floor. And no, Nolan, I *hadn't* left it hanging off the edge. I've been diligently not thinking about this the last couple of days. Assumed it was just one of those things."

Things do happen. Some of them inexplicable. We assume it's because we don't know all the facts. That there's an explanation, yes, involving "science," and we simply can't think of it right now. When three or four such events cluster together, it gets harder. But not impossible.

"Something else I didn't tell you before," Molly said.

"What?"

She hesitated, as though she wasn't sure this was a box she wanted to open. "Because I thought you wouldn't take it seriously. Before I saw the thing in the shower. I heard something. That's why I turned around."

"What was it?"

"A voice."

"Saying what?"

" 'I'm still here.' "

We'd reached the end of the road. "Let's just go find Pierre," I said.

It was now at least half an hour since Val saw Pierre heading toward the woods.

Kristy and Molly set off left, the direction that would eventually bring them around the back of town and toward the motel. Ken and I went straight ahead, because the right soon banked up steeply and it seemed unlikely Pierre would have chosen a course where he had to scale wet rock on hands and knees. Thankfully, the rain was holding off, but the sky was dark and there was a lot of mist between the trees.

Soon it was very quiet apart from the occasional snap of twigs under our feet. Once in a while we called out to Pierre. No response. Otherwise we walked in silence.

After about twenty minutes Ken said, "Okay, spill it."

"Spill what?"

"I dunno, do I. But something's on your so-called mind."

"I'm just trying to make sense of something. One of the reasons I brought us up here in the first place was Kristy sent me a picture of Alaina's Instagram. She uses a reversal of the name Lilith."

"Adam's first wife."

"How the hell do you know that?"

"I know almost everything, mate."

"I see. Well in that case you'll also be aware that idea actually came about pretty late—popularized in works like the *Alphabet of Sirach* and the writings of Isaac ben

Jacob ha-Cohen, some of which may have been satirical, before getting tangled up into Kabbalistic mysticism."

"Yeah, I knew all that as well. Obviously."

"Listen. The idea originally sparked off the fact that while Genesis 2:22 describes how Eve was created from Adam's rib, earlier in 1:27 it says God created man in his own image—specifying 'male and female he created them.' The Bible doesn't go near any of that, and mentions Lilith only once, in the Book of Isaiah, where something of that name is listed among eight unclean *animals*."

"Huh."

"And the interesting thing about *that* is the Semitic root of the word comes from the Hebrew *layil* and the Arabic *layl*—both meaning 'night.' In Hebrew-language texts, *Lilith* or *lilit* is generally translated as 'night creatures.' And in the Dead Sea Scrolls, the first time the name Lilith is used is in a list, again, of monsters."

"I assume you have a point?"

"I don't get why she'd pick the name. Why position yourself as the queen of monsters?"

"That's because you're a nerd, Nolan. You know this stuff and you cleave to the old-fashioned idea that words have histories and meanings and that people give a shit. Meanwhile she's a teenager and cares not a jot. She hears the name from some emo YouTuber or Ariana Grande puts it in a song and suddenly Lilith's all cool and rad."

"Not sure anybody says *rad* anymore, Ken."

"Well, they should. It's a rad word."

"Something else I turned up in the dark of the night. You know that abandoned bar outside town? Called Olsen's?"

"What about it?"

"It's built on the site of one of the earliest houses built

near Birchlake. You'll note I say 'near,' rather than 'in.' And one bonus fact: Alaina Hixon's mom, Jenny. Her maiden name was Olsen."

"You seem to be under the illusion that you're talking to Kristy, Nolan. I don't care about any of this. And I'm not sure why you do, either."

"Because," I said. "Hang on—is that him?" We stopped, peered into the trees, and I called out. "Pierre?"

"I don't see what you're looking at," Ken said.

"Past those trees."

"*Which* trees, Nolan? We're in a fucking forest."

I started in the direction in which I thought I'd seen Pierre. Ken followed, swearing quietly. The mist seemed thicker now—either that, or steadily declining light levels from above were making it seem gloomier overall.

"Is that what you saw?"

"Oh. Yeah."

It was a wall. A little under six feet tall. I'd seen the end, and—as it was about the same height as Pierre— mistaken it for a person. We moved around the side and soon saw that while it resembled all the others we'd seen in the mode of its construction, the shape was different. The previous ones had been semi-straight or wavy. Deliberately curved in one way or another. This had one long straight side, seventy or eighty feet in length. At the end of this there was a return, sharper than ninety degrees— and then a further straight line of about forty feet. Another turn, again not quite a right angle, leading to a further fifty feet or so.

"There's another one over there."

This wall had nothing straight about it. An imperfect semicircle, about four feet high. Imperfect partly because it looked like it had never been designed to be an exact half circle; also because, right in the middle, someone had pushed a hole through it. Rocks lay in a pile on the other side, leaving a gap wide enough to step through.

I did so, and squatted down on the other side among the rocks. "This happened recently."

Ken stepped through the wall, too. "How do you know?"

"Look at the lichen on this rock. There are scrapes when the rocks fell and crashed against each other. It hasn't had time to regrow."

"How long does it take?" He shivered. "Does it suddenly feel a lot colder to you?"

"I don't know how long lichen takes to regrow. But the cuts look fresh. And look at the corner of that other structure. There's a bunch of rocks missing from there, too."

We walked over and saw the same thing. Fallen rocks, with signs they'd been dislodged recently. And Ken was right. It did feel colder. I looked up. Through the mist and the trees I got a glimpse of the low, dark sky.

Ken shivered again. "Do you think it's that woman? The one who owns the space under Kristy's apartment? The numbers on the bits of paper with them—they could be GPS coordinates from where she found them."

"Val. Could be. But why would you knock holes in the walls and take away rocks?"

"Because she's a loony, Nolan. Because she lives in a small, boring town in the middle of nowhere and there's fuck-all else to do. Because..."

He stopped talking.

Mist often has a kind of motility to it, as microscopic droplets of water are swirled into motion by the wind, or breeze, or a movement of air too small for our skins to perceive. That wasn't what we were seeing.

We watched as the mist ten feet away from us moved. It looked for all the world like someone was walking through it, in a straight line. You could even see the mist curl lazily back around afterward, as if in someone's wake.

"Ken..."

"Yeah, I'm seeing it."

And then the movement changed. It was as if whatever was causing it suddenly accelerated—running down past the far end of the wall, banking around it to disappear.

For a few moments afterward the mist kept moving, then slowly returned to how it had been before.

"Air current," I said. "Temperature change."

"Science of some kind."

"Definitely."

But I don't think either of us believed it anymore.

CHAPTER
36

I don't think he went this way," Ken said. His voice was firm, but it sounded like he was speaking for the sake of it—as a way of not talking about what we'd just seen. "Do you?"

"Why don't we check in on Kris and Moll?"

"They'd have called if they'd found him."

"I know," I said. "I'm going to do it anyway."

"Good idea."

The tips of my fingers were turning white. There was no question it was a lot colder than when we entered the forest. Two bars of signal. I called Kristy. It rang but went to voicemail.

"Not answering?"

"No. Try Molly."

"You do it, mate. I'm keeping my hands in my pockets."

I hit Molly's speed-dial and waited. Her voice came on eventually, but only her voicemail message. Friendly but businesslike, her "I'm a nice person but don't even think of bringing me a problem" tone.

"Nope," I said.

Ken was frowning, however, and looking away into the trees. "Do it again. But take the phone away from your head."

I redialed then lowered the phone, holding it against my chest to muffle it.

"You hear that?"

I did. The faint sound of a phone ringing, some distance away in the woods. "Is that hers?"

"I think so." The sound stopped, as the call dead-ended in the message service again. "Must be. Do it again."

I redialed once more. The same tone, from the same direction. Ken and I turned on the spot, locking on to it.

When the call failed again I stuffed the phone back in my pocket and we started walking fast.

I called Molly again after about two hundred yards. The same tone, and definitely closer, but still some distance away and to the right of our current bearing.

We set off once more and after five minutes passed another wall, in a strange fish-hook-like shape. Stones had been dislodged from the middle of it, and again, it looked as though it had happened recently.

The mist was getting thicker, too. I know nothing about that kind of meteorological stuff, nor why it should be gathering more strongly. It was now sufficiently dense that it was hard to make out anything more than sixty feet away.

"Stop," Ken said.

I listened, expecting to hear Kristy's voice, or Molly's. Nothing for a moment, but then the sound of a twig snapping—from behind me.

I turned. Like most forests, this one varied in how the trees were arranged. Some parts were relatively open, others more dense. The area we'd just hurried through was somewhere in between. Trees ten to twenty feet apart. Not much in the way of bushes or undergrowth. Just the endless mist, curling between the trunks and around a few granite boulders.

I was about to say something when there was a similar noise—from the right this time. A short snapping sound. Exactly what you'd expect from someone treading on a thin, dry branch. A person, or a deer, or a dog. If we'd been able to see any of those things, then the noise would have been wholly explicable. We could not.

Some kind of unusually heavy rat, maybe, or the ever-popular "temperature differential" rationale. Neither felt convincing, Your mind may think it's smart, but your body knows the score. Mine did not believe we were alone.

"I was hoping that was Pierre," Ken said.

"I think we're going to have to let him find his own way out. We need to focus on finding Kristy and Molly."

Ken already had his phone in hand, and dialed. This time the ringing didn't sound so far away—and it was coming from straight ahead.

We went forward into the mist. Soon we came upon a bluff and had to scramble down. The lower ground was more uneven. More boulders, too—some of them pretty huge, gray eminences in the fog. We kept going, peering forward in hope of seeing a flash of color among the gray-green-brown. We called out, but got no response. "Are we close to the motel yet?"

"Don't think so," Ken said. "We walked out a long way when we first came in here, and we've been bending farther and farther out while tracking Moll's phone."

We were walking quickly now. Neither of us had encouraged the other to pick up speed. We were simply . . . walking fast. It felt like a good idea. "Are you sure?"

"Yeah. It's been bearing right all the time. We've got to be nearly a mile from town by now. Probably more."

"This is how you get lost in the woods," I said.

"Nolan, that's not helping. And we've got GPS and there's a compass on your phone and this is where the ringing was coming from—and so in general stop being a ponce and…"

Molly was sitting on the ground thirty feet away.

She was at the base of a tree, her back and head rested against it, legs out straight, hands in her lap.

"Moll?" Ken squatted down to one side. Her mouth was half open. Her eyes were, too. Her phone was in her hands, the screen full of missed-call notifications.

I put my fingers against her cheek. Her skin was warm. "Molly—wake up."

"Wake *up*? What are you talking about, Nolan? She's not asleep."

Her pulse was strong. "Then what's wrong with her?"

"I don't know. Call Kristy."

"We didn't hear anything when I tried earlier. I think she's left the ringer off."

"Just try it, mate. We need to get Moll back to town. *Now.*"

I called Kristy. It felt like I'd done this about fifty times in the last twenty-four hours without an answer. I didn't get one now either. "Stay with Molly," I said.

"Where are you going?"

"Whatever happened, Kristy's not going to have bailed on her. She'll be close by."

I walked a little way and called out Kristy's name. It sounded odd to me. When you shout in an open space, most of the sound happens in your head. There was something else going on here. "You hear that?" I asked.

"What?"

I called out again—noticing as I did so that Molly didn't flinch, even though it was very loud. "Like an echo."

"Trees. Or rocks."

Maybe, though it sounded more enclosed than that. I walked a little further. Then stopped.

"Ken, come look at this."

In the mist about forty feet away was another wall. This wasn't like the others, however. We walked to it together, then stood in silence.

It was tall, maybe about eight feet high. Easily the biggest we'd seen. But that wasn't the point. This wall wasn't made of lichened rocks piled on top of one another. It was made of concrete. The surface was flat and smooth.

"Fuck is this?" Ken said.

"The ruins of an old house?"

"Made of concrete? In the forest?"

"Or a storage facility."

"The hell do you store a mile or two into the woods? And it looks new, doesn't it?"

I touched the wall. Drew my hand back, touched it again. "Ken—there's something strange going on."

"No shit, Nolan."

"No, I mean—feel it. Feel the wall."

He did so, and immediately got what I meant. *"What?"*

"You're feeling it too, right?"

"It doesn't feel the way it looks. It looks smooth but it feels like those other walls. The ones made of rocks."

I drew my hand slowly over the surface, watching it slide smoothly across flatness. That's what my eyes told me, anyway. It's not how it felt. My fingertips were registering a far more uneven, scratchy material. Sharp edges and lichen.

I stood back and looked along the wall. It stretched seventy or eighty feet. By the end the mist was so thick that it disappeared.

I walked along it. Ken followed, casting a glance back to check on Molly. She was still gazing into space. At the end of the wall was a return, a precise right angle. It looked for all the world like the corner of an underground parking lot. "It's getting darker," Ken said.

"It can't be." It seemed that way, though. I looked up but couldn't even see the sky through the fog.

"I can hear something, too."

All I could hear was the sound of blood in my ears, powered by a heart that was beating hard. But then, yes— something else. Far away, very quiet. Music?

"Shit, Nolan," Ken said. "It's Kristy."

I followed him into the mist. Stopped as abruptly as he did. A little way ahead, the wall dead-ended in a sharp rocky bluff. The interface between the two was perfect, as though someone had put an inordinate amount of effort into making the join between wall and cliff as tight as possible.

About ten feet short of that, a huge boulder was embedded in the wall. Again, the joins either side were perfect, as if the concrete had been poured around it.

Kristy was leaning back against the bluff, apparently staring at the boulder. "Kristy? Are you okay?"

She blinked, slowly.

"What's going on? What happened to Molly?"

"Can you hear it?" Her voice was quiet.

"Hear what? Kristy, let's get back to town, okay?"

"Tell me you can hear it."

And I *could* hear it now, a little more clearly. Music. And it sounded familiar. I knew I'd heard it recently.

Ken suddenly turned his head to look back toward the trees. "Nolan—something's coming."

"Pierre?"

"Nah, I don't think so."

"Kristy," I said, reaching out to gently take her by the shoulder. "Come on. Let's just..."

"Steps," Kristy said.

I stopped because I realized why she'd been staring at the boulder. I don't know how I hadn't spotted it before, unless it was the change in angle.

The boulder had steps in it. Cut cleanly, as if with an angle grinder. Though, the more I looked at the boulder, the less it seemed like a natural feature. Like the wall, it looked more like poured concrete.

Kristy fell down. It was sudden, as though someone had pulled the plug. I managed to grab enough of her to break the fall and make sure she hit the ground fairly softly.

"Ken—*help*."

My shout echoed in a strange, flat way. Ken didn't come. He was standing weaving. He looked at me owlishly, as if very drunk. His voice was slurred. "Feeling kind of weird, mate."

"Tell me you can hear the music," Kristy said, softly. "I don't want to hear it alone."

"I can," I said. There was a flat echo on it, and her voice, as if I was hearing sound in a space with lots of hard surfaces. I was so close to being able to remember what the song was now. The lyrics were...

Kristy's eyes widened. "Oh no."

She was staring at a point above and behind me. I turned and found myself looking up the staircase in the boulder. It didn't look remotely natural now. There was a light at the top. Not some weird-ass ethereal light. Very mundane. As if there was a door up there in the mist, being opened as I watched—revealing a lit corridor beyond.

For a moment it also looked like there was someone standing in it—a woman, with brown hair.

Then they were gone, as everything went light.

CHAPTER
37

After she pulled on her hoodie—the backup, in gray—Alaina paused in front of her bedroom mirror. Her skin was moon-pale, a legacy (so her mother used to say) of Scandinavian blood. Or Scottish. Or maybe Russian. She'd spun the story a few different ways. Alaina had wondered about getting one of those DNA tests from the internet, maybe asking for her birthday, but knew her dad wouldn't go for it. He didn't want her thinking about bloodlines.

Didn't matter. There were things tests weren't able to show, areas where science—and fathers—didn't know shit. Dumbasses. The fact they *thought* they knew everything only meant secrets were better hidden.

One part of her mother's stories Alaina *did* believe was that her side of the family started out over east. She'd never said, but implied, that they came west with a following wind—in the sense of being encouraged to move along. A family of strong women, none more so than Elizabeth Olsen—the woman whose portrait hung on the wall of the sitting room, the first to live in Birchlake. Or just outside, of course.

Ladies who'd got in people's *faces*. Who knew how to

do the things that people weren't supposed to know about, or want to do. Women who shored up the walls.

But who sometimes exploded.

Alaina missed her mom every day. She'd not been easy to live with, and Alaina understood that, were Mom still alive, they'd be having regular and CNN-worthy fights by now. That happens when swords clash. Sparks fly. Nobody's going to back down—and nobody wants to admit that the new wave is here, and their time is done.

Mom solved that problem herself. Dark road, late night, too much liquor.

So people whispered when they thought her daughter couldn't hear. But Alaina knew better. She had been in the car on evenings when her mom had been too drunk to *speak*, and her driving was fine. She'd felt more scared sometimes when Mom was sober—and, despite what people might imply, her mom had been sober most of the time. Too much, maybe. Sometimes you need white noise. Sometimes it gets too hard. If you choose—or are destined—to live outside, you're going to withstand a lot more weather than other people. Dark rain will take its toll.

A companion for years, day after day and night after night. A whisper under the bed. A half-seen face on the other side of the room. Inaudible footsteps behind you, every night. Every day weakened by small and invisible acts of strength, tiny heroic acts of resistance that nobody else knows about. Because you can't tell. No one must ever know. They can't see the enemies all around.

When Alaina was young, her mom had a game she liked to play. She'd grin and thrust out her arm, fist clenched, elbow locked. "Get through that defense!" she'd declare. And Alaina would try, cupping Mom's fist in her hand (a hand that was tiny at first, but bigger as the years went by) and try to bend her mother's arm. She couldn't. A locked elbow is strong. It can hold a great deal at bay.

The last time they played was a couple weeks before Mom died, and as Alaina pushed she sensed that she *could* get through that defense. So instead she laughed, and stopped, as if it had been as impossible as always.

Her mom looked her in the eye and lowered her arm. There comes a point where it's better not to play.

It's the same. You spend years choosing not to give up, locking your elbow against it. Until one day or night you realize you're not strong enough anymore, or at least not tonight. You let down your guard and lower your head, and accept the rise of darkness with something like relief.

Mom did that, but with someone's help. That someone was going to pay.

And it wasn't going to happen to Alaina. On that final night in the woods, before she properly returned, she really had died and come back, or so it felt. And if you've died once, you don't have to do it again.

Nobody had noticed yet—least of all Dad, who was always studiously looking the other way—but she was getting paler by the day. There would come a time when, if she wanted, she'd be translucent. Invisible. Like them.

Alaina was going to live both sides of the wall.

Her dad was on the couch. Not reading. Not looking at his phone. Just staring into space. He looked straight-up exhausted. There'd been constant knocking on the walls and roof throughout the night, the sound of things moving around outside, crashing through the bushes, scampering over the porch. Trying to get in. To say hi. To do deals.

"Bad night's sleep?" She'd tried to keep a mocking tone out of her voice, but not hard enough.

He looked up, and her resolve briefly faltered at what she saw in his eyes. "You have to stop this."

"Too late."

"I should have hidden her journals better."

"They would have led me to them sooner or later."

"Destroyed them, then."

"You wouldn't have had the balls."

"It's not about balls. I just couldn't let all of her go. I *loved her too*, Alaina. For a lot longer than you've been alive. I lived the life and paid the price, and you have no idea what that's like yet. I should have set fire to them."

"It wouldn't have stopped me becoming."

"You *don't know what you're doing*."

"I'm a quick study," Alaina said. "As you're all going to find out. And I have friends to help me."

"They're not your friends."

"I thought you liked Maddy and Nadja," she teased.

"That's not who I mean and you know it. Don't trust them."

"Trust who? Say it."

Her dad looked her in the eye. "The things we can't see, Alaina. They killed your mom, and your grandma before her. They'll kill you, too."

The rain didn't bother her. Something kept pace with Alaina in the bushes as she strode down toward the highway. She didn't check to see what it was. When she got to the highway she walked out and stood right on the center line for a moment, looking up the misty road toward town.

Oh, this walk.

How many times?

At first carried. Then walking, with her hand held up to hold her mom's. Later, side by side. But it was different today. She wasn't the child anymore. And she walked alone.

Or maybe not. She saw something waiting for her, up ahead. Tall, thin, old. Then he was gone.

Alaina wished for a moment she was small again. That her mother was there to surround and protect her.

But she bit down on the feeling and started walking toward Birchlake, her head held high.

This was her time.

CHAPTER
38

Someone was nudging me—a finger gently prodding into my shoulder. I was impatient with this because I'd been doing something and it was important. And now they'd distracted me, and I couldn't remember what the hell it had been.

"Quit that, will you?"

I was surprised at how clear my voice sounded, because now I thought about it, my eyes were shut, which presumably meant I'd been asleep. Normally I sound like a bear when I wake up after even a short nap, a bear that moreover dipped its snout too deeply into the trough before passing out. But now I sounded like I'd spoken only moments before.

"He's back," someone said. Ken, His voice was on my right side. He sounded relieved.

I opened my eyes. Again, this wasn't hard, the heavy-lidded "Okay, let's face the world" movement of the recently awoken. It was like the upbeat of a blink. My mind was clear.

I saw two sets of legs in front of me, both wearing jeans. I looked up. Kristy and Molly. They were a few feet away and looking down at me with concern.

"What?" I said. I stood up.

Ken looked serious. "This is how we found you," he said, holding his phone up.

The photograph on screen showed me lying on my side on the ground, eyes closed. "What do you mean, found me?"

He looked at Molly. "Tell him."

"I was with Kristy," Molly said. "Looking for Pierre. We were close to giving up and calling you. Then...I don't know what happened. I...I thought I saw someone. Standing to one side in the trees. I thought it was just a shape in the mist at first but then it wasn't."

"Someone from town?"

Molly shook her head. "Someone else. Who can't be here."

"Who?"

She just shook her head again. "Next thing I know, I'm sitting on the ground. I saw another person, twenty yards away. It was Ken. Then he woke up—and we both saw Kristy. She was sitting there blinking. We couldn't see you anywhere. So we called out. Then we came looking."

"Have you got a cigarette?" Ken said. "By which I mean, of course you have, so give me one. Now."

His hand was shaking a little. I've never seen that in Ken before. "What is it?"

"You were about a hundred yards away," he said. "Right where you are now."

"That's..." I didn't know how to finish the sentence.

"Yeah. But there's more. Come on."

He started walking. We followed. After a minute I saw a wall. Tall, made of rocks. Ken pointed at it. "Recognize that?"

"No."

"That's the wall we were looking at before we all, well, fuck knows what happened."

"No. What we saw was a concrete wall."

"Exactly, mate. That's what we *saw*. That wasn't what was *there*."

I turned to Kristy. "What did you see?"

Her face was pinched. "Same thing, by the sound of it. Two concrete walls joined in a right angle. But I also saw a staircase."

"Leading upward. I saw that, too. There was a door at the top. It was opening. And it seemed like there was someone there. A woman. Brown hair. Did you see her?"

"No," she said. "I didn't see anybody."

"I'm cold," Molly said. "I need to be indoors."

My sense of direction is pretty good. Once in a while it will unpredictably fail and leave me even more stranded and lost than someone with no sense of direction, but this time it did not. Eventually a combination of GPS and cached map data confirmed we were headed in the right direction.

Ken had been right: we'd made it nearly a mile out into the forest.

"You haven't said anything about science yet," Molly said, when we were about halfway back to town.

"Gas."

"Excuse me?"

"Some kind of natural gas," I said. "Seeping up from the rocks. You were overcome quickly. The rest of us stayed conscious long enough to undergo mental effects."

"Are you *serious*?"

"I admit that as a theory, it needs work."

"Yeah, Nolan. Given that you, Ken, and Kristy seemed to hallucinate basically the same thing, it really does."

"I am famously open to new and unusual ideas. So give me your best shot."

"I don't *have* one," Molly said. "I am famous for being prone to say if it walks like a duck, it's a duck. Are you really going to have to hear it quack?"

She shook her head and kept walking.

Eventually we came upon a path that led us to a dead-end road at the edge of the middle of town. This had a trash can and recycling bin and a sign telling people to watch out for mountain lions and asking them to not set fire to things, and so was presumably the way most people set out into the woods.

We made our way around the metal barrier in single file and stopped, looking back into the forest. Even though the barrier was merely a horizontal metal pole, knee-height, designed to swing open to let a service vehicle through once in a while, it felt better to be on this side of it.

"Okay," Ken said. "So what do we have?"

"We went into the forest," I said. "And something happened."

"Nolan, that's crap. What just occurred was unusually strange. I'd like to feel we have a better handle on it than that."

"Well, I know what it *felt* like," I said. "But it doesn't make sense."

"Try me."

"Okay. I have smoked a little pot from time to time."

"Good for you. But unless you've got some on you right now, I don't know how that's relevant."

"I'm a pot amateur, is my point. Little baggie in my

sock drawer. A joint every now and then. But once at a party, five years ago..."

"God," Kristy said. "I remember that."

"I'm sure. It came up in marital discussions for months afterward. It was late afternoon, a party at an expensive house in Venice Beach. Good time being had by all. Maybe *too* good. Someone handed me a joint. I thought what the hell, I'd had a couple drinks already..."

"A *couple?*" Kristy said.

Probably the only thing worse than having your spouse edit your story in real time is enduring an ex-spouse doing it. "So I took a big puff, then another, and passed it on."

"I don't want to rush you, Nolan," Molly said. "But I really am cold."

"So then I turned to the person I was talking to, ready to get back into the conversation. They weren't there. I thought that was a little odd—it'd taken me a few seconds to take the hits on the joint, tops, why would they have walked away so quickly..."

"You *are* very dull, mate."

"Shut up, Ken—and then I realized *nobody* was there. And that it was dark. And I was outside, sitting with my back against a brick wall. In an alley. Half a mile away."

"I had no idea where he was," Kristy said. "One minute he was there, chatting. Then he was gone. For two hours."

"Whatever was in the joint was either very strong or simply didn't work for my brain chemistry. I blacked out. Kept talking for a while, then left the party. Walked along the walk, into backstreets. Eventually sat down."

"This is *precisely* why I don't do drugs," Molly said. "You could have hurt yourself."

"Maybe. But maybe not. I'd evidently been conscious

that whole time—in the sense of moving, talking to people, doing things. I had a new pack of cigarettes, which I'd clearly bought, somewhere—asking for what I wanted, paying for it, putting my wallet safely back in my pocket. I had no bumps or scrapes. I'd been awake and functioning. Just not present."

"'Know your dealer,'" Ken said, "has always been my mantra. But I get your point. What we all experienced was like a blackout. I've had a couple myself, which is why I now try never to drink more than a pint of bourbon in one sitting. Unless it's really good. But so... what caused ours? And don't give me bollocks about natural gas. Just not credible, mate."

"What else have you got? For it to have affected all of us, we'd all need to have ingested the same thing, more or less at the same time. Kristy and I had coffees earlier—but neither you nor Molly did. Kristy didn't drink at the Tap last night, either. None of us have eaten *anything* today. So what's the common thread, unless it's some kind of weird gas?"

"For God's *sake*," Molly snapped. "For someone who fronts a show on weird and spooky things you are *remarkably* bad at recognizing when they're *right in front of your face. Seriously.* Both of you. Stop trying to tie this up in a neat science bow when it's *not* and that doesn't *work*."

"Molly," I said. "It does."

"What kind of drug or gas makes three people hallucinate the same thing?"

"But we *didn't*," I said. "Yes, we saw walls. But we've spent a lot of time looking for walls over the last few days. So they're in our minds. But what the *brain* thinks of as a wall, when vision's unhooked, might be different. Brick walls. *Concrete* walls. We create a picture, confabulating not in memory but in real time. And then we saw steps: but I didn't see them until Kristy had said the word *steps*. So I caught my vision from her. And I saw a figure, right? But Kristy *didn't*. What I was probably doing was inserting the figure you thought you saw in your shower into the scene."

Molly had started shaking her head before I got halfway through. "No. What did the figure look like?"

"Female. Long brown—"

"Not what I saw in the shower. Or in the woods."

"Okay, but Moll," I persisted, "that's my point. I didn't see what you saw, so I put something else in. And remember when Pierre turned up at the Tap last night? He was groggy. Said he'd crashed out in his chair. Perhaps that was the same thing. So maybe the question is: what'd *he* do yesterday that we didn't?"

She looked me right in the eye. "He went into the woods, Nolan. Same thing Alaina did, before she disappeared. And like we just did. This isn't food or drink or gas. It's not science either. It's *something in the woods*."

Molly wanted to check back at the motel in case Pierre was there. Kristy volunteered to go with her.

"Good plan," Ken said. "For now, let's not do a Pierre. Stick together in pairs."

Moll smiled brightly. "In case we come across any random pockets of hallucinogenic gas in town. Gotcha."

We agreed that unless Pierre was back at the motel we'd meet at the Tap. Ken and I watched them head off down a side street. "Kristy's not saying much," Ken said.

"No."

"Any clue what's on her mind?"

"Not yet." In ways that I'd find it hard to pinpoint or

describe, Kristy had been behaving strangely ever since we'd arrived in town. There was a distance that hadn't been there when we'd spoken the night of the book signing in Santa Cruz. That had felt like old times. This didn't. I watched the back of the woman hurrying off along the street next to Molly, the woman I'd shared a house and bed with for eight years, and felt like I didn't know her at all.

"So what now?"

"You remember when we talked to the twins, we knew there was something they weren't saying?"

"What about it?"

"I'm pretty sure I know what it is."

CHAPTER
39

bout halfway back to the motel, Molly realized
Kristy was slowing her pace. She stopped and
turned. "You okay?"

"Look. This doesn't need both of us, right?"

"Ken said to stick together. Nolan agreed."

Ken's not the boss of me, Kristy thought. *And neither
is Nolan.* "I know. But I don't think Pierre's going to
be there."

"So what are you going to do?"

"I want to talk to someone about Alaina."

"Alaina's not missing anymore, Kristy. And she's not
my friend. Pierre is."

"What's your point?"

"I don't understand your priorities."

Kristy smiled tightly. "Well, you don't really have to,
I guess. I'll quickly do this, and meet you all back at the
Tap. Okay?"

"Sure. You do that."

"What?"

"It's been interesting to meet you, Kristy. I mean, I'm
sure Nolan can be a pain at times. But he's a good guy.
A kind and thoughtful guy, who always tries to do the

right thing. And so I never really got how he wound up separated."

"What's your point?"

"I think I understand now."

"Not sure I understand what you mean by that."

Molly smiled just as tightly as Kristy had. "Well, you don't really have to, I guess."

She walked away.

Kristy took a chance and headed straight for the school. Sure enough, the Subaru was in position in the lot. The doors to the school were locked. She knocked on the glass, then spotted a discreet doorbell.

The principal eventually emerged from the corridor inside. He seemed neither surprised nor enthusiastic to see Kristy. He unlocked the door. "You continue to be here."

"And growing less popular by the hour. I just want to ask a couple things and I'll be gone. When you covered witchcraft—how much detail did you go into?"

"Very little. Nothing sensational. My aim was to hook them with something they'd heard of, that's all."

"Nothing on specific spells, symbols, any of that?"

He laughed briefly. "Absolutely not."

"Did you direct the students toward further reading, where they could have picked up that kind of thing?"

"There's a whole internet out there, Kristy. Thirty seconds on Google would reveal more than you ever need to know, even if most of it would be wrong."

Kristy switched tack. "Gina Wright—tell me about her."

"A good teacher. The students like her. Married, no children. Her husband seems nice. I doubt she has any interest in witches whatsoever."

"It's not that. I had a weird confrontation with her this

morning. She seemed to think somebody was attacking her online. Any idea who that might be, or why?"

The principal looked concerned. "No."

"Final thing." Kristy got out her phone. "This was the last picture taken of Alaina before she disappeared."

"Kristy—Alaina's back. I'm at a loss to understand why you're still chasing this stick."

The principal put on reading glasses. Kristy altered position so she could watch his face carefully as he looked at the picture. "When she reappeared, she was wearing a coat."

"That's odd." His expression was that of a man who'd been confronted with something that didn't make sense but wasn't of any real interest. Nothing more.

Kristy decided she may as well say it out loud. "I was going to ask if you had any idea how that could have happened."

The principal removed his glasses and slotted them neatly back in his shirt pocket. This was a man who was used to modulating his voice when dealing with both students and teachers, to subduing emotion in pursuit of calm and productive communication: nonetheless, when he spoke, despite a carefully flat tone, it was clear he was angry.

"I assume you're asking if I gave it to her. Or if I was somehow involved in her disappearance, or played a role in her time away. The answer to all questions is no. And I'm becoming extremely tired of the implication."

"Okay, look, I'm sorry. I'm really just trying to work out what happened."

"For whose sake?"

"Excuse me?"

"I didn't tell you this, but I harbored desires to

be a journalist myself once. Even edited the college newspaper. Unfortunately, I discovered I can't write dispassionately. I wound up being too front and center in anything I wrote."

"Meaning?"

He opened the door, letting a cold wind into the building. "I get the sense this story is actually all about you, Kristy. So perhaps you should stop trying to pretend it's for anybody else."

Kristy checked her watch when she got back to the main street. She should head to the Tap to meet the others. She knew she was in a bad enough mood that it wasn't a great idea. And the worst of it was she was pissed because she knew the principal was right.

So she turned left and headed up the highway instead. She'd missed her run again. Maybe a brisk walk would help. The sky was dark gray and so low it felt as though she should be able to reach up and touch it. It was drizzling, faint speckles against the mist. The river sounded loud and the forest felt intrusive, as though it was trying to encroach upon the road.

She knew what she had in mind was probably a bad idea. Confronting Bryan Hixon with evidence that his daughter hadn't been alone in the woods was unlikely to be popular. He'd made it clear in the hospital that so far as he was concerned, this was over—and like the rest of town, he seemed oddly keen to keep it that way. He'd probably also be unwilling to confront the idea that if a man had given Alaina the coat, they might have interacted in other ways—ways she appeared to want to keep secret.

Kristy slowed. Yeah, this was a dumb thing to do.

As Nolan would sometimes say, no good would come of it. Even if Hixon listened, all she'd be doing was dropping a bomb into lives she'd be leaving soon. The quest for truth is all very well, but sometimes it simply isn't what people want to know—and there comes an age where you realize that other people's comfort may be more important than winning another small and bitter victory for facts.

So she should turn the hell around. Help look for Pierre, who—as Molly pointed out—was the one now actually missing. Smooth things over with her, too. And with Nolan, who she'd been pushing away since she got here.

Stop feeling she had to be right. Nobody cared.

As she turned to walk back to town, however, she noticed something ahead on the side of the road.

Olsen's looked bigger in the mist, more abandoned. It was even harder to imagine that it had once been a place where people came to have fun, to flirt, get drunk— undertake assignations of a type every town pretends don't happen.

Kristy left the highway and walked along the front of the building. The front door was securely locked, boarded over. No broken windows, all dusty, opaque and boarded over from the inside. She tried each of the sills. They'd all been securely fastened from the inside or nailed shut. Trying them reminded her that she'd still had no response from Val to the news that they'd broken the back door to her storage last night. Which was odd. But, whatever.

She walked around the end of the building. A door there also showed clear signs of having been shut for many years. And so then around the back. A third door. The same. Further windows, the same as the front.

But there, low down: a service hatch.

Kristy squatted next to it. An opening through which deliveries had been made into the building, presumably. Barrels of beer, bottles of wine, boxes of frozen Simplot Classic Fries. The wood was old and weathered. There was a D-loop to secure it at the front. The padlock looked a lot newer than the ones on the other doors.

And it wasn't closed.

Interesting.

Kristy removed it. Lifted the hatch cautiously, keeping her head back—she didn't want to surprise a raccoon or rats or any other brand of furry thing with teeth. When she was confident that wasn't going to happen, she opened it all the way. The smell of damp earth. She turned her phone light on and directed it into the space. A rusted metal ladder.

She was going to take a look, of course. But she'd seen enough horror movies to know how this shit worked, so she put the padlock in her pocket to make sure her next plot point wasn't finding herself trapped in the cellar by a psycho, or psychos, unknown. Or, zombies. She climbed down.

The ceiling was low. The floor was earthen but the walls were of old wood, and looked like they'd been patched many times. The space was only about twenty feet deep by twelve, nowhere near the dimensions of the structure as a whole. There were three old-looking barstools in one corner. Next to them, someone had dug a small hole in the ground. There was a flat, rusted metal box in it, open and empty.

Another metal ladder at the other end. Kristy climbed

the first two rungs of it and reached to push the trapdoor above. It resisted for a moment—wood warped by years of damp—but opened.

She pushed hard enough to flip it over: jumping at the sound of it slamming down on the floor above. Motes of dust fell around her, sparkling in the light from her phone. They seemed very bright—enough to make her blink and turn away.

She climbed. When her head was up through the hole she stopped and panned the light around. A smallish room previously used for storage. She climbed up into it. Bare shelves and cupboards. A chest freezer. Empty.

A door in the side gave onto a small kitchen area. Someone had done a reasonable job of mothballing it when the business shut, but it was still dark and smelled of rust and rancid cooking oil.

She went into the corridor. To the left was a bar area. A few glasses hung still from racks. Tables, chairs. The smell of mouse droppings and disuse.

She went right, into a larger space. There was a small bar on the side of this room, too, but it seemed like it had been more of a dining area. Not much furniture. The old rock fireplace at the end. The space looked old, and cold, in the pale and muted late afternoon light coming through cracks in the boarded windows. She blinked again—her eyes still hadn't recovered from the bright dust below.

A wooden staircase led up one wall, opposite the front door. Kristy took a look at it from underneath, decided it looked stable enough. Walked carefully up.

The higher level was structured around a corridor that ran the length of the building. As she'd expected from the window distribution from outside, there were two rooms on each side of the staircase. She went right first. Both held wooden double beds with bare, mildewed mattresses, and damp-looking rugs on the floor. Sinks in the corner. An invisible pall of old sex and subterfuge.

A further door at the end of the corridor revealed a small toilet with a tiny shower cubicle. She went back the other way. The third bedroom was the same.

And so was the fourth. Except that odd curling symbols had been written on the walls. And except for the fact that there was a sleeping bag on the bed, a small kerosene stove in the corner, a line of empty plastic bottles, a back-pack, what looked like an old journal, and an untidy pile of clothes.

Kristy moved the pile with her foot, turning over the dark item on top. It was a Birchlake School hoodie.

She went downstairs. There were a lot of questions still to be answered, but one thing was clear. She'd been right. For what that was worth. The only question was what she did with the information. Actually, she realized, as she wandered into the restaurant area, there were others. First of all, why?

Why would a teenage girl disappear herself, letting everybody think she was dead (or worse). And why would she then come back? Kristy knew the answer to the initial question—how widely her discovery should be shared—depended on the answer to these others. That meant talking to Alaina.

And she was already halfway to her house.

She was on her way to the storage room and the way out when she heard a sound. Footsteps.

From above.

CHAPTER
40

The door to the Hardaker house was opened by Nadja.

"There's only us here," she said. "Dad and Mom are staying down in San Jose tonight."

"That's okay. It's you we want to talk to."

"Dad's zero-tolerance about us letting people in the house when he's not around."

Maddy appeared behind her. "My friend Ryder found your show online. The comments section is a dumpster fire."

"Critical response is mixed," I admitted. "But—"

"We're not doing it," Nadja said. She seemed fidgety and distracted. "And you should go."

"We just need a couple minutes."

Maddy put her hands on hips. "You heard what she said."

"We did," Ken said. "And that's a good point." He pointed at the house next door. Then the one on the other side. Turned, a couple on the opposite side of the street.

"What are you doing, weirdo?"

"Just showing how many people are in earshot."

"So?"

"Ken's not always clear," I said, raising my voice. "But

I *think* the point he's making is if we start talking loud, the neighbors are going to hear everything."

"So?" Maddy sneered. "They'll call the cops."

"Maybe," Ken said, very loudly. "Maybe not. You know what people are like. They might get all *intrigued*."

"What's that even supposed to mean?"

He dropped his voice. "What it's even supposed to *mean*, love, is we know what you did. And we can talk about it here, or inside."

They led us into the living room. Nadja's eye seemed to be caught by something in the back yard, but both already seemed jumpy and I didn't want them distracted. "Was it your idea?"

"No," Maddy said. "It really wasn't."

"I didn't think so," I said. "And I don't think anybody needs to know about it. But my ex-wife is a journalist, and she's very good, and extremely persistent. She's all over this. If I can tell her what happened and she realizes it's no big deal, we can all walk away and let life go on as normal."

"How did you know it was us?"

"We didn't," Ken said. "Until you let us in."

The twins looked at each other. "Fuck," Maddy said.

"Not for sure," I said, "but you were the last people to see Alaina before she disappeared."

"But we didn't *know* then," Nadja said. "She disappeared in the woods. For real. And then we were caught in it and couldn't tell anyone."

"So tell us now," Ken said.

The girls looked at each other again. Nadja nodded.

"Okay, so looking back," Maddy said, quietly, "Alaina had been...unusually weird. For weeks. I mean, face it, she's always been pretty extra, especially since her mom died, but I don't know. It was different."

"She was *super*-intense," Nadja said. "Sitting off by herself at recess, drawing weird stuff."

"What kind of thing?"

"Symbols. Diagrams. Things she'd found in some old book. She set up a second Insta account and had us do dumb blank comments on her post."

"I saw that. Why?"

"I have *no* idea. She said it was a ritual, but it seemed kinda random to me. She was being odd all over, so we thought she was just making shit up. She'd be staring off into space in class. Super sad for no reason. We even wondered whether we should talk to Gina about it, because Alaina seemed like she was genuinely depressed."

"And she's emo enough to actually do something about it," Nadja added.

"Right. But then . . . she seemed okay again. Not happy, or sad. Just focused. We figured, okay, she's over it."

"Then that day we went walking," Nadja said. "Something we've done fifty times. Except she wanders off and doesn't come back. We looked. We looked *hard*."

"So that part was true," I said. "You couldn't find her. You came back, told your dad, he called the cops."

"We were freaked out of our *minds*. For three days. We went on all the searches. And everybody's, like, how come you two are here and she's not?"

"Did anybody actually say that?"

"No. But you could tell. It was *horrible*."

"And then what happened?"

"One afternoon after school we were in here doing homework," Maddy said. "Dad was down in San Jose as usual. Mom was at work. And..." She gestured out at the back yard.

"The door's open again," Nadja said. She said it quietly, and just to her sister. I glanced out into the yard. The gate in the back fence was ajar.

Maddy didn't turn to look. "I know."

"We need to *lock* it."

"I did," Maddy said. It seemed like she really didn't want to think about it. "It makes no difference."

"What were you saying?" Ken said, trying to keep them on track. "Alaina turned up in your garden?"

"Yes. Just standing there. So we went running out, like, *so* fucking happy to see her. She was freezing cold. Covered in mud. But she wouldn't come inside. And she said..."

"What?"

"She said she was Lilith now, and could talk to demons."

Ken and I stared at her.

"Well, right," she said.

"Why didn't you go straight to the cops? She'd been missing. She was clearly having...an episode. Why not get her indoors and call the police, or hospital?"

"We *tried*," Nadja said. "But she wouldn't. She said she met someone out in the woods. A man who wasn't there."

"That doesn't sound good," Ken said.

"I *know*. But she said he taught her stuff," Maddy said. "No, not like that. He'd told her where to find some old journals of her mom's that she'd buried somewhere. We still tried to get her to come inside. And then she..."

"What?"

The girls looked at each other again. "My mom leaves her purse lying around," Maddy said. "It is not unknown for us to take advantage of that fact."

"Not much," Nadja said, quickly. "Not often. But, yeah. And Alaina knows. She threatened to tell our dad."

"Unless?"

"We helped her."

"By doing what?"

"Not telling anybody. She'd been in the forest for two days and nights. She was freezing and starving hungry. She said she needed a little more time, and then she'd come back properly. She promised it would be one more night, two at most."

"So... we gave her food from the cupboard. And one of dad's old coats. And camping stuff from the garage."

"Seriously?" I said. "Even though you *knew* what people in town were going through? And her *father*?"

"You don't have to worry about him," Maddy said. "He's the reason she bailed in the first place."

"He's not," Nadja said. "Not like that, anyway."

"Whatever. Yes, we did it. And then we'd done it. And once we'd known about it for a day and not told anybody, people were going to crucify us anyway. So what difference to wait a day or two more?"

"I get it," I said. "The first lie you tell traps you into more lies. It happens to everyone."

Nadja nodded, looking grateful.

"Where was she hiding out?"

"She wouldn't say," Maddy said. "And it was 'just one more night' each time. Until then one day she didn't appear."

"Or the next," Nadja said. "We were *really* scared. We thought something bad had finally happened to her.

But then she came back. For real. And we thought it was over."

"Isn't it?"

"No. She's...she's being *really* weird now. Weird and kind of scary."

"Did she get you to take the picture of Gina a couple days ago?"

Maddy's eyes widened. "Shit—you know about that, too?"

"We do now. Why?"

"We don't know. She just wanted it."

"And also wanted Maddy's boyfriend to hack her Insta and post it. I have no idea why."

"Ryder's not my boyfriend."

"Really? Then maybe you should tell *him* that, and stop getting him to do dumb shit for you."

I sensed the conversation was getting away from us. "All this because Alaina threatened to tell on you? You really think your parents would have *cared* about that if they knew someone else's kid was alive after all?"

"It wasn't only that," Maddy said. She looked guilty but defiant. "She promised us things. Things we deserve."

"I don't want those things anymore," Nadja said.

There was a slamming sound from out in the garden. Everybody turned to look. The gate in the back fence was now shut. "It's just the wind," Maddy said, quickly. She sounded like she was trying to reassure herself.

"What kind of things?"

But both girls stood looking nervously out at the gate, and shook their heads, and wouldn't tell us any more.

Nadja showed us to the door.

"There was one other thing we didn't tell anybody."

"Okay," I said. "What was it?"

"On the day we went to the woods, when Alaina disappeared. You asked us if we saw anybody we knew."

"You said you saw Val."

"Right. We did. But also. Maddy and I went into the store to get a juice, and while Maddy was paying I saw Alaina over by the corner. She was talking to Kurt."

"That bartender guy? What about?"

"I don't know. *Obviously.* But when we came out he was gone, and Alaina looked pretty down. Or pissed. Or something."

Ken was staring at her. "Why didn't you tell the cops about this?"

"I asked her about it, and she said it was nothing. And once she was back, I knew it wasn't a thing, so."

"Sure," I said. "That makes sense."

"You said earlier that nobody needs to know what we did," she asked. "Is that still true?"

"I guess," I said. "Unless someone gives me a good reason to think otherwise."

"Thank you," she said. "Though really, it'd be best that way for you, too."

Ken raised an eyebrow. "What's that supposed to mean?"

"I mean . . . don't cross Alaina. Not the way she is now. Just don't get into it. It will not end well."

"We've dealt with some pretty weird stuff in our time," he said. "I'm sure we can handle one teenage girl."

Nadja cocked her head. "Wow. So it *is* true."

"What?"

"All men really *are* too dumb to live."

She slammed the door.

And locked it.

CHAPTER
41

Kristy remained frozen while she listened to the sounds above.

They started at the far end. And at first sounded like slow footsteps. As if someone was walking along the corridor above her head, toward the staircase in the middle of the building. Step, step, step.

Though...having walked that corridor herself, only minutes before, she knew there could be no one up there. She also knew all the doors on this lower level were locked.

She was going to have to go out the way she came in.

The noises above were quieter now. Maybe she was getting spooked over nothing. Maybe it was just science. Temperature differentials. Creaking wood.

Or an animal. A raccoon or possum that had been lurking in the attic. Would have to be a raccoon, of the two, judging by the weight of the footfalls. She'd disturbed a big momma raccoon. It'd come down from its lair to see what was going on, seeking to protect its brood.

Though...of course it didn't have to be an animal. It could be a *person*. Who'd heard her slamming open the trap door when she came in, and taken cover in the attic while she explored. And had now come back out, either not realizing the interloper was still in the building or else coming down to tell her to go the hell away.

It could be Alaina, in fact.

"Hello?" Kristy said, loudly. No response. She moved toward the door to the storage room and kitchen. "Look—if I've disturbed you, I'm sorry, okay? I'm leaving now."

The noise changed. Still kind of like footsteps, but with an odd rhythm. Not one-two, one-two. There was a sliding sound in it. So maybe an animal after all?

With a tail?

Then a loud crashing sound. Not from above—from the storage room. Kristy was in the doorway when it happened and in position to see what caused it.

The trapdoor slamming shut.

By itself.

She backed away, heart thumping. Though what she'd just seen—the door flipping over, with no one to push it and no one pulling from below—wasn't something she could understand, she knew that wasn't important right now and she needed to focus on getting out. She flashed on the fact that there had been a small, square window on the road side of the kitchen area. She'd seen it from outside. No one in their right mind (or a non-scared mind) would try entering or leaving the building by that route. So maybe there was a chance it hadn't been secured like the others?

But that still meant going through the storage area.

It would have to be a last resort: for now keep ignoring the fact that the trap door had shut apparently by itself—there was probably some rational explanation for that, too, she'd work it out in the bar later, with a fucking huge glass of wine.

She was going to have to break a window.

Rip off the boards, smash the glass. She'd need to be careful climbing out, but her coat was thick and would hopefully protect her.

Suddenly she realized her leg was hot. Very hot. She shoved her hand in her pocket and pulled out her phone. It was so warm she could barely hold it. A text notification on screen from Nolan. Something about Alaina and Kurt.

It cracked before she could read it, in front of her eyes, diagonally across the screen. Then went cloudy.

The sound above had reached the top of the stairs now. It paused. Kristy looked up slowly. Whoever or whatever it was had to be standing directly above her head.

Something moved behind her.

She turned, fast. Nothing there. But she *knew* that something had brushed past her. Something big, too. And there was music now. It was quiet, muffled. As if someone was playing it on a small speaker on the floor above.

Except then it didn't sound like it was coming from there. It sounded like it was coming from the bar.

A footstep on the stairs, at the top.

A heavy creak.

Kristy backed away along the corridor. As she kept backing away, still facing the staircase in order to be able to react quickly if something or someone suddenly came running down it, she glanced into the bar.

Her eyes were still sparkling from the dust. Still, or again. Sparkling worse. But it seemed like a couple of the old, half-broken chairs in the bar weren't empty anymore. As if figures sat in them. One very broad, the other horribly thin. They started to turn their heads toward her.

But when she turned back to the restaurant, deciding

she had to run in there instead and take her chances, she saw a hand near the bottom of the fireplace. The sparkling in her eyes was very bad, but there was definitely a hand coming out of the wall, about a foot from the ground, fingers moving slowly, as if trying to grasp something.

Footsteps coming down the stairs now.

Kristy's legs felt heavy. She lurched back toward the door to the storage area, knowing it was her only chance. She was going to have to risk trying the trap door.

But it was opening and shutting now, flapping like a butterfly's wings, silently.

Her legs gave out and she stumbled backward, grabbing at the wall to slow her fall. She managed to make it most of the way down under some kind of control.

Then she was lying on her back on the ground.

And everything changed.

CHAPTER

42

During the time we'd been in the Hardaker house the mist had thickened even further. The rain was mild but persistent. And it was cold. It was miserable.

"Fuck me sideways," Ken said, as we walked back toward the main street. "Well, in a development that won't make your day, it turns out Kristy was completely right."

"I already conceded that when I told her about the coat thing. Thought I'd get it over with."

"Wise. Not exactly in the way she was expecting, though. Are you going to let her know what Nadja told us about Alaina talking to Kurt that day? Sounds like there was a bit of a crush going on there, don't you think?"

"Yes. I just texted Kristy. No response. I'll tell her when we get to the Tap."

"That Alaina kid needs help. Maybe she had the same experience we did in the woods, but it hit her harder because she's got a puny teenage brain. Spent three days stumbling about, off her head on natural gas or whatever, then came back and saw the twins. Either way it's not our problem, mate. I'm sure Kristy will let people know that the kid needs an eye kept on her. We're done here."

I stopped as we turned onto the main drag. We were at the top end, past the point where there were many businesses. A closed-down appliance outfit and the liquor store. Which was shut. The other buildings were old, single-story wooden houses, most of which looked like they'd been here from the town's earliest days. No light in any windows, despite it being cold and rainy and dark.

I walked to the nearest and dipped to look through the window and saw that actually, there *was* a glow inside. But way in back. Away from the street. As if whoever lived there was keeping safely away from it all.

Ken came and looked with me. As we peered in through the window together, there was a fluttering sound.

A flock of birds came out of the mist and arced straight past us. They flew like birds, anyway, though went so fast it was more like winged scraps of black racing past. They disappeared into the mist—leaving a fluttering sound behind. It faded slowly.

"I'm not sure that's real mist," I said.

"Not... what the fuck are you talking about, Nolan?"

"It's raining, Ken. When have you ever seen fog this thick when it's raining?"

"I haven't. But that's because I live in LA, where people go outside and take selfies if it drizzles. Fuck knows what the weather gets up to here."

"It doesn't look right. There's too much of it and it's too dense and it's here and in the forest and everywhere."

"Nolan—are you feeling all right?"

"*Look* at it, Ken."

You could barely see half a block. The mist was so thick that the main drag disappeared within fifty yards, and what we could see seemed gray, desaturated.

"When you're tired," I said. "Or hungover. Or in a low mood. The world looks different. Doesn't it?"

Ken nodded. I passed him a cigarette. "Everything feels flat," I said. "You drop stuff. Bump into tables. Every damned thing's a struggle. People look pissed off or mean or sad. They're all playing bad music too loud or the silences are too long. It's too hot or too cold or windy or just not *right*. You know what I'm talking about."

"I do."

"But none of that's actually there *in the world*, right? It's not *happening*. It's in your head. That doesn't stop it seeming real to the point of *being* real, though. It doesn't stop it being your reality."

Ken walked forward, peering into the fog ahead. He turned his head slightly, side to side. "If that mist's not real, it's pretty fucking convincing."

"In the middle of the night, when all the phones went off. In the motel. And all our cell phones. At the same time. How would that work? How would someone do that? Are we sure we actually heard it?"

"We heard something, Nolan."

"And something else. Since we've been here...how have we been? Especially the last day or so? Pierre's gone weird and disappeared."

"True. And it's not just him. Kristy's not like she's been when I've met her before. Even Moll's been bad-tempered and strange."

I pointed at the house we'd peered into. "There's people in there, but in back. Like they're hiding."

"From what?"

Just then there was a sound from down the street. A thud. Muffled, but loud. Then a harsher, crashing

noise—like a trash can being hurled into a wall.
Very hard.

"Maybe...*that*," I said.

We took a few steps back.

"What the fuck *was* it?" Ken said.

We watched as a portion of the mist ahead of us seemed
to detach itself. It was similar to what we'd seen in the
woods earlier, but lower down, near the ground. Like
something crawling, but crawling fast—something a foot
or two high. As it left the mist behind it became hard to
tell where it went. That didn't make it any better at all.

"Wind current?"

"If you say so."

There was the sound of a window breaking, some
distance down the street. Then silence again.

"It's not *that* windy."

"Ken—the Tap's down there."

"I know, mate."

"And that's where Molly and Kristy are."

"The logic of the situation is not escaping me."

"How are we going to do this?"

"Head to the left. That's the side the Tap's on. And if
we've got walls and storefronts on one side, we only have
to worry about the other."

We headed quickly over to the left sidewalk, on a diagonal course. When we got there we positioned ourselves
right up against the building. "How far is it?"

"Block and a half," I said.

"I think we should just get on with it."

"Quick sounds good."

Ken went first, walking into the mist, staying about a
foot from the wall. I followed close behind. When you

walk into fog it generally retreats—or appears to, at least. The part that seemed thicker from afar becomes less so, and you turn back to look at where you've come from, and it seems more dense back there. You change how it seems through your position in it. This mist didn't do that: the further we went, the thicker it seemed to get.

"It's cold against the skin," Ken said. "And wet."

"Because that's what we think it should feel like."

"Imaginary mist? Come on. Nolan, we're knackered. Neither of us slept. It could just be real mist. With...noises in it."

"Shh."

"What?"

"I thought I could hear footsteps."

"Not ours?"

"No." I called out, not too loud. "Hello?" My voice sounded odd, flat. There was no answer.

We started walking again and within a couple of minutes made the end of the storefronts, near the corner. We stopped, listened. Nothing to hear. I felt tired and very wired and was beginning to feel kind of dumb. Maybe it was only mist after all—though it was now so thick that we couldn't see the other side of the road—and the noises we'd heard would have been totally explicable if we could just see what had caused them. Somebody in a temper kicking a trash can. A garage door closing too fast.

I believed these possibilities were almost certainly true, but even the sidewalk didn't look right. I was pretty sure that it had been pocked, multiply patched, showing the signs of many years' use. Now it looked smooth, like some kind of indoor walking surface.

"We going to cross the street or what?"

Just before we stepped out, something went past us

in the mist, as if running along the street we were about to cross. It was fast and made a skittering noise—which faded as it hurtled along the street and into the distance.

"A deer," Ken said.

"It sounded heavier than that."

"Deer are heavy, Nolan."

"Whatever you say, boss. But you remember when we went to Alaina's house to see her dad? The night she reappeared?"

"Yeah. That was pretty similar."

"No mist then. And we didn't see a deer. Or coyote. Or anything at all."

"Nolan..."

"I'm just saying."

"Well, *stop* saying things, and cross the street, okay? You look left, I'll look right."

"If anything comes in either direction that fast..."

"Nolan."

We walked, each carefully watching our own side. The mist was an impenetrable cloud now. There was some variation in density, swirls when you could see six feet, other portions where it was only half that. We both tripped on the curb on the other side of the road.

"Nearly there. And they have beer, remember."

We moved back up close to the building on the left. I knew exactly where we were now—in the last several days I'd been up and down this stretch of road many times. Opposite our current position would be the little organic market. Another hundred yards down, the place where Kristy was staying, and the coffee shop we'd been in only hours before. It felt different now. It didn't feel like any place I knew.

"There's that sound again."

He meant the footsteps. "I know."

We stopped. Deadened silence. We started walking again, slowly, and within moments could hear the footsteps.

"Sure that's not an echo? Everything sounds weird."

He was right—and I'd been noticing it for a while. Flat—as if we were walking in a contained space, rather than a street open to the sky—but with a hard edge, too, like tiles or something. The footsteps might have been our own, rebounding from the buildings on the other side of the street. "I dunno. Could be, I guess."

Except then they started up again, and both Ken and I were standing still.

Ken and I tracked the sound. It started off on the right.

"Pierre—is that you? Stop fucking around."

The footsteps stopped. For a moment, a movement in the mist revealed a patch back in the middle of the crossroads. It looked for one strange second as though there was an ornamental fountain there, slap in the middle of the intersection. I even thought I could hear falling water, though it must have just been the rain.

Then it was gone, and a figure stood there instead. Largely obscured, but tall and thin, with a slight stoop in his shoulders. Hands down by his sides.

"That's not Pierre," Ken said.

"Who's there?" I said, with a cheerfulness that sounded as forced as it felt. "Heck of a mist, huh?"

The figure did not respond. The mist continued to swirl, slowly, and after a few seconds it didn't seem like it was there anymore, and it was hard to be sure that it had ever been. "Keep moving," Ken said.

And we did, our backs to the wall and moving as

quickly as we could, fixing our eyes on where the cross-road would be if we could see it. Soon we could hear footsteps again.

"There's more than one set now, isn't there."

"Yeah," Ken said. His face had a complicated expression on it. Unnerved, but also as if he wasn't sure whether he was overreacting. I'm sure I looked the same. We moved faster, sidling along the storefronts, until there was a sudden noise behind us.

"Oh, thank God," a voice said. Molly's voice.

And then hands were pulling us out of the mist.

CHAPTER
43

Derek was in the living room.
Again.
He was watching television.
Again.
Slowly sipping a glass of wine.
Again.

And, once again Gina was in the kitchen by the sink staring unseeingly out into the yard. The mist was so thick that she could barely see the back fence. There were no leftovers, so she needed to cook something. She couldn't imagine what. There were plenty of ingredients in the fridge and cupboards. She'd bought them herself. She understood that they could be combined to create something to eat. She was finding it hard to remember how, or why. The idea of connecting things seemed ludicrous. Better to let everything remain separate. If you take away the habits between us, all that's left is empty space and people standing far apart.

Derek's voice floated into the kitchen. "Are you coming in?"

"In a *minute*."

It wasn't the first time he'd asked. He'd done it ten minutes before. And last night. And most nights. It was always him asking her to come in. It was a wonder one or other of them didn't get the message.

And it was raining, again.

It was always fucking raining now.

And she was always standing at this counter with a glass of wine, delaying the moment. It even sounded like Derek was watching the same TV show as the night before. The same voice droning on. She poured another glass of wine, then got out her phone.

Three messages via their app had gone unanswered. She'd tried calling, twice. Voicemail. She hadn't left a message. She'd now waited twenty minutes to see if he'd respond to the missed call notifications his phone must have shown him. Didn't seem like it.

She hesitated, then sent a text.

Two minutes later, a reply came back: I'm gone. Blocking this number. Thanks, but bye. K

She read the text three times, nodding. Turned the phone over in her hand. The phone she'd sent messages from, to organize meetings. The phone she'd received ones on, too. Confirmations. Private jokes. The kind of thing that keeps the pot boiling. All over now.

She considered throwing the phone to the ground, stamping on it. But what a pain it would be to get a replacement. That's how you know you're a grown-up. You only allow the emotions that are convenient. You carry on.

Meanwhile, Derek kept turning up the sound on the TV. Louder and louder. The demise of out-of-town shopping complexes. Again. Who cared? Things come and they go. Old things die. New things arrive. And then they run away out of town, leaving you all alone.

Derek's voice: "Are you coming in?"

Had he actually said it this time, *again*, or had she merely heard it in her head? And why was he still turning up the TV? The music was so loud now it felt like someone stabbing things into her ears. It was killing her. *He* was killing her. Killing her softly, with his love, with his forever *being there*, with being so calm and fucking reasonable *all the time*, about everything, until all you wanted was something dumb instead, that didn't matter, something you could stay apart from, instead of feeling like you were forever being sucked deeper into soft and loving quicksand.

And even though it never meant much, having it taken away still made everything vastly emptier. All the little cuts life visits upon you, making it harder to hold back the world, with all its stupid things you had to do and say, all its dumb questions. Because there's only ever one answer.

More wine.

Except now she was standing out in the yard drinking it.

In pouring rain. Enveloped in mist. She could still hear the television, so very loud. She could still hear the song, going round and round. And voices now, too.

Lots of voices. None of them saying anything important—everyday conversation as people wandered around. Hey, why don't we go in there? Hey, why don't you buy this?

They were too close. Gina couldn't see them but she could feel them. Brushing up against her, behind her, past her. A constant flow, flying over the fence, coming from out of the forests, coming to find her at last.

She heard her name being called. Derek was standing in the back doorway, confusion and shock splashed all over his face—an expression so big it was comical.

She laughed at him. Who *was* he? Why was he living in Gina's house? Was the building even hers? Was it really a house? It didn't look like one. Garish light designed to pull people in. All the other houses on the street were the same. Buy into life. Buy into the endless bullshit.

Derek ran out into the rain toward her. "Gina—what are you *doing*?"

"I can't do this anymore," she said.

She turned from him and ran—sprinting full speed into the back fence, crashing into it, face first, her head jerking back, blood spurting from her nose.

Derek got to her in time to catch her as she hit the ground. "Gina—what's wrong? What's *happening* to you?"

But though her eyes were open, staring up into the mist and rain, Gina wasn't there.

CHAPTER
44

It was Molly who'd pulled me into the Tap. Ken was hauled in immediately afterward by a woman I recognized—Val. Once we were both inside she quickly locked the door.

"You guys okay?"

"I have no idea," I said. "What the hell is going on?"

She smiled, briefly. "Ah, there's the question."

"Is it anything to do with that wall in the space under where Kristy's staying?"

"No," she said. "It's got *everything* to do with it."

"Wait—where *is* Kristy? Isn't she here?"

Molly shook her head.

The next thirty seconds were chaotic, as I tried to get back out onto the street. I tried hard, too, but Molly and the other woman turned out to be a strong combination—not to mention the door was locked. "Give me the key."

"Not going to do that."

"Why?"

"It's not safe."

"Nolan," Ken said. "Look on Find Your Friends. Could be she's nearly here. And at least you'd know where to go."

"He's not going *out there*," Molly shouted.

I got out my phone and fired up the app. The indicator swung around lazily for a few seconds. Then: NOT FOUND.

"Shit."

"That's not reliable," Val said. "It may mean something's happened to her phone. It might mean she's out of data range. Or it could, at this point, indicate neither of those things—but instead that your feelings toward her are conflicted and you're not sure what she is to you anymore."

"What are you *talking* about?"

"Can I trust you not to do something stupid?"

"Probably not. Why?"

The woman hesitated, then reached in her pocket and pulled out the key. I put out my hand. She shook her head. "First turn around and look."

"For God's sake..."

"Just do it."

I turned to face the street windows. Blinked. Ken came to stand beside me. "I don't..."

But then he ran out of ideas for what to say. There was no mist outside now. None. It wasn't raining, either. It looked like a crisp early winter's late afternoon, old storefronts in dark blue light. "So it *wasn't* real?"

Val unlocked the door. "You tell me."

She opened it. The mist was so thick out there that you could barely see the sidewalk—and it was raining hard.

I glanced out of the window, and saw what I'd seen before. Cold, clear. I looked at my clothing and confirmed, however, that it was soaking wet. "I don't...*what*?"

"Nolan," Molly said, "there's things you need to hear."

Val told us to sit at the table by the window, and brought a pot of coffee. I could see Ken eyeing the bottles of vodka behind the bar and deciding now wasn't the time, but putting a pin in the idea for not much later.

She brought something else, too, which she placed in the middle of the table. It was a large-format book, leather-bound and water-stained, and it looked old.

"What's that?" I asked.

"Take a look," Val said. "From talking to Molly, I think you're going to know."

I opened the volume at random near the middle. It wasn't actually a book, I saw, but a notebook or journal. About half of the surface of each of the two pages I could see was covered with small, dense, very untidy handwriting in an old-fashioned style. The rest was filled with drawings.

I turned the page. More drawings on the left. The right appeared to be a rough map. There was some labeling, but the writing was even smaller and much of the page had suffered water damage. A shape that could have been a river, others that might be mountains. I turned another page. Abstract shapes, some curves, some straight lines with kinks in them. It was pretty obvious what they looked like.

Finally I turned to the front of the book. There, in the same handwriting, was a name. Mary Paula von Tessen.

"Jesus," I said. "This is real? This is her notebook?"

"One of them," Val said. "There are supposed to be seven. We have three others in our possession, already digitized. This one was only found very recently."

"Where are the others?"

"Nobody knows. Most were damaged in a flood at the mission in the 1940s. We're lucky to have any of them. It's possible the remaining three were destroyed. I hope not."

Ken leaned forward. "Care to bring me up to speed?"

"He told us in the car on the way up here," Molly said.

"Nolan says a lot of things, Moll. I don't always listen, to be honest."

"Sister Mary Paula von Tessen was a member of the Dominican order at the mission in San Jose," I said. "When I was researching the walls I found a single reference to her, claiming she'd made a study of them. I didn't believe it was necessarily true, because I couldn't find any corroborating evidence—even of the fact that she ever existed."

Val sat in the remaining chair and poured herself a coffee. "She was real. And for over a decade in the early 1900s she studied the walls in a level of detail that nobody else ever has, even covertly getting some of the Indians at the mission to go out and search for them."

"Is that the kind of thing nuns normally do?"

"Not most nuns," Val said. "But Sister Mary wasn't like most nuns. Though she was a member of the Dominicans, she also had an allegiance to the Knack."

"Is that an acronym?"

"No. Comes from the Old German *knak*, meaning a crack, or blow. But it came to mean a deception, or trick."

"And eventually, the facility for doing something," I said. "I know. Okay, so—what does it mean in this context?"

"An organization. To which I also belong."

"Instead of waiting for us to ask the right questions, how about you just lay this out? And quickly. Because if Kristy's not here in ten minutes I'm going back outside even if it means kicking down the damned door."

"That would be a mistake."

"Mistake is my middle name. Seriously. Talk."

"You broke into the area underneath my Airbnb."

"Yeah," Ken said. "We did. We heard a weird noise and thought somebody might be hurt in there."

"You didn't hear the noise," Val said. "You *felt* it. If someone had made an audio recording of the street at that moment, then played back the tape, the noise wouldn't have been on there. Same with the sound Kristy 'heard' a couple of days before."

"I saw a glow in there though," I said.

"Same kind of thing. Wouldn't have shown on a photograph. You could just sense something was in there."

"And on our way here just now. We heard something similar—in the mist. Was *that* the same?"

"Yes. It's not a sound, or sight. It's an experience. It's feeling something and not having any way to process or name it. You file it in your mind as best you can, though there's a theory it's actually the big mat of neurological material in the midriff that does most of the processing. The stomach brain. The old, pre-verbal mind, the site of gut feelings and unease. Same with the phones last night."

"You heard them?"

"It wasn't 'hearing.' No phones actually rang. You may have been seeing odd things in the last couple of days, too. And feeling nauseous."

"I saw someone in my shower," Molly said. "And Ken heard knocking inside his closet. Nolan heard it, too."

"Not real sounds, again," Val said. "It just meant something was nearby. You know it's there, but you can't *see* anything, so your mind resolves the conflict by positioning the source somewhere hidden. That motel is right by the woods, which is where they live. You may also have experienced sudden temperature drops. Though those are real. I mean, it's all real. But there are different reals happening at once."

"Great," Ken said. "We've found the one person in the world who talks even more bollocks than Nolan."

"I've been doing what I can, including trying to replace the wall originally sited here in the middle of town. It's not my real job, but it was going okay until the last few days. When it all got badly out of hand."

"Does this notebook show the walls in this area?"

"Yes." She got out her phone and showed me a series of photos of pages in the notebook, stopping on one that showed a drawing of a wall with a slight curve. "The local walls in their original state. Or at least as they were a hundred years ago. That's the one I'm trying to replace. It was destroyed when the town was built."

"Who made the walls?"

"Nobody knows. They've been patched and amended over the centuries but the original designs have been here for thousands of years. From long before European settlement. It's possible they even pre-date the Native Americans."

"Then what are they for?"

"You're going to have to be pretty open-minded."

"That won't be a problem," Ken said. "Nolan's mind could do with being a lot more *closed*."

"But you've only got five minutes left," I said.

"Okay," she said. "What do walls do?"

"Form a barrier," I said. "Put a wall through an area, and you've changed it. It turns one side into the inside and makes another, even if only inches away, an outside. Where before it was all the same thing."

"Exactly," she said. "That's good. But it's more than

that. Starting to build walls was the beginning of human-kind. Nothing we've done to the environment since is bigger than the making of the first wall. It was the birth of here, and there; of in, and out. Also, of us, and them."

Ken frowned. "You mean of having enemies?"

"Partly. Before, humans were nomads. Small groups, intermingled families with shared goals, wandering in a huge open world. Using parts of it season after season. Centuries before Birchlake appeared on a map, local Indians would stop here at certain points in the year. Because it was convenient. Because they had become accustomed to it, and each generation passed on the habit to the next. That didn't make it theirs. But it made it a *place*. And when you build a wall..."

"That makes one side yours," I said. "And after that, anybody on the other side isn't you—and you can pretend it isn't there."

"You're a smart guy," she said. "I'm surprised that YouTube show of yours isn't a lot better."

"Oi," Ken said.

"You've seen *The Anomaly Files*?"

"Of course. As soon as you came to town I made it my business to find out who you are. I keep an eye on everybody."

"Was it you who wrote the message on our car windshield?"

"I thought it would be in your best interests to leave town at that point. I was right."

"Why would you even care about us?"

"Walls aren't only a barrier between people," she said, carefully. "They can be a boundary between people... and things that aren't people at all."

"What... kind of things?" Molly asked.

"The things we can't see, but are there all the same."

"*Invisible* things?"

"Yes."

"If something's invisible," Ken said, irritably, "it doesn't exist."

"Why? What makes you think things have to be visible?"

"The fact I'm not bonkers. Next question." Ken looked at me for backup, but could see that I was taking her seriously. "What? Nolan, don't tell me you believe this bollocks."

"Things exist in the dark," I said. "Molecules exist even though they're too small to see. Feelings exist, and run our lives. But you can't point to them."

"That's different," Ken said.

"Is it?" I said. "We see things because of light. Unless an object produces its own, then we only see an object if light from an external source bounces off and reaches our eyes, after which electrical impulses provoked by the interaction of light with our retinas pass along the optic nerve to the brain, which interprets the signals and presents the result to our minds as an image. Which sounds simple, right?"

"Not really," Molly said.

"Exactly. And then think about what each of those stages involves—and bear in mind Darwin himself admitted that he couldn't imagine how natural selection could have produced something as complex as the eye. 'Interprets the signals and presents the result to our minds as an image'? Easy for you to say, my friend. Most of us have only the vaguest idea of how that happens on a computer screen. In our heads, there's no screen. So where *is* the image? Somewhere in our minds. And nobody's really sure where they are, either. Without light to bounce off an object, it's gone. It's no different, it's still there, just no longer visible."

"That doesn't mean it's actually invisible, Nolan," Ken said, though he sounded less convinced.

"I know, but remember: we've only got our nerves' and brains' word for it that what we think we can see is actually there, too. We don't apprehend things directly. Bounced light, electrical blips along specialized tissue, conjured in our brains with the aid of short- and long-term memory to patch in details, together with a host of cognitive functions like having your attention drawn by something fastmoving or a contrasting ability to tune out events that seem unimportant. We have amazingly little idea of how this all works. And so we build walls around the stuff we do understand, and declare everything outside to be nonsense. We make it invisible to the mind."

Ken rolled his eyes, but Val nodded. "There are walls like this all over the world," she said. "Humans have been building them for tens of thousands of years, maybe longer. In the distant past the design process was understood far better—the shapes that will hold back the things we can't see and have no way of dealing with."

Molly looked unnerved. "But what are these things called?"

"A hundred things. They've had a different name in every culture and language that's ever existed."

"Just one or two will do, love," Ken said.

"Monsters." Val shrugged. "Or demons. Take your pick."

PART THREE

Our psychological energies are reflexive in character, invisible to the mind's eye, even as their consequences in the world are visible.

—James Hollis, *Living an Examined Life*

This was a winter visit,
with the wind north-west.
We see things not as they are,
but as we are ourselves.
—H. M. Tomlinson, *The Gift*

CHAPTER
45

As Alaina approached the Hardaker house she saw two silhouettes side by side in one of the upper rooms, watching out the window. It was the only building in the street where you could even tell people were inside. Everybody else was skulking, lights low. Watching television. Scrolling through their phones, scroll, scroll, scroll. Even reading, maybe, some of them.

Hiding from the world. From themselves. Doing something—anything—to transport their minds and feelings elsewhere. Put up a fragile wall and curl up like a baby bird in your shell. Don't be here, be there. Pretend it's all okay.

Did they realize?

Of course not. People have no idea what they're up to half the time, or why. They tell themselves stories about what they're doing, concoct plans and schedules, but they're not the truth. Everybody makes up their own fairy tales so they don't know why they're anxious or depressed or happy or sad. They're just *there*, those feelings. They prowl, the troops of Midian. Sometimes they put their arms around you. There's nothing you can do about it.

If you want to see what's really going on, if you want to be safe from people, you have to live outside.

Don't ever trust the village. They lie.

Alaina had walked the entire circumference of the town, counterclockwise. She cut her finger with her pocketknife and allowed drops to fall in various places, as her mother had done twenty-five years ago. There had been something emphatic in one of the journals about urinating on the bridge near the motel, but that seemed weird and it was really cold and raining, and she'd decided it could wait for another night.

Nothing felt any different, though.

It wasn't working the way it was supposed to.

Everything just felt empty and sad. The streets reeked of loss. There was something else going on here that she didn't understand, and it was stopping things working. Somebody else had control of the narrative. Somebody was screwing this up. It was time to get this thing reframed. Make it hers. Get it right.

The first step was punishment, and for that she needed witnesses.

It was time for others to step up.

But they didn't answer the door.

Alaina rang the bell again. And a third time.

They'd seen her coming. They must have. Alaina walked back from the front of the house and looked up at the window where Maddy and Nadja had been standing before. They'd turned the light off.

But she could tell they were still there. There was a darkness against the darkness inside. Why weren't they coming down? Why weren't they opening the door? It wasn't because of their parents. Alaina knew they were out of town. So WTF?

She texted Maddy. It was delivered. Then read. On-screen receipts for both events. But nothing came back.

She texted again, this time just ?

Thirty seconds later Maddy replied: Go away

Alaina stared at the screen. Then texted: ???

Maddy: everything is fucked up

Alaina angrily thumbed a response, having to redo several words because of rain on the screen: I told u it would be this way, its how it works

A pause, then from Nadja: we don't want your gifts

From Maddy: youre not normal

Alaina blinked, staring at the screen, feeling the back of her head start to throb. Then carefully thumbed: last chance, bitches

She watched as two further messages came on screen.

From Maddy: We're blocking u

Then, from Nadja: bye

As fast as she could, Alaina replied: FUCK U

Then she turned and stalked away down the road. She didn't see all the lights in the Hardaker house suddenly come on, glow brighter and brighter, and then blow out. But she heard things laughing in the corners, on rooftops and in the drains.

She stopped, and spoke quietly to the invisibles. "Don't piss me off. That would be a mistake."

By the time she turned into the main street she came shrouded in darkness. She could feel things rubbing against her, flying over her head, and hear them jumping on parked cars. Every now and then a glimpse of form, of faces.

She heard shouting, too.

A man was standing outside the liquor store, enveloped in mist. He looked like he'd been there a while. He was soaked. He was shouting at things he couldn't see, waving his arms, creating sparkling trails in the light from the sign, which was blinking on and off.

"Hey, handsome. Pierre, right?"

Pierre stopped, turned to peer into the mist. "Who's there?" Anybody who knew Pierre would have been able to spot immediately that his voice didn't sound right. "Who are you?"

"We met before. The night I came back."

"I don't remember."

"So let's meet again. My name is Alaina. But all you need to know is that I'm the boss of you."

Pierre blinked. "I don't understand what's happening. What's inside me?"

"I have no idea. Just do what it wants. It may tell you to hurt people. And that's okay. Go nuts."

She walked away, leaving Pierre standing in the middle of the road like an empty coat.

Once more there was a single building with lights in it. Not a house this time, but a place she knew well. Better than anyone below the age of twenty-one should.

She stopped on the opposite side of the street.

Only a few people were in the Tap. The barmaid with gray hair. Val. Another woman, younger, and two guys. The other people who'd been here in the street the night she came home. So everybody from then was right here, now, except one.

The woman who'd driven her to the hospital, and then come the next morning.

Why wasn't she with them? Did that mean something? Was *she* the problem here?

The woman's friends were all looking out of the window of the Tap, but Alaina couldn't imagine why. The fog was thick and getting thicker. The rain didn't feel like it would ever stop. They didn't seem like they were looking at her, or as if they could even see her.

The window glowed. It looked warm in there.

Alaina blinked. For a moment it had seemed like there was another person in the Tap, cozied up against the bar, her back to the world, happy for a while.

But that wasn't real. And there was no sign of the one person she *wanted* to see. He'd turn up to work sooner or later. Or if not, then Alaina would go to Plan B. If he was hiding from her, she'd bait the trap harder.

But what until then?

Alaina stalked away into the mist, figuring she may as well go piss on the bridge and see if it helped.

CHAPTER
46

Sounds. Music. Muted conversation. Quiet laughter.
Kristy opened her eyes.

She was lying in the corridor between the two
main areas of Olsen's. There was a rug underneath
her now, however, against her face—whereas the floor-
boards had been bare before. The rug was red and
threadbare. It'd seen a lot of use, the passing of many feet.
It smelled of dust and spilt beer.

She pushed herself upright, put her back against the
wall, legs out straight in front. Sat blinking for a moment. It
felt like when you zone out on a long drive and come back
to realize you've steered the car safely for five miles with
no recollection of what you saw or did, or the decisions
you made. Or like an entire year of your life, during which
you've lived the same way, like a driverless car piloting
down the highway with no idea where it's going, or why.

The noises were coming from the bar. There were
more chairs and tables in there now, and people. Not all
of them looked like they were one hundred percent there.
Their edges were translucent, like those old photos where
the exposure time was very long and people didn't know
the picture was being taken, or realize they had to stand
still, and so appeared as curious blurs.

Someone walked past.

They came from the restaurant, stepping over Kristy's legs as though it were no big deal to find someone sprawled there. They walked along the corridor and into the bar. As they arrived, the room became empty again.

Kristy stood. Cautiously took a few steps toward the bar. The bar was fully stocked, and you could smell bourbon and beer and the lower note of some kind of food. And the room wasn't empty after all. She simply couldn't see who was in there, or understand why they were looking at her with what felt like generous pity.

Kristy was getting scared now.

She went the other way. Hesitated a moment outside the storage room—the shelves were now full, though none of the labels looked modern. The trap door was closed. A woman stood over the sink, her back to the door, shoulders bent, gently shaking. A house dress out of the 1930s.

By the time Kristy got to the restaurant she'd started to hear music again. The air was hot, stifling, muffling everything. The restaurant was devoid of people, but there were tables and chairs. The tables were small and round and red, and the room smelled of burgers and fries. The bar on the side looked more like a counter, the kind where you'd stand and select from the menu on the wall behind the servers and take a number and wait for your meal to arrive on a red tray.

The windows on the side were different, too. No longer boarded over. They were big sheets of glass.

The front door was ajar.

Kristy went through. It should have let her out into the parking lot, but it didn't.

CHAPTER
47

Ken nudged me, pointed at the window. It was snowing now.

"I'm going out that door in two minutes," I told Val. "Is that what I'm going to find?"

"No. It'll be the same as before. It is actually raining. In real life. And the mist, we can't do anything about. Some of that's real, too. The snow you're seeing may be because Molly's feeling cold."

"I don't understand."

"It's not there to be understood."

"That's cute but doesn't sound like it actually means anything."

"Everything we think 'means something' feels that way because it sticks to the path, right? And you've never walked this way before."

"Fuck is *that* supposed to mean?" Ken asked. He was looking back at the vodka bottles with the air of a man who was close to deciding that *later* could also mean *now*.

"It means," I said, looking at Val, "it doesn't fit with the way we believe the world works—which is a function of the shape of our minds and of the structures of language. Right? When we come up against something that doesn't mesh, can't be expressed, everything breaks. Stuff stops meaning and can't be understood. Not consciously, anyway. Is that close?"

"Surprisingly close."

"So. You're saying things we can't see have always existed side by side with us. Creatures that don't fit in our world, or our understanding of it. And so we're afraid of them, like we're afraid of the dark."

"It's because of them that we *are* afraid of the dark. When you're not distracted by all the things you can *see*, it's easier to feel the presence of things that you *can't*."

"Okay. And when we *do* encounter them, we don't have the slots in our minds to deal with them, and so our imaginations do whatever they can to incorporate these things into some kind of picture—even if it means hearing things that aren't sounds, and seeing things that aren't there, or seeing them wrongly. Yes?"

Val nodded. "Hence myths, ghosts, monsters."

"So why is this happening? And why now?"

"Alaina is . . . causing a lot of problems. Breaking some of the walls—or getting other people to do it. She's made contact with forces she's simply not equipped to deal with yet. Using spells she doesn't understand."

"Is her whole 'Lilith' thing basically a witch fantasy?"

"It's not a fantasy," Val said. "She *is* a witch. Natural born. There's nothing she can do about it. And that's why I'm here."

"I don't believe in witches."

"That's a shame, because up until now you were on a good streak of saying smart stuff."

"Try me instead," Molly said. "What are they? Witches?"

"The term's been used to describe different things in different cultures at different times. Could be an older

woman with wisdom and experience. Can just be someone who knows herbs. But it can also refer to people with
the knack."

"Of seeing the things that most people can't?"

"Yes. Though other people can sometimes do it intermittently. Children, though they lose the ability early
these days. People in certain kinds of mental distress.
Animals—especially cats. The difference is witches can
do it all the time. Not just see, but communicate."

"Seriously?" Ken said. "And how would that work?"

"We're not sure," Val said. "But at least part of it
is genetic. Many of the differences between humans and
Neanderthals relate not to the genetic code we have—a
vast amount is the same—but which parts are switched
on. Some genes associated with diseases, especially com-
plications of the mind like schizophrenia, autism, and
Alzheimer's, were present in Neanderthal DNA too—but
not activated. Turning them on rewired our brains to evo-
lutionary advantage, but at a cost: it's easier for us to live,
but we're not seeing the whole truth. Some people have a
touch of it still, the ones with the sight—and that's why
the facility is often associated with mental challenges, a
tendency toward madness and depression. That's not the
only reason why those things happen, but sometimes. If
you have it your whole life, and receive guidance, you
can get accustomed to it—and learn how to use it."

I stood. "And so where do you come in on this?"

"I was a doctor. I had a patient who was presenting with serious mental health issues. A young patient.
She'd been referred by the school, and her mother was
extremely resistant to me giving her drugs. After a while
I came to understand why. I stopped being a doctor and
joined the Knack. Our job is to help witches. In ancient

days that was largely a matter of physical protection. Helping them escape bad situations. Now it's more of a support network. Alaina's mother died before she had the chance to help her daughter understand who she was. I was moved into position to be on hand to help when the time came."

"How'd that work out for you?"

"Very badly. Something triggered Alaina earlier than it should. I don't know what—though the principal's class might be part. Either way, the knack started to come on her early, and it came on *fast*. And then she disappeared, and while she was away made contact with things that are supposed to stay the other side of the wall."

"When she came back she said she was dead."

"Ascending to witch-hood is often framed as a rebirth. You go away, you change in fundamental ways, you come back. And while she was in the wilderness some of these things convinced her to disturb the integrity of some *physical* walls—so there are spirits abroad now that shouldn't be."

Molly had remained silent for most of the discussion, listening hard. "She released *demons*?"

"The things we give that name to, yes. That's why everybody's indoors tonight. They know something's wrong. There are parts of the world where the danger is higher, because far more of these other things live here. Walls were built in those places—here, Europe, the Middle East, across the world. To keep the others on the outside. Something like this happened here fifty years ago. The people in town don't know *what* is going on right now—only that the best thing is to turn away."

"So why doesn't the world look right?"

"These things get in your head. And we *feel* that—but

our minds don't have the tools to frame it. So they paint the closest picture they can. The closer you are to people, the more likely you are to experience it the same way. If what you're confronted with is too big, or too sudden, the mind just shuts down. To stop itself from going insane."

"That's what happened to you in the woods earlier," Molly said. "And—"

"Great," I said. "That's all been extremely interesting, and I look forward to mulling it over at my leisure. But time's up. I'm going back out there."

"I really wouldn't do that," Val said.

Ken stood. "He's right, love. We can't just sit here like lemons. We have to do something."

"And this is why," Val said, wearily, "it's a blessing that most witches are women. Sometimes randomly 'doing something' is the biggest possible mistake."

"Look," I said. "Two of our friends are missing. If there are actual *demons* out there, I'm not abandoning my people to them. If that makes me some kind of patriarchal asshole, so be it."

"What he said," Ken added, firmly. "Only, with a lot more swearing in it."

"It's a bad idea."

"We've got to do something, Val," I said. "So I'm asking your advice on what the best thing would be."

"To be clear," Ken said, "that doesn't mean we'll take it. In the last ten minutes you've managed to make Nolan sound almost normal, and that's a first."

"The only person with any power over this situation now is Alaina," Val said.

"Fine," I said. "I'll add her to the list."

"You'll only make things worse."

Molly stood up. "I'm with you guys. Let's go."

CHAPTER
48

When she stepped out of Olsen's, Kristy was braced for rain. Even welcoming the idea, after the stifling, trapped air in the restaurant. It wasn't raining, though—because she wasn't outside, or not completely.

Instead it felt like she'd come out into some kind of contained space, like a big corridor. It was hard to tell how wide it was because it was dark and thick with mist, but it was clear what direction it was headed. Back toward town.

At first the boundaries of the area were nebulous, formed by her sense of the highway on the right, the cold river beyond, and Olsen's on the left, all under a ceiling of low cloud laced with branches that curved around her like long fingers.

As she got farther the space started to feel more concrete. Literally so—the mist looked a lot like a wall of brushed concrete. It began to feel claustrophobic again, too, as if she were underground. And also as if something was coming.

She looked back, but couldn't see anything. That didn't mean it wasn't there. She started to walk more quickly.

What had been rough ground under her feet became

asphalt. She could still hear the river on her right, swollen by rain, but that too seemed to change as she realized she was hurrying along tiles now, and what she'd thought was the sound of rushing water was actually the beat of her shoes, echoing off walls of dusty concrete. She started to run.

Kristy could run fast, and she knew after a few minutes she should be approaching town. She started to see something ahead, but it wasn't Birchlake.

It was a staircase, dimly lit at the top.

She didn't want to go up. She'd watched enough horror movies to know that, whatever else you do, you don't go look in the small room at the top of the stairs.

And she hadn't told the truth in the woods.

She *had* glimpsed the figure at the top of them. It wasn't there now. But that didn't mean she wasn't waiting, whoever she was.

Kristy turned and looked back, but the corridor she'd come along was lost in mist barely ten feet behind. She could hear things in it, glimpse flashes of darkness, though she couldn't tell how far back they were—as if her mind were struggling to form a picture of something that wasn't there to be seen.

She didn't want to go up the stairs, but she didn't want to deal with whatever was causing the flashes, either.

She ran up the stairs.

There wasn't a room at the top, or more corridor, but a much wider space. It looked a lot like the main drag of Birchlake, in fact, except that it had a roof.

And everything along the road was different...

...though also the same. She recognized some of the older houses. She spotted other buildings she knew, too, as she walked, though they'd changed. Most had striped awnings and old-looking signs in firm, blocky typefaces. The windows of some stores had prices written on them in white paint. All were dark. The doors were shut.

She passed a newsstand with fifty different papers and magazines spread out over racks. A hardware store, with pots, pans, and utensils hung in rows and piled in baskets and boxes on the sidewalk. One of these had a handwritten sign saying 6¢. This store was dark, too; the door shut.

The next sold musical instruments. Violins, acoustic guitars. Sheet music with engravings of the singers on the front. She passed a small fountain in the middle of the crossroads. The water had frozen into shape, so she could snap off a piece as she went by.

Kristy finally ground to a halt on the other side of it, shivering.

On the corner where the grocery should be—the place where she'd bought snacks on her first night in town—was a small store with a sign saying R ADAMS, GROCERIES & MEATS. The sign for the Stone Mountain Tap was now one for the Stumptown Saloon. The signage looked Victorian. The coffee shop was now a small store selling old radios and clocks, 1930s style—except the radios and clocks in the window all looked brand new.

And there, the building that held the apartment Kristy was staying in. The old general store. The stucco looked fresh and the display windows at street level were no longer whitewashed. They held rows and rows of dresses, displayed on wire frames.

The door was open.

Kristy approached cautiously. Her holding assumption was that this was a dream. Or Nolan's idea about some natural gas leak. Or... something. She still had to be careful. Dreams are real when you're inside them. Emotions, too. If something scares you, then you're going to be scared, and Kristy felt she was scared enough already without putting herself in the way of something that might be even worse.

But this was the only open door on the street, and she didn't want to be outside. It was cold and the mist was getting thicker. She felt bad and it seemed like she'd spent a long time out on the street, maybe years, trying to get in. She didn't want that anymore.

She paused on the threshold. She knew the space beyond. She'd seen it when she and Nolan and Ken had broken in. That must be how her dreaming mind was able to fill in the rough dimensions of the interior. It was dark, but she could tell it was full.

Dresses on racks. Dresses on mannequins. Dresses folded on the shelves. Far, far too many dresses.

And... there was someone in there.

Kristy knew this before she could tell how she knew. There was something different about the darkness, as though something was making it even darker from within.

Then she heard a faint scraping sound.

"Hello?" The word was out of her mouth without thinking. She immediately wished she hadn't spoken.

No response. That didn't mean she was alone. Not getting a response is what makes you feel alone when you're not. She took a single step into the store. Though dresses crowded in from every side—even hanging from the ceiling, in row after row after row, on old wooden hangers—there was a narrow pathway through the middle.

She took another step. Glanced back at the door to

the street. Though she didn't want to be out there, she didn't want to be trapped in here, either. She looked around for something to brace the door with. Couldn't see anything.

It'd be okay. She'd wake up eventually, right?

And, Kristy thought as she took a few more slow steps into the store, now would actually be a good time to wake up. A great time, in fact. She didn't care how lame it was—and she knew for a fact that Nolan got fired once for suggesting it as a fix in a script (after six months of rewrites he'd stopped caring)—for Kristy it was getting to the stage where the *Oh, it was all a dream* reveal couldn't come soon enough.

"No," said a voice. "Not that one."

Kristy froze. A woman's voice. She couldn't tell where from. Somewhere in the dresses.

"No," the voice said, again. More emphatically.

Kristy glanced back at the door again. Still open. Did that mean it was going to stay that way, or was this a last chance she'd better take? She didn't know her subconscious well enough to guess what game it might be playing.

"No, no, *no.*" This was quieter, and the voice hitched hard on the last "no." The three words together were enough for Kristy to get a rough fix on its direction.

Near the back of the store, on the right. As she looked that way, a dress flew up into the air. It sailed slowly back into the darkness.

Silence for a moment, then that quiet metallic sound again, like something being scraped against something else.

Kristy took another tentative step along the path.

"*Obviously* not," the voice said. It wasn't addressing Kristy. It was talking only to itself. "You will *look like shit* in that."

A ripping sound, cloth being savagely shredded, then the scraping noise again. "And in that."

The scraping sound. "Even worse in that." Scrape. "Don't even joke, you ugly *bitch*."

The words were increasingly hard to understand as the hitching in the voice grew more pronounced. More ripping. Another dress flying up into the air. More scraping.

And sobbing, mixed in with a low moan, the sound of a body or soul in pain.

Kristy carefully parted the dresses in front of her. This revealed a small clearing in the dresses, like one between trees deep in the woods.

A woman stood in the middle of it.

It was Gina. She was wearing a worn-looking house dress. Her face was wet with tears. There were scratch marks down her cheeks, from her own fingernails.

She looked blearily at Kristy. "What the hell are you doing here?"

"This is a dream," Kristy told her. "And I'm going to wake up now. You should, too."

"God, you're dumb," Gina said. She sounded tired, wretched, old. She sat down abruptly on the floor. "Of course it's not a dream. This is how it always is."

CHAPTER
49

The rain was still lashing down outside the Tap. It still wasn't making any difference to the fog. After the things Val had told us, this combination felt less strange—in one way at least, but a lot stranger in many others. It was nearly dark now.

I stepped out, staying under the awning. Ken joined me. Through the noise of rain hammering onto the fabric above our heads, I heard barking, some distance away. The sounds were very low, however, spread far apart.

"That's not really a dog, is it," Molly said.

The sounds suddenly got closer together and higher in pitch, until they sounded much more like hysterical laughter.

"Nope," Ken said.

I turned to Val, still sitting inside at the table. "Which way should we go?"

She shrugged. "I have no idea where your friends are, Nolan. They probably don't know either at this point. Like I said, the only person who—"

"I heard. But why does Alaina have power over them?"

"Witches do. Sometimes. It's the reason they were tolerated down the ages. They arrange for these things to get what they want, to keep the peace. Objects. Animals.

Even people, sometimes. Children. It's not nice, but that's the way it works. And that's why they were never trusted, and often made to live outside town. Put there to form a barrier against the outside things, like a human stop sign."

"Olsen's," I said. "That abandoned bar up the road. What's the history?"

"Her family used to own it. It was popular, in a sketchy way. Then some bad things happened there, and it was never the same. Closed a long time ago."

"But why's it outside town?"

"Bars often are," Molly said. "Zoning, or to keep whatever happens there out of plain sight."

"True. But what did Val just say? About living outside town?"

Val blinked. "Huh."

"That really never occurred to you?"

"You're losing me this time, Nolan," Ken said.

"Kristy was right," I said. "We know that. Alaina wasn't out in the woods the whole time. Maybe the first two days. She got provisions and equipment from the twins after that, but they didn't know where she was hiding out."

"You think she was in that bar?"

"Because I wonder if that was the original site of her family's house."

"But the cops would have looked there, surely."

"Of course—on day one. And maybe again on day two. When *she wasn't there*. But then it's been searched and proved empty, and nobody goes back. So she moves in."

"Jesus," Val said, looking pained. "It's a shame I didn't start talking to you guys earlier."

"Doesn't mean she's there now," I said. "But it's a

place to start—and on the way to her dad's house. Matter of fact, it might make as much sense to start with him."

"True," Ken said. "We assumed he was boarding up the house last night to keep things out. It could be he was doing it to try to keep Alaina *in*."

"It won't have worked. And you'll get nothing from Bryan Hixon," Val said. "He's spent the last eighteen months trying to stop Alaina from going down a road she can't avoid."

"Didn't her mother die in a car accident, while drunk?" I asked. "Maybe that was the road he was trying to steer her off."

"It's not an easy life. That's why the Knack is here to help."

"How'd that work out with Alaina's mom?"

"I wasn't here then."

"You're here now."

Val looked down at the floor, breathed out heavily. Then stood up. "Okay, you're right. Let's go talk to him."

As soon as the Tap door was locked behind us, the mist got thicker.

"Quicker the better," Ken said. "It's going to be full dark soon, and I doubt that will improve matters. If we can't see anything, then what we *think* we see is going to get even worse."

Yet none of us moved. It didn't feel good out there. It felt unsafe. It felt like walking into an after-hours bar on a back street in some city you didn't know, and being able to tell immediately that strangers were not welcome. The kind of place where there would be old blood stains on the carpet and a stray tooth in the urinal, where people always left in a worse state than when they arrived and yet still came back again. Maybe that's no coincidence. Maybe there are unseen things living in some of those bars.

I went to the edge of where I was still protected from the rain. I thought I heard the sound of crying, not too far distant—but a gust of wind swept it away. "Let's go."

We started off in single file, keeping close to the wall. Within seconds we were soaked to the skin again. The rain was like a hail of tiny little bullets. It didn't take long to get to the corner. The rain suddenly got even harder, and thicker, pouring in from the right.

I turned against it and saw why. A large fountain loomed in the mist at the crossroads, benches around it. It had been there before, briefly, but was now much bigger, and the wind was so fierce that it was blowing the water as far as where we were standing. It made no rational sense for it to be there, which might mean it made some *other* kind of sense, but I was too beset to work out what it might be.

We ran across the road. As we reached the other side there was a loud, low thudding noise from a couple of streets away—accompanied by a shudder that was enough to send Val sprawling. I grabbed her arm and pulled her with me to the side of the next block, where we all huddled together for shelter against the wall.

Molly had to speak loudly against the sound of the wind. "What's big enough *to do that*?"

"Nothing," I said. "It's not a real vibration. But it means it's something we *really* don't want to see, even if we could."

"You learn fast," Val said.

"Have you dealt with something like this before?"

"No. Much smaller events. A single demon on the

loose. People think they hear a knocking, or see a ghost. That's the most I've ever had to cope with."

"So you have no useful advice at this point?"

"Sorry." The thudding sound again, but with a tearing note to it—and it seemed closer this time. "Keep moving. That's all I've got."

As soon as we were around the corner the wind dropped. The mist opened up for a moment, too—but only to reveal that the next stretch of road was gone.

In its place was an expanse of tiles that stretched from building to building across both sidewalks and the street. The tiles were utilitarian, cream-colored, once shiny but now scuffed and chipped.

An object drifted across the space. A shopping cart— one of those that are fashioned like a small truck or fire engine—designed for you to push small children around in, to keep them happy or at least patient while you wander.

It sailed down the street toward us in a series of grace-ful revolutions, wheels squeaking. When it was level with us it stopped. We watched it carefully. It was motionless for five seconds—and then hurtled in our direction.

We split two ways—Ken and Molly falling back, Val and I jumping forward. The cart went slicing through the gap and smashed into the wall. And disappeared, leaving only the sound of laughter spiraling up into the rain and mist. Then the sound of feet or paws running away along the roof.

"We need to be faster," I said. "They know where we are."

But Molly was blinking now. She staggered. Ken got his arm around her and kept her moving forward. "What's the matter with her?"

"She's blowing out," Val said. "Too many things, getting too close. We need to get her out of this. We *all* need to be out of this, or we'll be next."

We kept plowing on. Molly got her shit together, and soon the four of us were double-timing forward into the mist, still trying to keep it close to the wall, in the hope that'd stop. We got as far as the liquor store before...

"Christ," Ken said. He stopped in his tracks, staring down at the tiles in front. "It's a fucking leg."

A human leg, unclothed. It looked like it had been severed, none too cleanly, just below the hip. It was lying on its side and trying to bend at the knee.

"I don't want to know what that really is."

We started to run. The rain was now coming from the front, driving straight into our faces. The heavy, grinding thudding noise came from behind—once, twice, and then again, getting closer each time.

It made you run faster. You couldn't help it.

After a few minutes I noticed Ken breathing hard behind me. I run a little, and I know Molly does, too. Ken doesn't. He was starting to fall behind.

"Keep going," I shouted to Molly and Val. Molly turned, started to say something, but I shook my head firmly. "Just *do* it. We're coming."

Val grabbed Molly's arm and encouraged her to keep jogging forward. I dropped back beside Ken.

"Don't be a dick," he panted. His face was red and blotchy. "I neither need, nor fucking want, your charity."

"Hell are you talking about? We're the menfolk."

"Sexist, mate."

"Sue me. If something's coming at us, it's our job to be in the way. That's the only reason I'm hanging back."

He was forced into a smile. "You're a lying bastard," he said. "But you lie nicely."

"Well, there is another thing. To outrun the monsters, you don't have to be the fastest, remember. Just the second-slowest. You're my insurance policy."

"Oi."

"Just keep running, you tool."

A couple more minutes took us to the top end of town and onto the highway—still a ribbon of incongruous tiles heading forward into the mist. Trees pressed in hard on the right, at the side of the road, but they didn't feel like protection. Anything could be in those woods, and there was nothing to stop it coming out at us.

"Head toward the center of the highway," I said.

Ken had no breath left to talk by that point, but nodded. Then he frowned, as if hearing something. "Wassat?"

I could hear it too. Music. Except then I realized that it was the sound of the river, on the left of the highway. This made me remember the dark shapes I'd seen in it in the night and understand that this thing had already started then. And before, in fact... I no longer had any doubt that Molly had seen something in her shower—which knocked it back another day.

And, even *earlier*... the homeless guy I'd seen outside the liquor store, on the very first night. He'd shouted into thin air. Homeless guys do that, sure. But why? What are they doing? And the way he'd reeled back, as if confronted with something much bigger than he'd bargained for...

And just after I'd seen *that*... there'd been the shape in the window of Kristy's apartment. The shadow I'd seen up there, despite it turning out that she was already in the Tap.

This had been going on since the day we arrived.

Had we helped *cause* it, somehow? Or at least *frame* it? Give it shape?

Ken stopped. I assumed he'd finally run out of running, but—though he was now nearly purple in the face—that wasn't it. "Can't hear them," he panted.

"What? Who?"

He gestured. Up until a moment ago we'd been able to hear Val and Molly running, not far ahead. Now there was only the river and rain pattering down on the tiles. Both sounded different, too—flatter, with an echo.

I called out. "Molly?"

Nothing.

"Nolan—what if it came from the front?"

"What if *what* came from the front?"

"Whatever we thought was behind us. Moll!"

Suddenly there was a scream. Two screams, in fact—at the same time. I started forward but Ken grabbed my arm.

"Easy," he said. "Not so fast."

Something came smashing out of the woods. It went so fast I didn't even see it, but the beat of its wings was enough to nearly knock both of us over.

Then it was gone. A moment later, the sound of two near-identical screams again—this time from behind.

"That's not them," I said. "How did you know?"

"The deep inner wisdom of the overweight and winded."

"If you hadn't held me back . . ."

"Sometimes the race goes to the slowest, mate."

The screams came once again—from behind us, and a lot closer. Ken and I turned.

About thirty feet away, shrouded in swirls of mist, were the twins. Maddy and Nadja. They weren't screaming in fear, however. They were screaming because they were fighting each other, slapping at each other's faces as if oblivious to everything else in the world. The movements were odd, stylized—but the viciousness and anger wasn't. It looked like they wanted to kill each other.

Nadja slapped Maddy again. Maddy seemed to be trying to grab something off Nadja's neck.

Ken took a step toward them. "Wait," I said.

At the sound of my voice the girls immediately stopped fighting. They turned toward us, smoothly. Smiled, at the same time—and tilted their heads in the same way.

"Shit," Ken said. "That's not them…"

And then they vanished—though they weren't gone. The girls weren't visible anymore, but movements in the mist showed they (or whatever they *really* were) were headed in our direction, so quickly that we had no chance to even start running.

We stood frozen as one curled around Ken, the other around me. It felt like a very large cat rubbing itself against me, around my legs, up to waist height, and there was a smell like garlic and cinnamon.

"Ken!"

The voice was Molly's. "Stay back!" Ken yelled.

But she and Val came running out of the fog, each grabbed one of us and started pulling. "There's more of them," Molly said. "And they're getting more solid. We have to get inside."

Trying to move against the things weaving around us was like wading through a heavy current. The smell was getting more acute, too—as if the garlic was burning, turning rancid and bitter. The sweeter note in the smell was cloying to the point of stomach-turning.

"Stay."

The voice was quiet—and seemed to come from around my waist. There was nothing there—nothing visible at least.

Val was getting greater traction with Ken, and he was now on the move with her toward the side of the road. I kicked at the thing moving around me as Molly and I backed away, but of course that made no difference.

"Stay, Molly. You belong to me." The voice was insistent. The voice of someone who loves you but is becoming unhappy. Angry. Who is growing willing, if you force them, to consider hurting you, really *hurting* you, to demonstrate just how big their love is.

Molly could evidently hear it, too. "Go *away*," she screamed. "Just *leave me alone*."

I grabbed her hand and yanked it, pulling her toward the abandoned bar I could now see looming in the mist. It was hard to get her moving, but I kept dragging until we made it to the parking lot—at which point Moll dug her heels in and couldn't be pulled any further.

"Always mine," said a voice. "Always."

Molly screamed into the mist where it'd come from— her voice so cracked and out of control that I couldn't even make out the words—and then spat at it.

"Moll—let it go."

But she kept screaming, fighting against me so hard that it was almost impossible to move her. It was inch by inch, and a wind was picking up now, slashing through the mist on the road—though I knew it wasn't really wind, but things getting closer and stronger.

Then Val was at my shoulder, panting. "Around the back—there's a way in. Come *on*."

We each took one of Molly's arms and dragged her around the back of the building, where Ken was squatting by a hatch nearly at ground level. Opening it revealed a basement area that was very dark.

"Fuck knows if this is a good idea."

"Anything's better than staying out here," I said, as he and Val shoved Molly down onto the ladder.

I was wrong, of course.

CHAPTER
50

Kristy lowered herself to the floor a few yards from Gina. The other woman had drawn up her knees and wrapped her arms tightly around them, head down.

As Kristy sat, the dresses disappeared. The space now looked as it had when she and Nolan and Ken broke in the night before. Dusty, old, populated with piles of rocks. That half-built wall, whatever the hell it was doing here.

Real, in other words.

Did that mean she was actually here?

Maybe one way of telling would be to try the back door. If this was real, it should still be openable. Though of course that didn't necessarily work...if this was a dream, she could have simply dreamed it that way, too.

So how could you tell when things were real? Now, or ever?

"Gina? How did you get here?"

The woman whipped her head up disconcertingly quickly. *"What?"*

"How did you come to be here?"

Gina's eyes were wild and red-rimmed. "I can't remember. I was going to be something. People were going to know my name. And now it's just 'have you done the assignment? What's for dinner tonight? Is it time to load the dishwasher, or *un*load it? What's for dinner *tomorrow*?' The fun never stops, right?"

"No, I meant, here. Physically. In this store."

"I was…I was in our yard. Then Derek was there, and…I don't know. I was running after that. And there were bees."

"Bees?"

"Black bees. Coming after me."

"In the rain?"

Gina frowned. "That does seem weird, looking back."

"I really didn't take a picture of you, by the way. And I most certainly didn't hack your Instagram account."

"I believe you."

"So who did? Who'd know how to be able to do that?"

Gina shrugged. "No idea. Maybe one of the kids."

"Who?"

"Only one I can think of would be Ryder. Dan's son. He's pretty much the only geek in town."

"Can you think of a reason why he'd do it?"

"No. He's a nice kid."

"Maybe somebody else had a reason, and got him to do it for them."

"I think he's theoretically Maddy Hardaker's boyfriend. Or hopes he is. But Maddy and I get on fine, too. Why would she do that to me?"

"For the one thing, teenagers, and especially teenage *girls*, don't have enough of. Power."

Gina shook her head. "I don't see it."

"What was the big deal about the picture?"

She didn't answer. Kristy waited, listening to the rain drumming onto the road outside. Real rain? Presumably. Eventually Gina spoke quietly. "I did a stupid thing."

"To do with a guy?"

"How'd you guess?"

"It's the stupid thing people of our age do. I've been there. And the picture was evidence?"

"Barely. But whoever took it could only have done it because they knew what was going on."

"Who was the guy?"

"Kurt."

"That *bartender*?"

"I know. I know."

"Was it a real thing?"

"You've met the guy, and you ask that question?" Gina shook her head. "Just dumb, dumb, dumb. And he's already bailed. Run out of town."

"As in, permanently?"

"Yes."

"Good. Because it sounds like you already know what it was worth."

"And the truth will set me free? Please."

"No. The truth may fuck you up. Believe me—I know. But at least it doesn't own you anymore."

Gina stared at Kristy. "Yes, it *does*."

"Why not?"

"Because *somebody else knows*. You know, for a smart woman, you're not very smart."

"I understand that. Which is why you have to get out ahead of the story. It won't fix everything, but—"

Gina blinked. "Alaina," she said.

"God," Kristy said, as the pieces dropped into place.

"*Yes*. Nolan texted something about them earlier. If Alaina had a huge crush on Kurt, then somehow found out about the two of you...you said she got distant before she disappeared...Jesus. That's *it*."

But Gina was staring over Kristy's shoulder. "No— she's *behind you*."

CHAPTER
51

The cellar was dank and smelled of earth and dust and something else. A low reek that was meaty and ancient. The odor seemed to exist deep in your head rather than coming in through the nose, though, so perhaps wasn't really a smell after all, but something hiding in there. It wasn't good, either way.

"This looks old," Ken said, as we headed to the ladder on the other side.

"Probably from the original dwelling. The cellar of a witch's house."

"I don't like this place," Molly said. "At all."

Ken gestured her toward the ladder. "Me neither, love. But it's better than being outside."

She climbed, holding her phone up. As she raised her head into the space beyond, she gasped. "Christ, Nolan."

I quickly followed. The ladder emerged into a kitchen storage area lined with empty shelves, shadows, and the smell of rust. Molly was crouched in the corridor beyond.

Kristy was sprawled along it. Her eyes weren't entirely closed. Molly had her fingers on her wrist. "Pulse is fine," she said. "Fast, but strong. She's not unconscious. Like she's awake, but just...not here."

Ken looked at Val. "What's happening to her?"

"It's similar to the trances mediums go into," she said. "If you're trained, or an actual witch, you can keep control. Remember where you really are, and be in both places at once. Anybody else, if there are too many of these things around...the mind bails on the real world. Retreats into the closest picture it can make instead."

"Real-time confabulation," I said.

"I guess."

"There were a ton of other things out there just now," Ken said, dubiously. "But we kept it together."

I lifted Kristy's head gently. Her skin felt cold. "Barely," I said. "And there's safety in numbers. We shore up each other's reality. Kristy was alone."

"So what do we do?"

"*Nothing*," Val said. "If you try to shake her out of wherever she thinks she is, it's going to break her mind. It's better to let her—"

There was a loud crashing noise on the roof. Then the sound of tiles sliding off to smash onto the ground outside. "That was real," I said. "As in, an actual impact."

"They know we're here," Molly said.

There was another crash—but from the other end of the building. Silence. Then something that sounded like huge wings, beating above our heads, before heading away.

"Going to fetch more of them."

"Shut up, Ken," Molly said.

A rattling sound from the front of the building. All heads turned toward it. Rattling again.

I moved cautiously along the corridor and into the area at the end, which had once been a restaurant. All the windows were firmly boarded over. The rattling sound was coming from the front door. The handle was twisting back and forth.

It stopped, then started again—even more violently.

Then a series of thumps along the wall, moving from the door, along the building, toward the end wall. Then along that wall, past the chimney. As if something was banging a fist against it. A fist, or something else.

"It's looking for a weak point," Ken said.

We followed the sound as it traced around the building. Something strange was happening with my right eye. It seemed to be going in and out of focus, though the left remained clear. This made it hard to judge distance, especially with so little light. Yet when I glanced at my hand it looked sharp. My brain knew what my hand looked like. It wasn't sure how to process everything else.

The knocking turned the corner and continued along the back wall, toward where we stood, changing from intermittent thumps to a consistent rapping sound.

"Nolan," Ken said. His voice was slurred. He pointed into the storage room. Tried to say more, but couldn't get the words out. Instead he pointed more vigorously.

"Christ," Molly said. "The hatch we came up through. The entrance to the cellar is back there. *Outside.*"

Val ran through into the storage room and slammed the hatch shut. The rapping in the walls stopped, suddenly.

She made a face. "Should have done that quietly, huh."

The rapping started again, now coming from all around the building. And then there was the sound of footsteps on the roof.

Ken was leaning against the wall now, and looked as vague as I felt. "Secure that hatch."

"How?"

"Put something heavy on it."

We looked around. A few chairs, none substantial enough to stop anything determined from pushing its way up. I heard the sound of the hatch outside, the one which gave access to the cellar from the parking lot, creaking open.

"Us," I said. "We're heavy."

I stood on the hatch. It felt weird, as if it was tilting, but I was pretty sure that was just in my head. Until I almost fell over. "What about her?" Val said.

"Who?"

"Kristy."

"Are you kidding me?"

The rapping all around the building was getting louder. Some sounded as if it was coming from *inside* the walls. Maybe that was merely my head trying to express the knowledge that bad things were getting closer and closer. Or perhaps something was in the actual walls. I sensed it was an increasingly unimportant distinction.

Molly was helping Val move Kristy's body into the storage room. "Val's right. She's not doing anything else."

"For fuck's sake," I said, angrily. "You're *not* using Kristy as a... wait, what's that?"

A soft clonking noise—but not from the walls. I felt in Kristy's pocket. Something metal. A padlock. God knows what it was doing there. "There we go."

The ring on the hatch was rusty and none too strong. But I put it on, and it was better than nothing—and better than my ex-wife being deployed as a human sandbag. "Ken—are you okay?"

"No," he said. He was half-sitting in the corridor. "I feel... unusual. Furious. Or sad. Can't work it out. Fuck's up with your eyes?"

I was blinking again. Slowly. There was more darkness

in my vision than the flicker-visions provided by Val shining her phone screen around. My right eye was entirely out of focus now, too, very blurred. And I was afraid. "I can't see properly."

There was a soft thud from under the floor. "Something's in the cellar," Molly said glumly.

I sat on the hatch. I felt very sad but also incredibly anxious. And I didn't know what to do.

"Is everything okay?" Ken said. He was now half sprawled in the corridor. "Is everything okay?"

"I don't think so," I said. Everything felt jagged and sharp and out of control. "I don't think it ever was."

"*Stop* it, you two," Molly shouted. "It's bad enough without you freaking us out."

"How close are those guys?" Val asked Molly. "Nolan and Ken. I mean, as friends?"

"Well, they're guys. So I have no idea. Why?"

The walls sounded as though they were full of ticking insects, but I still heard the noise of someone stepping onto the metal ladder below me. A metallic *thung*.

Ken was blinking too now. Heavy, slow, up-and-downs of his lids. Val patted him on the cheek, quite hard. Then did the same to me. I could barely feel it.

"They're blowing out together," Val said. Her voice had a flat echo on it—the same I'd heard in the street earlier. "Molly, we're going to have to secure this place ourselves."

I stood up, unsteadily. Saw Ken trying to do the same. "No, I'm fine," I said. "And so is…"

The last thing I heard was something banging very heavily on the back wall of the building. Hard. Then everything went gray.

*   *   *

Nolan and Ken collapsed at the same time. Molly tried to get to Nolan, but he collapsed into the side wall of shelves, crashing off it to fall to the ground.

She rolled him onto his back. Nolan's legs were moving, very slowly. His fingers were rubbing over the wooden floor, as if feeling the texture.

"Are they *okay*?"

Val didn't answer. Molly looked up to see the other woman was by the boarded-over window in the corridor, face pushed up close to a gap between the planks. "Shh."

"What?"

Val gestured. Molly went over, bent to look through the crack. The mist was thick outside. And somebody was standing there.

A dozen feet away. Unconcerned about the pouring rain. As Molly and Val watched, he raised his head. Staring straight at the window.

It was Pierre. But he didn't look himself.

He ran straight at them.

CHAPTER
52

Kristy stood to look out through the front windows. The street outside was still thick with fog, but where before it had been shadowed and gloomy, now it seemed softly lit—as if by moonlight, though not from above.

Alaina was in the middle of the road. A dark figure, head lowered, in a hoodie.

"She's going to hurt me," Gina said.

A swirl of fog obscured the girl, then revealed her again, making her look taller and thinner. Then back to Alaina. "I'm not sure that's even her."

Gina stood too. "It is. She's come for me."

Kristy went closer to the window. It was Alaina. But also not. The person out there was Bryan Hixon's daughter. But more than that. Different. She looked far more three-dimensional than everything else. "Go talk to her."

"Are you *kidding*?"

"I don't think this can be my dream," Kristy said. "It must be yours. Alaina has nothing on me."

"This is *not a dream*."

"Well, whatever the hell it is. Either way, I don't give a damn about Alaina. But you do."

The windows at the front of the store shattered. The glass wasn't blown inwards, however, but outwards—as if from pressure from the inside. Kristy glanced at Gina and saw she was shaking, hands trembling violently.

But then the glass was back.

The girl outside was closer to the windows now.

Gina ran into the darkness at the back of the store. Kristy hesitated. Everything told her to stand her ground, but she was as scared as Gina. There were dark shapes moving in the mist behind Alaina. Huge dark shapes. And things coming in under the door. Small, like cockroaches—skittering into the room. Wholly black, scraps of shadows. They were as bad as the things outside, she knew—part of the same huge thing, as tiny ants are part of a single colony fifty miles wide.

She hurried into the corridor, but it was empty. Kristy turned back, to see if Gina had somehow slipped back past her again. Couldn't see her—just Alaina's silhouette outside, now right in front of the door.

Kristy heard a sound from the side room on the left. Gina was huddled in the corner. Eyes wide. "She's going to get me."

"No, she's not."

"Someone will. I've *broken everything*."

The skittering sound from the main room was loud now—one much bigger and louder sound, broken up into little bits, a thousand cuts.

"Yeah," Kristy said. "You did. So now what?"

"I always fuck everything up."

"A few years ago I screwed up too, Gina. *Really* badly. And I believed that when something's broken, it's broken for good—that however well it's fixed, breakage remains. And that's true, but I was wrong about what it means. If you break something then sure, you can throw it away, feel hurt, betrayed, furious at yourself. Or you can gather up the pieces and glue the damned thing back together. There may be bits missing and of course it will never be the same. But it'll *still be there*."

Before Kristy could get close, Gina suddenly darted around her, and out into the corridor. "I have to get out."

Kristy followed, to find the other woman tugging in vain at the door at the end. Turned out that here, wherever *here* was, the latch hadn't been broken last night.

"There's no back-door escape," Kristy said. "You can't sneak out that way. You have to walk out the front."

Gina kept desperately yanking at the handle. "I don't understand you. Stop *saying things*."

Kristy kept trying. "I've had a lot of time to think about this, Gina. And I know that decision to *not* throw the broken thing away, but to repair and keep, to treasure it because of what it means, not because it's perfect...that actually gives it more value, not less. Before, it was just a thing you had. Now it has you woven inside it— through the effort you gave to fixing it. You don't own it anymore. You have joined with it. It's not perfect. But nothing ever is."

Gina turned from the door. "So what—turn and face the monster? And it's all suddenly fine?"

"No," Kristy said. "We're both old enough to know that's self-help bullshit. You're the monster. I'm the monster. We're all monsters, once in a while."

Another big thud from out in the street. "I'm scared," Gina said.

"Yeah, me too."

They stood together and looked along the corridor. The fog in the street was flashing now, as if lit from

within by a strange kind of lightning—the muted flicker
of overhead lighting about to fail.

The shadow in the hoodie, right outside the door.

"Say sorry," Kristy said. "Then forgive yourself. Then
move on. It's all you can ever do."

Gina took Kristy's hand.

But after three steps Kristy realized Gina wasn't there
anymore.

Outside, Alaina held up her hand. A ring with two keys
on it dangled from her finger.

Kristy took a step back. The girl opened the door and
pushed it wide. "Where'd she go? Gina?"

"I don't know."

"I want to talk to her."

"I think you've done enough, Alaina."

The street behind the girl now looked like it should.
Misty, rainy, but real. On the other side, shuttered stores.
Further up, the Tap. The glow of lights in its windows. It
looked warm, welcoming, the kind of place you'd hurry
to on a night like this. Hunker down. Get a local beer
and some nachos. Feel like you were part of somewhere
for a while, even if in reality you were only listening to
an echo. Over the course of an evening you might get a
couple of glimpses of the actual place. The rest would
only be in your interpretations. In your head.

"How come it looks normal out there?"

"I'm really here," Alaina said. "You're not."

"But how does that work?"

Alaina shrugged. "Who cares?"

"You don't actually know, do you."

"No, I don't, and so what. I spent ten days trying to
figure it out and then thought—fuck, just roll with it."

"You're going to make mistakes."

"Spare me," Alaina said. "Old people, Jesus. You always think you know the score, that the world is the way *you* think. When you can't even *see* it. You've been looking through stained glass so long you don't even realize."

"And you see it clear?"

Alaina took a step toward her. A fourteen-year-old. Taller than Kristy by an inch, nearly two. Bigger, taking up more physical space in the world, but still half a child. Both things true at once. "Yeah," she said. "I do."

"If this is real, how come you have a key?"

"I was walking down the alley a month ago and they were hanging out the back door. Senior moment of Val's, I guess."

"So why'd you take them?"

"Wanted to see what she was doing in here."

"Did you mess them up? The rocks?"

"Maybe."

"Why?"

The girl smiled. "Why not?"

"Because it *screwed everything up*. Because sometimes you can do things that you can't put back, and there'll be no grown-up you can run to—because by then you'll be the grown-up and it's *all on you*. Sure you're ready for that?"

"It was going fine until you got here. *You're* the problem, not me."

"Says who?"

The girl turned her head. Someone was standing out there, down the street. Tall, thin. Old. Waiting. "He does."

Kristy felt cold all the way down her back, a feeling that moved down through her muscles and into her stomach, locking it. For a moment, as on her first night in town, there was a faint shadow of familiarity over the figure.

"Who...is that?"

"I have no idea. But here's an idea: why don't you let me build out *my* world, and you deal with *yours*."

"Fine by me. But leave Gina alone. She's done with Kurt. He's yours, if you want him."

"*Want* him? What are you talking about?"

"Personally I'd run a mile, but that's old person wisdom talking. Very bad idea at your age anyway. And super illegal. And he's left town, FYI. For good."

Alaina stared at her. "No."

"Yes."

"No, no, no," Alaina wailed. "That's not *fair*. He *cannot* be gone."

"Love is a..."

"Love? *Love?* God, you're stupid. I don't love him. He's an *asshole*. I want to *pull his fucking head off*."

Alaina turned suddenly and went running out into the street, vanishing into the mist. Leaving only the impression of a tall, thin man, face obscured, a black hole of nothingness. A void into which a life could disappear.

"Oh no," Kristy said, finally realizing who he might be, just as he disappeared.

CHAPTER

53

I t felt strange but familiar. For a moment all I could make out was a flat plane of undifferentiated gray, but it was the kind of space I knew. Also something I'd seen recently—maybe even thought I'd *been* in, however briefly.

"Is that you?" Ken said.

"I hope so," I said.

He came toward me out of the gloom. This helped me get a handle on the space, settling it into three dimensions. A long, wide area, fading off into blackness and shadows in all directions. Concrete all around, pillars every forty feet or so. Very dim, flickering fluorescent lighting above—or at least, the effect that kind of fixture would have: no lights were actually visible. "Is this…a parking lot?"

"Looks like one. But hang on." I bent down, felt the floor. "Feels like wood. We're still in that storage room."

"So now what?"

There was a sudden, piercing scream from the deep shadows off on the right. Not close, but also too close.

"We could leave?"

"I think that's a solid plan. How, though? By which I mean, which way?"

"Your guess is as good as mine, Nolan. But how about we start by going the opposite direction to the screaming?"

"See, that's why you're the director and get the big bucks." We started backing away together.

"It's barely *bucks* plural, mate."

"Not now, Ken. Wait—can you hear something?"

"Music? Yeah. Head for that."

We kept backing, glancing over our shoulders to make sure we weren't heading in the direction of something dangerous—and to avoid the concrete pillars. It was the same song I'd been hearing over the last day or so—in fact, pretty much since we'd been there in town. Which again made me wonder how long things had been bending, and why: and how much of the last three days had actually *happened*. I'm not one of those music nerds who can pick out a song from the first semiquaver, but I'm not bad. I could hear all the notes, and recognize them, but it was as if there was a barrier between them and the tune. It was a song that should have sounded sweet and wistful, I knew that much. But it didn't. It sounded guilty and sad.

"Ken."

"What?" he said.

I stopped walking. "That wasn't me."

"Don't be an ass, Nolan."

"I didn't say your name."

"Ken."

We were looking at each other that time, and so it was very clear that neither of us had spoken. The voice had come from the left. A man's voice. Conversational. Nonthreatening. Apart from the fact there was no one there.

"Is that you?" The same voice. It now sounded as though it was coming from behind the nearest pillar.

"Let's go faster," I suggested.

"Right you are."

We turned and started walking quickly—still with no obvious sense of where to go. It was no longer clear whether the gray all around us was concrete or fog, though the fact it felt increasingly damp, as though we were hurrying through heavy drizzle, made it feel more like the latter. It got thicker as we tried to head for the music, but that faded in and out in no apparent relation to the direction we took.

Footsteps over on the right.

Nothing to see except mist. We kept walking, bearing away from the sound. Then we heard footsteps from the left, too. We stopped, and they stopped—but a beat later. It wasn't an echo.

"They're herding us," Ken said, as we started walking again, more slowly. "Which means..."

"Yep. On three."

We kept walking for a moment, as Ken counted under his breath. Then we turned and ran in the opposite direction.

Very soon it was clear we weren't in a parking lot after all. We were in woods. The concrete pillars had really been trees. The mist was heavy, but swirled thick and thin by a strong wind, and it was still raining.

"Nolan—where the fuck are we going?"

"I don't know." I paused, whirled around on the spot—and thought I could discern a thinning in the forest on the right. "That way."

We ran in that direction, narrowly avoiding tumbling down an unexpected slope, and passing a long stretch of curving dry stone wall, and then—the highway.

When we arrived on it we stopped, looking left and right. "Now what? Back to Olsen's?"

"It's not going to be there," I said. "This still isn't real. Look." I pointed at the road. Instead of the rough and cracked surface of the highway, it was a stretch of badly weathered tiles. "Are you seeing tiles?"

"Yeah. But mate—things were *attacking* Olsen's when we checked out. Moll and that woman are there. And Kristy."

"I know," I said. "But I'm pretty sure Val could kick my ass, so there's no reason to think they can't look after themselves. And don't even *think* about splitting up."

"Nolan, as I've had cause to remind you..."

"You...were a horror director. Right. Maybe that's it."

We looked at each other. Ken frowned. "Are you saying..."

"That we're in your head? No. I don't understand how that would work. But perhaps you're coloring it somehow. *The Undying Dead* has that whole long sequence in an underground parking lot, right?"

"Nolan—look." He was pointing up the road toward town. "Is that what you saw earlier in the woods?"

There was a staircase in the middle of the road.

We walked toward it. By the time we were within fifty feet, the environment around it had changed. I could still see the tiled road and woods either side.

But the staircase—simple, utilitarian, the edges of each step long ago painted a now scuffed white—led up to a doorway. A glow beyond. And once again, music, faintly, echoing as if against a hard surface. And for a moment I believed I caught a glimpse of someone up there. A woman.

Ken and I looked at each other. Then we started up the stairs.

CHAPTER
54

After Pierre ran at the back of Olsen's the first time—crashing into the wall and bouncing back—he did it again, hard enough to make the wall shake.

Molly and Val shrank back across the corridor. They braced for a third impact, but it didn't come. After a minute, Molly crept back to the window. Peered through the crack. He wasn't out there. "He's gone."

"I doubt it," Val said. "Or, not far."

"So what do we *do*?"

Val looked at her. With both their phones off, the younger woman was little more than a deeper shadow in near darkness. And Val didn't know what to tell her.

This kind of event—whispered of, obliquely mentioned in old texts, sometimes even making it to general news— was one of the things that the Knack was supposed to help prevent. But you couldn't tell where it would happen, or when—and so, often they failed. The Irish Fright in 1688, when villagers in parts of England and Wales armed themselves and tried to fight nonexistent groups of Irish soldiers. The Great Fear in Paris in 1789. Tales of Spring-Heeled Jack in London in the 1830s: a tall, thin specter who could leap from building to building—but

for whom no piece of physical evidence was ever found.
The nonexistent Halifax Slasher in 1938. The New England vampire panic of 1892. More recent mass attacks
of fainting or hysteria or seeing things that aren't there,
everywhere from Tanganyika in 1962 to the West Bank in
1983 to Kosovo in 1990, including widespread claims of
evil clown sightings in 2016: all attempts by the body or
mind to frame things they had no way of encompassing.
Usually they were one-offs, when barriers were breached
accidently.

This wasn't. This was it happening *again*.

Val had heard rumors from the oldest Birchlake locals
as they sat at the bar (where, by all accounts, Alaina's
mother had spent more than a few afternoons in the years
before she died) late at night and got deep into the head-
spinning local IPA. The rumors implied that something
similar happened decades ago, when Alaina Hixon's
grandmother lost control of herself for a while and let
wild things roam. A night nobody remembered clearly
except for a sense that very bad things had happened, and
a pervading sense of anxiety, a fear of the invisible. Only
for a few hours, though, by the sound of it. And nothing
like tonight.

Val was unqualified to deal with the current situation
and knew it. "I don't know," she admitted.

The building shifted around them. As if it stirred in
its sleep—as if all large structures had only ever been
drowsing animals, and at times like this they could awake.
The wood in the walls and ceiling creaked, as though
stretching, the sound of long-hidden things moving.

They heard the front door being tried again. Then a
muffled voice. "Molly—it's me."

Pierre. He sounded afraid. "Ignore it," Val said.

"But he's my friend."

"He just tried to smash his way into the building, through the wall. That the kind of thing he normally does?"

"I can't just *leave* him out there."

"Yeah, you can. That's *precisely* what you should do. I'm sorry, Molly—but we have no idea what you'd be dealing with. Something's gotten inside him. I don't know what, exactly, but I can guarantee you it's not a good kind of thing. And three of your other friends are lying in here. It's our job to protect *them*."

A sudden burst of music from the bar area. Grotesquely loud, but scratchy—like a 45 played on a jukebox desperately in need of a service—distorted to the point where it was impossible to tell what it was.

"That same *goddamned song*," Val said. She felt worryingly close to losing it. The walls were creaking ever more loudly, as if wooden bones were close to breaking—as if the building was trying to break apart to expose them to what was outside. "What *is* it?"

"I don't *know*," Molly said. She was staring down the corridor toward the bar. Suddenly she shouted: "Go *away*!"

The music stopped like a record scratch, changing to very loud, mean-sounding laughter.

"Whatever it is," Val said, trying to sound calm, "whatever you think you're seeing, ignore it. It's not there. It's just how the things in the walls are making you feel."

Molly knew that. She knew the man she kept thinking she glimpsed in the shadows—the same person she thought she'd seen in her shower at the motel, and she'd fought that realization hard, but couldn't any longer—could not be here.

She knew that because the man's name was Peter and he was dead.

He'd thrown himself off Santa Monica pier after a three-month period of stalking Molly. He'd texted her half an hour before he killed himself, warning that he was going to do it, and she—despite the fact they'd never once gone out, and she'd never given him the slightest reason to believe there was something between them, despite Peter having scared the hell out of her by doing everything from sending two hundred emails a day to standing outside her apartment in the night, staring up at her window—had gotten down there as quickly as she could.

But too late. She'd watched his body pulled out of the water, feeling hollow with a terrible guilt that no amount of rational thought since had been able to mute.

So she knew it wasn't him, but that only made it worse. Because it meant the horrible, bottomless sense of attack, of being under threat by something that felt it *owned* her, could only be coming from her own mind. It meant that feeling was already inside, bedded like a maggot burrowing in her soul. Peter buried it there and then fled reality and died.

"We could run," Val said. Molly just looked at her. "Yeah, I know. Just making sure we're considering all options and making choices."

Molly began dragging Ken into the storage room. "Help me."

By the time they'd got him propped against the shelves next to Nolan, the noise around them was cacophonous. Banging, clanking in the pipes. What sounded like…

"Jesus," Val said, rearing back. In the space above the very lowest shelf on the left, a yard away from Ken, a hand had appeared. The fingers were moving, as if trying to grasp something. Its wrist disappeared into the wall.

Molly scooted back along the floor. "Is it real?"

"Real enough." Val's head hurt. She knew what the hand reminded her of. A hand that used to come creeping under the covers of her bed when she was small.

Molly was blinking, slowly. She'd had enough too. "We're going to have to—"

A banging sound from underneath. Something or someone hammering so hard on the hatch to the cellar that Val bounced up and down. The D-ring attachment was already splintering. "Stop it," Molly screamed.

It stopped. The hammering on all the windows stopped too. Even the structure of the building stopped creaking. The silence was very loud.

"Molly, it's me. I'm okay."

The voice came from the cellar. Molly turned to look at it. Val shook her head, firmly, but found she couldn't actually say anything. Her vision was blurring.

"I was weird for a while," Pierre said, earnestly. "I know that. But I'm okay now. There's really freaky things out here, Moll. I need to come inside."

"Is it really you?"

"Yes. I promise. It's me. I'm fine now."

Val was still shaking her head, but her eyes were nearly closed now.

"Pierre," Molly said, crawling over to the hatch. "I want to believe you. But I don't know."

Val's head suddenly nodded forward, and she slumped down across the hatch. Molly was alone here now.

"I'm scared, Moll."

Molly could barely see anymore. "But what if you hurt us?"

"I'd never do that."

She pushed herself to her knees, started rolling Val off the hatch. "Okay. I'm doing it."

"Thank you. I'd never hurt you. I just want to be with you."

Molly froze. She knew those words.

"Molly. Let me in. Please. I've been in the ocean. I'm so wet, and so cold. Let me in."

"No," she whispered. "That's not you."

CHAPTER
55

We came out of the top of the stairs into a corridor. There was no mist, no rain. It was just a corridor. Cream tiles. Gray walls. Light from panels in the ceiling, flickering. Double doors at the end, the kind with horizontal metal bars. They were shut.

We walked up to them and listened. Music, and something else. A low, echoey hubbub. Hard to tell what it might be. I tried pushing one of the bars. The door was stiff. "I don't think there's any half measures here," I said. "If we open this, we're going in."

Ken answered by pushing on the other bar until the door opened, and walked straight through.

I followed. We both stopped after a few feet.

"What the hell is this?"

We were back on Birchlake's main street. That's how it felt at first, at least—as if we'd just stepped out of the Tap. After that initial impression, however, it became clear that we weren't. Or that we *were*, but...

The light was low—lit with candles, dotted everywhere. The street was thronging with people: individuals, couples, families with children. Many were carrying baskets or bags. The cloud cover was low, and looked like the roof of a huge tent. People were talking, shouting, calling out. The loudest of these cries came from people working stalls crowded in front of buildings on both sides of the street.

A place selling metal pans and earthenware pots. Another busy with livestock—and as we stood there, staring, people passed us with a live chicken or two in their bags—along with a row of strung-up rabbits, still with fur, and what looked like whole sides of pig, or boar.

Further up on the right was a huge stall selling bolts of brightly colored cloth, though everybody around us was dressed in dark and muted hues. Behind us, we discovered, wasn't the Tap—but a low, dark room where people lounged drinking coffee and dark tea from small glass cups. To one side of the room was a stall selling food—a young woman dolloping steaming spoonfuls of what looked like tagine into bowls.

"I've been somewhere like this," Ken said, as we stepped off the sidewalk and into the crowd. "Me and the wife went on holiday to Morocco years ago. It's a souk. Or…something."

He was right, on both counts. It did feel like a Middle Eastern covered market, but the longer you looked the less that made sense. It was more like the *idea* of a souk than the reality. Everybody was white. No black or brown skins—making it seem more like a medieval square on market day, somewhere in Europe. But as we made our way through the people, unsure of what to do or where to go, I realized some of what I'd thought were candles providing the glowing spots of light were actually gas lamps. And some of the light was actually coming from long, horizontal candles hung from the arcing canvas a few feet above our heads. Candles that glowed along their entire lengths, a lot like fluorescent tubes.

It was noisy. It was crowded. But. "There's no smell."

Ken frowned. Despite all the food, the animals—someone walked past us leading a goat on a length of thick twine—the crush of men, women, and children, people grilling meats on open fires...there was no smell, apart from fresh rain and a hint of pine and fir. "You're right."

A low howl came from down the street. I heard something sniggering behind me.

"Also, these...aren't people," Ken said.

I glanced back into the Tap. It was dark, full of muscular shadows. More than there had been before. Some were wearing tall hats. Others huddled together as if in secret conversation. I saw something slide out of the door, like a fat black sausage, two feet thick. Then it was gone. My mind was flickering like the spinning wheels on a slot machine, trying to find a temporary visual reference for things I knew were unpleasantly close, but unseeable.

"And none of this is real?"

"It's real," I said. "We spend half our lives in interior landscapes that can't be seen or photographed."

"Yeah. Dreams. Memories. But—"

"Something doesn't have to be visible to be real. And there's always more than one 'real' going on. We've just never been looking at this one before."

The faces in the shapes around us were changing. Even though I knew they weren't actual *faces*—a woman hurrying past with a small child looked, for a moment, remarkably like a middle school teacher who gave me endless hell, and I realized the guy working a stall selling bottles of rose-colored ale looked a *lot* like one of the baristas in the Starbucks in Santa Monica, who suddenly wasn't there one day, arrested after his girlfriend found a horrific stash of pornography on his laptop.

"Christ, Nolan—over there."

He started pushing his way into the crowd before I'd seen what he meant. Then I saw it. Up at the crossroads, where previously there'd been a fountain, stood a statue. A huge cross, in battered and weathered stone, looming over the street and looking like it had done so for a thousand years. And there, on the other side, I spotted someone trying to shove through the crowd. A flash of color among clothing that was all gray or brown or dark and murky blue. A real face, that I recognized.

Kristy.

I followed in Ken's wake, shouting her name. It was like trying to wade through a sea of molasses. Every now and then it felt as though something was paying attention to me, and that didn't feel good—the rest of it coursed around us like heavy currents, with a sense of glee, of unconfinement.

Soon I was right behind Ken, and we shoved forward together. I kept calling out, but Kristy either couldn't hear or wasn't listening. Resistance to our movement was getting stronger and stronger, the faces around us uglier. A man with both eyes sewn shut, a woman with a missing nose, a child with no lower jaw at all. No canvas awning above us any longer, just the low, dark sky, and it was raining once more, the ground turning to mud, tugging at my shoes.

"*Kristy!*" I shouted, again.

This time she heard, and stopped, and turned—and suddenly there was open space around us. "Nolan."

"Didn't you hear me?"

"I thought it wasn't you." She looked impatient,

anxious, unhappy to have been stopped from hurrying onward.

"What are you doing?"

"Him," she said, pointing up the street. "Oh no."

The street disappeared into darkness. "*Who*, Kristy?"

She was fidgeting from foot to foot, desperate to go. "The man I saw on my first night here. It had already started then and I didn't even realize."

"Who is he?"

"I don't know. That's why I have to talk to him. Dan was right."

"It's okay," I said, though I had no idea what she was talking about. "We'll help."

"You can't help. You don't know. This is all about *me*."

Ken held up his hand. "Nolan...do you hear that?"

All I could hear was the hubbub of all the "people" milling around further down the street. Though the road was clear on this side of the huge cross, it remained as crowded on the other.

Then I heard Ken's name being called.

"Ignore it," I said. "It'll be like what we heard in the parking lot. Kristy—everything will be okay. Whatever it is, we can help."

"You can't," she said. "This is from before."

I thought she meant from before we'd met. "So what? Why would that matter?"

"Because *this*," she shouted, grabbing the cross on her necklace and holding it up. "Because *that*." She jabbed a finger at the huge, crumbling cross at the crossroads.

Another shout from the other side. My name this time—loud. Ken took a few steps back down the street.

"Nolan, that sounds like it's really them."

Kristy looked desperate, very young, like someone I

hadn't met yet. "Nolan, this is nothing to do with you, so just leave me alone. It's nowhere out there." She stabbed a finger at her forehead. "It's only in here."

Someone shouted my name again. "Nolan," Ken said, "that's definitely Moll."

"It can't be."

"It is," Ken said. "She's down there."

"Go," Kristy told me. "Help her, Nolan."

"We are *not* splitting up again."

The noise from the other end of the street was getting louder and louder, less like the hubbub of people going about their business, and more like a mob. Shouts, chanting, harsh laughter.

Then my name, and Ken's, shouted together. But this time a scream. "Kristy," I shouted, "come with—"

But she was gone. She ran, taking advantage of my momentary inattention. I could hear footsteps running fast off down the side street. Off on her own.

Another scream from down the street. *"Ken!"*

Ken has faults. He'd be the first to admit this and happy to start listing them. Lack of loyalty isn't one, however. "It's up to you, mate," he said, as he started trotting back toward the crossroads. "But Moll's in trouble."

I went after him.

The statue of the cross now had fountains around it again. The crowds were thicker still—and whereas they'd been shapes in passing before, people going about their business, they were far more boisterous now. Leers and cruel smiles, a sense of hectic cheer, as if a dark and exciting game had been announced. It felt much as I imagine it would have felt five hundred years ago, in a crowd that had been promised a public hanging. Or the burning of a witch.

Ken went charging into them like a sheriff trying to break up a bar fight. "Out the way, you demon arseholes."

That backfired quickly. The "people" around us changed from feeling as if they were anticipating something to seeming like they'd decided it had already arrived. In the shape of me and Ken.

Faces turned our way. Most of the lights in the roof—which now looked even more like fluorescent lights—blinked off. We were jostled, pushed toward the side of the road.

"Christ," Ken said, swatting at something. A child. It was throwing itself at him, and with the press of bodies around us, very hard to push away. "Look, bugger *off*."

It looked up at him—at us—and smiled broadly. Its face was moon-shaped and pale and its mouth was full of sharp gray teeth. It grabbed hold of Ken with both hands, its fingers far too long.

"It's not a kid, Ken," I shouted, as I grabbed it around the throat and shook it. The other things around us responded as though I *had* grabbed hold of a child, however. Something large and hard banged into me from behind, shoving me up against Ken. The smaller thing let go of him and started trying to bite me instead.

Ken punched it hard in the temple. It made no difference. It was like having a four-foot piranha with legs trying to take a chunk out of you.

There was chanting all around us now. Very loud, in a complex rhythm, or two at once. One that was heavy, slow—the other lighter, faster, like a melody line. And something was coming toward us through the crowd. It was making a different kind of noise.

Two notes together, harsh, like screaming.

I managed to throw the smaller thing back and grabbed Ken's shoulder, trying to pull him away with me. I had no idea where to go, no clue what might constitute shelter in this situation. Possibly nowhere, but *anywhere* had to be better than being confronted with whatever was making the sound that was getting closer and closer.

The bodies around us were elongating, changing. Some "people" growing taller. Others wider. Heads staying the same size on bodies that were grossly distorting. Ken and I were now face-to-face, shoved up against each other.

"Ken, we've got to get out of this."

"I know, mate."

I twisted my head around, trying to tune out the screaming noise, looking for something—anything—that might help. It felt increasingly unlikely we'd be able to get out from under the things pressing in all around, starting to loom over us. I was starting to panic. It was like claustrophobia but worse—hemmed in and crushed by a darkness that had *things* in it. I felt something biting at my hand but couldn't look down to see what it was...so I just slammed my knee into it as hard as I could. It was getting hotter, too, partly from the press of bodies—but I could also smell smoke.

I felt my hair being tugged from behind—really hard, like something was trying to pull my head off. *"Nolan."*

Molly's voice.

"Is that you? Really?" I twisted my head an inch— all I could manage—and caught a glimpse of her blond hair. And behind her, someone with shorter gray hair. Val. "Ken," I shouted. "Grab hold of me."

"I can't move my arms, mate."

"Do it. And you two—form a circle, heads together."

It took a few seconds to shove and elbow the swarming

things aside, but then it was done—and for a moment the crush around us felt a bit less tight. "Back up," Val shouted, leaning into me. "I'll push—Molly, you too."

"Why?"

"Just *do it*."

I braced myself and pushed backward. I could feel Ken doing the same. Meanwhile Molly and Val shoved us from the front. The momentary advantage from being together started to fade, and I could feel panic beginning to rise quickly again. Not just in me. In all of us. The things knew it, too, and started chanting louder.

But we kept slowly moving backward, in a growing cacophony of noise—it seemed like it was getting darker and darker, at least on the sides. Then I realized we'd been retreating into a recessed doorway.

"Now," Val shouted—and she and Molly shoved us.

There was a moment of resistance and then something opened behind our backs.

Ken and I went sprawling. Val tumbled forward too, but Molly kept her feet and turned to slam the door shut.

It was quiet. None of the things were in there. It smelled of dust and was half full of rocks. As Ken and I got to our feet, I realized where we were. The former department store. It didn't look like something out of a souk or market. It looked exactly as it had the night before, when Ken, Kristy, and I broke in.

Outside, shapes were still crowded up against the window and the door. "Why aren't they coming in?"

"We're not really here," I reminded him.

"Whatever, Nolan."

Val pointed at the rocks. "Fragments of the original wall. Tiny sections I've managed to put back together, as they should be, or as best I can, from Sister von Tessen's notes. It's weak, and it's not really here, of course, but the fact I know it exists is holding them away for now."

"Rebuilding that wall may have been a mistake," I said.

"Oh," Val said, angrily. "Why?"

"Because you've built a *new wall*, effectively. And I doubt you have any understanding of how the shape of it affected things here in town."

"What do you mean?"

"Kristy heard or felt something happening down here before Alaina even came back. What if that's when it started? What if the shape you made here was a *door*?"

Val blinked at me. "I..."

"Whatever," Ken said. "I'm glad you did. It saved us."

"No it hasn't," I said. "Or not for long. What was the last thing you remember, Molly, before you found yourself here?"

She frowned, trying to recall. "Val slumped over. I was sitting on the hatch to the cellar, because..." Her face fell. "Oh God. Pierre was trying to get in."

"Right," I said. "Now we're *here*, and all that's left *there* is five unconscious bodies. With no one to stop him."

CHAPTER
56

Principal Broecker was sitting in the living room of his house. He was alone.

Ryder was in his room. The days when he'd regularly stay downstairs after dinner were long gone—though he'd linger an hour or two, once in a while. Dan knew there was likely a hidden reason on those occasions, that those nights weren't entirely random and their child was feeling uncertain about something, or insecure, or simply young. Dan had the sense not to ask. When a fourteen-year-old wants parental company you just let them have it, rather than risk scaring them away.

It was barely nine o'clock, but his wife was already in bed. Usually she stayed up as late as he did, reading by the fire. Tonight she'd abruptly said she was tired and gone ahead, as though at a level below the conscious she'd decided to retreat from the world, turn her back.

Dan felt very awake. Some of this was a churning feeling of guilt. Partly for being short with Kristy Reardon in their conversation. He knew that had come about because of a far larger guilt, also, concerning Alaina Hixon.

He'd heard the rumors. Of course. Though parents often treat a principal like a policeman, becoming circumspect in behavior and speech in the fear that they will be judged, others are different. Especially older residents, those whose families had been there for generations. They understand that the teacher is one of the archetypal building blocks of a town. Teacher, preacher, doctor, lawman—the pillars that make a place real, as structuring as a church or main street. If one of those people is new in town, the elders will sometimes let things slip. To inform, to bring them up to speed.

And so he'd heard it suggested that Alaina's mother killed herself, and that depression and years of drinking had not been the only cause. That she had spent years performing her secret role, the fifth essential pillar of community, the one that's seldom acknowledged out loud—because nobody believes in that stuff anymore. Or so we claim. In the end it burned her out. As, he'd further heard it implied (by Bob Maskill, who owned the motel on the edge of town), the mantle had also eventually consumed Alaina's grandmother, though she'd at least made it into her seventies before suffering a massive stroke. On a night long ago.

A night like this.

And so Dan's decision to cover witchcraft in his elective—after Alaina had signed on—had not been an accident. He'd hoped it might help, provide a way of showing her that her family's tendency had a place in history, and a venerable one—whether it was real or not. Back then he'd been convinced it wasn't real. He was far from sure of that tonight. Perhaps it didn't even have to be one or the other. He'd long ago learned the concept of polysemy, the observation that words and phrases could mean more than one thing. That they often meant several things at the same time, in layers of simultaneous and coexistent meaning.

"Dad?"

Dan looked up. Ryder was standing in the doorway. For a moment Dan saw a six-year-old, awake in the night, needing to be walked upstairs and coaxed back to sleep, a child who cared a very great deal about dinosaurs and wanted to tell his father all about them, all the time, even if that father was busy or tired. But Dan also saw the gangling young man who already understood computers and phones far better than he ever would. And he realized: reality is polysemic, too.

"What is it?"

"Maddy. And Nadja."

"Are they okay?"

"I think so. But...they're really freaked out. And their parents aren't home."

Dan considered saying something bland and going upstairs, putting in earplugs, getting in bed beside his wife and pretending nothing was happening.

But it was too late for that. "Okay," he said.

He got his coat from the rack. Not because he was sure he could do anything, or that it would be safe for him to even try. But because when children are scared, that's what grown-ups do. You try to help.

Otherwise there's already no point to you.

He managed to convince Ryder to stay at home. To be there for his mother, in case she woke.

He drove through town along dark, rainy streets, keeping his eyes firmly on the road. There were noises in the sky, and not all of the shadows seemed to be behaving as they should. He ignored them and the sense that things were tracking his progress, loping alongside in the mist. Especially ignoring the strong impression that something was riding on the roof of the car.

He parked in front of the Hardaker house and knocked on the front door. It opened almost immediately.

Maddy and Nadja stood just inside, tall shadows in candlelight. Dan felt a beat of disquiet. Not just because of what was going on tonight—but because the young often instill that feeling in their elders. The next thing coming down the road of history, the one that will eventually sideline you into old age and irrelevance. That sense teenagers have of being unknowable, untamed, of coming from some other place and not being susceptible to control.

"We're scared," Maddy said, however.

"We don't know what to do to stop this," Nadja added. Again Dan saw a version of what he'd seen in his own home. This time, a pair of ten-year-olds wearing grown-up bodies. "You have to do something."

"I don't think I can."

"But you *have* to."

"I'm a dusty old book, Nadja. Neither of you believe I'm actually real, do you, or that any grown-up is. You may even be right."

"But we have to do *something*. Or she's going to hurt people."

"I know. Come with me."

"Where?"

"To find Alaina."

"But *then* what?"

"Then you talk to her," he said. "She's not going to listen to anything I say. It's you she needs."

"She does *not*. She hates us."

"No, she doesn't."

"But what can we do?"

"You have to pull her back. Or else go onward with her."

"What? But why?"

"Because you're her friends. And nobody can do life by themselves."

CHAPTER
57

"What are we going to do?"

"We've got to get back to Olsen's," Ken said.

He looked at Val for confirmation, but she shook her head. "We're all still *in* Olsen's, physically," she said. "I don't see how you can travel to somewhere if you're already *there*."

"You know, for an alleged expert on witches and demons and stuff, you've been surprisingly little help."

The crowds outside were buffeting harder against the windows. It didn't feel like it would be long before something broke. The sad scrap of wall in here could be all that was keeping the exterior of the building—or at least the panes of glass—intact. The walls of this building weren't even real—just the lingering defenses we still had up in our minds against the things outside. The more Ken hassled Val, the weaker those defenses would become.

"She's doing everything she can, Ken."

"We don't know this stuff *works* anymore," Val shouted. She was pissed, and scared. Ken was being more in-your-face than usual—because he was also pretty scared. The knowledge that we were all lying on a floor unconscious and unprotected was hard to take calmly. "Most of us assumed the whole flying demons deal was a metaphor. Or at least that you'd be able to see them, and fight properly. Not that you'd wind up lost in your head and unable to get out."

"Stop talking," I said. "Please."

Val glared at me. *"Seriously?"*

"He means 'let me think,' love," Ken snapped. "And we should. We need out-of-the-box thinking right now, and Nolan's brain is further outside the box than most."

"It actually kind of is," Moll said.

Something in what I'd last thought, and something in what Val had last said, were trying to make sense together in my brain, like two strangers in a bar glancing each other's way. There was a crawling sensation along the back of my neck that was making it hard to think, however, and a faint but acrid smell—that, and the three people urgently waiting for me to say something, along with the sound of things thumping around on the tiles of the roof above.

Except...there was no roof above. Or not an external one, anyway. There was the apartment Kristy had stayed in. If I was hearing something on a roof, it was the roof of Olsen's.

And with that realization came a moment of near clarity.

"Moll, Val," I said. "First, we need to check this place is secure. Ken and I broke in here last night. Let's make sure nothing can get in the back door."

"Christ," Moll said. "Good point." She and Val headed quickly into the corridor.

"Nolan," Ken said, "even if it's locked, in our heads or whatever, it's not going to work against—"

"I know," I said, quickly. "I just didn't want them to try to follow me. And you're not going to, either."

"Follow you where?"

"Val said we're stuck in our own minds. But that's not right. At least not *individual* minds. The four of us are in the same place right now. It's a *shared* place."

"Okay, but so?"

"It's *not* just ours. There's stuff we're seeing that's nothing to do with us, and that means it's coming from somewhere else. Or *someone*. I'm beginning to think Kristy was right about what she said out there. I'm going after her."

"You have no clue where she is, mate."

"I know."

"And the town is crammed with demons."

"I'm aware of that also."

"So what exactly are you going to do?"

"No idea."

"Excellent. Knew you'd have a coherent plan."

I heard Molly and Val trying the door at the back and knew I didn't have much time. "Ken…"

"If you're not back in fifteen minutes…"

I reached for the handle on the door. "Stay *here*."

"Bugger that, Nolan. Do what you can—and do it fast, or I'm coming after you. And don't die out there, because that would just be annoying."

I opened the door, slipped outside. Then realized everything had changed.

The market stalls were gone, along with everything else. No people. No animals. Just a wide, open concourse. Tiled, dirty. On the other side of the street, vacant storefronts with big, grimy windows. A ceiling a few feet above my head. Most of the lights in it were broken. The space was murky, cold, and very unwelcoming. Tendrils of mist clung to the shadow spaces, moving as though they had muscles and bones.

I turned back to the door and found it barred. It had once been a clothing store, glass across the whole front-age, now painted over. A big red sign saying GOING OUT OF BUSINESS SALE. I grabbed the handles, shook hard. They wouldn't open. Rapped on the glass. No response from inside. I was on my own now.

As I headed out into the street it became more clear what this place was. An abandoned mall. The large cross was still there, but no longer made of stone. Now it looked more like a piece of civic art, fashioned from twisted, rusting iron. It stood in an ornamental pool with small fountains evenly spaced around it. The pool was dry.

The mist was thicker on the other side. The street con-tinued to look like a concourse, with side arms branching out. The first of these on the left was about the same position as the street Kristy had run away down. Did that mean she'd still be along there somewhere?

I ran up to it and looked. More abandoned storefronts. The mist was thick along there. There was something else about it that made me hesitate to enter, but I couldn't figure out what.

"Nolan."

A man's voice.

I turned. Nobody there. Not close to me, anyway. On the other side of the fountain, way down the street, I could see people again now. They weren't heading my way. They didn't even seem aware of me. They were wandering slowly around the concourse, shambling.

"I don't want to do this."

The same voice, and now I recognized it. It was

muffled, fuzzy, and coming from the side road I'd been looking down before. "Pierre?"

"I don't want to hurt anybody," he said. "Let me in, Nolan. Let's talk."

Mist was starting to seep out into the main concourse now—pooling so thickly down the side road itself that it was almost black.

Except...*maybe it wasn't mist.*

From the way I wanted to back away from it, even run—and from a tickle in the back of my throat—I was beginning to wonder if my brain already *knew* it was something else, the central deep mind that didn't care what reality looked like but understood it had only one important job to do. Protecting the body that held it.

"Okay, Pierre," I said. "Let's talk."

I walked into the mist and within a few yards my eyes began to sting. I started to cough. I felt my arms twitching, and legs too—as if trying to push away from something. A sudden, visceral fear.

And then I blinked and found myself lying propped up in the storage room in Olsen's.

Something was thumping against the floor, from beneath.

And the place was on fire.

CHAPTER
58

Those two impressions came straight at me—rapidly followed by awareness of the fact that Ken was propped up alongside me, Molly and Val sprawled out in front, Kristy out in the corridor, like a bizarre slumber party.

The transition was instantaneous, with an abruptness that might have made a lesser man pause. Okay, to be fair, I sat blinking for a few seconds, my mind literally *hurting*, before locking in.

More thumping from the floor increased my focus—and there was enough light coming in from the small, high window to see Molly's body was bouncing up and down as the hatch underneath her took heavy impacts from the other side.

I crawled over. "Pierre?"

"Nolan," he said. "Seriously. Just let me in."

"I don't think I'm going to do that."

"Why?"

"To be honest—you're sounding kind of weird."

His voice had an odd doubled quality. The fuzziness I'd heard came from the fact it sounded as if two voices were overlaid, one at least a tone higher than the other.

"I set a fire," he said, and this time it was even more

clear. The higher voice was a little slower, finishing the word *fire* a beat after the one that sounded more like him. "It's not big yet. But it will be. It will burn this place to the ground."

The light coming through that window wasn't moonlight, I realized. "You set a fire *in the cellar*? Where you *are*?"

"No, out front. I'm not *dumb*, Nolan. I know you all think I am. But I'm *not*."

"We don't think you are," I said. "You're . . . a hugely valued member of the team. You know that."

"Without me," the voice said, and this time the higher tone was clearly dominant, "he wouldn't have noticed that you avoided the question. But I'm in him now, so he does. Let me in."

"Pierre—why do you want to get in here? Do you know?"

"To kill you."

"Well, exactly. That was my fear. Though you did say before that you didn't want to hurt anyone."

"I don't," Pierre said, suddenly sounding miserable, in the lower tone. "But I'm not just me anymore. And the thing inside wants to hurt you all very much."

"Why?"

"It's what it does."

"Can I talk to it?"

"It hears."

"Listen," I said. I could smell smoke more strongly now. "I genuinely don't think Pierre's dumb. Not to mention that he's saved my life in the past and is one of the bravest and most good-hearted people I've ever met. So fuck you, demon. How about you stop making him do things he doesn't want to—and get out of him and leave him alone?"

Pierre's throat laughed, but it wasn't him. It was a bad, high-pitched laugh—the kind of laugh bad people make before doing very bad things. "I like it in here. It is wet and warm. Let us in."

"I'm really not going to do that."

A barrage of thumps—as he/it/they tried once more to force their way up through the hatch. Then it stopped, just as suddenly.

"If you don't," the voice said. "I'll hurt him."

"No you won't. You just said you like it in there."

"Listen."

A hard thump against the underside of the hatch. A pause, then another. And one more.

"Okay, so what?"

"That wasn't his fists," the voice said. "It was his head."

"Pierre," I shouted. "Are you okay?"

"I don't know." Pierre's real voice, but slurred and vague. "Maybe."

Something went skittering by in the corridor, trailing laughter. Creaks came from the walls, building in intensity, the kind of noises it might make if being gently squeezed in a giant fist. I realized that though the thing in the cellar wanted to come up here and get at us on its own account, it was working in concert with others. Keeping me occupied while they renewed their attack.

A loud thud from the underside of the hatch.

"He's bleeding from his head now," the voice said. It was sounding less and less like Pierre, and less like a sound, too. I was understanding what it meant, but not through words. "A lot. And don't forget the fire."

If you have your people, they're your people. You don't throw anybody off the boat—especially if it's not their fault—unless or until there's no other option.

I rolled Val off the hatch and pushed Molly off the other, while keeping my weight on it. The effort, and the smoke, made me cough my guts out, and I had to wait a moment before I could speak. "Can you hear what I'm doing?"

"Moving bodies."

"A gesture of good faith. So now how about you go put out the fire, then I'll let you in, and we can talk."

"There is no good faith. Only different color lies."

"I don't have time to master demon rhetoric. The smoke is very thick in here now. I have no idea what you have in mind, but I'm assuming that it's not getting in here to find five people already dead of asphyxiation."

Not all of the thickness in the atmosphere was smoke. There were things already inside the building, and I knew from being buffeted by them in the marketplace that they could interact physically. Unless it'd only felt that way because I was in a space conjured to deal with their nature, and out here they needed to be inside someone. I didn't have time to work that out.

I could feel my mind failing to cope, becoming confused, sliding sideways under the weight of the things in the building—the ones running along the floor like invisible rats, lurking in corners like dangerous chairs.

"It's up to you," I said. "Put out the fire or you're not coming in. I'll open the door when you've done it."

"If you do not, I will tear Pierre's skin off his face with his own hands."

"Just *put out the fucking fire*."

A pause. Then I heard Pierre letting go of the metal ladder and heading toward the exit to the cellar. Soon as I heard his feet heading upward on that, I rolled Val and Molly back onto the hatch and added Ken for good measure.

I went into the corridor, stepping over Kristy. Her face was pale and her eyelids were twitching fast. It seemed like whatever she was into inside her mind was a lot worse than the others, and given what was happening to them, that didn't seem like good news at all.

The smoke was thicker out here. There were faces in the floor and walls. My head was pounding. I staggered through the restaurant to the door. Yanked at one of the planks nailed across the glass, getting a hand full of splinters in the process.

I couldn't move it far, but enough to see through the gap that Pierre was out there robotically stamping on something. He looked like a puppet being worked on strings.

My stomach was cramping. Smoke or fear. Couldn't tell, didn't matter—the effect was the same and it needed to stop. Even if Pierre/the thing truly put out the fire, the smoke wasn't going to disappear immediately, and without fresh air in here very soon we were all going to die.

I kicked at the lock on the door. Kicked at it again. The third blow started the damp, semi-rotten frame splintering, but it was still pretty solid.

I leaned to the side to give vent to another gut-wrenching bout of coughing. By the time I'd finished there were stars in my eyes. "Pierre," I shouted. It was more of a rasp. "You're going to have to help."

There was a near-immediate crash from the other side of the door. Then another. The frame splintered. I wondered why the thing inside Pierre hadn't thought to try this before, instead of coming in through the cellar. Maybe demons just aren't that smart. Or maybe it was hard for them to break through walls. Any kind of walls. Maybe they needed human help. Maybe that was how all this started.

Another kick. It was close to breaking now. There was something I had to try first. "Hey Pierre," I said. The sparkling in my eyes wasn't from the coughing anymore. I was close to sliding over again, close to blowing out.

A couple of the planks broke, and the glass shattered. Crash—the door flew open. Pierre stood outside. His upper lip and chin were covered in blood. There was a deep gash across his forehead. "What?"

"Remember rowing down the Grand Canyon?"

I took a step toward him. My legs felt wobbly and insecure. My vision was cutting in and out, either because of the things all around in the building, or the specific one now only a yard from me, inside my friend.

Pierre's eyes were cloudy. "Of course. What about it?"

"Just checking. That was pretty cool."

I had no idea if my idea was going to work. It was all I had. I grabbed a shard of glass from the floor. "Remember that river. Picture it in your head."

The other voice from Pierre's mouth, or in my mind. "What are you doing?"

"Just talking. To Pierre. Nothing to do with you."

I put my arms around Pierre's shoulders and pulled him close, pressing my forehead against his. "You and me, Pierre, and Molly and Ken. We're a team. Right?"

"Help me," he whispered.

"Come with me," I said. "Let's go find them."

CHAPTER
59

Then we were in the main street of Birchlake. We arrived in the echo of an enraged howl. Pierre pushed back from me, looking very confused. "What's *happening*?"

It was still grimy, stores closed, and mistier and darker. A few of the streetlights were working, but flickered badly, like strobes. There were a lot more people wandering around on the other side of the crossroads now.

I could feel something sharp against my fingers. I focused on it. Kept the sensation in the front of my mind.

"Hurry," I said. I didn't like the look of the crowd.

Pierre was bewildered. "Hurry where? Where *are* we?"

"Your body's where it was. In Olsen's. And there's likely something still inside you there. But for now, you, the real *Pierre*, is here with me."

"What?"

"Just go with it." I walked fast down the street to the fountain. The huge cross was still in place, less rusty than before. The pool was full of stagnant water, and sickly looking liquid was leaking from the fountains. There were long splashes and smears of blood on the tiled road.

The closer we got, the easier it became to hear low moaning sounds from the figures crowding into the next section of the street. Men, women, children. Shambling around, not looking at each other. Staggering as if in search of food.

"Nolan...what the hell are those people?"

"Did you ever see Ken's movie *The Undying Dead*?"

"No," Pierre said. "He says it's crap."

"It's actually not. I mean sure, it's a total rip-off of *Dawn of the Dead*, but it has its moments. I finally got around to watching it a couple weeks ago. And basically that's where we are."

"We're *inside Ken's head*?"

"No, thank God. But because I left, I think everything skewed more toward how he sees things. A mall. Danger. And so now zombies."

"I don't get it."

"It doesn't matter." As we got around the fountain area there was a discernable change in the atmosphere. One by one, the things lurching around the other side seemed to sense that something unlike them had entered the area.

Heads were raised, sluggishly. A child on the left turned in our direction. How this felt in my head made me confident I was seeing another interpretation of the demon that had been trying to bite Ken and me before I left.

I focused on my right hand. Didn't look down at it, because I knew I wouldn't see anything but my fingers—and this would deflate the sense of a realer world. I tightened my hand. It hurt, but that was good.

"Uh, Nolan..."

Pierre nodded toward the child. Its mouth was hanging open slackly now. Both eyes were dripping. It was slowly raising a hand to point at us.

"Shit." I realized that it wasn't a wholly good thing that the figures were clustering on the right side of the street. They were at their thickest right outside the store where I'd left Molly, Val, and Ken. "Pierre, we need to get on this fast."

The child was pointing directly at us now. More of the shambling, rotting figures were arriving, too—out of the darkness down the concourse/road. They were starting to cluster, to arrive in far greater numbers.

They knew we were here, and they were hungry.

For the moment, apart from the child, they still didn't seem to have a clear fix on us. I led Pierre quickly toward the storefronts on the right.

"We need to stay...very, very quiet," I said.

At that moment the door to the store smashed open and Ken came barreling out, waving a wooden chair and shouting.

Really loudly.

Ken skidded to a halt, holding the chair like a baseball bat. Molly and Val were right behind, also holding makeshift weapons. Every head in the street turned to look. They looked like something out of a 1980s movie poster.

"Whoops," Ken said.

Mouths were dropping open all around us. Feet shuffled as the figures turned in his direction.

"For fuck's sake, Ken," I said. "I told you to *stay inside*."

He saw me, grinned. "And I told *you* fifteen minutes, mate. Alright, Pierre? Stopped being weird yet?"

"Come toward us," I said. "Quietly. And *do not* make any more sudden moves."

Ken sized up the situation and elected to sidle along the front of the buildings rather than cut straight toward us through the things thronging the street. They were starting to move in a more concerted fashion now. Most toward Ken, a few toward Pierre and me. It was clear we didn't have much time.

I focused on my hand again—though by now it was beginning to really hurt. The child started to moan. Quietly at first, but getting louder, still pointing.

Ken carefully moved to a position where he was about a yard out from the storefront and gestured to Molly to slip behind him. "You too, Val," he said.

"God you're a sexist asshole," she said.

"You want to be in front, be my guest," Ken said. "But bear in mind they'll also come from the side, and maybe *behind*. Which is why I thought it'd be a good thing if you're there. And if they do, don't screw it up."

"Shh," I said. "Just *move*."

They started to sidle along the wall toward us. Heads turned jerkily to follow their progress. Molly coughed, tried to stifle it. When Ken glanced toward me to gauge how much farther there was to come, I saw his eyes were red.

The kid stopped moaning. But then started to scream. This worked like a siren for the others. They started to move, to close in on Pierre, who was still standing there, confused, blood dripping down his face.

"Pierre, step *back*."

Val was coughing too now, unable to hold it back. Molly joined her, collapsing against the wall. Ken was managing to hold it in, but barely.

"Okay," I said. "This isn't working. Change of plan. Ken—come here. Just you. Now. Do it fast."

"Nolan..."

"Trust me."

He hesitated, but then swung out at the nearest figures with the chair, swacking several across their heads. This created enough of an opening that he could crouch down and drive into them, fast.

I tensed my fingers. Coughed. It hurt, but I knew why and what it was, and so it might help.

Ken was within a few feet of me now. Molly and Val were coughing ceaselessly. Pierre was surrounded by the figures, in a circle, staring silently at him, jostling, crowding him. His eyes were watering and he looked very scared. I wondered why they were paying more attention to him than the others, and then remembered—he still had something else inside. One of them.

"Alright, now what?" Ken said, as he reached me. The figures around us were reaching out for us now, a sea of arms, waves in danger of rolling over us.

Just at that moment Pierre stopped looking afraid, and slowly smiled. He started pushing through the other figures toward Molly and Val.

"Molly," I shouted, "get Val back in that building and stay there. *Forever.* Okay?"

"But what about Pierre?"

"He's being controlled by the thing inside him again. *Leave him outside.*"

She nodded, still coughing horribly, and started to retreat. I looked Ken in the eyes, tightened my fingers and felt the pain of the shard of glass still in them—and then jabbed it forward into his thigh.

"What the *fuck* are you . . ."

Flat on my back. Eyes stinging. A weight across me. For a moment I thought it would be Ken, but of course it wasn't.

I threw the shard of glass away. I rolled, shoving Pierre's unconscious body off me. Put my hand over my nose and mouth. The smoke was very, very thick. The thing that had been inside Pierre hadn't put it out properly. Of course.

This wasn't residual smoke. The fire was still burning.

I heard a hacking cough from further inside the building. Hauled myself upright and stumbled into the corridor.

Ken had made it out of the storage room, coughing badly. "That really hurt," he said. "You berk." His leg was bleeding, but not too badly.

"Best idea I could think of."

"Think a lot harder next time."

He took Kristy's feet and I got my arms under her shoulders. We got her outside the building and into the mist and drizzle. Then did the same with Molly, and finally Val. The fire had grown enough to be blackening the front of the bar. Part of me wondered whether it would be better to let the place burn down, but it wasn't the building's fault and that wasn't my decision to make.

I kicked the fire, spreading the burning parts, stamping on them. Ken helped. But then held up a hand. "Something's coming."

"Christ, seriously?"

We retreated to where we'd laid Kristy, Molly, and Val. I was light-headed from the smoke, and my lungs and guts hurt. My hand was bleeding freely. I felt very, very tired. I honestly didn't know how much fight I had left.

A glow was coming down the road, sparkling out in the drizzled mist. Two glows, in fact. Sallow yellow eyes. The eyes were pretty big.

"What are we going to do?"

"We can't run, mate. Or I can't. So I think we're going to have to fight."

It kept coming toward us, bringing a wet, slick sound.

I couldn't imagine what would make a noise like that. It seemed impossible that it could be anything good. "Fight with what?"

"Fire?"

"We put the fire out."

"Oh. So we did."

Then slowly the noise resolved. My mind had spent so long trying to make sense of the unknowable that something more prosaic had thrown it for a temporary loop.

It was the sound of tires on a wet road. And the yellow eyes were headlamps.

A truck. It braked rapidly, pulling to the side of the road. Bryan Hixon jumped out. "Is she in there?"

"Who?"

"Alaina," he said. "I smelled the smoke from the house. *Is my daughter in that building?*"

"Why on earth would we have left someone in there?"

"Because people *do*," he shouted. He looked like he hadn't slept in days. "Sure, they'll tolerate them when they need them. But then they *forget*. And then they *burn them*."

"Nobody set fire to your wife."

"Yeah they did." Hixon got right up in my face. "Not literally. You're not allowed to *do* that anymore, right? But you can whisper. Behind their backs. Treat them like they've a disease. Like there's something not right about them. Better not have that woman or her child over for playdates. Or do more than quickly say hi in the street and then move on. Because we all know they do a job, but there's something weird about them, and nobody wants to get contaminated. *Right?*"

"Did you know what you were getting into? When you married her?"

"Of course I did, you asshole. But I *loved* her. And this town killed her. They're not killing my daughter."

"You can't protect her from what she is."

"There is nobody here who gives a damn about her, except me. They'll use her when they need her. The rest of the time, nobody cares."

"You're wrong," I said. "Val is in town specifically to protect your daughter."

"Great," he snarled. He pointed at Val's unconscious body. "So how's that going?"

"Not well," I admitted. "But you should know that it seems like Alaina started this whole thing. Over a man she had a crush on."

"Because she's a *teenager*," Hixon said. "Which is why she needs *protecting*."

"She does," I said. "But not just by you. It can't just be you. It's a time of big emotions, big mistakes. When kids do things that..." I faded off. "Shit."

"What?" Ken asked.

"We have to find Kristy," I said, finally understanding what was going on. "And Bryan, you're just going to have to trust we're on your side."

CHAPTER
60

laina stood in the rain looking through the window of Gina's house. They were inside. The teacher and her husband. Sitting on the couch together. But not close. Gina's hair was wet and she'd been wrapped in a blanket. She was staring down at her hands as they twisted in her lap, over and over each other, like unhappy animals. He was sitting in silence. She was saying something. She was saying a lot of things. You could see the tears rolling down her cheeks, and Alaina felt terrible.

Gina looked up tentatively, after a few minutes, toward her husband. Saw Alaina outside. Her eyes opened wide. Alaina made a knocking sign with her hand, and headed for the front door.

But when it opened, it wasn't Gina. Derek seemed very calm. "What do you want?"

"Has she told you?"

"We are talking right now. About something that's none of your business."

"Not my *business*?"

Derek smiled faintly. "That's how it seems to me. Or were you sleeping with him, too? If so, that's something

the cops need to know. That'd be serious jail time for
Kurt, and trust me—right now, I'm here for that."

"No, I was *not*."

Derek smiled. Alaina could see the remnants of shock
in his eyes, and that he was trying to be nice. "I have to
go back inside now. My wife needs to talk."

"And you're going to listen? After what she did?"

"Gina makes my life worthwhile, Alaina. She makes
these walls a home. If anybody is at fault here, it's me,
for forgetting to remind her every day that's not all she
is. For hoping that coasting along would be enough. And
that's all you're getting from me right now. You have no
place in this conversation."

"I have to say sorry. I didn't mean . . . I didn't want this
to happen. I was trying to get at him. I just wanted to
mess him up. I *have* to talk to her."

"You really don't. You can't bust your way into other
people's lives. You have to build one. Out of real stuff.
Otherwise it's all just make-believe."

"I can make you regret talking to me like that. I have
power you don't understand."

Derek nodded, but not in agreement. "I'm sure you
will, one day. Not yet. I know your world is very
real to you, Alaina. But to be honest—I can barely
see you."

He gently closed the door.

Kristy was lost.

More lost than ever in her life. She'd run after where
she thought the man had gone, run so far and so fast
that she had no running left. For a long part of it she
had run down streets with houses. Then along dirt tracks
with shacks.

Now she stumbled, all out of running, around a large open space.

It felt like an island.

The river winding around it. Forest along the other side. Trees here too, but smaller, and more widely spread. Brush, small bushes. A path through the center. Not wide, not obvious. Only used at certain times of year, as part of a tribe's seasonal wanderings. They had fished here, off the bluff that now formed one side of the park where Kristy talked with the principal on her first day, and also from the one that now formed the boundary of the motel parking lot. They ate their catch in the clearing at the center, under the stars, around fires, they talked long into the night. They stayed a few days and moved on.

But before they left, they did something else.

None of them knew why the walls existed. They only knew they were here, as they were in the woods for miles and miles around, and had been for all time. They were part of the world. The shapes meant nothing to them. Like the bend of the river that formed this place a million years before, like the form of the clouds that changed moment by moment, like the sounds and voices you heard sometimes deep in the woods, they simply were what they were.

And if something is, you respect it.

So before they moved on, higher into the mountains on their way to other spots they had always visited, on the long walk through winter in search of spring, they would tend the walls. Put back any stones that animals or the weather or people with less respect had dislodged. For hundreds, thousands of years they had done this. It was part of the ritual of being in this place. They did it because you do.

That short section, over there. The one that Kristy noticed when she arrived at the park to talk to Dan.

A longer, lower portion. Nobody now remembered that it had been incorporated unchanged into the foundations for the liquor store, and had been made safe that way, because people are always going to need beer and potato chips.

But then that bigger one, right in the center of the clearing at the middle of this semi-island.

Kristy wound up in front of this wall, trying to figure out where it would be now. She couldn't remember, couldn't think straight. All of us want to be alone sometimes, but being truly alone is a precarious state. Dangerous. It takes you out of the shared place. It throws you back on your own understanding, into your own lonely house. Your own memories. Your own self.

The things only you know.

A wind was building in the forest. Shifting the leaves, branches, whole trees. There was music in it, of course, that same old song.

Talking, too. A feeling of old recognition. A reality, a thing, that had been real and had very real consequences, that she alone knew. That she had revisited ten thousand times down the years, walking along a faint path only she could find, to that event, to a moment with a population of one.

She sat down by the wall. Closed her eyes and let the sounds build up around her. Conversation. Falling water.

The echoes of a fight.

Alaina meanwhile stood in the here and now, at the top of the main street, looking at the buildings and houses she'd known all her life. When she was small, her mom walked

her down this street many times. They left their house.
Walked past Olsen's, situated carefully outside town: the
spot where their family first lived, Alaina was told, before
her grandfather built the bigger house, selling the land to
a guy from out of town who'd built the bar—not realizing
the whole reason they wanted to move was the scraps of
things from the other side smeared inside it.

They'd walked down through town. Her mother would
nod to people, and some would say hi. They'd pick up
groceries and other things they needed. Get a sandwich
and soda at the place that was now a hipster coffee shop.
And wind up for at least a couple hours in the place that
four years ago was renamed the Stone Mountain Tap.

Alaina's memories of it were all warm, up until that last
time. In the Tap, her mother seemed to relax. She'd talk
more, get a little wild. The people in there seemed to treat
her differently, too. Others in Birchlake would usually be
reserved with Jenny Hixon, as if they didn't want to get
too close, or appear *too* friendly—and Alaina's mother
would mutter about that sometimes, saying sure, they're
that way now, but you watch, my girl, there will be nights
when they'll turn up at our door and they'll be plenty
polite then, you bet, and nervous, and bring gifts, because
they want something from us that no one else can give.

Although you never get any thanks.

But in the bar the lights would be low and cozy and
people would smile at them and bring snacks, and it often
seemed that Alaina's mother wound up with a few drinks
she didn't pay for: as if it were her due, and the people in
here—people the more upstanding members of the community often didn't take seriously—understood that. You
don't pay a witch with money. You pay in other ways.

As she got older Alaina's mother would sometimes

say the time was soon coming when she'd start to explain. Let Alaina know how things worked. The rules. The power that was coming. How to walk in the light and the dark.

But she only said those things when they were out alone together, so Alaina's father wouldn't hear. Then one night, after they'd made this walk together for what turned out to be the last time, Mom went out in the car and didn't come back.

They'd fought hard that night, too. Over what? Homework. A piece of math homework that didn't matter now and hadn't even really mattered then.

And Alaina had not said goodbye.

The street was empty tonight—of people, anyhow. Alaina could feel the other things, catch glimpses of them in passing, like gleeful ghosts. Running along the street. Dancing on rooftops. Squatting on parked cars. Shouts, laughter. A full-scale invisible carnival. Because of her. Because she'd taken life into her own hands.

But it didn't seem like these other things were in the business of giving thanks, either.

"Go," she said, quietly. Then again, louder. *"Go."*

Suddenly there was silence. They were still here, but knew the party was over. And she felt it then, felt it like she'd never felt it before. Like a tingling in her stomach. Like those days when you know you want to make something, create something, but you don't know what.

Without Mom, how was she going to learn to do it right? How was she going to learn how to grow up?

She stopped outside the Tap. A few lights were on. No customers. Nobody behind the bar. Just an empty space littered with shadows and memories. She stood in front of the window and looked in, as she'd done many times over the last year and a half. Glancing toward the bar, in case he was working.

But not because she had a crush on him.

Because Kurt was the guy who'd kept letting her mother drink that last day. Who kept topping up her glass, time after time. The other bartender stopped after a while, even though he was usually generous with her mom. But Kurt kept them coming. And not, Alaina knew, because her mother had been giving him the idea that there was a chance of getting her to bed. Even though they argued, Mom had loved Dad fiercely. But Mom had been on a mission that night, drinking hard.

And something else had been going on.

Even back then Alaina's sight had been coming upon her. And that afternoon, she believed, she'd seen something in the air around Kurt, a shadow guiding his pouring hand. Getting the sad witch drunk.

Too drunk.

She didn't know for sure. Didn't do anything for a year and a half.

But when, two weeks before she walked out into the forest, Alaina happened to catch a glimpse of Kurt slipping into Gina's house in the late afternoon, she'd decided...yes. Kurt had bad things inside him. It was time for her to learn how to stop the bad things. To punish them. And him. Him most of all.

But she'd failed.

And hurt someone else instead.

Alaina tried the door to the Tap, wanting to go stand where her mother used to sit, to see if she could feel her one last time. Turned the handle, tugged at it, rattling it hard. It was locked. She couldn't get in.

No getting back there, no more. She couldn't get past that defense.

She turned away, let her back slide down the door until she was sitting on the cold, wet sidewalk. To stay there a while, and then walk back to the bridge again.

It was high and the water was deep.

Mom would understand.

CHAPTER
61

We loaded the others into the back of Hixon's truck, using a strap to hold their bodies securely and covering them with a tarp. That felt weird, but I didn't know what else to do. We couldn't just leave them lying in the lot. Ken and I joined Hixon in the front of his truck.

As we entered the top end of town, he slowed. It seemed normal. Raining. Foggy. The road looked like road and the buildings were the ones that should be there.

"Just to be clear," Ken said. "This is real now, yes?"

"I guess," I said. "Or it's the way we usually see things, anyway. I don't know if that counts."

Hixon didn't ask us what we were talking about. I got the sense that he knew.

"So where have the things gone?"

"I don't think they have," I said. "Not all of them, anyway."

"But most. Why?"

"You got me."

Hixon slowed to a halt. He stayed that way, leaning on the steering wheel. "Last thing Jenny said," he said, quietly, "before she drove off that night. 'Take care of our baby.' It came after a fight with Alaina, and I thought she meant…let it go tonight. Even if she's being a pain in the ass. Later, when the police arrived at my door to tell me about the 'accident,' I realized she'd meant something else."

"That must hurt like hell."

"It did. But I couldn't blame her," Hixon said. "I saw how hard it was. How she struggled. A *lot* of days. I did what I could. She tried. But being that way breaks your mind sooner or later. And the *one* job she left me with was taking care of our girl. And I got it wrong."

"Wrong how?"

"You can't keep them small. You can't keep them from being who they're going to be. You can't protect them from the world. All you can do is try to point them in the right direction and then forever have their back. True for any kid. Ten times truer for Alaina. I fucked that up."

"I would have done the same thing," I said. "Fatherhood isn't just about being the guy everybody whines to when the Wi-Fi goes down. Being a mom isn't only saying, 'Sure, honey, whatever you feel, here's a snack.' Sometimes you're going to believe it's your job to put yourself in the way of the bad things, even if it kills you. That you're the one who's got to be the…"

I stopped, mouth open. "What?" Hixon said.

"Wall."

Ken pointed. "What the heck's happening down there?"

A Subaru was parked along the street. A guy I didn't recognize was leaning against it, smoking a cigarette like he felt he needed it.

Nadja and Maddy Hardaker were kneeling next to each other by the wall of the Tap, with their arms around someone.

* * *

Hixon covered the rest of the street in two seconds, slamming to a halt in the middle of the road. He jumped out of the truck and ran to his daughter, where she sat with her back to the wall, knees pulled up tight. The Hardaker kids moved aside. Alaina saw him coming and reached up her arms.

Ken and I headed across to the store. "Are we sure this is going to do anything?"

"I don't know what else to try."

As we walked into the store I remembered something I'd thought on our first day here, about walls. How I'd been right, but also wrong, and the desire to try to fence something off was little more than a symbolic statement of fear about something you generally couldn't do much about, and often shouldn't—and every time you build a wall you're cutting yourself off from life, from the past, and a future.

No man is an island, and anybody who tries to be one will slowly sink beneath the waves, alone and forgotten.

We weren't alone in the store.

You could tell, not least because the walls of the place seemed insubstantial. It was misty inside, and there were trees all around in ranks in every direction. I assume they were trees, anyway. They were very treelike. But maybe we've simply decided that's the way those things look, the closest we can get to seeing what they are. They didn't seem to want to cause trouble, so we let them be.

But there were other things there, too. Disturbances in the mist. Soft voices on the shelves. Something that looked like a bird but pretty definitely wasn't: it came arcing out of the corridor, flying sideways. It stopped in front of our faces, hovered in space, not moving its wings, and then sped off again. It seemed to go right through the ceiling.

I don't know why they weren't attacking. Maybe they never *had* been. Maybe we'd just been scared, and a feeling of being attacked is simply how you interpret the actions of the things that scare you. Fear of the unknown.

Then we were just standing in a dark and dusty old store. Rocks on the floor, rocks on the shelves. "So what do we do?" Ken said. "Just rebuild the wall?"

"I guess."

We squatted down, picked up a couple of rocks each, started experimenting with placing them on top of each other, ignoring the increasing sense that things were coming closer, watching intently—and some of them didn't want this to happen.

"Ow," Ken said, after a few minutes, turning irritably, and swatting out with his hand. I'd felt it too, something that felt like being stung by tiny bees.

"Just ignore them."

Then we heard it. Music. The same old music, and this time there seemed to be less in the way between me, and it, and I knew what it was. "Killing Me Softly with His Song." Not the Roberta Flack version. One with a heavier beat.

"Wait a second."

"I hear it, too," Ken said. "And I'm tired of it. Let's just finish fixing this bloody wall."

"No," I said. "Look."

It was standing in the shadows of the corridor at the

back. And I say "it" because however convincing the appearance—that of a man in his late sixties, wearing a black coat, with a gaunt face and sallow bags under his eyes—that wasn't how it actually was. He looked too sharp around the edges, preternaturally *there*.

It looked that way because he meant something, though not to me. I was now pretty sure I knew who he must mean something to.

"What do you want?"

"I tried to warn her," he said. His tone was dry, not unfriendly. The accent wasn't from around here. "First night in town. Wouldn't listen."

"Kristy makes her own decisions."

"And everybody just *loves* those who go their own way, right? Let's hear it for the go-getters, being their best selves every damned day. Only problem being, once in a while they're going to get it *wrong*, and other people always pay the price. Some of those go-getters need to learn to walk before they run."

"Like Alaina."

"Her most of all. Back in the day, things were done different. A lot of head-to-head and war. Especially around here, in the early times. Didn't work then, sure as hell won't now. Alaina's young. She'll learn. But for now, we need to put the genie back in its box. Last thing we need is this situation spreading further. Not good for you, not good for us."

"So who are you? Or what?"

"Me? I have no idea how I look to you. What I am in reality is *our* version of an Alaina—but I've been doing it a lot longer than she has. I'm not your problem right now and neither is she. But I think you know that. And the woman who *is* the problem, the one who made me look like this...the only person she's going to tell, is you."

Then he/it was gone.

I stood there by the half-assed low wall of rocks Ken and I had built, trying to work out what the thing had meant. What I was supposed to do.

"Nolan."

I turned. The door to the store was open. Someone was standing outside. A teenage girl in a hoodie. Her father was behind her, his hand on her shoulder. I thought at first that he was trying to hold her back.

"Let her do her thing," he said, however.

Alaina reached into the back of her father's truck, and rested her hand on Pierre's forehead for a moment. Then she came inside. She walked to where I was standing without giving Ken a second glance. She looked very tired, and very young.

"Just go through the wall, dumbass," she said. "She's waiting."

And she pushed me.

CHAPTER
62

Everything was bright and clear. A concourse stretching out in front and behind. Clean tiles on the floor. A fountain ahead, splashing sounds mixing in with the low hubbub of people talking, to the point where it was hard to tell where one ended and the other began. People on benches around the pool. Others walking by. Big hair. Palms in big pots. White metal trelliswork. Diamond motifs on the floor and columns, with a pair of initials in each. The nearest store was a Waldenbooks. Next to it, a Radio Shack. From somewhere, the faint smell of Chinese food.

A couple of women walked past carrying shopping bags. One wore a suit jacket. The other a sweatshirt with a big CK logo. That song in the background. Overlaid for a moment, a peal of laughter. That flat echo of hard surfaces.

A sign saying WELCOME TO THE GARDEN MALL.

Saturday afternoon. Some people here to get things in particular. Many just here to be here. Families wandering along, kids wanting things, parents saying no. Individual women on more of a mission. Couples hand in hand, or with arms around each other. Nobody was talking on a mobile phone, and nobody was staring at a screen. People on benches were speaking to each other or gazing peace-ably into space, taking a breather, resting their feet.

I caught a glimpse of eyes in the crowd, looking at me. A woman's eyes. Molly's eyes, I was pretty sure.

I followed, pausing at the fountain to look down into the pool. Coins glittering in the water. I bent and picked one out. A bright cent. It was wet. It seemed very real, and I wondered how many other things in life had only seemed that way. When I'd thought something was happening when it was not, or the other way around. Someone fails to answer the phone. You assume it's because they don't want to talk. That interpretation changes the world, and can't be wholly reversed even if you later find out they were merely in the shower. You're forever somewhere else now. You encounter a grim-looking man and assume he's just a grouchy guy, a pain in the ass. You have no idea he's lost in regret for the ways in which he feels he could have been a better father. Doesn't matter. To you, he's Grouchy Guy. That's who he is.

Even though, so far as his son was concerned, he was a pretty good dad.

I caught someone else looking at me, a man this time, turning to glance back at me in the crowds. Good-looking enough to be Pierre, though it wasn't his face.

So I kept walking up to the next intersection, where there was another fountain just like the first. Exactly like it, in fact—even the pattern of coins in the pool was the same. You can't remember everything, or understand everything either. So you fill in the gaps as best you can.

A woman with short gray hair separated from the crowd ahead and headed off down the side concourse.

I hurried after her, but by the time I got there it was empty. Or almost so. Ahead on the right was the record

store you used to see in every single mall. Seeing its
sign now made me realize I couldn't remember when I'd
stopped seeing them, and in fact that so far as I was
concerned, all malls still have a Sam Goody. I'd assumed
their continued presence even though they weren't there,
thinking that I just kept accidently failing to walk past,
when in fact they were gone. Like Faulkner wrote: the
past is never dead; it's not even past.

Level with the store, in the concourse and facing the
other way, was a bench. A teenage girl was sitting on it.

Her head was lowered. From a distance I thought at
first it was Alaina. But as I got closer I saw she was too
slight, not tall enough, and her hair a different brown.

When I came around the side I saw her cheeks were
wet. Her right fist was clenched very tight.

It was Kristy. As she'd been back then.

As she still was and always would be, out of reach
of anybody but herself, in a shard of the universe with a
population of one.

I sat. Didn't say anything. Wasn't sure what I should
do. Sitting near your wife the way she was over ten
years before you even met her will make you unsure of
many things. I remained silent, looking ahead along the
tiled floor of the empty concourse at pillars that looked
like trees.

"His name was Jim," she said, eventually. Her voice
did not sound like that of a fourteen-year-old. It sounded
as she normally did.

"Jim Vaneski. I wanted him to be mine. I wanted to
be his. I wanted that to mark me out. In everybody's
eyes. But especially hers. Helen, I mean. Two sides of the
same coin for years. And for a long time that's what you

want, right? Security. But then it's not. You want to be
different. Not *too* different, not actively *strange*, but you
want the world to get that...you're unique. You are what
you have. Who you have, especially. You want to have
things and people that are yours and nobody else's. You
become competitive."

It was empty back at the intersection of concourses now.
No people. Nothing but us in the entire place. Silence.

"She'd been weird all day—on the walk, while we'd
been wandering around, during lunch. Like she was
bubbling to tell a secret. Like something had made her
five minutes older than she was before. Senior to me,
somehow. Then finally, just as I'm about to go buy the
CD for my dad, she holds up her necklace. And yes, I'd
already noticed it. I assumed she'd bought it herself. I
mean, it was just a cheap thing. But no.

"'Guess who,' Helen said to me. I shrugged. And so
she told me. And, I mean, it was like...they'd been on
two dates. That's all. Not exactly married, right? But he'd
given her this thing. And for a moment I just stared at
her, because, I didn't even know how to *process* it. Jim
Vaneski was the guy, the *one* guy in the entire school, the
sole guy that we knew from *anywhere*, that I liked. She
knew that. She *totally* knew it. She did not know I'd spent
enough time doodling his name that I'd even come up
with a joint monogram for the letters *J* and *K*. She didn't
know how many kids we were going to have, or their
probable names, or what color we were going to paint our
cute little house. I was still undecided on that. But she
sure as *hell* knew what she was doing when she shoved
that necklace in my face."

"Kristy," I said. "She—"

"I know. I *know*. She was just excited and wanted to

share that with me. Her best friend. And it's not like I
owned him, right? I get it. I know that *now*. But we were
so close, Nolan. It was like finding out you couldn't trust
yourself. That you are totally alone in the whole of cre-
ation and cannot for a moment ever feel secure that your
view of what's real, or who can be trusted, is true."

"So what happened?"

"I called her a bitch. She...*smiled*. I can see that smile
in my head like a photograph, and I'm old enough *now*
to see the uncertainty in it. The dawning realization that
she'd screwed up, really badly. That even if she actually
did want Jim—and I have no idea what the truth was
there—and even if she really *was* just happy about the
situation, not crowing, she'd blown the delivery."

"And hurt you."

"Yes. But I *didn't* see that, didn't see the layers, didn't
know it could mean more than one thing, all at once.
I only saw the smile. And...I totally lost it. I swore.
I called her everything under the sun. I slapped her. In
the face. More than once. And she tried to slap me back
but I was faster and blocked her and I slapped her again
and then I grabbed at that necklace and yanked it off her
dumb neck."

The fist in Kristy's lap was still clenched, so tightly the
knuckles were white.

"I felt a pure black joy and I knew she wanted to hit
me now, hit me *hard*, but there were people coming up
the concourse so she couldn't. I turned and stormed into
Sam Goody. Bought the Fugees CD for my dad. Bought
it fast, because I was still good and pissed and I got even
more pissed while I was in there and thought of a whole
bunch more things to say. But when I came out, Helen
was gone."

"Where?"

"I didn't know. Stormed off, I assumed. I waited: thinking, screw her, she needs to come back and apologize to *me*. Managed to keep my anger stoked for quite a while but then started to get upset, too. With what she'd done, but also over what had happened. Because she was my *friend*. My very best friend. The Kristy and Helen Show was my entire world. Even mad as I was, I didn't want it to end. So finally I went looking. Couldn't find her. Couldn't ever find her. And so she never left this place."

"Did you really think anybody in the world would blame you, if they knew what actually happened?"

"They blamed me *without* knowing."

I could hear footsteps. In the distance, but heading our way. "Not really, Kristy. And you know it's not your fault. Not in any way that makes sense. She stormed off, angry and upset and scared by realizing how she'd fucked up. The Helen and Kristy Show was her world, too, remember. She probably just wanted to get home fast. Work out how to start fixing it."

"I know."

"And who knows what happened then. Maybe some guy in the lot saw a pretty girl stomping home and offered her a ride, and it all went dark after that. Could be that, could be something else. You're never going to know the truth. And it's not on you. It's *not your fault*."

"Yes, it *is*. If I hadn't done what I did, she wouldn't have left, Nolan. Don't pretend that's not the truth. I'm the thing that made the next thing happen. I got her killed. I *vanished* her. *One second* of my life, boom, and everything's broken. Forever. I can't fix it. Never have been able to, and never will."

"No," I said. "You can't fix it. So you're just going to

have to let it go. If there's truly nothing that can be done, you have to let it be and let it go."

"But it's *my fault*."

"Yes," I said. "And that sucks. It is your fault. But it's also *not* your fault. That's even worse. You didn't do it, but you did. They're both true at once and the future splits right in that moment. Because in the end you're the only person who can choose which of those worlds you live in, now and for the rest of your life."

"I already live in—"

"No, Kristy. It's a choice. Your choice."

I put my arm around her, and she rested her head on my shoulder. She cried quietly for a long time. I listened to the sound, and wished I could do more to help.

Suddenly she stopped.

I looked up. A woman was standing in front of us.

Kristy was staring at her. For a moment—as long as it takes to think the thought or perform the action that colors the rest of your life—I saw the woman, or thing, as Kristy did. Not as a woman in her mid-thirties, an age Helen never got to be, but as a young girl who'd made her own mistake. Not even a mistake, really, just an action with repercussions in a world that can be unkind. I glimpsed Helen as she was before she slipped behind a wall and never came back, before she became condemned to live the rest of her life, to grow older, nowhere except in Kristy's head.

The woman smiled. It was a small smile, a painful smile. A smile too complex and private for me to read.

Kristy seemed to know what it meant. "I'm sorry, too," she said. "So sorry."

She opened the hand in her lap and held it up.

The woman took the necklace that was lying there. Hung it around her own neck. Leaned close and kissed Kristy on the head.

Then she turned and walked into the darkness at the end of the concourse, where a tall, gaunt old man was waiting.

Kristy caught her breath.

Then she was gone, and it was darker and colder, and I was lying facedown on the floor of a disused department store that smelled of dust and rocks.

"Thank Christ for that," Ken said, as he helped me up. "Thought we'd lost you this time."

Molly, Pierre, and Val were standing to the side. Alaina and her father were outside, with him holding her tight. As I got to my feet I saw Kristy suddenly sit upright in the back of Bryan Hixon's truck.

She turned and said to me: "I know who he is."

CHAPTER
63

When I got up next morning it was clear and bright. It was early and there was no one else around. I stood outside my motel room with a cup of coffee, looking up at the cold blue sky. Trying to figure out whether it was really clear, or if the town simply felt that way today, and so that's what I saw. I eventually realized I had no way of knowing.

I had the same feeling intermittently over the next two days. I still get it sometimes now.

We spent those two days in Birchlake helping repair the walls. It's hard to tell whether we got it right. Hard to be sure what getting it right would mean. All I know is that when we left town the walls looked a lot more like they had in the sketches in Sister Maria von Tessen's notebook, and the one in the old general store was a consistent height along its length. Val had bought the building on behalf of the Knack, it turns out. That wall is now safe.

As Pierre and I worked on one of the other walls out in the woods—a wall he'd kicked around while he wasn't himself, so we had at least some idea of what it was supposed to look like—I got a feeling of someone watching us. I didn't turn to look. It wasn't a bad feeling. It wasn't the things from over the wall. I wonder perhaps if it might have been people who'd tended these walls before, way back in the day.

I know that doesn't make much sense. It was probably just imagination. A lot of things are.

That afternoon I ran into Dan, the principal, and exchanged a few words. I get the sense he'll be keeping an eye out for Alaina. After he left I noticed that though there was a faded painted sign on the side wall of the market on the corner, the name wasn't Vaneski. It was Adams.

And though there were a line of decorative tiles along the front of the coffee shop, there were no J&K initials on them.

When Ken and I arrived at the Tap late that first afternoon, Kristy's rental was no longer on the street. I asked Val if she knew where she was. She said Kristy dropped the key off an hour earlier and said goodbye.

Bryan Hixon was sitting at the end of the bar with some food and a beer. He nodded at me. That was it. After I left, I glanced back and saw him back in conversation with Val. I have since done some research on the Knack. There's nothing whatsoever about them on the internet, which implies they know how to do their job. Quietly. I think Alaina will be offered the guidance she needs. All she has to do is take it. But then, she's a teenager.

The teacher, Gina, was in a booth in the back with the guy I'd seen her with before. She was talking, and he was listening. At the end they laughed together, then stopped. She looked hesitant in the silence, as if unsure it was okay for things to be okay. He reached out and put his hand on hers, and she smiled.

After a while I tried calling Kristy. She didn't pick up. I left a message.

She didn't call back.

Mid-evening I was outside smoking a cigarette. Three women turned the corner up by the grocery store and walked down the street toward me, talking, laughing quietly, trailing a cloud of smoke. At least, at first I thought they were women. Then I realized it was the Hardaker girls and Alaina Hixon. Nadja quickly slipped something in her pocket.

"Oh," she said, as they got closer. "It's only you."

"Who did you think?"

"I thought you were my dad."

"On his behalf I'll tell you that getting into vaping is a bad idea."

Maddy stared at me. "Dude, you are literally smoking. Right now. In real life."

"Do as we say, not as we do."

They did their simultaneous eye roll number and walked on. Alaina stayed behind a moment. "Thank you."

"For what?"

"Helping fixing the walls. And the mess I made."

"Sounds like you'll be spending the rest of your life doing something similar for other people. We're good. But in exchange, tell your friends from me that adulting isn't as much fun as everybody says."

"That's like a rich guy telling a poor guy that money isn't everything."

"It's really not. As you'll find out. Don't be in too much of a hurry to get where I am, is all I'm saying."

"Take life one day at a time, right?"

"I don't know a better way of tackling it."

As we were packing our stuff into the car next morning, the motel owner drove into the lot. He parked up and got out.

"Good visit with your sister?"

"Nope," he said. "She's a pain in the ass. Always has been. So—did I miss much?"

"Nothing whatsoever," Ken said. "This is a very boring little town."

"And that's just the way we like it," the guy said. "Don't forget you owe me an extra five hundred bucks."

A few days after I got back to Santa Monica, Kristy emailed.

She was in Lavenda, her hometown. She had spent three days trying to get the police to listen to her, without success, about a man who'd lived by himself a few doors down from Helen's family in the 1990s. A neighbor she'd only seen a few times, from a distance. He died in 2004. His former house had changed hands twice since.

The new owners were a nice young couple with a new baby, and Kristy didn't even ask them if they'd be open to the idea of digging up their yard. She knew it was unlikely Helen would be there anyway. There are a lot of woods around Lavenda.

There was a photo attached to the email. It was an archive clipping from the local newspaper. An obituary. It showed a guy in his late sixties, with dark hair, a gaunt face, and bags under his eyes. A face that Kristy had stored in the back of her mind, somehow knowing without knowing. Or guessing, at least. How? I have no idea. I doubt she does either. Maybe he looked at them a beat too long one afternoon, or at Helen, and Kristy's mind stored that away, far back in the shadows of her mind.

She might even be completely wrong.

After I'd read the email I tried calling. Again, she didn't pick up or respond to the message I left. The next day it occurred to me to check whether she was still in Lavenda. I hoped she'd decided to leave it be. If not, I hoped I might be able to convince her to move on.

I booted up Find Your Friends. I didn't even get a LOCATION UNKNOWN.

She'd unfriended me.

The next night the four of us met up in Venice Beach to eat and try to figure out what to do next on *The Anomaly Files*. We agreed there was nothing to say about Birchlake or the walls. Nothing that people needed to hear, anyway, or would understand or believe. It had already occurred to me, when I saw Val and Bryan Hixon in the bar, that they were the only adults who knew something had taken place. For all the rest it was just a dark, rainy night, when everyone stayed indoors and perhaps felt anxious or sad, but then felt fine the next day.

Pierre still had the remnants of two black eyes and the cut on his forehead from where his face had been smacked into the underside of the hatch in Olsen's. "Can the next show at least not involve the threat of physical violence?" he asked. "Because it always seems to be me who gets hurt."

"Pierre, you tried to set fire to us," Ken said.

"I was possessed."

"Well, next time, be more careful."

After the other two had left I told Ken what had happened with Kristy, including the fact that I had no idea of her whereabouts or any way of finding out.

"She'll be back," he said. "Or she won't."

"Gee, thanks."

"Sorry, mate—that's all I've got. Seems like the person you used to know isn't there anymore. Not in your head and especially not in hers. You told her she gets to choose which world she wants to live in now. You were right. That's going to take a while to play out."

"I see. Any further advice?"

"Yes. Buy me more beer."

He was right. If a story finishes, you can't simply pick it up and start again. You can't reread it, because you know how it ends, and that it *does* end. You can't simply start adding fresh new pages, either. Getting back together is a sequel. What went before is going to be relevant, but any further story has to function on its own merits. Even I, celebrated emotional klutz though I may be, understand this.

So I guess I'll wait and see what happens next.

A couple nights ago I got a call from Molly. She asked me to meet her on Santa Monica pier in the early evening.

I wandered over and we walked together to the very end. She stood there for a while, looking out over the ocean, and then she said something to it.

"No," she said. "I belong to *me*."

Then she turned away. "Do I need to know what that's about?" I asked.

"Nope. Just wanted a witness. With a witness you know something's really happened."

"Well, sometimes," I said.

She laughed, and asked if I wanted to go find a drink. I said yes. As we walked back up the pier I was pretty sure I heard, from a distance, a song I recognized.

I didn't mention it.

ACKNOWLEDGMENTS

With many thanks to my agents, Jonny Geller and Jennifer Joel, my thoughtful (and patient) editor, Wes Miller, and everybody at Grand Central and Bonnier for all their hard work and enthusiasm.

Thank you also to those who supported and encouraged me in various ways through the process, including: Paula and Nate, Stephen Jones and Jim Haley, Ellen Goldsmith-Vein, Neil Gaiman, and my father. And with no thanks to our cats, Stark, Maybe, and Ginge, because honestly, you were no help at all.

ABOUT THE AUTHOR

Michael Rutger is an acclaimed short story writer whose work has been optioned by major Hollywood studios. He lives in California with his wife, son, and two cats.